Chronicles of Nethra

Book One

Star Spire

Chronicles of Nethra: Star Spire

For Carolyn,

Thank you for pushing me to make my

dreams a reality.

Acknowledgments

Firstly, thanks to Alana Joli Abbott for providing the copy edits for this book. Thanks also to Josh Alquist, Don Roath, and Dave Tobey for reading through early drafts of the story. Your feedback is what has kept me going. Last, but certainly not least, thanks to my wife and kids for all the hours they've allowed me to slave away at the computer. We did it, guys.

"What did you expect? They're assassins. You can't be too surprised when they stab you in the back. It's kind of in their job description."

Braccus Kai flexed his hands on the tablet in frustration. He was thankful that the newest models were more durable than their predecessors. They'd had to switch suppliers to slow the rate at which he churned through the devices. The medications that were supposed to help with his anger were obviously not working as advertised.

"You say that like it's a trait exclusive to the Ghenza," he growled. "In my experience, trust has no safe harbor in all Terran space."

Rico's laugh was more resigned than sardonic. "True enough. You seem to have had a rough run of it as of late, Kai."

"Indeed—something I might largely credit to your own prestigious family."

"Oh, come now, you've made out all right in the end. Don't let past business cloud your eyes to future possibilities!"

At this moment, Braccus was seriously considering the possibility of putting the tablet through Rico's skull. "How do I even know this is real?"

"You don't," the young man replied. "But it's yours to keep. Have your men verify it."

That he *would* do. Information this damning was not to be taken lightly, and the requisite response should be measured carefully.

For the sake of this conversation, Braccus decided to entertain the idea that the intel was at least partially correct. "Why would the Ghenza turn around and sell the Conduit to House Valadar?"

Rico shrugged. "Why would Valadar want to buy it in the first place? That's the question you should be asking. Honestly, you should have been suspicious when the Ghenza first approached you. Their inter-system monitoring stations work fine without investing in cutting-edge power disbursement tech. I'm surprised you didn't ask *that* question sooner."

True, though Braccus knew exactly why he hadn't. The Ghenza Collective had a way of making sure that your mind was occupied by other things instead of contemplating their end game. He'd enjoyed the partnership the Inheritors had struck with the assassins. He'd also enjoyed some of the fringe benefits proffered by the Collective's representative.

A calculated move in retrospect. This meant his mind had been more focused on Aria's body instead of her ambitions. He'd taken her for a simple creature with simple needs. It now seemed that he'd been quite mistaken.

"What do you want for this information?"

"Pardon?"

"Nothing in this universe is free, Rico. What is it that you seek in return?"

Rico smirked. "I think that should be obvious. I want to buy the Conduit instead."

"And why do *you* want it?"

"Aside from keeping it away from my father's most powerful rival? Oh, I don't know. Perhaps I'll use it to power my yacht."

Braccus eyed the smug little noble. Despite the fact that the man might have actually brought him something of value, he still wanted to crush that perfect face of his. The political ramifications would be significant, but the greater part of his temperance came from the figure looming to Rico's right. That silent brute eyed him up like a predator stalking its next meal.

The man was tall for a Terran, more on the level of one of the Maur or Orchallen. It was typical for those other races to tower over their Terran counterparts. Such was the reason the Great Houses and other Terran factions favored them as enforcers or bodyguards. Rico's guard was bald, with eyes that seemed too small for the rest of his face. Thick lips and a grayish cast to his skin made Braccus think he might have some Orchallen in him after all.

A half-breed, maybe? Or perhaps one of his parents was the halfie. Most half-breeds were sterile, but Braccus wouldn't place a bet on the accuracy of that information. Plus, with recombinant technology so commonplace, who knew what was possible? Perhaps the brute in his office had been cooked up in a lab somewhere.

Braccus looked back to Rico. It didn't matter what the smug asshole wanted the Conduit for. It wasn't worth anything to Braccus other than a payday.

"What's your offer?"

"I'll match whatever the Ghenza are paying."

"You'll have to do better than that. Even if they are aligning themselves with House Valadar, betraying the Ghenza is not something I do lightly. If I sell the Conduit to you, my arrangement with the assassins comes to an end. That means you must bear part of the cost of breaking the deal."

"Fair enough. Name your price."

"Forty million."

"Done."

"*And* a formal alliance with House Chronos."

Rico hesitated. "I don't necessarily have the authority to…"

"That's my price, Mr. Chronos. Do what you have to do to make it work."

An angry look crossed the young man's face. *Finally, an actual display of backbone.* "You overstep, Kai. I'd advise you to remember your place."

"My place? At last calculation, my place was that of the seller, and yours that of the buyer. It is my right to demand the price I wish. If the proposition is not to your liking, take your corporate stock and governmental influence elsewhere."

Rico balled his fists. His jaw tensed like he might grind his teeth. "I could just take the Conduit, you know."

"You would have to find it first. Don't think for a second it's here with me now." Braccus paused, staring Rico down and letting that bit of truth sink in. He leaned back in his chair, taking a sip from the tumbler on his desk. "By the way, threats will get you nowhere with me. Even if you were to have your lapdog over there strangle me, you'd never make it out alive. So, let's avoid any mention of unpleasantness, shall we?"

Rico was fuming now. "Why you…"

Braccus slammed a fist on the nearby desk. "You sir, are in *my* house!" Lowering his voice, he growled, "I don't care how much money and influence your father has placed in your pocket. A full bank account and a handful of parliamentarians do not a great leader make. It is best you learn that now, while your ailing father is still alive to make amends for your indiscretions."

Rico hesitated again, a pause that lengthened into an awkwardly tense silence. As Braccus had imagined, invoking the man's father had provided the necessary sobering influence.

Gods help them all when Don Chronos finally succumbed to his illness, for they all knew the man had not paid proper attention to his succession plan.

Rico drew a deep breath. "Forgive me. Your point is well taken. It does not change the fact that I will have to confer with my family before extending our protection."

Braccus smiled, though he doubted it reached his eyes. "Most certainly. You have one week, Dorian standard, to close the deal. I am appointed to pass off the object in question to the Ghenza at that time. Absent a better offer, I will be forced to go through with that transaction."

Expression teetering between skepticism and consternation, Rico asked, "You would truly transfer such a powerful asset to an enemy faction?"

"My enemies abound Mr. Chronos." Braccus waved his hand dismissively. "As you pointed out, my faction has had a run of ill-luck lately. Though House Valadar represents a dangerous adversary, my list of allies runs thin. If I am to begin betraying those few that I have, I will need to line up replacements."

Just entertaining Rico's proposition was enough to put Braccus on the receiving end of an assassin's blade. He was putting a lot of faith in the room's scramblers to prevent Rico from recording this conversation. He could always claim a recording was a forgery, but it would still do much to weaken his ties with the Ghenza.

Rico's brow knit with concentration. "Are you sure there isn't something that I can arrange more immediately? A transfer of company stock, perhaps. Shares in Vega Major are surging quite nicely at present."

"I'm not worried about finances alone, Rico. My offer stands. Rich men are overthrown every day. I need something that grants me position—something to cement my place in this system. If you are unable to secure a formal protection agreement, then my position remains one of vulnerability."

The sag in Rico's shoulders put the truth to Kai's words. Truthfully, the compensation Braccus demanded was so valuable as to turn this little betrayal on its head. A protection arrangement from House Chronos would provide the Inheritors a leg up on all other minor players in the system. The House was arguably the only major player left in the Ravian System with House Barkay gone.

The Ghenza were formidable in their partnership, but they worked in the shadows. House Chronos was currently the dominant player in the system and would soon be a contender for the title of the most powerful House in the sector. No one would cross Braccus with the threat of Chronos's wrath hanging overhead. To secure such a contract, Braccus would have written an indenture contract for his own mother—gods rest her soul.

"Very well," Rico sighed. "Give me a few days to secure consensus. I will either reach out to you at the time to confirm payment or arrange a counteroffer."

Braccus made a mental note to double his guard until he heard back from the young noble. If the Don was not amenable to Kai's terms, then the counteroffer would likely take the form of a bullet sent from a nearby rooftop.

"Agreed," Braccus extended his hand. "A pleasure doing business with you, Rico. May this only be the first accord of a long and fruitful partnership."

CHAPTER 1

[ACCESSING COGNIS.DATAFILES...]

SIF — *PLANET (TERRAN SPACE)* — THE THIRD AND PRINCIPAL PLANET OF THE FREYVIAN SYSTEM. KNOWN FOR ITS MANUFACTURING, CYBERNETIC TECHNOLOGY, AND GENETIC RESEARCH INDUSTRIES. HEADQUARTERS FOR VALADAR HOLDINGS INC. AND ITS NUMEROUS SUBSIDIARY CORPORATIONS. THE NEOCONSERVATIVE POLITICAL LEANINGS OF THE CURRENT PARLIAMENT HAVE CREATED AN IDEAL ENVIRONMENT FOR THRIVING ECONOMIC POLICIES. THIS HAS COME AT THE EXPENSE OF SOME BASIC CIVIL LIBERTIES AND DEMOCRATIC FREEDOMS.

[CLOSING DATAFILE...]

Markus watched the hulking figures unloading crates from the shuttle transport through the scope of his rifle. The six men wore a form of polymer battle armor, the kind of gear that just screamed "merc."

This wasn't much of a surprise. After all, privateers made up one of the largest employment pools on Ascension. Even if there had been some sort of public defense entity on the planet, corporations usually liked to bring in external forces from time to time.

This was especially true when the activity in question was either too illegal or too deadly for the tastes of tenured employees. Bringing in a little external cannon fodder was not only good for plausible deniability; it also did wonders for employee morale.

Focus. Having watched these mercs for the better part of ninety minutes, it was a little understandable that his mind might wander. That didn't change the fact that inattention was a nice way to get yourself killed.

There was a shit-ton of contraband coming out of this particular rig. Plus, the crew here was taking their sweet time getting it onto their little skiff. Must be getting paid by the hour.

Markus took his right hand off the trigger of his rifle and slid it down into a pouch at his waist. With his eye never leaving the scope, he fumbled around until he found a small cassette. He pressed on the cassette's clasp and pulled one strip of film from the dispenser.

With the film pressed between his thumb and forefinger, he brought it to his mouth and pressed it to the skin on the inside of his lower lip. The strip adhered readily to the scarred tissue opposite his gums. As it made contact with his saliva, the film dissolved into a sticky substance that left a peppery taste on his tongue.

The results were quick. As the stym hit his system, he was able to make out the fine detail of the mercs' armor. The black polymer took on a blue tint in the artificial illumination of the safety lights gleaming from the shuttle's ramp.

He drew in a deep breath, the euphoric effects of the drug washing over him. Boredom gave way to keen alertness. His heartbeat quickened. He flexed and released his shoulders, discharging the tension building in his back and arms.

Just in time. A pair of the armored goons brought out the last of the crates and placed it onto the hovering skiff. Another man scanned the barcode with a device built into his armored gauntlet while their leader signaled for the others to wrap things up.

Markus spoke quietly, but loud enough for the comm in his ear to pick up his words. "Winter reporting in. Cargo is secure. Confirm readiness to approach."

"Confirmed, Winter," came Sahar's growled response. "Beast is ready for approach."

"Ruby here," Aaliyah chimed. "Inbound in thirty seconds."

Good, everyone was in position. "Confirmed," Markus acknowledged. "Advance on target."

He began to countdown.

Twenty-nine. Twenty-eight. Twenty-seven...

When he hit twenty-six, he squeezed the trigger. The rifle hissed as the suppressed bullet surged from its barrel. Markus immediately pulled back on the bolt, chambering the next round.

The first bullet hit its mark. An emerald fizzle shimmered in a vain effort to stop the shot. The unfortunate merc's head exploded in a shower of red.

Twenty-four. Twenty-three. Twenty-two...

Markus squeezed the trigger again. There was another green pop as the bullet exploded through his second target. Markus reloaded.

Seventeen. Sixteen. Fifteen...

The remaining four mercs were now taking cover. A few dialed in the zoom on their visors, trying to pinpoint their assailant's location.

Markus popped off a couple more rounds to keep them undercover, landing a glancing blow off one of the armored figures. The target's shields saved his ass, but the force of the impact sent him sprawling onto the ground.

Nine. Eight. Seven...

The merc with the barcode reader scurried to the side of the skiff, diving into the cockpit. The lights near the craft's thrusters switched from red to green.

Four. Three. Two...

A loud crash echoed back up to Markus's position as a figure in an armored mech suit slammed into the front of the hoverbed.

Sahar was right on time.

Her tall, muscular form was made all the more imposing by the mech exoskeleton she wore. The mech's arms clenched onto the front of the skiff, holding it fast. Weighted clamps sprung out from the armored legs and anchored both the mech and the hovering craft into a locked position.

Now the remaining mercs took aim at Sahar. Markus went back to work, sending off round after round into the armored warriors. A few of the mercs still got a couple of shots off, but they bounced harmlessly off the armored mech.

The brave soul in the cockpit leaned out. A rod, shimmering pale blue with an electric charge, extended from his hand.

Markus's next shot caught the merc in the shoulder. The green flare of his shields caught enough of the bullet to keep him alive, but the rod he was holding spun off into the distance. The merc looked from side to side for the discarded weapon.

Markus's second shot put him down for good. Only three to go.

Where in the nine hells was the rest of their team?

"Ruby? ETA?" No response.

Shit.

Markus flipped channels. "Wraith, you got eyes on the shuttle?"

Eli's voice was calm on the other end of the comm. "A little bit of drone trouble, but they're clear. Inbound in three, two…"

The roar of jet engines cut off Eli's countdown. Markus switched back to the open channel.

It looked like the shuttle would slam into the concrete platform below. At the last possible moment, the ship's reverse thrusters fired. The sudden shift of inertia sent ripples of air and dust across the ground, knocking the few remaining mercs off their feet.

As if being jettisoned by the force of the maneuver, a woman in a tight blue bodysuit dove from the craft's open cargo hold. The black cord fastened to her belt slowed her descent and stopped her just above the hovering skiff. The mechanism holding the cord on her belt whirred, flipping her in a backward somersault to land expertly on her feet.

Skye raced toward the skiff, disconnecting the cable and sliding under the craft. A second later, her voice rang out over the channel. "Charges placed! I'm clear!"

"Got it," Aliyah responded. "Detonatin' charges"

A muffled explosion. Lights on the skiff flared and died as it came offline. Sahar released the craft. "Let's bag her up!"

Netting flared from underneath the vehicle. Skye emerged from the far side and quickly bound the ends together. The shuttle hovered closer, and she grabbed the cord, attaching it to a ring at the top of the netting.

"Package secured," she reported, attaching her own safety line to the central ring. "Reel me in."

"Roger, Sapphire," Aaliyah answered. "Hold on tight."

The cord on the shuttle began to retract. The skiff groaned as the bed of the vehicle detached from the rest of the frame.

Then things started to get messy.

Aerial drones, menacing, hawk-like things, began to drift in from between the surrounding buildings. This must have been the trouble that the shuttle had run into earlier.

Markus barked a warning. "Ruby, you have drones incoming."

"Can't see them, Winter. Direction?"

Fragging everywhere? That probably wasn't a helpful response. "Clusters at your one o'clock, your nine, and your six."

Aaliyah let loose a stream of curses.

Sahar chimed in. "I'll hold them off. A little help, Winter?"

It was going to blow his cover, but Markus didn't see any better options. "You've got it. Let's go."

The mech launched toward a group of drones coming from the west. Sahar's arm turrets hummed, unloading a hail of bullets into the bots.

Markus covered her flank, taking out the drones emerging from the south. His first round took a bot in the engine, detonating it on contact. A second went down as he put a round just under its left wing.

They were turning now, having sussed out the second threat. The defense bots didn't have the most sophisticated AI, but at least they were smart enough to know when someone was shooting at them.

A third round reported from his rifle. It struck its mark right as his target's shields flared protectively. The drone stayed airborne. Another round in damn near the same spot took it out of the sky.

Just one more. Markus pulled the trigger.

Click.

He spat a curse. The magazine was empty.

He scrambled to eject the mag and pop in his spare. Eli's voice cut into his focus. "Winter, they have your position. Three drones en route. Get out of there."

Markus double-checked his scope. "Three? I only see one more."

"Check your nine o'clock."

Markus swung his scope around. Sure enough, three more birds were heading his way.

Nine hells. It was time to go.

He fought a moment of vertigo as he pushed himself up to his feet. He slung the rifle over his shoulder—no time to disassemble it. Turning on his heels, he rushed toward the door that would get him off this roof.

Blinding spotlights lit up his position. The roar of thrusters filled his ears.

The drones opened fire.

The bed of the skiff surged into the air, taking Skye with it. For not the first time, she was thankful for her cybernetic legs.

Without those, the sudden shift in momentum would have sent her careening off the package—or smashed her right into the cargo.

She steadied herself as the shuttle rose rapidly, simultaneously reeling in the stolen goods. Things were going according to plan.

And then the drone struck the crate.

"What the—"

Another impact. Rather than trying to shoot the shuttle down, the bot was trying to knock the cargo loose. Skye sprawled backward with the force of the second blow. Inexplicably, the line to her safety clip snapped.

Her body lurched off the floating platform. With a desperate swipe of her left arm, she sunk a gauntleted hand into the side of the nearest crate.

Pain coursed through her back and neck as her muscles strained to keep her shoulder from dislocating. Her arm itself was fine—another win for cybernetics—but now she dangled helplessly on the swaying parcel.

She flung her other arm back onto the crate, fingers scrabbling for purchase. Another blow sent the cargo careening sideways. The boxes and crates slid. The netting holding everything together strained against the shifting bulk.

Don't break, don't break, don't break!

Aaliyah's piloting skills saved Skye from being smeared across the side of a nearby building—barely. The crate and its passenger swung perilously between the steel and glass skyscrapers. City lights whipped past Skye in a frenzy. A wave of nausea welled up in her abdomen.

Skye finally gripped the edge of the netting with her other hand and pulled herself back on top of the cargo. She made it back onto her feet just in time to see another set of lights racing toward her.

Reflexively, she snagged a slender disk from her belt and pressed firmly on the center. Blades flared from the device. A red light indicated the weapon was armed. She sent it whirling at the drone.

The target swerved to miss the blade. Its shields flared defensively—just enough to detonate the projectile.

Not enough to take it down, but it slowed long enough for Skye to draw her pistol.

She fired right into the drone's adjusted path. The charged blasts flared with brilliant light as they collided with the bot's shields. Sparks flared from the drone's damaged hull, but it kept coming.

Then, seemingly out of nowhere, a gigantic form crashed into the drone. Another flash of light. The sound of tearing metal.

The bot detonated.

Sahar's mech hovered falteringly in the air. Sparks sprang from its joints, and the rear thrusters sputtered ominously. At least she was airborne, though the mech had definitely seen better days.

"I thought for sure I was going to be scraping you off the concrete after that last hit," Sahar teased.

"You could have just shot it down!"

"Out of ammo. I had to get creative."

"That's one word for it."

Her teammate chuckled. Then, more seriously, she asked, "You all right?"

Skye let out a relieved sigh. "Oh yeah, I totally had it under control."

"Sure you did."

The mech's engines flared precariously. "Might want to get inside?" Skye suggested.

The shuttle was right above them now, with no drones in sight. They were safe.

Sahar didn't respond, which showed she knew how bad a shape the robotic armor was in. She laid hard on the thrusters, pushing the bulky rig up and into the open shuttle bay.

Skye blinked at her helmet's interface to reactivate the comms. "This is Sapphire. We're clear. Ground team report in."

She waited a few long seconds. No response.

"I repeat, this is Sapphire. We are clear. Winter, Wraith, please acknowledge."

The hollow sound of static was the only reply.

Chapter 2

[ACCESSING COGNIS.DATAFILES...]

SAHAIA — *RACIAL PROFILE (SAPIENS)* — *SAHAIA* IN ANCIENT KINTARI, TRANSLATES ROUGHLY TO "ASCENDANT" IN THE INTERGALACTIC STANDARD LEXICON. THIS RACE OF BEINGS BEGINS LIFE AS TERRAN. THEIR PSIONIC PROFILES ARE ENHANCED IN A MANNER THAT DRASTICALLY MODIFIES THEIR GENETIC MAKEUP. THOSE WHO SURVIVE THE PROCEDURE BECOME SOME OF THE MOST FORMIDABLE PSIONIC ENTITIES IN KNOWN SPACE. THE MECHANISM FOR THIS TRANSFORMATION IS LARGELY UNKNOWN, BEING KEPT INTENTIONALLY SECRET BY THE COVENS THAT COMPRISE THEIR SOCIAL HIERARCHY. THEIR SECRETIVE BEHAVIOR AND PRETERNATURAL APPEARANCE, HAVE PROMPTED MEMBERS OF OTHER SPECIES TO CASUALLY REFER TO THE SAHAIA AS "SHADOWS."

[CLOSING DATAFILE...]

Gunfire tore through his leg. Markus collapsed to the ground. The stym running through his system amplified the burning sensation to the point of agony.

Drawing his sidearm, he rolled and attempted to blind-fire the pistol at the drones in pursuit. Emptying the clip, he took down the nearest bot. Unfortunately, that still left three on his tail.

Well... shit.

Not much of a final thought, but he'd never been much for poetry. The drones opened fire. Markus braced for the inevitable.

In that same instant, the door he'd been rushing toward blew right off its hinges. Now a soaring projectile, it flew straight into the farthest drone.

The air in front of Markus coalesced into a foggy barrier, refracting the searchlights of the pursuing drones. Bullets flashing from their machine guns bounced harmlessly off the translucent shield.

Eli's deep voice shouted at him over the clatter of the bullet storm. "You really shouldn't shut off your comms when under fire."

Markus looked up at the speaker. The man's dark armor was lighter and sleeker than mercenary standard issue. It wouldn't even stop small arms fire, but Eli had always favored mobility. Plus, he probably didn't need as much physical protection with all those psionic tricks up his sleeve.

"Didn't know I had!" Markus shouted.

"An oversight in a moment of panic, perhaps?" The mocking tone was obvious, even under the roar of gunfire.

"Tease me all you want, Eli. Just keep saving my ass while you do it."

He was damn lucky Eli had found his way onto the balcony when he did. Unfortunately, that also meant their street team was completely without cover.

Eli helped him to his feet, but he kept one hand extended toward the forcefield. "Are you able to stand?"

Markus put weight on the bad leg. The surge of pain told him that was a definite "no." "I'll live. Might be a little slow on the extraction. Everyone else make it out all right?"

"Of course, but you would know that if you hadn't shut down your commlink."

"Thanks for the lecture, teach. Got any more words of wisdom? If not, would you mind dealing with our metal-plated friends before more of Valadar's toys show up?"

Markus could practically see the eye roll through his friend's reflective faceplate. With a forceful gesture from his extended arm, Eli sent the shield flying outward.

A wave of concussive force shot straight through the hovering drones as they continued to fire. When the shockwave struck, they exploded into two bright flashes. The remains of the drones fell from the air in a shower of sparks and debris.

Eli considered the tableau of destruction for another moment. "Done," he sighed. "Come on, let's get you inside."

He slung one of Markus's arms over his shoulder. As they started to limp off, Markus gestured back the way they'd come. "Hey, can you grab my rifle?"

With another sigh, Eli flicked his fingers at where the rifle had fallen. The weapon sprang up and floated into Markus's outstretched hand.

"Anything else, boss?"

"Well now that you mention it…"

"Should I remind you that we are still on this roof? Everyone would believe me if I said the drone got you."

"Point taken. Let's go."

Markus's leg was messed up enough that Eli had to carry him to the door. Once they were inside, his friend forced him to take a seat in the stairwell.

"Let me see it," he said as he removed his helmet.

"You really think now's the best time?"

Eli fixed him with those black-in-black eyes of his. Those eyes were creepy enough on their own, but they really popped against his alabaster skin.

Most of the time the features didn't bother Markus. That was how all Sahaia looked. In the dark of the stairwell though, with that serious look on his face, the composition was a bit unnerving.

"I think you're losing so much blood that you'll pass out before we can make it to safety. Now please, let me see it."

Markus leaned back on the stairs and allowed Eli to inspect his leg. He fought not to wince as the Sahaia pulled back on the shattered armored plating.

"Shit, Markus. You'll be lucky not to lose the whole limb."

"Don't be so dramatic. I've been shot before. It's not like the bullets hit any vital... *ah*!"

Eli's hand was hovering over the wound. Something—several somethings—were shifting inside the open sore. There was a small spray of blood as the bullet fragments were sucked out of his leg and into Eli's waiting hand.

"If your femoral artery was hit, then you'll be bleeding out in short order. I don't know whether you would characterize that as 'vital' or not, but it doesn't change the fact your injuries need to be treated."

Damn Eli and his rationality. "So... what's the plan? Are you going to hit me with some more of your mojo? Patch me up a bit?"

Eli's eyes flicked up at Markus in annoyance. "I'm a telekin, not a biokin. None of my abilities are going to be of much use in 'patching you up.' Not unless you're interested in being bonded."

"Aaliyah seems to like the benefits."

"Are you entertaining the offer?"

And give Eli open access to his thoughts and feelings? Frag that. He liked the guy, but that was a bit too intimate. "I think I'll pass thanks."

"Then sit still."

He reached into his pouch and drew out a fist-sized spray can. Pressing the nozzle against the wound, he pressed down on the container.

Searing pain filled Markus's leg as the pink foam entered the wound. Within seconds that pain gave way to a tingling sensation as the analgesic compounds started numbing the area.

Even under the effects of the stym, Markus could hardly feel that entire part of his leg.

"There," Eli sighed. "That will keep you patched up until Z can take a look at you."

"I think you meant that to be reassuring, which just shows you've never had the pleasure of experiencing the medical drone's bedside manner."

The Sahaia's half-grin was more than a little sardonic. "What can I say? I'm more durable, and I get shot less."

Markus rolled his eyes. If he could stop bullets with his mind, he'd get shot less too. "So you say. Now, if you're done fretting over me, let's get back to business. Have you contacted the team?"

"No, I've been too busy saving you from defense drones."

Then that was the first order of business. Markus blinked at his helmet interface to pull up their coordinates. There was a brief moment of panic when he couldn't connect to the shuttle. "Eli, I'm not seeing them on the network."

"They're probably out of range by now. With this much drone pressure, they'd do best to try and break atmosphere as soon as possible."

Okay, that was a much better line of thought than the one Markus had just been pondering. Gods, when had he gotten so jumpy? "All right, I'm good with that idea. So, we just need to make for the safe house as planned, right?"

"Agreed. Let me just check in with Aaliyah to let her know you're still breathing."

Maybe it was the blood loss, but now Markus was confused. "I thought you said the comms were out of range."

Eli tapped his forehead. *Oh, right... more shadow tricks.* Eli didn't need comms to communicate with someone he'd been bonded to.

The Sahaia closed his eyes. He was silent for several seconds, almost like he was praying. Markus waited quietly, not wanting to disrupt his focus.

Another few seconds and Eli opened his eyes. "Message delivered. They're all fine, by the way. The package is secured. Now, let's get your gimpy ass off to the safe house."

CHAPTER 3

[ACCESSING COGNIS.DATAFILES...]

MAUR — *RACIAL PROFILE (SAPIENS)* — THE MAUR ARE CHARACTERIZED BY THEIR LARGE, MUSCULAR BUILDS AND FACIAL FEATURES CONSIDERED SOMEWHAT BESTIAL BY OTHER SAPIENT SPECIES. THEIR SKULL AND FACIAL STRUCTURES ARE FREQUENTLY DESCRIBED AS EITHER FELINE OR URSINE IN CHARACTERISTIC. THESE FEATURES, ALONG WITH PATTERNS IN FUR COLOR AND TEXTURE, DEMARCATE CLAN ORIGIN AND HEREDITARY LINEAGE. THE MAUR FEDERATION ATTEMPTS TO PROMOTE HARMONY AND COOPERATION AMONG CLANS, THOUGH ONLY SEVENTY PERCENT OF MAUR FACTIONS HAVE ADOPTED GOVERNMENT STRUCTURES RECOGNIZING THE AUTHORITY OF THIS CENTRAL GOVERNMENT.

[CLOSING DATAFILE...]

Skye tossed her head as she removed her helmet. Sweat covered her face and matted her blonde hair. She took a cloth off a nearby bench and wiped the mist off the helmet's faceplate.

They still hadn't heard from Markus or Eli, and it was bugging the shit out of her.

"You said he fired on the drones. Then what happened?"

Sahar, who was struggling to free her bulky frame from the confines of the damaged mech, looked back her way. Even through her helmet, Skye could tell she was annoyed.

"I was a little busy blowing up drones to keep tabs on him. Look, he's probably fine. He always makes it happen. That guy has the devil's luck."

Putting aside the fact that it was weird to hear Sahar using Terran slang, Skye still wasn't so sure. "We're all pretty lucky in this game—right up to the point when we're not. My helmet link lost his signal way before we broke range."

"You know Markus. He's never gotten used to the retinal interface on these new fragging helmets. Keeps blinking out of the group channel. Him and Eli are probably grabbing a drink with Vallus before linking up for the resupply."

As she spoke, Sahar finally managed to wiggle free of the mech exoskeleton. She'd had to shut it down and force the thing open manually since it wouldn't stop sparking while the power was on. That hadn't been ideal with her and Skye crammed in the confined space of the shuttle bay along with their new cargo.

The thick cords of her muscles rippled under her gray skin suit. After taking a second to stretch, she reached up and pulled off her helmet. A coy look played at the corners of her feline maw.

"I thought you two were done, anyway. What's up with the sudden well of concern?"

Skye wanted to wipe that smirk right off her lioness face. She knew better than to try, though. Cybernetic limbs or not, Maur strength trumped that of any Terran. "We *are* done," she insisted. "But he's still our captain and a friend."

"Uh-huh… do you fret over me like this when my comm is off?"

Skye's response was cut off as Aaliyah shouted back from the cockpit. "Just got word from Eli. Him and Markus are headin' to the safe house. Guess Markus got shot, but he'll live. He ain't gonna be runnin' any foot race, though. Eli said they might be a little late."

"Thank the gods," Sahar growled. "Now blondie back here can relax."

Skye didn't bother replying. The Maur might put on a tough front, but she was likely as worried as any of them. Everyone had to rely on their own defense mechanisms if they wanted to stay sane in this job.

There had been more drone pressure than they had anticipated. House Valadar must have been pumping some serious cash into their efforts with their defense contractors.

Skye set aside all the what-ifs and close-calls that played through her head. Instead, she focused on wiping down the flight gear she had been wearing. When she finished, she stowed it in one of the lockers in the shuttle's cargo hold.

Taking a cue from Skye, Sahar had pulled her clothes out of a nearby locker and was attempting to peel off the skinsuit. "Damn, is Valhalla always that hot this time of year? I figured with it being so far north that even the summers would be cool."

"That's what they say," said Skye. "I hear the winters are still brutal."

"You'd think the corporations would pump a bit more money into climate control," Sahar grumbled. "I mean, I get that your governments don't do shit anymore, but who wants to live in a place like that?"

"I didn't think it was so bad."

"Guess it's a little different when you don't have to deal with fur. That shit wouldn't fly on a Federation world."

As the Maur managed to free herself from the skinsuit and began toweling off, Skye tapped into the shuttle's front viewscreen from her tablet.

Their destination was just coming into view.

Despite the clutter of ships and satellites in Sif's low orbit, the *Vandal* was easy to spot. The K-class freighter was one of the largest vessels allowed this close to the planet. If it were any bigger, they would have had to park it in one of the shipyards farther out.

The ship wasn't sleek, and it definitely wouldn't go far in a firefight. A trio of defense turrets was mounted on the underside of its long, armored bulk. Those worked more for clearing away space debris than actual combat. They'd installed torpedo bays and railguns along with a few other aftermarket mods, but those had yet to be tested.

Though it wasn't much of a fighter, it was one of the best transport ships to grace the market. According to the documentation required by the Dorian Gate Commission, the *Vandal* acted as a supply transport based out of Sigma-4. As legitimate as their registration was, the crew had to take precautions to keep the DGC from looking too closely at the ship's manifests.

Hard to believe Markus and Skye had dug her out of a junkyard so many years ago.

Aaliyah's voice rang out from the cockpit. "Hey Dan, ya read? We're on approach. Mind openin' the door for us?"

A young man's voice responded from her console. "Confirmed, Aaliyah. Opening hanger doors. Welcome back."

Clicking sounds echoed from the cockpit as Aaliyah flipped the switches to engage the auto-pilot. Once that was done, she unstrapped herself from the pilot's chair and wandered back into the shuttle bay.

The shuttle's pilot—who also served as the ship's resident mechanic and engineer—ran a hand back through her frizzy mess of red hair. She'd already stripped off the top half of her flight suit and tied it around her waist, leaving her runic tattoo visible on her left forearm. The black symbol popped violently against her pale skin.

Despite looking the part of the frumpy mechanic, her angular facial structure was striking. A smattering of freckles spread across high cheekbones provided an attractive accent to her chocolate-colored irises. Somehow that girl still managed to look good even with the evident lack of effort put toward her appearance.

A look of disgust distorted her features. "Lith's tits, Sahar! What the frag did ya do to my mech?"

The Maur tried to play it cool. "It's just a little combat damage. You know that's always a risk on these missions."

"Combat damage? What did ya do? Just stand there and let them shoot ya? Ain't ya never heard of 'evasive maneuvers?'"

Skye lifted a hand to hide her spreading grin as she murmured, "Using it as a battering ram to take out drones probably didn't help."

Sahar glowered at Skye as Aaliyah launched into another stream of curses. "How am I supposed to fix this? There ain't a fraggin' part on this whole gods-damned thing that doesn't need replacin'!"

"I'm sure you'll manage," Sahar replied dismissively.

The shuttle buckled slightly as the autopilot landed them in the *Vandal's* cargo bay. Aaliyah was still fuming as the craft's ramp lowered.

Skye slung her backpack over her shoulder. "Do you guys need help with the mech or the cargo?"

More cursing from Aaliyah.

"We're good," Sahar replied. "I know how to get a hold of you if we need you."

That was what Skye had hoped to hear. Normally she would stay and chat, but she was exhausted. Plus, aside from providing another set of hands to lift the heavier stuff, Skye didn't bring much to the table in terms of technical skill.

Her two crewmates were already in the thick of it as Skye stepped out of the shuttle and slunk out of the hangar. She contemplated placing a bet with the other crew members as to whether Aaliyah would try to save the mech or scrap it for spare parts.

The rest of the ship seemed unnaturally quiet. Only the sound of her boots striking the grated floor and the soft buzz of the life-support systems kept her company. She occasionally passed one of the ship's maintenance bots. The simple programming on the spider-like drones seemed to not even notice her.

Soon she came to her cabin. When she palmed the access pad, the door hissed open to reveal a chamber that was comfortable if not incredibly spacious.

All crew members had their own rooms with the basic utilities: closet, bed, desk, and bathroom with a shower and toilet. It was about the same size for most of the crew, save for Markus, who'd claimed the captain's cabin. Even the smaller accommodations were a lot better than what most crews dealt with.

When she and Markus had first picked up the vessel, the cabins had been designed for double or triple bunking crew members. Under that configuration, the *Vandal* was capable of housing just shy of two score crew members. With only the six of them currently manning the vessel, the accommodations were practically luxurious.

A new wash of fatigue hit Skye like a tidal wave. One of those slow, aching headaches she'd been dealing with was starting to build. Without even removing her flight suit, Skye stretched out over the sheets of her mattress.

She laid there for a moment, staring up at nothing. Despite being so tired, her thoughts would not leave her alone.

Markus not checking in after she had reached the shuttle had affected her more than she was comfortable with. It brought up feelings that were complicated, and certainly not welcomed.

It doesn't mean what you think it means. You'd be worried about any member of the crew. Nothing else. You're done with him. Really, it's done.

And gods knew it would be done permanently if Markus knew how she'd been spending the last few weeks getting over him.

As powerful as these emotions were, her exhaustion proved more intense. At some point in her internal deliberations, she finally fell asleep.

Eli's little surgery hadn't done anything to help Markus's mobility. The Sahaia had to support him all the way back to the safe house. It hadn't been a short walk, either. They'd been limping along for the better part of an hour, keeping to the shadows of largely unoccupied streets.

Although the sun had set hours earlier, the summer's heat was scorching. Even without the armor, which Eli had helped Markus stash inside the backpacks they now carried, Markus was pouring sweat.

They had been trying to look casual: just two space jockeys stumbling back from a night on the town. *Please ignore all the gear strapped to our backs. We take it everywhere.*

"Did Ora have to hide this place in the ass-end of nowhere?" Markus grumbled.

"I would imagine that a secret hideout in the middle of the main thoroughfare would hardly suit its clandestine purpose," Eli replied.

"That's my point though! No one's looking for a syndicate to set up shop in the mercantile district. It's the perfect cover."

"Perhaps." The Sahaia's expression did nothing to convey how he actually felt about the subject, though Markus was suspicious he was just blowing him off. "I, for one, am currently grateful for our benefactor's level of discretion. It seems unlikely that we'd be passed off as two travelers who've had a bit too much at the tavern given how much equipment we're carrying. Then again, if you continue to neglect to shave, you might pass as a homeless vagabond."

Markus rubbed one hand up his two-day growth of stubble. "I was thinking of growing it out, actually. It's kind of nice not having to run a razor over your face every day."

"If you say so."

Markus's foot slipped on a piece of rubbish lying on the sidewalk. He grunted in pain as a fresh flare of agony went through his leg. "We almost there?"

"Just a bit farther."

The banter ran dry after that. It was hard for Markus to keep talking while putting all his energy into staying on his feet. Plus, his sense of humor waned as the stym left his system.

That was the thing about the drug: when it cleared, the pain in his leg would lessen, but the withdrawal symptoms would come on quickly. He'd rather deal with a gunshot wound than have to work through those.

They stopped in front of a nondescript steel door. Eli pounded on the door twice and paused. After a moment there came an answering knock. In response, Eli struck the door once again.

A piece of the neighboring wall slid away to reveal an access panel. While still holding Markus up with one arm, Eli pressed his palm against the blue screen.

The device chimed approvingly, and the door clicked open. Eli pushed gently on the door, swinging it inward.

A burly sand-colored Maur stood just inside, rifle trained on both of them. He might have passed for the same clan as Sahar if not for the darker stripes along his forehead and neck.

"Just you two?" he growled.

"Yup," Markus grunted. "As planned."

The Maur's eyes scanned the area behind them before going to Markus's leg. "You look like shit."

"Good to see you too, Vallus. Can we come inside now?"

With a nod, the Maur stepped aside. Markus and Eli limped through the door, which slid shut behind them.

"Apologies," Vallus whispered. "Standard precautions, you understand. Have to keep them enforced even for the ones that Ora trusts."

"And we make that list?" Markus asked.

"If she hires you more than once, you know you've made the list."

Huh...

Markus had never thought of it that way. Working for Ora had been one of the stranger experiences in his running career.

Despite this, he hadn't considered her any choosier than the half-a-dozen other crime bosses they'd run for.

Vallus's brought a hand to his shoulder. He caught Eli's eye. "Here, let me take him."

Markus's friend was a little too quick to relinquish control. Before he knew it, Markus found himself swept up in the arms of the super-strong alien enforcer. "This is a little intimate, Vallus."

"I could always drop you."

"Please don't."

"Then shut your mouth. Your friend looks tired, and your Terran hide is hardly a burden for me. Don't read too much into it. You're not my type."

"Wow, way to let a guy down easy."

"You're welcome."

Vallus carried him through another door into a lounge of sorts. The place was empty, which Markus didn't mind. He wasn't keen on anyone getting a glimpse of him being carried like a bride across the threshold.

The Maur set him on one of the black couches that lined the walls. "You're just in time. We've got a supply shipment going up to another vessel in low orbit. You can hitch a ride on that one, and we'll drop you off at the *Vandal*."

"Thanks, Vallus," said Eli.

"Not a problem. You guys *did* get what Ora wanted, right?"

Markus rolled his eyes, more than a little annoyed at being questioned. "Yes, we secured the shipment. The rest of our crew is inventorying it as we speak."

"Good," Vallus replied. "Not that it would change anything, of course."

"No, we get it. Ora wants her reassurance that she's successfully pissed off House Valadar—though gods know why she'd want to do that in the first place."

"That's the thing about Ora: if you thought on her level you'd be calling the shots instead of risking your asses running the Nethra."

Fair point, but there wasn't anything this side of Terra that would convince Markus to trade places. Ora might have more money, but her notoriety brought more than its fair share of problems.

"How much longer until that ship lifts off?" Eli asked

"Thirty minutes. We'll have you on a land transport in ten to take you to the spaceport." Then, almost as if he would have forgotten, Vallus added, "Oh! Here, I've got something else for you."

The Maur reached into his pocket and drew out a small data chip. He handed it to Eli, who looked at the thing like it might self-destruct.

"What's this?" he asked.

"A message confirming that you are inbound to Sigma-4. Transmit this when you get up into orbit and are in range of the gate."

Eli still eyed the chip suspiciously. A moment of tense silence set in. It was Markus who finally spoke up. "So, Ora's looking for immediate confirmation on our jobs now?"

Vallus chuckled. "Nah, nothing like that. Ora just wanted to know when you were coming in. It's a good thing."

"How do you figure that?"

"Well, apparently there's something waiting for you back at the station. Something about another job and all that. She wants you guys on it, but it's time-sensitive. You know how that goes."

Despite the assertion, Markus didn't know anything of the kind. "Time-sensitive?"

"She didn't tell me any more than that." Vallus clapped a big hand on Markus's shoulder. "Relax, big guy. You guys are always looking for more trouble, right? It looks like it's going to find you a bit sooner than expected."

CHAPTER 4

[ACCESSING COGNIS.DATAFILES...]

JUMP-GATE — *TECHNOLOGY INVENTORY* — DORIAN JUMP-GATES REPRESENT THE MOST FEASIBLE AVENUE FOR FASTER-THAN-LIGHT TRAVEL IN THE SAPIENT SYSTEMS. JUMP GATES SUSTAIN A HOLE IN SPACETIME THAT ALLOWS FOR THE SEAMLESS TRAVEL OF MESSAGES, SUPPLIES, AND SPACECRAFT BETWEEN INHABITED GALAXIES WITHIN SECONDS. THE DORIAN HIGH COUNCIL EARNS THE MAJORITY OF ITS TAX REVENUES THROUGH THE COLLECTION OF GATE FEES FROM PERSONS WHO CHOOSE TO USE THE GATE NETWORK TO NAVIGATE THE STARS.

[CLOSING DATAFILE...]

Aboard the *Vandal*, Daniel Ratemacher sat staring at a discrete holodisplay he'd positioned above his lap. He tapped his foot along with the light-hearted music that drifted from the console speakers: Old Terra Jazz. Not something that his crewmates would have appreciated, which is why he waited until they were all gone on missions to indulge.

Though Skye, Sahar, and Aaliyah had arrived, none of them had stopped by the cockpit to check in on him. Dan didn't mind; that just meant his tunes kept playing. Besides, they were probably busy with other things right about now.

And, as fortune would have it, Dan had something very important he needed to check in on as well. The *Vandal* had just moved in range of the Serpent Gate, which connected back to the

Ravian System. For the next ten minutes, he could bounce messages back through the gate to Sigma-4.

[ARE YOU THERE?] he typed.

Long seconds—close to a minute—before the reply popped up on his screen. [YES.]

Dan's heart fluttered in anticipation. His fingers worked furiously at the keyboard. [I'VE SECURED THE PAYMENT YOU REQUESTED. DO YOU STILL HAVE THE ITEM I WANT?]

He held his breath. If his contact had already sold the drive-chip to someone else, that was going to represent a lot of wasted effort.

It was mere luck that Dan had stumbled on this contact in the first place. What he was looking for wasn't exactly available on the open market. Sure enough, as soon as the contact had been able to confirm that the item in question was available, Markus had them leave for a new contract.

Dan found himself on his way out-system before he could confirm that he was still interested. In hopes that he'd get another shot at buying the item when they finished up their job on Sif, he'd still had the krets liquidated from his account.

That had been quite a feat without setting foot on the actual planet. Come to find out, it was difficult to liquidate sixty-thousand krets into an untraceable form. It was doubly hard to do so from orbit. The transactional fees had been insane—pure thievery.

Which Dan found ironic, of course, given their stated purpose in this system in the first place.

[I HAVE THE ITEM.]

Dan let loose a sigh of relief. It looked like things were coming together.

A second message: [WHEN CAN YOU MEET?]

That was a good question, the answer to which was largely dependent on factors outside of Dan's control. Their shuttle had returned with half the crew members, but he had no idea when Markus and…

"Daniel, this is Eli. Do you read?"

Now *that* was good timing.

"Yes, I read you, Eli. Go ahead."

"Markus and I are en route with the resupply. Markus suffered a bit of an accident on loading. Can you have Z prepped and ready to receive him in the medical bay?"

Dan doubted Markus's injuries were actually from loading supplies. More likely Eli was keeping the conversation inconspicuous on these open channels. Between the DGC, Valadars, and fates knew who else, they didn't want to get tied to what had happened down in the shipyards that evening.

"Roger that, Eli. Can I get your ETA?"

"Our pilot says we should be docked in about an hour."

"Confirmed. See you soon."

Dan muted the comms channel and started doing the math in his head. If he gave supply transport a full two hours to arrive, unload and depart, then added in the two, maybe three hours it would take to make it over to the Serpent Gate…

It could be as late as five hours before they were even in Ravian space. Factoring in the inevitable traffic, he was looking at as much as ten hours before they docked at the station.

He took a couple more seconds of running the calculations, scenarios, and converting time zones before Dan typed his reply. [THIS EVENING, 23:00. WHAT LOCATION?]

Another long, agonizing wait for a response. Dan looked at his timer, half-worried he'd moved out of sync with the gate.

The response came. [R-1. EXACT COORDINATES ATTACHED. COME ALONE.]

There was a mapping file attached to the message. Dan scanned it, reviewed it, and routed the file to his MoDAC before cutting the connection.

He could hardly contain the smile that he felt stretching the limits of his face. At long last, he was going to have the missing piece to his pet project.

This time tomorrow, he would be busy turning his elusive dreams into reality.

The feeling of acceleration was almost imperceptible, but it was still enough to jostle Skye from her impromptu siesta.

After re-establishing that she was, indeed, still on the *Vandal*, she relaxed a bit. Bad dreams, again. It seemed like she was having a lot of those lately. Almost as frequently as she was having headaches.

Groaning, she pressed her palms to her forehead just above her eyes, trying to relieve the latest round of brain pain. She needed to remember to talk to Doc Li about getting back on the meds.

How long had she been out? Long enough for Eli and Markus to make it back if they were leaving. An hour or two?

With trepidation, she glanced at her MoDAC. She'd been out for nearly four hours. She'd practically slept the night away.

Skye rolled to the side of the bed, stood up, and stripped out of her flight suit. The synthetic fiber had to be peeled off her skin. Her gray underclothes were still completely saturated with sweat, despite the cool air in her quarters.

It all felt extremely nasty. With a grunt of disgust, she pulled off the rest of her clothes and gathered them absently into a sopping heap on the floor. She couldn't believe she'd fallen asleep in those things.

Her mouth split with a massive yawn. Why was she so damn tired?

It must have been the jump. It had been a while since she'd done one of those maneuvers. They had been coming in a little too fast this time, too.

The gear she wore helped keep the g-force from tearing her apart, but she could tell she wasn't in as good of shape as she'd once been. Even with her cybernetics enhancing her strength and durability, conditioning still played a huge role in her ability to pull off those acrobatics.

She hadn't done a great job of keeping up with her training regimen lately, and she wasn't getting any younger. Shit, how old was she now? Thirty-two, maybe thirty-three standard cycles?

It was hard to keep track when they kept jumping to different systems. Regardless, she wasn't the daredevil recruit she had been over a decade ago.

Pushing that thought aside, she wandered over to the shower and hit the controls to start the cascade of water. A three-minute timer appeared on the control panel, and she jabbed a couple more buttons to override it. Today's jump definitely earned her the right to supersede the standard water ration.

It had been a long day, and there was no doubt about it: she needed a break.

There was always the next conflict—the next mission. The faces and other details changed, but the core of it was always the same. They were blowing something up, stealing something, or knocking off some group of lowlifes who had pissed off the wrong person. It was always about that next payday.

Yup, running the Nethra was getting old. Back in the day, when it had been just her and Markus, she hadn't exactly been focused on the grand design. A part of her, though, had always thought this would be temporary.

In her mind, the mercenary gig was a natural extension of the skills they'd picked up in the Colony Wars. They'd run jobs for a few years and then move on to something better.

That wasn't how things ended up playing out. Not with her life, and certainly not with her and Markus.

And now you're thinking about him again…

Why did that keep coming back up today? Seriously, why now? The guy fails one check-in and suddenly she's stumbling down memory lane? *Grow up, Skye. It's been weeks.*

She didn't know how long she stood pensively under the running water. Eventually, she pressed the keys to stop the shower and wrung out her hair over one shoulder. She was reaching back to grab a towel when a voice made her jump.

"Nice job today."

Her heart leaped at the unexpected noise. Even after she realized who it was, her adrenaline continued to surge. *Enter romantic problem number two.*

"Shit, Eli!" she hissed in surprise. "Knock much?"

Eli held up his hands placatingly. "Apologies, the door was unlocked. I took it as an invitation."

"Are you serious?" she huffed. "No, that was not an invitation. The damn thing must be on the fritz again."

"Might be a problem with some of the changes Dan has been making. I'll ask him to look into it."

Skye studied his expression. He was using that tone of voice that he often did: incessantly polite and unfailingly calm. It did a lot to help mitigate her frustrations with him.

He must have been back for quite some time now because he had managed to get himself cleaned up. Then again, Eli never seemed disheveled. Did Sahaia physiology make it so you didn't sweat?

Despite the awkwardness of the situation, Skye found herself lost in his handsome features. There was no doubting that Eli was a looker with his sleek black hair and black-in-black eyes. Though some found the look unnerving, especially in contrast to the ultra-white skin, Skye thought that it added to his mystique. Strangely, the pale skin didn't carry a sickly cast, like when Terrans grew too pale from lack of sun exposure.

No, there was an odd beauty that could be found in the preternatural appearance of the Sahaia. Skye had never considered herself a xenophile. Not until a few weeks ago when she and Markus had split, and she'd decided to recruit a little help with moving on.

Best way to get over someone, right?

Well, Skye had never claimed she had the best foresight. Part of her had been hoping she'd get drunk, get slick with some guy she'd just met, and move on. She hadn't expected Eli to find her that night. She certainly hadn't expected that this little arrangement would still be going weeks later.

And now she realized she was staring at him. He stared right back, and Skye blushed as she realized that she was still very much undressed. She fought that I-wasn't-prepared-for-you-to-see-me-naked, impulse to cover herself up. After all, it wasn't anything he hadn't seen before. Like, plenty of times now.

"Any chance you could hand me a towel?"

Eli cleared his throat. "Um, of course," he answered, eyes suddenly desperate to focus on anything but her body.

Damn it, she hadn't wanted to make this awkward.

As he handed her the towel, he planted an ironically chaste kiss on her cheek. "Everything okay? I'm sorry if I overstepped. I just… I missed you."

And, there it was. If she hadn't felt like shit before…

She turned her face and pressed her lips against his. "Yeah," she whispered into his mouth. "I'm good. Just a little in my head, that's all. I crashed hardcore when I got back in…"

"In your head, hey?" Their mouths came together again. His hand caressed her bare hip, nudging her closer. "Maybe there's something I could try to help clear your mind?"

Skye's heart thudded faster at the suggestion. Part of her, at least, thought that was an excellent idea. "A little risky," she breathed, "doing it on the ship with the whole crew on board, don't you think?"

"Markus is in medical. Probably will be for a few more hours."

"But there's still everyone else we need to worry about."

"So what if they find out?" he protested. "Maybe it'd be better if we were a little more open about our…"

He trailed off. Perhaps because he wasn't sure exactly how to describe their situation, seeming to suggest that she should help him out here.

I mean, the first time she could've called an accident—maybe even a mistake. The second time she'd done it to prove it wasn't. By the third time, the fourth, the fifth, it was pretty fair to say they were in a…

"Relationship?" she suggested.

A smile spread across his dark lips. "Yes."

Her spirits lifted at the sight of that smile. Then, as she realized the implications that brought it there, she grew anxious.

Markus was going to be pissed. Yeah, some people might be able to shrug it off and move on in a few weeks, but not Markus. He was a man of enduring passions, with a very distinct idea of loyalty. If there was any chance of salvaging that friendship, they were going to have to be careful about how they broke the news to him.

Skye planted another gentle kiss on Eli's lips. It was done in a way that was affectionate but sent the message for him to cool his jets.

"We'll be back on Sigma-4 today. Let's reconnect tonight, okay?"

Eli smiled politely, but those ink-black eyes gave away his disappointment. "All right," he agreed. "Tonight."

He wrapped the towel around her and took a step back. Skye could tell he was trying hard to make his warm expression look sincere. He almost even succeeded. "I'll leave you to your reflections then. See you when we dock?"

"Yeah," she agreed, flashing him her own smile. "See you then."

Chapter 5

[Accessing COGNIS.Datafiles…]

Mobile Data Access Card (MoDAC) — *Technology Inventory* — MoDACs are the most popular personal communication and data storage devices among sapient user groups. These handheld devices are durable, flexible, and slot most commonly utilized data storage chips. They enable voice communication, text transmission, financial transactions, and numerous other functions through various applications available on digital markets.

[Closing Datafile…]

"Agh! Damn it, Z!" Markus roared. "What in the nine hells are you doing down there?"

The medical drone seemed unconcerned by his outburst. The bot kept stitching away at his injured leg, which was held fast to the examination table by magnetic clamps.

"The nature of your injury requires that I replace damaged nerve tissue with threads of cylian alloy, the properties of which…"

"I could give a damn what the properties are! Can you go a little easier on the stabbing? Or maybe numb my leg first?"

"Your leg was numbed before the procedure. As I was attempting to explain: you are experiencing the result of the newly established connections. I've bridged your existing neurons with a cylian alloy splint that will help to regrow your nervous tissue. The emergence of pain is a sign that the procedure has been effective."

Markus groaned and lay back on the table. He should have opted for an actual sedative. That dose of harpy he'd downed a couple of hours ago wasn't cutting it anymore.

The medical drone continued diligently with the knitting actions of its needle-like appendages. In absence of any further protests from Markus, it prattled on in robotic cadence as it worked.

"As a potential point of interest, I've detected significant amounts of amphetacyrine in your bloodstream. This might contribute to an enhanced pain response in conjunction with the surgery."

"Ampheta-what?"

The drone clicked as it registered the query and switched over to its medical dictionary. "Amphetacyrine—more commonly referred to by the street name 'stym'—is a metabolic and neurosensory enhancement agent frequently abused by sapiens with a proclivity for adrenal stimulation. Would you like to learn more about amphetacyrine?"

Markus groaned again. "No…" He knew plenty about the drug. The fact that he hadn't had a dose since the safehouse was one of the factors contributing to his worsening mood. "Just hurry it up, would ya?"

"Already done, sir," the drone replied as it looked up at Markus and rolled backward. "The pain will subside in approximately thirteen point two minutes. The numbing agent will metabolize in another thirty seconds. You should be able to use the leg at that time. How may I be of further assistance?"

Gritting his teeth, Markus forced himself up into a sitting position. "I think I'm good. Thanks, Z." The robot intoned a perfunctory, "You're welcome. Have a wonderful day." With its function now served, the cylindrical bot rolled back to its charging station.

Z-426—or Z, as most of the crew referred to it—was the closest thing they had to a physician on the *Vandal*. Like most primitive AIs on the market, it was all autonomous processing and very little bedside manner.

The thing gave Markus the creeps. He'd been optimistic about buying it when their last medic had decided to give up the running game and try her hand at a normal life. That optimism had long since given way to the cold reality of having an AI caregiver. The thing could calculate medication doses to the tenth decimal, but the awkwardness of dealing with a machine when you were sick or injured left much to be desired. Gods, he missed Nikki.

Now that he was thinking about it, maybe he should have Dan adjust the bot's calibration to be on the more generous side when it came to the pain meds. It certainly felt like Z had short-changed him on this procedure. Sure, it might have been the stym heightening his senses, but he didn't remember it hurting this bad the last time he'd gotten shot.

"Damn, and ya weren't even near the real action!"

Markus turned to see Aaliyah striding through the door to medical. "Nice to see you too, Red. And you're welcome for taking care of those extra drones for you."

Aaliyah's smirk was unwavering. "I'm sure we could've handled them."

"Guess we'll never know."

"Yeah, guess not."

Markus shook his head. At least she wasn't losing any sleep over his wellbeing. "What's up? I imagined you'd be tied up taking inventory right now."

"Already done. I've got the report right here." She waved her MoDAC pinched between her thumb and forefinger. "I wanted to check somethin' with ya real quick though. Was that the full list ya gave me?"

"List of what?"

"The cargo we should be expectin'."

"Only one I had."

"No last-minute updates from Ora? No changes to the manifest?"

"No…" He dragged the word out. Now she had him curious, and more than a little bit nervous. "Why? Was something missing?"

Her smile broadened. "No, nothin' missin'. Actually, there was a little somethin' extra. Have ya ever heard of j-krysts?"

He arched an eyebrow at her. "Jakra-Kul crystals? Only in passing. Why? Did you find one tucked into the shipment?"

She passed her card over to him. "Thirty."

Markus choked. "Come again?"

"Ya heard me."

Even looking at the image she'd snapped, Markus could hardly believe their luck. A single j-kryst was a nice payday. Thirty would have made the job worth pulling even without all the other shit Ora had them pick up.

"So," Aaliyah continued. "My next question is, are we obligated to hand them over to Ora if they weren't on the manifest?"

Now *that* was a serious question. If Ora and her Grey Wings had missed such a serious line item in that shipment, were the odds pretty good that it wasn't supposed to be there? Maybe it was something slipped in off-the-books. With no record, there was nothing to say that they were ever there in the first place.

"Stash them in the hold," he said, handing Aaliyah back her mobile. "If Ora doesn't make a fuss, we'll pretend like it never happened. We can try and fence them next time we're off station."

Aaliyah hesitated. "Actually, if we get to keep the goods, I've got a little project I wouldn't mind tryin'. That is if we don't need the money right away."

"Now you've surprised me twice in as many minutes. I thought you were all about the payday?"

"I am! I just… I think that, with a little help from the kid, I might be able to cook up somethin' even more valuable than a few more krets in the bank."

There was no need to ask who she meant by "the kid." Dan was the only crew member that still looked like he was grappling with puberty. Markus had to admit, though, that he wouldn't have expected Aaliyah to partner with him on a project.

Dan was still the newest member of the team. Although he was starting to fit in, he didn't spend a lot of his time socializing with the rest of the crew. Right now, he was spending all his free time getting the ship's systems integrated. Maybe a break in that project would be good for the kid's morale.

"All right, it's fine by me. Remember: only if Ora doesn't say anything. If she brings it up, we're handing over the crystals. We don't need to be sowing bad seeds with our best client."

The redhead beamed. "Great. Thanks, boss."

At that moment, Dan's voice rang out over the ship's intercom. "Approaching jump gate. Estimated fifteen minutes until the crossing."

Aaliyah sighed. "Have ya given up on tellin' him we don't need the travel updates?"

Markus shrugged. "I don't know, I've kind of gotten used to them. Helps me make sure I stay on top of shit."

He attempted to twist his foot. Seeing that the limb was at least sort of working, he unbuckled the clamp on the table and slid off the edge.

"I think I'll go sit with him for a bit. It's been a while since I've spent any time on the bridge."

"All right gimpy," Aaliyah teased. "Need help hobblin' up to the ol' captain's chair?"

Markus gently tested the leg against the floor. It held. "I'll make it. Thanks, Red." As he slipped on a pair of dark pants and jacket, he turned back to her. "How's everyone else doing? You didn't mention anything, so I'm assuming everyone else is okay."

The engineer eyed him strangely, even as she shrugged. "Sure. Unless ya count the mech. That thing's toast. But yeah, you're the only one who came back with any damage."

Markus nodded. "Good."

He forced himself to start moving again and resisted the urge to ask about Skye.

She said everyone was fine. Hells, it wasn't like Skye was sitting around worrying about his sorry ass, right? Right.

Fighting to keep his limp imperceptible, he meandered out the door and down the hall toward the bridge. Aaliyah went off in the other direction.

When she was out of sight, Markus reached into his pocket and pulled out the stym cassette. It wasn't like his drug use was any secret among the crew—Skye had seen to that—but he still didn't like to use too openly in front of them.

He closed his eyes as the film dissolved into his gumline. The effects of the rush were even stronger when he went this long between doses. There was nothing quite like those first few seconds of euphoria. Despite the heightened perception, the pain in his leg didn't bother him as much with his buzz on.

At least, until he stumbled over the drone that crossed into his path. "Shit!" he spat, as he tumbled onto the grated floor.

The spider-like bot flipped over in the collision. It landed with a metallic clang, and its spindly little legs swiped at the air in frustration. Rolling onto his back, Markus gave the fragging thing a solid kick with his good leg, sending it spinning off into the far bulkhead.

Gods-damned things were getting even more glitchy lately. Dan needed to hurry up and get them integrated with the rest of the ship's new operating system. Maybe then the annoying little things would be smart enough not to wander out into the middle of the hall.

Still grumbling, he pulled himself to his feet and punched the access panel leading to the bridge.

Inside, a boy that looked way too young to be hanging out with mercenaries was absently entering commands into the ship's navigation console. An array of holodisplays and control panels surrounded him, seeming to envelop him in a kind of cocoon.

Unlike the rest of the crew, Dan hadn't been on the original team's roster. They'd picked up the kid after an incident on Beta-9 had left them short-handed. It was strange to come across someone like him on a station like that, and Markus might not have believed the kid's story if it hadn't been so strange.

Dan claimed to be a born and bred spacer, though he didn't have the typical credentials to support this claim. He lacked Aaliyah's folksy accent, and he didn't carry himself like someone who'd been brought up in an indenturement academy. Despite being less than sixteen cycles in age, he carried himself with a maturity that frequently made him see out of place.

As it turned out, that was because the kid was a certified super-genius. When he was old enough, his parents had offloaded him to the Prodigy program for a quick payday. He claimed there were no records of the transaction, so there was no way to identify who'd sold him as a glorified brain slave.

Markus never did get a good answer on why Dan had left the camp—or how he had left it, for that matter. He'd never questioned Dan's decision, though. He knew better than anyone what it felt like to give the finger to the corporate overlords and carve out another path.

The fact that Dan was out and on the loose when they had found him was an anomaly, but that wasn't the only strange thing about him. For some reason, the standard nutritional sups had not taken to his physiology. The kid clocked in at a meter and a half and couldn't have weighed much more than forty kilos.

Even stranger, Dan wore glasses. Granted, they were some high-tech model with all the trimmings: state-of-the-art analytical tools, environmental scanners, universal integration capability, and gods knew what else. But still… *glasses*?

That was almost unheard of ever since biomods gave civilization the ability to cure any kind of visual impairment.

Whatever corp had scooped Dan up to put him in a camp was not going to hold onto damaged goods. Was that why they'd been so careless to let him get away?

Well, whatever. Their loss was Markus's gain. That was exactly the way he liked it.

He slid into the larger chair right next to the kid's hollow-panel cocoon. Dan didn't acknowledge Markus's presence. He remained, instead, absorbed in whatever incremental adjustments he was making. Markus had flown this ship plenty of times before Dan was on the scene. He was pretty sure that all the brain-power the kid was squandering on this relatively simple routine was not necessary. With a sigh, Markus gazed out the viewscreen. "How's it going, Dan?"

The boy started at the greeting. Apparently, he hadn't seen Markus enter the room. Damn, that was some good focus. "Oh… ah… yes! I mean, good… it's good… everything within normal limits."

"I expected nothing less," Markus chuckled. He hadn't meant to throw the kid into a tizzy.

"We should be passing through the gate in…" Dan paused, searching frantically for the holodisplay that would give him the exact figure.

"Dan, it's fine. I was just popping in to say hi. Go back to what you were doing. Pretend I'm not here."

"Um… okay."

The teen went back to tinkering with the figures on the display, but not nearly as enthusiastically as he had been moments earlier. Markus sighed again, and half-contemplated leaving the kid to his business.

Then again, his leg was starting to hurt after the altercation with the bot in the hallway. "I may have fragged up one of your drones, by the way. Sorry about that."

Dan blinked. "Huh? When? What happened?"

"Oh, back there in the hall. Wasn't watching where I was going. To be fair, I wasn't expecting it to be crawling in the middle of the walkway."

Dan grimaced. Markus couldn't tell if it was for him, or for the drone he might need to replace now. "Apologies. I think the last system update messed with their ability to synchronize their task lists with existing operating parameters. I've noticed several of them out of position lately."

"System update, hey? So, that will be fixed when you get your pet project online?"

"Lexa, you mean?" Dan asked using his nickname for the LX-Alpha operating system running the ship. "Yes, actually. I think I'm on the verge of a breakthrough. I just have to pick up a new part when we're back on station."

"Yeah? What are you grabbing?"

Dan hesitated. "Well, it's a different kind of drive chip. Without getting too technical, it'll give me the power I need to integrate the rest of the peripheral systems. That includes the maintenance drones. I should be able to get Z linked in too."

Markus raised his eyebrows in surprise. "That's... pretty cool. Good for you, Dan."

He'd been working on the project for a while. As installed, the LX-Alpha was a rudimentary AI that handled basic ship functions. It did a fine job of flying the ship but required a ton of patches and auxiliary programs to handle the systems they were running today.

They'd been dealing with the shitty system ever since he and Skye had acquired the *Vandal*. Dan hadn't exactly been enthused when Markus had challenged him to upgrade the program. Lately, though, he'd been complaining about the project a lot less. In fact, he almost seemed to be enjoying it.

The holodisplay to Dan's left beeped, and a vibrant blue sphere appeared in the far corner of the translucent panel. "Gate command center transmitting," Dan reported.

A chill swept up Markus's spine. "Why? Did our auth-codes not check out?"

"No, everything's reading like it's fine."

"The kret transfer went through?"

Dan was looking as frustrated as Markus at that moment. "Yes. *Everything* is normal. I don't know what this is about."

Markus leaned back into the chair. Good thing he'd decided to wander up here for a bit. "Patch it through."

A holodisplay popped up in front of Markus's seat and a video feed appeared in its center. The feed showed a woman's face with warm brown skin. Her dark curly hair looped back behind a pair of horns that arced backward from her temples.

Dorians, like the woman on the feed, were an elusive race that held interplanetary commerce under their complete control. This was, in part, thanks to their daringness in challenging the laws of physics and having the cunning to turn it into a microeconomy.

Their monopoly on interstellar travel was a huge source of resentment for the other races. That, along with their unique appearance, had earned them the derisive moniker "satyrs."

The slur was usually whispered well out of their range of hearing. To do otherwise tended to attract unwanted attention. No one wanted the Dorians, particularly those associated with the Gate Commission, up in their business.

Which was why the fact that the woman on the screen was an old friend did little to soothe Markus's anxieties. "Markus Frost," she greeted, a smile spreading across her face. "It seems the universe is too damn small."

"Llana," he replied, doing his best not to sound stiff. "How's my favorite DGC officer these days?"

"Know many Dorian officers, old friend?"

"I'll admit, you're one of only two I've kept in touch with. Can you see now why you're my favorite?"

She laughed—a *genuine* laugh. At least that was a good sign. "Have you run into Turan much lately?"

"Nope. I stay away from the Taurus Gate, and he leaves me alone." Markus swallowed hard and hoped he didn't look as nervous as he felt. "As good as it is to see you, I have to ask. To what do I owe this pleasure?"

Llana's friendly face darkened slightly. "It seems that there was some kind of incident on Valhalla last night. A VIP has requested that all traffic leaving the system be scanned." She sighed. "We, of course, weren't *staffed* for that kind of effort. Which is why you have the pleasure of talking to me instead of the technician that would normally be doing this."

"My lucky day," Markus chuckled. "What are you scanning for?"

"Don't worry, it's something pretty unusual. It'll only take a moment. Do I have your consent?"

Consent was a funny thing in this kind of situation. Either they consented to be scanned or they consented to be boarded. Authority was all on the DGC's side here. After all, using the gate network was a privilege, not a right.

"Of course," Markus replied. "Go ahead."

Alerts popped up on both Markus and Dan's holoscreens letting them know the vessel was now the subject of an active scan. Markus risked a glance at his pilot. The kid was looking so shaky and pale that Markus would have paged for assistance had they not been in the middle of an inspection.

The alert disappeared. Llana's brow furrowed as she studied the results on her end.

Markus held his breath.

"All right!" she exclaimed, her smile returning. "Everything checks out. Nice seeing you again, Markus. Have a safe trip."

"Thanks, Llana. Good to see you too."

Her image blinked out. Markus exhaled hard.

"Were they looking for us?" Dan asked.

Markus could only shrug. "Maybe. I guess we'll never know." The unique storage capabilities on their little smuggler's ship were designed to block some scans used by the Dorians, but not all of them.

There was a decent chance that the satyrs had been looking for someone else. There was an even better chance that they'd just gotten very, *very* lucky.

"Oh!" Markus exclaimed. That reminds me…"

He fished the data card Vallus had given him out of his jacket pocket. "Send this message to Ora with an attachment that mentions the Dorian scans. Say that's why we didn't send it when we were in range of the gate."

Dan arched an eyebrow, even as he complied with the order. "So, we're telling her it's because of the DGC when in reality you just forgot?"

"Yup. Much better story, don't you think?"

"And what would you have said if the DGC weren't running scans?"

"I don't know. Good thing they were, right?"

Dan shook his head and muttered something to himself that sounded suspiciously like, "Devil's luck."

Even if Markus had taken offense at the comment, it would be hard to argue with him. Inwardly, he was cursing himself for not seeing this taken care of as soon as he'd been brought on board.

Damn Eli and his mothering. He'd been so intent on getting Markus into medical that he'd almost landed them in hot water with their client. While Dan busied himself with that task, Markus took a moment to admire the distant image of the station.

The three-tiered satellite was typical of Sigma-class stations. Larger than most moons, the silvered station consisted of fifteen rings—five for each tier. It wasn't his favorite design, especially given the disparity in relative comfort and safety between each tier. Then again, it was hard to complain when the lack of security in the lower rings made it a prime area for individuals in his line of work.

Scratch that—he was being unfair. Crime was probably just as rampant in the upper rings. It just took on a classier facade.

Another message hit the *Vandal's* system almost immediately after Dan had sent his own.

Well, that was quick. "What's the word, Dan?"

The boy studied the screen for a second. "New docking instructions. Ora's slotted us in the R-3 concourse just outside of Annex." He glanced sideways at Markus. "That's highly irregular."

That was an understatement. Part of the reason Markus took advantage of the *Vandal's* merchant-class permit to dock in mid-tier was to provide a healthy distance between the Grey Wings and whatever he happened to be shuttling for them. If Ora was deviating from protocol to have them dock in the lower tier of the station, then expediency must be taking priority over discretion.

"Yeah," he agreed. "Patch me through to the rest of the ship."

Dan entered the appropriate commands in the prompt. Markus's holodisplay opened a new window to show the intercom application.

"All right team," he began, "We'll be docking at Sigma-4 in…"—He hesitated as he glanced at Dan who mouthed the ETA.—"three hours. We've been instructed to dock in the lower levels just outside of Annex. The client has asked that we check in with her immediately. Eli, I need you prepped to disembark right after we dock. Everyone else has leave until further notice. Keep your mobiles handy. Everyone's share will be wired directly to their accounts as soon as the client pays up. Remember to use standard encryption protocols when sending communications to team members."

He paused again, trying to think of anything he might be forgetting. "I guess that's it. See you all when we arrive."

"What do you think the rush is?" Dan asked as Markus closed the application.

"Not sure," he admitted. "What's your take?"

Dan shrugged, "You would know better than me. I just work here."

"See, that's what I like about you, Dan. You've got that 'speak only when spoken to' thing down. I feel like a proud father."

"Frag off, Markus."

"Such language for a boy of your tender years!" he clapped the kid on the shoulder. "I'll be back in a minute. Just have to go check my gear."

The crew quarters were one deck down. Even with a limp, Markus managed to get there in a matter of minutes. Inside his cabin, he quickly shed his clothes and snagged a quick shower. The leg injury seemed to be healing nicely, despite how much he'd bitched about the little surgery.

When he got out, he gave a little more consideration to his wardrobe than he normally would have. It wasn't like a trip to Annex necessitated anything formal, but he never wanted to look like a slouch when he met with a client. He kept his dark jacket but traded out the rest of the ensemble for something clean.

Instead of his gun belt, he strapped on a shoulder harness that allowed him to discreetly pack a pair of slender dirks. Firearms weren't allowed on station for good reason, and energy weapons were all but useless in a fight where your opponent would be packing a static shield. He didn't care for blades, but they were better than nothing.

Lastly, he checked his stym cassette. The thing was getting a little low, but it should be more than enough to get him through the night. He'd have to remember to pick up some more while on station.

One last survey of his person and his quarters, and he was out the door. He arrived back on the bridge just as Dan was pulling up to the concourse.

Holographic signals guided the ship through the containment fields and to their assigned docking platform. It was easy piloting because there were hardly any ships docked in this area. Most of the merchant-class freighters would be unloading at R-6 or higher.

While there might not have been many ships in the way, there was still something surprising waiting for them.

"Are those Ora's people?" Dan asked.

Markus nodded. "It looks like she was serious about getting us over to Annex ASAP."

"Umm… am I seeing things? It looks like they're armed."

Armed?

Shit. The kid was right. Those were definitely firearms being hefted by the Maur enforcers. And it may have been his imagination, but it looked like the station defenses were tracking the *Vandal* as it coasted closer to the platform.

It didn't surprise Markus that Ora had that kind of connection at the R-3 dock. What *was* surprising was the level of attention they were getting. This was not S.O.P.

Dan must have read the expression on Markus's face because he started tapping his leg nervously. "Are you sure you haven't done something to piss her off?"

"With Ora, I'm never sure. Nothing specific comes to mind this time, though."

"Should I set the engines for standby?"

There was a pause before Markus replied. "No. We'll be all right."

That wasn't exactly how he felt, but the net result was the same. If Ora had decided to knock them off, this show was over anyway. They wouldn't make it off the platform.

CHAPTER 6

[ACCESSING COGNIS.DATAFILES...]

HOUSE VALADAR — *FACTION PROFILE* — ONE OF THE FIVE REMAINING GREAT HOUSES OF TERRA. AS WITH ALL THE GREAT HOUSES, HOUSE VALADAR'S PORTFOLIO COVERS A VAST RANGE OF POLITICAL, SOCIAL, AND ECONOMIC INTERESTS. THE CURRENT DON, CYRUS, SON OF THE LATE EZEKIEL VALADAR, MANAGES THE MAJORITY OF THE FAMILY'S PROPERTIES DIRECTLY ALONG WITH HIS THREE SIBLINGS: JULIA, JOAQUIN, AND TESSA. VALADAR'S INFLUENCE PREDOMINANTLY LIES WITHIN THE FREYVIAN SYSTEM. YET, RECENT POLITICAL AND BUSINESS DECISIONS INDICATE A SHIFT TO A MORE AGGRESSIVE POSTURE. THIS HAS RIVAL HOUSES NERVOUS WITH THE PROSPECT THAT VALADAR IS SEEKING TO EXPAND ITS INFLUENCE.

[CLOSING DATAFILE...]

"Where do ya think you're goin?'" Joaquin asked as he pawed at Aria's waist.

She shot him a playful grin. "I need to be getting dressed, love. I've got a business call in five minutes."

He wasn't taking the hint. Instead of letting her go, he inched up and pulled back her long, dark hair. "What, you think you can use me like that and just go about your business?" His tone was equally playful, and his kisses along her neck might have changed her mind if the meeting hadn't been so important.

She relished the moment of temptation briefly. As lovers went, Joaquin was one of the better ones. Not that it meant anything, of course. It was just sex. Still, that man knew how to move his body. It must have been the gods' way of compensating for his lack of brains.

With one final, indulgent kiss, she pushed him back on the bed and stood up. "Don't tempt me, dear. Besides, don't you have somewhere else to be? I believe Cyrus was expecting to hear from you before it gets too late."

His face scrunched in a disapproving look. "My brother can wait. Despite what he's grown to think, we don't all start hoppin' the moment he shouts 'jump.'"

"Well, he *is* the Don." She pulled on her undergarments and reached for a pair of black leggings. "Besides, you don't exactly have the best excuse to be tardy on a check-in. How would Cyrus feel about you fraternizing with one of your new business partners?"

Joaquin let out a derisive snort. "Like he has any room to talk there, what with the way he's paling around with that buddy of yours."

"Which one?"

"That Citza chick. You know, tight abs, big tits…"

"Sydney?"

"Sounds right."

"Well, part of her *job* is keeping him satisfied. This here…" She leaned over and ran a hand down the man's rippling stomach, stopping just shy of the more interesting bits. "This was just a bit of recreation."

Joaquin laughed. He must have resigned himself to the fact that he wasn't going to get a repeat because he rolled off the bed and disappeared into the bathroom. A few seconds later, Aria could hear the shower running.

She'd shrugged into her top and was running a comb through her hair when her MoDAC beeped. Braccus was on the line.

A glance in the mirror verified that she was presentable. She slipped in her earpiece and brought her mobile to the docking station at the far corner of the room. Making sure that the camera angled away from the tousled bedsheets, she took the call.

Braccus Kai appeared on the screen. "Ms. Hendrix," he greeted.

"How *are* you Bee-Kay?" Her disarming smile and the use of the pet name were laying it on a bit thick, but it felt necessary. Like the rest of her client load, Aria tried to keep things intimate.

The look on *his* face was far from amicable. He looked pissed.

"Feeling a bit harried, I'm afraid. It seems a recent shipment was lost on its way through customs."

"Oh?" Aria feigned ignorance. The Collective had already briefed her on this possibility, and—in a way—facilitated it.

"Yes, the DGC locked down the entire Freyvian system. My understanding was that your associates were taking steps to ensure that wasn't going to happen."

Well, Braccus had *asked* that it be handled, and Aria had relayed the request as promised. The problem was that the messenger he had requested be dispatched worked for House Valadar. Unfortunately for Kai, Cyrus was paying the Collective far more than the Inheritors could afford.

Aria couldn't let Braccus in on this little fact, however. "I'm so sorry, love. I will report this back to my superiors. We will deal with this failure accordingly. Do you require documentation of the disciplinary action?"

Translation: *"Do you need to see the body?"* Of course, the Ghenza had not assigned an operative to the task. That meant there was technically no one to execute, but they would identify a creative solution to that problem at a later time. They would if Braccus demanded it—which Aria hoped he would not.

Braccus did not disappoint. "No need. To my knowledge, this is the first time you have not delivered on a contract. Your assurances that the problem will be addressed are sufficient."

"Thank you for your continued faith in our partnership." With that bit of nastiness out of the way, she moved on to the next order of business. "Are you still in the Helion system?"

"For the moment, yes."

"Will you be tarrying for much longer? Perhaps we could rendezvous and make the trip back to Khonshu together?"

A lustful gleam reflected momentarily in his eyes. "I would like that." Sobering then, he continued. "But I'm afraid, that won't be possible. I will be making the crossing in about an hour. My ship is already en-route to the Taurus Gate."

"Such a shame." She wasn't sure if that was a total lie or not. Braccus wasn't the best lover she'd had, but making the five-day journey with him was better than just having Treska for company.

"Indeed. It seems we have missed each other on this trip. I was disappointed that we were not able to cross paths on Ares."

"Alas, important business always seems to pop up at the most inconvenient times."

"So it seems. I trust no such business will delay our next appointment?"

His remark came off as somewhat peevish, but Aria chose not to react. "Darling, I wouldn't miss it for the world."

It was true. Her next encounter with Kai had been given top priority by the Collective. Failure was not an option for *that* particular mission.

"Good," he said, appearing satisfied. "See you soon, my dear."

"Bye, love."

As she logged off, Aria noticed Joaquin standing in the bathroom door. He was towel-drying his medium-length hair as he studied her and putting absolutely zero effort into modesty.

Looking at the lines of his lean muscles, Aria reconsidered her decision not to take another quick tumble before getting on with her evening.

The sound of the locks on the door put a stop to that little fantasy. Treska stepped quietly through the portal, shutting it behind her. Reflexively, the Maur woman unbuckled her harness and dropped her weapons onto a chair near the door. She was in the room for almost a full minute before she noticed the naked Terran man among them.

She didn't say anything as she sized up his sculpted body. After a moment, she seemed to realize she was staring. Her eyes went to Aria, then back to Joaquin. "Am I interrupting something?"

"Yes," Joaquin replied quickly.

"No," Aria corrected. "Joaquin was leaving. He just seems to have misplaced his clothes. They're over there by the table, love."

His laughter was genuine. "And so they are!" He tossed the towel aside and gathered the cloths that had been hastily discarded sometime earlier. Garments in his possession, he wandered back into the bathroom.

Treska started in on Aria. "Him?" she hissed. "*Really?*"

Aria let her mouth hang open in mock offense. "What? He's gorgeous!"

"He's a client!"

"His brother is the client, and you're just jealous."

The Maur extended her middle finger in response. It was true that Treska had a thing for Terran men. Though that would raise some eyebrows in more conservative cultures, it wasn't so uncommon in the Collective's circles. The real problem was that the Maur's tastes were a bit too violent to be on display for their clientele, much less for her to ask any of them to partake.

When Joaquin emerged from the bathroom again, he was now reasonably dressed. "I suppose it's just as well. I need to be heading out to Minos anyway. Those shadows will lose their minds if they send for me and I'm not at their beck and call."

Treska cocked her head to the side. "You have business with the Sahaia?."

His eyes widened in alarm. "Potentially. Can't really say more than that, I'm afraid."

Truthfully, he probably shouldn't have even let that much slip. House Valadar seemed to be sinking their claws into everything across Terran space. Cyrus was a very ambitious man.

With one last lecherous glance at Aria, Joaquin made for the door. "Catch you next time you're in the system?"

"Only if I'm lucky," she purred.

When he was gone, Treska went back to removing her weapons and armor. "I swear, one of these days your sex drive is going to get us both into some shit we can't fight our way out of."

"Oh, come now. You know there's no such situation."

Treska sighed, bringing a clawed hand up to cover her feline visage. "I know you believe that, but still. If you're going to get slick with a new partner every time we dock, could you try to pick out someone who's *not* paying us?"

"But that's half the fun!" Aria laughed. "Speaking of, Braccus called."

"Don't you mean '*Bee-Kay?*'" Treska laced as much disdain as possible in her pronunciation of the pet name.

"What? He likes that. I think it adds some authenticity to our relationship."

"He likes seeing you naked. He puts up with the nick-name so that he can continue to do so."

Aria waved off the comment. "Whatever. Anyhow, he confirmed the package is still on Khonshu. We need to start heading that way to pick it up."

Her Maur companion groaned, throwing herself on the unused bed on the opposite side of the room. "So we have to travel all the way to Geb? That will take a week!"

"Oh, you're exaggerating."

"No, I'm not. It's two days to Gaia, a day to refuel, and another two days to cross the gate and get to the far side of Geb."

"That's five days, not a week."

"Five days constitutes a standard week in Maur systems."

"Well this Terran space, so that makes me right—as usual."

The low rumble in Treska's throat made it sound like she wanted to continue the debate. Instead, she said, "Fine. What's the plan then?"

"I'll make arrangements for us to leave tomorrow, I just have to see what the Collective has available for us."

"What? Why can't we take the ultralight we came in on?"

Aria rolled her eyes. "That thing? I would go crazy if I was trapped with you on that little boat for a week."

"I thought you said it was five days?"

"You know what I mean. Besides, there's nowhere to hide this shipment on an ultralight. We need something big enough to conceal the cargo in case we get inspected."

Treska lifted her head to glare at Aria in frustration. "You know that Delta-2 is not one of the ports the Collective typically operates out of. Ares isn't friendly territory for us. There's a decent chance they don't have anything here that meets our needs."

She was right, but that didn't bother Aria. "That's fine. If that's the case, we'll just have to acquire one on our own."

"'*Acquire*,' huh?"

There was no need to elaborate. The wicked smile Aria felt spread across her face was all the answer she needed to supply.

CHAPTER 7

[ACCESSING COGNIS.DATAFILES…]

SIGMA-4 — *STATION (TERRAN SPACE)* — THE FOURTH AND FINAL STATION CONSTRUCTED FROM THE UNPOPULAR SIGMA-LINE. THE STATION ORBITS GEB, THE PRINCIPAL PLANET OF THE RAVIAN SYSTEM. THOUGH A HANDFUL OF WEALTHY MERCHANTS AND RETIRED POLITICIANS MAKE THEIR HOME IN THE STATION'S UPPER TIER, THE REST OF THE STATION SUFFERS UNDER RELATIVE SOCIAL AND ECONOMIC SQUALOR.

[CLOSING DATAFILE…]

Skye hadn't been assigned to the pick-up detail, but she wasn't about to let Markus and Eli deal with their armed escort alone. Aaliyah must have felt the same way because she was already down in the hanger when Skye arrived.

The engineer shot her a quick smile. "So, I'm not the only one who didn't think the boys could handle this one alone."

Skye returned her smile. "We worked hard to land this score. Best not let them screw it up at the finish line."

"Heard that," Markus intoned behind her. He and Eli marched in, exuding the all-business vibe they typically assumed when dealing with clients.

Skye donned a look of feigned innocence. "I'm just saying, usually the buyer is happy to see you. Does an armed escort scream 'happy' to you?"

"It would if this were the Federation," Sahar shouted as she entered the hanger. "An armed greeting means they take you seriously. The soft escort is reserved exclusively for unpopular politicians and fools."

Eli cocked an eyebrow. "Why unpopular politicians?"

"Invitation for assassination," Sahar shrugged. "Usually."

Markus rolled his eyes. "Well, we can only hope to aspire to Maur-level hospitality. I tell you what, I don't know whether I should be touched or offended you all showed up. Keep this punctuality going forward, and we might actually start our team meetings on time."

Aaliyah snorted. "Nah, Captain's always the one runnin' late. Ain't nobody gonna fix that problem."

After a few grim chuckles, the five of them stood in silence. There was a small bump as the craft connected with the docking equipment and then a clang of metal as the ship was secured.

Dan's voice came over the comm. "Docking procedure completed. You are clear to depart."

Markus slammed a button on a nearby console. With a hiss of hydraulics, the hangar doors slid open. Skye braced as the docking ramp extended from the platform, bridging the gap between them and the waiting party.

A dozen or so armed individuals stood in loose formation ringing the ramp. Their weapons weren't directed at the crew, but each member of the escort seemed strangely tense. They looked like a street gang in their varied assortment of dark leather outfits and mismatched pieces of armor.

When the doors were fully open, Markus strode forward, a smile plastered across his face. "Tashania! So good to see you." He made his way toward the figure at the front of the entourage.

Tashania was a Terran woman with skin the color of mocha and short, spiked hair. She was the only one who wore any kind of identifying mark—a pair of silvered wings on her lapel that served as the symbol of her faction.

To Skye's surprise, the woman's stern face broke into a smile. "Markus, it's good to see you back in one piece."

She embraced him and planted a kiss on his cheek. The show of affection seemed odd for someone who had seemed so menacing moments ago. The remainder of the leather-clad escort appeared pleased with the pleasantries. Several of them visibly relaxed on seeing the exchange.

Markus broke the embrace. "What brings Ora's right hand down to meet a few privateers? Surely the boss hasn't decided we're the type to go sour on a contract?"

"Relax cowboy," she chided. "You're not in trouble. Quite the opposite: she seemed pretty excited when she got your message." Shifting to a more business-like demeanor, she continued. "But, since we're here, let's go ahead and grab that shipment, shall we?"

"Most certainly. Sahar, would you do the honors?"

The Maur pushed the levitating cart holding the neatly stacked contraband. Her figure was imposing in her own black leather getup, complete with a top that left her muscular arms bare. She had no weapons, but that didn't mean anything. Maur didn't need any weapons to be deadly.

Tashania continued. "So, will your entire crew be joinin' us for the meetin'? I apologize, but we should get goin' quickly. Ora was very explicit about wantin' to see you as soon as you arrived."

Markus's reply was surprising in its honesty. "Well, Shani—I hadn't been planning on it, but I've got to be honest: you guys showing up with an armed escort got us a bit spooked. You're an old friend, so I'll ask you straight: Do I need a little extra protection on my way to Annex?"

Skye's eyebrow creased with a disapproving scowl. What kind of a question was that? What was Tashania supposed to say? *Yes, Markus, we plan to wipe you out to tie up some loose ends, so you might as well bring everyone to the party so we can get this messy business out of the way!*

"Not unless you want them there for the theatrics," Tashania replied. "The armed escort isn't to haul you in. The business is changin' a bit. We're under some pressure right now, and we've had a couple of mishaps with our contractors this past week. There have been some other issues too. In fact, Ora's in the middle of dealin' with one of those right now."

"So, you meet all your runners with weapons in hand now? That's got to get expensive when bribing station security."

The woman shrugged. "I just follow orders."

Markus's smile was charming, but Skye could see that it didn't quite reach his eyes. "All right, Shani. You've never given me a reason to distrust you in the past, and I'm not inclined to start now." He turned back to the crew. "Eli, I'd like you to join me as planned. The rest of you, please, enjoy your evening. I know you all have places you would rather be. I'll be in touch."

Eli started forward, but Skye grabbed him by the arm. "Are you sure you two have got this?" she whispered.

The Sahaia smiled. "Don't worry. There are plenty of things to be concerned about on this station, but Ora's not one of them. She's loyal as long as we're loyal."

Markus, meanwhile, seemed to be giving Sahar a similar pep talk. Once he had her convinced, she relinquished control of the cart with the stolen goods.

Before Markus got too far, Tashania's hand came to rest on his. "Don't worry about that Markus. We've got people for manual labor. Besides, we can't go walkin' right through the station with all that contraband. Even Ora's bribes aren't *that* good. You and your friend come right along."

With a nod, Markus relinquished control of the cart to two of the Maur in Tashania's escort and followed her onto the concourse. Eli fell into step behind them, and the entourage made their way to the gates that would take them to Sigma-4.

Sahar's eyes never left the group the whole way out of the concourse. She realized her vigilance was in vain. It wasn't like she could do anything about it if her friends were gunned down at this distance. Still, she couldn't bring herself to look away. There was an odd feeling in the air tonight, and she was in the habit of taking such premonitions seriously.

"They have it covered, right?" Dan asked. He had just made his way down to the cargo hold as Eli and Markus disappeared with their escort through a metal door exiting the hanger.

"Yeah Dan," Sahar replied. "They've got it covered."

"Eli seems pretty relaxed," Aaliyah noted. She absently rubbed at the rune on her forearm, the tattoo which cemented her metaphysical connection to the Sahaia.

"And Markus has had a good working relationship with Ora and the Wings for a long time," Skye added. "I think it'll be fine." She walked to the side of the hold and grabbed a plain-look gray backpack which paired nicely with her gray leggings and jacket.

"Where are you off to?" Sahar asked.

"Got an appointment for my tune-up." She gestured to with her natural arm to her cybernetic shoulder. "I'm a little early, but Li is squeezing me in after hours. I don't want to keep her waiting." With a sigh, she slung the bag over her shoulder. "You guys good here?"

Sahar glanced at Aaliyah and Dan before responding. "Yeah, I think we're good." As she watched her go, she whispered to Aaliyah, "She seem a bit off to you?"

"How ya figure?"

"I don't know. Ever since the shuttle ride, she's been a little… tense, maybe? I thought she might be worried about Markus. What do you think?"

An odd expression spread across Aaliyah's face. "Maybe," she replied. "None of my business, I suppose."

The engineer was right, of course. It was probably none of Sahar's either. Markus and Skye's breakup still felt so fresh. Sahar understood Skye's reasoning—the drugs bothered her too—but she couldn't help but notice how unhappy both of them had been these past few weeks.

But Aaliyah was right: it was none of her business.

"You heading out too?"

"You bet," Aaliyah answered, bobbing her head once for emphasis. "Got someone special at home, and I don't want to keep her waitin'." With a smile and a wave, she heaved up her bag and made her way onto the concourse.

Sahar turned to Dan. "What about you, big guy? You all booked up for the evening as well?"

The question had been rhetorical, and she had expected him to reply in the negative. It was usually just the two of them left hanging out together the first night back on station. Dan was reclusive, but she liked the kid, and she genuinely enjoyed spending time with him.

Which was part of the reason why his response surprised her. "Yes, actually. I've got an appointment to acquire a specific part I've been looking for. I should probably leave soon to make sure I'm there on time."

The Maur arched one furry eyebrow. "Parts for your pet project?"

Dan hesitated before answering, "Yes, that's right." He didn't offer any further explanation.

It was strange to see him being cryptic. Dan hadn't made it a secret that he was working on the ship's operating system. Markus had asked him to do it, and they could all see the improvements in functionality over time.

Which meant something was up.

"Mind if I tag along?" she asked.

He hesitated again. "I'm kind of supposed to meet the contact alone."

Alone? What kind of tech merchant only worked one-on-one?

"Um… all right. Maybe I could catch a ride with you to mid-tier then? We could grab something to eat after you settle up—"

"The meeting isn't on mid-tier," Dan interrupted.

Now, *that* was a red flag. "Yeah?" Sahar didn't bother to hide her surprise. "Where is it?"

Dan gave the ring designation, and Sahar sputtered.

"Say that again?" she asked, hoping she'd heard wrong.

There was an edge of frustration to his voice at having to repeat himself. "Ring One, District Seventeen."

Obviously, this arrangement had been made on the station net. Dan's affect indicated he had absolutely zero familiarity with the kind of people who set up shop on R-1. Sahar didn't even go there if she could help it.

Security forces were essentially non-existent on the lower tier of the station, but that shit was taken to an extreme on the lowest ring. Every time she'd been forced to go down there, Sahar had left at least one body in her wake.

"Dan, I don't know how to tell you this, but going down there alone is a really bad idea."

"It can't be that bad. Sure, the area is poor, but that doesn't mean there's anything to be afraid of. They're just people like you and me."

"No, Dan. They're not."

The kid donned a judgmental look. "Are you saying that poor people are dangerous just because they can't afford to live somewhere nicer?"

"No, I'm saying the people on R-1 are dangerous because they are *dangerous*."

Now he was rolling his eyes. "I'm surprised and sorry to hear you feel that way. I assure you—I'll be fine."

Yup, the kid had no idea what he'd gotten himself into. Sahar sighed. "You know, maybe you're right. I'm sorry Dan. Look, maybe I'll just head down there for an attitude adjustment. I'll let you run your deal and we can figure out where to go when you're done. Sound fair?"

"Fine," he huffed. "It's not like I can stop you anyway. But I meet with my contact alone, all right?"

Sahar smiled down at the kid. Gods willing, this might turn out to be a decent lesson for him. "Deal. Just let me grab a few things first."

CHAPTER 8

[ACCESSING COGNIS.DATAFILES...]

GREY WINGS — *FACTION PROFILE* — A MINOR FACTION ARISING FROM THE OVERTHROW OF THE VALKYRIE CRIME SYNDICATE. OPERATING LARGELY ON SIGMA-4, THE GREY WINGS OPENLY CONTROL A SUBSTANTIAL PORTION OF THE LEGITIMATE ENTERPRISES OPERATING IN THE THIRD, FOURTH, AND FIFTH RINGS OF THE STATION. THOUGH IT IS WIDELY ACCEPTED THAT THE FACTION IS INVOLVED IN MANY OF THE STATION'S ILLICIT ACTIVITIES, COORDINATED PUBLIC RELATIONS EFFORTS AND THE CELEBRITY STATUS OF THEIR LEADER—ORA MONROE—HAVE CREATED A SOCIAL AND POLITICAL CLIMATE THAT DISCOURAGES PROSECUTION OF THEIR ALLEGED CRIMINAL TIES.

[CLOSING DATAFILE...]

Markus and Eli filed right by the maglev and customs stations on the way to their destination. "No need to worry about checkin' in," Tashania had assured them. "Ora's taken care of the paperwork. Didn't want you to be delayed."

"A guy could get used to this VIP treatment," Markus noted with a polite laugh. Even to his own ears it sounded forced. It must have sounded force to Tashania too because she declined to comment.

They exited the docking area and were soon in the heart of the station-proper. Tashania smiled back over her shoulder at them. "Welcome home, gentlemen."

The station might have been their base of operations, but it was definitely not home. It was kind of hard to think that anyone would be forced to call this place, "home."

The inhabited areas of Sigma-class stations were located on the inside of the spinning rings. The original idea was that this took the strain off the installation's gravity grids by enhancing it with an appropriate amount of spin. As gravity technology got better, the Sigma-class station design was rendered obsolete.

Markus, who was not born on a station, was still mildly uncomfortable with the unusual curvature of the structure. In the enclosed areas, such as shops or other buildings, it wasn't so bad. It was the open areas that made you realize you were marching inside a massive tube with an inverted horizon. Apparently, people could get used to any kind of torture if they were subjected to it for long enough.

In the more prosperous areas of the station, dynamic holograms were used to give the illusion of terrestrial structures–lakes, mountains, etc.–which lay just out of reach beyond a border of buildings.

No such frills were present on lower levels. R-3, like the other five lower rings, lacked adequate open-air lighting, creating the unfortunate illusion of perpetual night.

And with the perpetual night, came the indulgences best enjoyed in the dark. Pubs, brothels, and nightclubs were plentiful on this ring. Annex, which was thought to be Ora's residence and the base of operations for the Grey Wings was one such nightclub.

Markus had always thought it an odd choice. Why house a crime syndicate in a building filled with so many of the station's denizens at any given moment? Further, why would so many people still frequent such a location? It seemed like most clientele would steer clear of such an infamous locale. But one look at the line outside of the club, and it was clear that this was not the case.

Annex's looming structure was comprised of swirling arcs of dark metal. Dim red lights dotted the underside of the metallic plates, creating an aura of diabolical menace. The snakelike structures parted in the center to frame the arched entrance. Inside the portal, metal swoops coalesced to form the walls, tables, and even furniture. It gave the impression that Markus was walking into a forest of sinuous, metallic trees.

Above the entrance, a holoscreen played a clip on loop. The scene showed silhouetted shapes of muscular men and curvaceous women dancing in and out of dark laser-light projections. The word Annex burned prominently in the center of the scene.

Tashania led them right past the line, nodding to one of the Maur bouncers who stepped aside to let them through. There was a private elevator behind a reception desk, but Markus had scarcely seen it used. Whenever he came here on business, they always approached Ora's private lounge by passing through the club.

And that was where they were headed next—right through the center of the party.

The thrum of dark, ambient music punctuated with the rhythmic force of bass poured out from every wall through embedded speakers. A massive throng of dancers writhed in the dance pit just below the club's entrance.

Overall, the exposed area was four stories high. The second floor, where Markus and his escort stood now, was dotted with tables and lavish couches. The men and women, who sat at these tables had the look of modest wealth acquired by illicit means.

Exotic dancers moved suggestively across the tables and couches in various stages of undress. Servers offered a wide selection of alcoholic beverages and drugs, which prompted the separation of small fortunes from the hands of those who succumbed to these vices. It was a little overt for Markus's tastes, but he could see the appeal.

On the third floor, dancers and revelers—many of whom moved with professional expertise—covered a series of irregularly dispersed catwalks, cages, and balconies. The paid performers must have been there to encourage the establishment's paying customers to let loose.

Each floor was connected by spiraling wrought-iron staircases. Bouncers stationed at each junction examined the club's patrons for any hint of hostile intention. They also removed any excessively intoxicated revelers or other disruptive occupants. It seemed a strange concession to safety in this dark menagerie.

At the apex of it all, there was a single gated entry-point to the uppermost tier. This was where Ora was frequently seen, looming over the gate in quiet contemplation as she gazed down upon her masterpiece of debauchery. More than a handful of club-goers came here solely for that reason—the chance to catch a glimpse of the fabled Silver Queen of Sigma-4.

Yet tonight she was not at her usual perch. Instead, two functionaries dutifully opened the gate to grant them passage. One of them passed a whispered message into Tashania's ear as she went by. Turning back to Markus and Eli, the woman explained the situation.

"Apologies, Ora is still dealing with that other matter I mentioned. She said I could bring you back anyway. This shouldn't take much longer."

Exchanging uncertain glances, Markus and Eli followed Tashania through the gate. They entered a tunnel lit with wrought iron fixtures reminiscent of millennia long-forgotten. Ora was a student of many things, including history. Markus knew that much like the earthly queens of old, she had constructed her personal palace to her unique tastes.

The sounds of the club dimmed as they made their way down the hall. At the passage's end, Tashania signaled to the Maur guards who swung another set of double doors open in unison. In the room beyond, Markus could finally see their illustrious host.

Ora Monroe had a reputation for being beautiful, but Markus wondered if the rumors didn't sell her short. It wasn't just that she was pretty, or sexy, or whatever. Something was mesmerizing about the way that she presented herself. It was something primal yet paranormal; something enticing yet dangerous.

Her skin was light in tone, but still tawny enough to provide contrast against her white clothing. She wore slacks snuggly cut to accentuate her muscular legs. The waistband of the garment rested below her hip bones, and her top exposed her sculpted midsection. Her bare, muscular shoulders showcased her level of fitness but did nothing to detract from her femininity. The same was true for the long, lean muscle of her arms on which she wore matching bangles constructed of silver.

The jewelry was a near-perfect match to her hair, which shimmered radiantly even in the low light of the room. One could not mistake the silver locks as a byproduct of age, nor did they have the look of a cheap color alteration. Markus figured Ora had a cosmetic gene mod. Gods knew she could afford such luxuries.

Though her hair was shorter, Markus noticed that she was built much in the same way that Skye was—a perfect balance of elegance and athleticism. He had once scolded himself for the comparison, but not too harshly. Ora had that effect on people. It was something that she went to great lengths to accomplish. That was Ora in a nutshell: powerful, sympathetic, beautiful, and deadly.

And currently, she was kicking the shit out of someone.

The hapless victim was a shabby-looking Terran. Over and over she hammered a booted foot into his gut before finishing off with a quick kick across his jaw. Blood splattered in an arc, creating spray patterns on the floor and Ora's formerly pristine white slacks.

"Last chance, Shift," she snarled, addressing the man on the floor. "Someone of your reputation doesn't pick his targets on a whim. Why were you caught in my servers? What were you looking for?"

The man on the floor spat out a coughing chuckle. "Ah told ya, Ora. Ah was lookin' fer the sex tape!" Her foot collided again with his gut, which only served to amplify his laughter. "Nah, really! Ah had a tip there was cam footage o' ya gettin' slick with Rico Chronos back on…"

He didn't finish. Ora's boot connected with the man's face. Immediately his disheveled form collapsed in a heap. Ora turned to a burly Maur who stood off to her side.

"He's all yours. You know where to take him."

"Yes, ma'am." The Maur signaled two of his underlings to pick up the limp form and drag him out of the chamber.

As they did so, Ora turned to the two other figures in the room. "Thank you, Kadath. You have delivered the package as promised and the payment has been wired to the account number you provided."

The man she addressed had dark hair and crimson skin. Though Markus was starting to recognize many of Ora's usual associates, he had never seen this guy before. He would have remembered him if he had.

From the skin tone, the man must have been part Kintar. That was the only species Markus was aware of were naturally that shade of red. Still, Kintar were hard to come by in this sector. To come across a half-breed was even more unusual.

"My pleasure, Ms. Monroe," he responded smoothly through a confident smile.

"It's Ora," she corrected—politely, but firmly.

"Ora," he repeated, bowing his head in deference. "May I ask you something?"

"Certainly."

"Is there actually a…" He let the sentence hang with implication.

"Sex tape?" She let out a quick chuckle to convey how she felt about the idea. "No, it's a baseless rumor—something taken straight from last month's tabloids. Why so curious?" She said the last sentence with a suggestive look that would have rendered most men speechless.

Despite the flirtation, Kadath never missed a beat. "Merely assessing the odds that there's a recovery op you could use us for. We are currently in an open contract, and have enjoyed the privilege of working with you on this assignment."

Markus wasn't sure what impressed him more: Ora's ability to go from murderous rage to flirtatious suggestion in a few short sentences, or this strange mercenary's ability to roll with her punches.

Ora laughed. "Alas, I have no need of you on *that* assignment, but new opportunities come up frequently. Perhaps if you don't range too far from the station, you'll hear from me soon."

With a bow, Kadath replied, "I will remain hopeful that this is the case." Taking her last remark as a dismissal, the halfbreed turned and took a step toward the exit.

Immediately on his heel was the other figure, clad entirely in black. The second mercenary's hood was up, and Markus's eyes could not penetrate the darkness of the cowl. Perhaps the figure was wearing a mask. He or she could have been of any gender, any race. With that kind of outfit, no one could tell the difference.

Both mercenaries nodded politely as they marched past Markus and Eli. When Ora gave her a quick hand signal, Tashania moved to escort the strange pair out of the room. After the trio of Maur bodyguards that had also been in the room left, carrying the unlucky hacker with them, Ora was the only one remaining.

The smile with which she greeted them was disarming. "Markus Frost. Eli Ren'Dahl. What a pleasure it is to see you both."

"As usual, the pleasure is ours." Markus let slip a genuine smile. Despite knowing how dangerous Ora was, there was something about her that inevitably disarmed him. "Though I'll admit, you spooked us a little bit with the welcoming party. Everything okay?"

Her response was another dismissive laugh. She strode toward him as she spoke. "That's what I like about you, Markus: you seem to have the intuition to know when to cut the bullshit and say what's on your mind. Most other crews would be walking in here trying to pretend I didn't just scare the piss out of them but you…"

She stepped close to him, reaching out a hand and letting her fingers play lightly against his chest. The touch was gentle, almost intimate. Despite his efforts to control it, Markus felt his heart accelerate. The feeling was strange—equal part desire and apprehension.

"You…," she continued, "just get right to the heart of the matter." Her hand traced the line of his collar bone, then up the side of his neck.

Markus found himself suddenly lost in her vibrant eyes. Amethyst—evidently another gene mod. Had they always been that color? Why did he feel like he was just noticing now?

Then she withdrew her hand and batted those gorgeous eyes at him. It felt like she was scolding him for all the thoughts that had come unbidden into his mind.

She spun on her heels and began to walk to the back of the room, beckoning for them to follow. After some prodding from Eli, Markus did so.

They came to a set of furniture arranged in a semi-circle. Ora slid onto one of the plush-looking couches, leaning back and crossing her legs. Markus's eyes went to the lingering dark splatter of blood that marring the white expanse of her slacks. If the mess bothered her, she did nothing to show it.

Markus and Eli seized two neighboring chairs. The three of them sat clustered to one side of the arrangement, but not uncomfortably close.

"Well, gentlemen," Ora began again. "As you've been informed, I was very eager to have you here to speak with me. Let's get right to it, shall we?"

CHAPTER 9

NEUROSIM — *TECHNOLOGY INVENTORY* — A COGNITIVE PROJECTION DEVICE. NEUROSIM UNITS USE CEREBRAL SCANNING TECHNOLOGY TO PROJECT IMAGES DIRECTLY ONTO A PERSON'S SENSORY CORTEX. THE PROJECTION CAN CONSIST OF NUMEROUS FILE TYPES RANGING FROM SENSORY RECORDINGS TO ARTIFICIAL ENVIRONMENTS. CONVERSELY, ALTERED VERSIONS OF THE TECHNOLOGY CAN BE USED TO RECORD OR PROJECT THE SENSORY IMPULSES OF AN INDIVIDUAL WHO WEARS THE DEVICE.

[CLOSING DATAFILE...]

Aaliyah swiped her mobile on the console and stepped onto the maglev. The display on the wall made it clear that this line only ran between Rings One through Five. A recording made it clear to passengers that they would have to board a separate system at R-5 if they wished to travel to the second tier.

Aaliyah tuned out the voice. She wasn't going that far. Mere minutes later, the rail was at her stop.

Stepping off the train, she emerged into a largely residential district. The buildings in this area were not as nice as those in the middle and upper tiers. As far as the lower tier went, though, it was hard to find much better than this.

The large plaster and steel structures were clumped close together on narrow streets. Unlike R-3, these streets were clean and reasonably quiet this late in the afternoon.

Or was it evening? Aaliyah couldn't be certain of the exact time. Like the rest of the lower tier, the artificial skies on this ring were afflicted with a perpetual bleakness that made it difficult to discern day from night. At least here they had overhead lights to keep every twist and turn from looking like a back alley.

Aaliyah marched up the street at a determined pace. After working her way across several blocks, she finally found the building she was looking for.

The entrance was crisp, clean, and without adornment. Two black-trimmed lights protruded out from the building's gray face between a series of identical light-blue doors. The door in front of her was flanked on both sides by small square windows that leaked bits of warm yellow illumination through the gaps of the drawn curtains.

Good. Someone was still awake.

She took a deep breath, exhaling slowly as she approached the entrance. Composed now, she rapped lightly on the door.

Clicking locks, then the sound of a handle turning. A set of dark brown eyes, about waist high on Aaliyah, peered out through the opening. On seeing her, the eyes widened, and the door swung wide open.

"Momma 'Liyah!"

The brown-skinned child squealed with delight and launched herself at Aaliyah, who caught her up in her arms and hoisted her into the air. Warm tears gathered at the corners of Aaliyah's closed eyes as she squeezed the child.

"Little Mona," she whispered, using her pet name for the child. Supporting the girl in her arms, she leaned back to look at her face. "What's Momma Nikki doin' lettin' ya open the door like that?" Noticing the child's nightclothes, she added, "And shouldn't you be in bed?"

A woman spoke up from inside the apartment. "Momma Nikki put her to bed an hour ago, but it seems like someone was trying to sneak into the kitchen for a bedtime snack."

"Nah-uh!" Monica protested. The child shook her head so earnestly that Aaliyah had to stifle a laugh. "I knew Momma 'Liyah was comin' home. I waited on her."

"Uh-huh," Nikki replied skeptically, stepping into view, her deep umbral skin providing just the slightest contrast to Monica's sepia tone. "Why don't you go and warm the oven up. I'm sure Momma 'Liyah is hungry and we should make her something to eat."

"Okay Momma Nikki," Monica responded. Aaliyah set the child down. As the young girl scurried off to the kitchen, Aaliyah turned her attention to Nikki.

Nikki was just as beautiful as Aaliyah had remembered. Her dark curls were still damp from the shower, and she had thrown a purple bathrobe over her ivory shift.

The woman's smile was warm and genuine. "You'd think if the little twerp could really feel you coming then she'd do me a solid and tell me to keep my makeup on."

"I like ya just the way ya are now," Aaliyah replied.

"You have to say that." Nikki swung the door wide. "Well, you going to come in?" Aaliyah didn't need to be asked twice. Shrugging off her backpack, she dropped it to the floor just inside the door.

Nikki shut the portal and pressed closer to Aaliyah. She gently grabbed the front of Aaliyah's shirt and kissed her softly. "I missed you," she whispered.

"I missed ya too."

Another kiss then—this one deeper, longer. "Will you be back for long?"

With a sigh, Aaliyah replied, "I don't know. There was some weird shit goin' on when we pulled in. We might be headin' out again soon."

Nikki tried to hide her sad expression by nuzzling her face against Aaliyah's neck. "It feels like you've been gone non-stop for months. When do I get to have you back home?"

Aaliyah winced at the well-intended remark. "Soon, I hope."

The conversation died after that. Aaliyah broke their embrace, giving Nikki another quick peck on the lips. "I have to keep my girl in the life she's grown accustomed to. Don't want some other spacer to come in here and sweep ya off your feet because my broke-ass can't pay the rent."

Nikki laughed softly. "I don't think you need to worry about that." She stroked Aaliyah's cheek and captured her gaze with her warm brown eyes. Those eyes could melt any heart, even one as hard as Aaliyah's.

It was only then that Aaliyah noted her cheeks were starting to hurt from the grin on her face. "Ya have to say that."

Nikki kissed her again. "Makes it easier when it's true."

Ora sipped from a glass of red wine as she began. "Firstly, good job on Sif. I just got word from my people that all supplies are accounted for. Well done."

"Our pleasure," Markus replied. "Though I've got to say, the whole job has me a bit perplexed."

"How so?"

"Well, in looking at that manifest, there wasn't anything on there that you couldn't source elsewhere. Don't get me wrong, we appreciate the pay-day, but why go through all that trouble to have us steal those goods and bring them across system lines?"

A knowing smile slid into place as Ora sipped again from her glass. "Sometimes, Markus, it's not about the goods. Sometimes it's about sending a message."

"And what message were you trying to send?" Eli asked. "I wouldn't have thought you'd want House Valadar as an enemy."

"And you would be right. I *don't* want Cyrus as an enemy, I want him as a client. By having you rip off this shipment, I'm sending him the clear message that his current security is inadequate. As it so happens, I've recently submitted a request to supplement that security. Now, I think, he'll give my proposal the attention it deserves." Still smiling slyly, she glanced at them conspiratorially. "I trust I don't have to worry about you boys letting all this get traced back to me."

"Of course," Markus replied dryly.

"Don't feel patronized Markus. I have to say these things, or I can't tell you that I warned you later."

She reached over to a small end table sitting next to the sofa and grabbed her mobile device. She swiped her thumb across the screen before returning it to the table. "As I mentioned, your fee has already been wired to your account, along with an additional twenty-five thousand kret quarterly retention payment."

Markus's brow furrowed. "Retention payment?"

"For your continued cooperation and availability for future tasks I may require of you. You can still contract with other clients, of course, but I want the understanding that you'll do nothing that jeopardizes your relationship with the Grey Wings. That also means I get first priority on your time if something unexpected comes up."

"I don't…"

"Just take the money, Markus," she said with a touch of annoyance in her voice. "It's something I'm doing for all my regular crews now. The Grey Wings are expanding, and there are some less reputable parties I use that need a little bit of extra incentive to stay in line. I know you don't need hush money, but there's no sense in cutting you out just because your team is made up of real professionals."

"Thank you?" Markus hadn't intended it to come out as a question, but it did.

"You're welcome," Ora replied, ignoring the questioning tone. "Now, if there are no other questions or concerns, we need to move right on to the last item on our agenda. I hurried you out here today because it's a time-sensitive matter. It was my good fortune that you happened to report back when you did. I need my best contractors on this one."

"Yeah?" Now Markus was openly skeptical.

"Yes, someone with a knack for solving difficult problems, and who doesn't mind transporting dangerous cargo."

Well, with those kinds of compliments, who was Markus to argue? "Let's hear the specifics then. What do you need us to move?"

Ora reached again to the side table and grabbed three disk-shaped objects. Markus knew the devices well, though that certainly didn't make using them any more comfortable.

Neurosim units, if configured correctly, were an immensely secure way of sharing data. The device projected information right onto your brain. Anyone using the little disks gave the device's programmer license to make them see whatever they wanted.

Ora's technicians had created a unique simulation environment specifically for sharing sensitive proposals. Besides making the presentation one-hundred percent secure, there were some fringe benefits.

Since a neurosim had direct access to your brain, any memory written onto your memory by the device could be extracted the same way it had been put in there. With the appropriate security mods, they could even bypass implants and memory backups. If you watched the presentation and decided you didn't want the job, no hard feelings. The device erased any memory you had of the presentation and you were free to go.

Ora handed Markus two of the disks, the second of which he passed to Eli. In unison, they placed the devices on the sides of their heads, right at the temple. Ora did likewise with the controller disk, activating the simulation with a touch of a button.

The lounge around them disappeared as the world in front of them went dark.

The environment generated by the neurosim was blank at first. Soon though, Markus became aware of the other two in the session. It was a strange sensation in that he could not see Eli or Ora as much as he just knew that they were there.

<All right then,> came Ora's voice in his mind. <Let us begin.>

Her presentations were always simple and to the point. This particular session was no different.

A piece of machinery materialized in front of Markus's eyes. The main body of the device was a long cylinder with metal prongs extending from the central shaft. The six prongs flared out to the side before bending back in to form a point at the tip, giving it a spear-like appearance. At the base of the object was a metal stand that clung to the center.

The image was so realistic that Markus felt he might have been able to reach out and grab it. That was, of course, if he had had a body in the simulation. As it was, he could only study the item from his disembodied point of view.

<Are either of you familiar with this object?> Ora asked. When they both replied in the negative, she continued. <It's called the Starfire Conduit—experimental tech commissioned by House Barkay from the Prodigy camps on Anubis. It's able to wirelessly transmit certain forms of energy short distances through the use of specialized sensor nodes.>

<Nice piece of hardware,> Markus noted. <Looks expensive.>

<Yes, it is,> Ora responded. <It's the most powerful far-field transmission conduit ever designed. According to our intel, the first three firms Ulysses Barkay contacted said it couldn't be made. The impossible nature of the task made it that much more appealing for the Prodigy program. Unfortunately, with the recent collapse of House Barkay, it never made it to the party which commissioned its construction.>

<And you have it now?> Markus asked. It was probably too much to hope that this would be a simple smuggling job. Bring the expensive equipment from Point A to Point B and collect your paycheck. Not the usual flavor of task Ora signed them up for, but he could still make wishes.

<If only. No, the conduit is currently being held by this man.>

A window popped up in Markus's vision showing a picture of a Terran. He was middle-aged, black hair, olive skin, clean-shaven, and slightly overweight in the way that formerly athletic men tended to be.

Ora continued. <This is Braccus Kai. Used to be a high-ranking dealer under the flag of House Barkay. When House Chronos dismantled Barkay's operations, Kai went into business for himself. He's done quite well as an independent. I've bought from him a few times myself.>

<So, you need us to be your contacts for the purchase?>

<I wish it were that simple.> If Ora were frustrated by the fact that Markus had now struck out twice, she didn't let on. On the contrary, her tone was almost sympathetic. <This particular item never went up for auction. Kai already has a buyer. He won't even open negotiations for a better deal.>

<Who is the buyer?> Eli asked.

<The Ghenza Collective.>

Now *that* was odd. <The assassins?> Markus asked.

<They do a little more than just kill people for money, but yes—that's who I'm referring to.>

That didn't make any sense. The Ghenza were heavily networked in the criminal underworld in Terran space. If you wanted someone dead, there was no better operative for hire than a Ghenza assassin. However, they wouldn't have been on Markus's list of interested parties for technology like this.

Eli seemed to be running on the same line of thought. <They must be an intermediary. Who are they purchasing it for?>

<I don't know,> Ora admitted. <I can't confirm that they aren't purchasing it for their own purpose, but my suspicions are the same as yours. There's another player here that doesn't want to advertise their interest in the conduit.>

Now that *did* make sense. If Braccus Kai had prior connections to the Great Houses, he likely had a list of enemies longer than Markus's arm. If one of those adversaries wanted to get their hands on Kai's tech, they'd have to work through an intermediary.

The unfortunate reality of the situation was becoming clear to Markus. <So, you want us to steal this thing?>

<Exactly.>

Oh boy. <Just so I'm clear on this: You want us to steal this piece of tech from the *Ghenza*? The same Ghenza that have made their names on their ability to kill any person in the sector short of a High Council member?>

<I wouldn't recommend you attempt to steal from the assassins,> Ora answered blandly. <That's where the time-sensitive component comes into play. If I were you, I'd attempt to get the conduit *before* Kai sells it to the Ghenza.>

<So that's why we're in such a hurry. You need us to get on this before the transaction takes place.>

<Now, you're catching on.>

<And where will this transaction occur?> Eli asked.

<The Star Spire on Khonshu.> Ora paused dramatically. <In five days.>

Markus and Eli cursed in unison. The Star Spire was technically a public facility, but it was massive. Finding where the device was stored—not to mention figuring out a way to extract it—was nigh impossible in that amount of time. The fact that the Ghenza were thrown into this mix made this fragged-up situation that much worse. This was impossible.

<Too much for you, boys?> she teased. <Before you answer, I should probably show you the take from this little operation.>

A number counted up in the bottom left corner of Markus's vision. He admitted to himself that he had been about to tell Ora it couldn't be done. No way were they going to be able to rip off an ex-arms dealer from one of the Great Houses in the middle of a deal with the most dangerous assassins to ever run the Nethra with a five-day lead time.

Thirty million krets changed his mind.

Chapter 10

[ACCESSING COGNIS.DATAFILES…]

RESCHE — *CULTURAL INVENTORY* — A CEREMONIAL SHORT BLADE OF SOCIAL AND RELIGIOUS SIGNIFICANCE IN MAUR CULTURE. THE BLADE HAS A JAGGED EDGE THAT EXTENDS ABOUT THE LENGTH OF A STANDARD MAUR FOREARM. IN BATTLE, THE RESCHE IS EASILY WIELDED IN CONJUNCTION WITH A SECOND BLADE. CULTURALLY, IT IS FREQUENTLY INTEGRATED INTO MAUR SACRIFICIAL AND ALLEGIANCE RITUALS.

[CLOSING DATAFILE…]

The "few more things" Sahar had grabbed were an assortment of blades strapped to her back, arms, and legs. Dan had protested at first, noting that she looked like she was out to assassinate a public official rather than make a simple transaction.

He wasn't protesting now.

The masses in the street were dirty. Many of them looked sickly, and they all looked like they'd open your throat if you looked at them the wrong way.

Most areas of the station spoke predominantly in ISL or some easily recognized version of the common language. Here the station's occupants shouted in a dozen different garbled dialects of their numerous native tongues. The effect was unnerving, and Dan's eyes were wide behind his glasses.

A collision with a massive, bear-like Maur nearly knocked the scrawny Terran on his ass. The snarling male was a head taller than even Sahar and was clad in tatters of black cloth that might have once been a robe of some kind.

Taking in the size of the creature unfortunate enough to cross his path, a grin split the Maur's maw, and he made a move toward Daniel.

Sahar rested a single hand on the boy's shoulder, steadying him as she stared down the would-be assailant. She didn't reach for her weapons. She didn't even say anything. The message was received, and the large male shuffled off in another direction.

"Thank you," Dan murmured sheepishly.

Sahar dragged him off to one side of the milling throng. Safely away from the herd, Sahar crouched so that she was eye-to-eye with the boy. "Dan, are you ready to tell me what we're doing here?"

His face contorted with a look of protestation. "I told you, we're…"

"No, Dan. Why *here*?"

He hesitated, his eyes flicking about in that way that made him look dishonest. Dan rarely lied outright—which was good, because he wasn't great at it. However, it wasn't uncommon for him to obscure the truth by talking over everyone else's heads.

"The item I'm looking for," he replied, "is not a commodity readily available through conventional channels." He wrung his hands and glanced sideways, looking uneasily at the disheveled masses. "I'll admit—I may have slightly underestimated what I was getting into down here."

"Good, I'm glad you recognize that. Now, let's get out of here."

"No!" he blurted. "My contact should be just ahead. Once we have completed the exchange, we will leave. Please, Sahar— just a few more minutes."

A growl of frustration bubbled up from her throat. "Dan, you're not getting it. Think about it: we steal and transport contraband for a living. When have you ever seen one of us set up a deal on R-1?"

"I don't see how that's relevant to…"

"It *is* relevant, Dan. We don't set up deals down here because that's not the kind of shit that happens here. People don't come to R-1 to buy and sell illegal goods. They come here to hide the bodies."

The boy set his jaw. A war of emotions played behind those youthful eyes. What in the nine hells was down here that the kid wanted so badly?

"Fine," he sighed. "Let's go."

Thank the gods. Sahar stood and glanced over her shoulder. "Stick close. There's another maglev station ahead. We'll hop on there and travel back to R-3. Once we're there we can decide where to go next."

Dan didn't respond. Obviously, he was sore at her for ruining his plans. That was fine—she'd make it up to him once they made it out of here.

"Look, Dan, I…"

Fear surged in her as she turned back to where the boy was standing moments earlier.

He was gone. He was *fragging* gone.

"*Shit!*" she spat. "Dan! Daniel Ratemacher! I swear to the gods and all that's holy…"

It was no use. The boy had given her the slip.

And with all the people clogging this part of the ring, she had no idea how in the nine hells she was going to find him.

Dan hated leaving Sahar like that, especially since he had seen that the danger she'd warned of was quite present and *very* real. That said, there was no way he could tell her the importance of what he was here to do. Not without giving away more than he wanted to.

It was okay though. This would just take another moment. He was almost to the location his contact had identified. He would settle the transaction, find Sahar, and the two of them would be on their way again.

Having convinced himself of the rightness of his action, he pressed through the crowds to his destination. It turned out the coordinates he was looking for didn't lead to a shop. It didn't correspond with a building of any kind.

It was an alley.

A new sense of unease crept into his stomach. This had not been what he'd imagined. Given the nature of the item he was looking for, it would have been a stretch to say he was surprised. He wondered if he might be less uneasy if Sahar hadn't been so persistent in her warnings.

The figures waiting in the shadowed passage did nothing to soothe his anxieties. They were cloaked in the same tattered dark clothing as the rest of the ring's occupants. This rendered their appearances indistinct, but two of the figures were large enough to be Maur or Orchallen.

A half-dozen persons lingered in the alley, but it was hard to say if they were affiliated. A few of them loitered distantly and might not be associated at all. With so many people in such close proximity, why had his contact been insistent on Dan coming alone?

One of the figures glanced around as if he were looking for someone. He held a black case in one hand. Dan was betting this was his contact.

"Mereth?" Dan asked, giving the name his contact had used on the net.

The figure glanced down at him. His eyes widened as he took in Dan's appearance. "Ratemacher?" The word had a sizzling quality as it slipped from his tongue.

At this range, Dan could make out his contact's features. The face was hairless, covered in scales of mottled gray and green. Darker scales accented the yellow hue of the man's reptilian eyes.

Hissak.

That was highly unusual for this region of space. Though he didn't consider himself xenophobic—his closest friend on the crew was Maur, after all—the man's strange appearance deepened his unease. It wasn't just the alien visage that plied at his nerves. Those reptilian features held a sinister cast, along with something else that Dan couldn't quite place.

"That's right," Dan responded. "Do you have what I'm looking for?"

"Perhaps…" the man hissed. "You has the payment?"

Dan held up the kret card and Mereth reached for it. Dan pulled it back away from the man's grasping claws. "I need to see the chip first."

Mereth let slip a growl of frustration even as he lifted the case. "Open it," he ordered, passing it to Dan.

Dan unzipped the padded parcel, glancing inside to confirm the presence of a single metal chip buried in protective black foam. He brought his MoDAC near that chip and tapped the screen to scan the device. When it beeped approvingly, he passed the kret card to Mereth.

"Looks like everything is in order," said Dan. "Take care."

The Hissak's clawed hand shot forward, grabbing Dan by the shoulder. "Don't be so hasty, my little friend. I admits you are not what I's expecting. What is it, exactly, that you plans to do with that chip?"

Dan jerked backward. "That's none of your concern."

He realized, then, that two of the cloaked figures were moving behind him. That cold, familiar dread he'd been feeling a moment ago returned to his stomach.

Mereth grinned wickedly from the concealment of his hood. "You don't looks like one who comes here often. You's better served to show some courtesy in your business dealings in this part of the station. The consequences of impoliteness are quite... *severe.*"

The two other strangers had boxed Dan in. Firm hands came down on his arms, holding him in place. "I... I-I'm sorry!" he stammered. "I m-m-meant no disrespect."

"I'm sure." The Hissak's words were punctuated by the hiss of metal as he pulled free a slender dagger from the folds of his robes. "But I thinks a more thorough lesson is in order—just to assure you remember it well, yes?"

Dan's heart pounded in his chest. He struggled in the arms of the robed men as they plied the case from his hands. "No!" Dan shouted. "Please!"

Sahar spotted the kid just as the black-clad thugs seized him by the arms. The gleam of a knife flickered from within the folds of one of the men's robes. A growl of fury tore from her throat.

She surged from the crowd and into the alleyway, resche sliding into her right hand. The blade tore through the first figure, a spray of blood following the weapon's arch as it swept through the air.

So abrupt was the first blow that it caught the other two off guard. They stumbled back, the one closest to Dan dropping a black parcel to the ground in favor of his blade. Sahar grabbed Dan by the shirt and jerked him forward, out of the assailant's reach.

The remaining figure, a Hissak, shrieked in rage and stabbed wildly at Sahar. The move was clumsy and easily parried. Sahar's foot came up to collide with the creature's gut, sending him sprawling backward.

The second moved for her now. This one she met with a flash of steel across his forearm. He dropped his weapon as Sahar brought hers back around. A thrust to his face ended his life.

Now the other dark figures had sprung into motion. Blades, long and short, flashed as they descended on Sahar.

She sidestepped the first thrust, grabbing the attacker's arm. With a quick jerk and a sickening pop, the limb broke. The assailant screamed in pain and anger, even as Sahar used the body to block an incoming dagger.

With a heave, she sent the body careening through the air to collide with the tiny mob. The would-be muggers scrambled to hold their footing. Sahar pressed the attack.

Her resche whistled through the air. She chopped her next victim in the arm, severing it clean from his body. His howl of pain was silenced as the blade arced back up and into his torso.

His companions were regrouping, trying to get around her. Still holding her resche in her dominant hand, Sahar slipped out a second blade—this one a long, slender thing she'd started practicing with recently. It was time to put that training to work.

When the first of the thugs rushed her, she parried with her resche and sank the second blade into his eye. Immediately she withdrew it, spun, and slashed at an attacker on her right.

This one was big, even bigger than Sahar. He wasn't as fast, though. He came at her again with a stab that Sahar dodged easily. Her resche arced up, slashing a deep gash across her opponent's abdomen. He clutched at the wound for a single gasp before she dispatched him.

The third assailant didn't fare any better. He slashed at her wildly, almost landing a hit against Sahar's leather vest by sheer luck. When he stumbled off balance, Sahar smoothly opened his throat.

These were not trained fighters—just a bunch of street-toughs who'd stumbled onto a mark that was far more than they were prepared to handle.

Looking down the alley, it seemed that the others had come to the same conclusion. Even the Hissak who had looked to be the ringleader for this little bunch had turned tail and run. A second later, scurrying shadows were the only indication that anyone else had been there at all.

Sahar turned to find Dan wide-eyed but safe on the opposite side of the alley. The kid had scooped up the black case that she'd seen dropped at the beginning of the fight and was cradling it to his chest.

At least it looked like he'd gotten what he'd come for.

Wiping the gore from her blade on the leg of her leather pants, Sahar couldn't help but laugh. Despite all the noise generated in the brief encounter, not a single person on the street had stopped to take the measure of what was going on. At the mouth of the alley, the mass of people continued to churn indifferently as they went about their separate lives.

"All right kid," Sahar growled, locking eyes with Dan. "It's time to cut the bullshit. What in the nine hells were you looking for in this alley?"

Chapter 11

[Accessing COGNIS.Datafiles…]

Half-breeds — *Cultural Inventory* — A term referring to any individual born of two distinct sapient species. Though technically referring to individuals who are sired in equal parts by two different sapien species, the term is commonly applied to any being of mixed blood. At one time, these individuals were quite rare. As the integration of intergalactic communities continues, they are growing increasingly common due to the proliferation of cross-species relationships. Individuals with a greater than fifty-percent proportion of mixed-species heritage are significantly less common, as half-breeds are typically born sterile. Despite continued proliferation, the existence of half-breeds is a taboo subject in much of society.

[Closing Datafile…]

As the neurosim session terminated, Ora's private lounge blinked back into focus. Markus removed the black disk from his temple and placed it on the table in front of him. Eli twirled the disk in his fingers as he contemplated the information they'd received.

Markus broke the silence. "We'll do what we have to do, but five days planning for an assignment this dangerous is a tall order."

Ora nodded. "The compensation for the assignment has been calculated with that in mind."

"Oh, of course! And the pay is fantastic. Still, we have absolutely zero time to scout the site. Nine hells, it'll take two days on full-burn to even reach Khonshu."

Their host's smirk never faltered. "I'm aware. That's why my informants have pulled together a full dossier and permissions kit for you."

She pulled out her MoDAC and removed a data chip, tossing it to Markus, who slotted it into his own device. He cast one last uncertain glance at her as the files loaded onto the card's screen.

Sure enough, it seemed that the Wings had done all the homework for them. All Markus and his crew needed to do was go in and pass the test.

"So you've done most of the hard part," he muttered. "Not that I'm not grateful for the opportunity, but why didn't you just have your team nab the goods?"

"These informants are intelligence operatives, not smugglers. They do what they do exceedingly well, but I know better than to burn quality assets by asking them to accomplish something outside of their skill set."

"Fair enough," Markus conceded.

"Are we bringing the target back here?" Eli asked.

"No," Ora's smile faded and she straightened in her seat. "Not right away, at least. You are to check in with me for further direction after you secure the conduit."

Well, that was nebulous—and more than a little disconcerting. Markus didn't mind letting that be known. "How long will we have to hold onto that thing?"

"Just until I can arrange for a safe transfer," Ora insisted as she reached for her glass on the side table. Taking a sip of wine, she added. "Technology like this will find a buyer quickly. That being said, its unique nature makes it a prime target for customs. I'd prefer to avoid the hassle of sneaking onto the station just to smuggle it back out again."

If Markus didn't like the idea of stealing something out from under the Ghenza, he *really* didn't like the idea of holding onto it while Ora found a buyer. This was one area, though, where he was going to have to put some faith in Ora. She'd likely factored this particular term into the size of their payment as well.

"Fine," he agreed. "We'll need another full day to resupply and make repairs. Can I count on the Wings for requisitions?"

Ora's smile slid back into place. "Certainly. Get me a list of what you need by tomorrow morning, and we'll have it transferred to you within the day." She glanced back and forth between him and Eli. "Anything else?"

Markus looked at Eli, who shook his head. It was the best they could hope for on such short notice.

Ora reclined back on her couch, taking another long sip from her glass. "A pleasure, as always, gentlemen. I trust you can see yourselves out."

Skye lay on her back, resting on a plain white operating table. The padding conformed to her shape so that she was comfortable while remaining firm enough around her limbs to hold her stationary. She wore only a simple modesty cloth that had been draped over her center, covering her breasts and pelvic region. At this moment, she was feeling very exposed, but it wasn't from the lack of clothing.

The artificial skin covering her cybernetic legs and left arm had been peeled back to reveal the circuitry beneath. Wires and metallic rods lay open to the air, still glistening with the circulatory fluid lubricated the mechanisms. Where in normal limbs there would have been muscle, her limbs had an assortment of durable pads and springs. Where there should have been nerves, there ran a complex network of conduction fibers. The neural conductors in this latest model were state-of-the-art. They mimicked her old tactile sensations perfectly—much better than the cheap and clunky prosthetics she'd had at one time.

Her surgeon-slash-technician was Dr. Li Su-Yang, a young-looking woman with the demeanor of a cranky old veteran. She was maybe two or three cycles Skye's junior but talked like she was at least twice as jaded.

The doctor's blue-black hair was tied up tight under a teal surgical cap, and her severe features were hidden behind a white mask. Not a blemish of blood or other fluid marred the clean appearance of her green-tinted scrubs. The lack of mess was indicative of the doctor's precision. That's why Skye always came to her. If you were going to have someone tinkering with your nervous system, you wanted to know you were in good hands.

She sighed and leaned back into her headrest. Unfortunately, there wasn't much to do during these tune-ups. Consequently, she always found herself reflecting on things she'd rather not think about.

Today, she was going right back to the memory of how she'd gotten the prosthetics on her first freelancing job with Markus. After the Colony Wars, their unit had been stranded on a broken-down station orbiting Colony 13—called Dracari by the locals. They hadn't been running their own crew back then. Lack of options and opportunity had them working for the first set of crooks with a decent offer.

During that first operation, they'd had the bad luck of coming across a nasty little creature in the swamp that was intent on making a meal out of the crew. Skye never did learn what was called, but its vine-like appendages had carried a localized neurotoxin.

One close call, no more than a few miserable seconds, had left her without the use of her legs and arm. As sad as it was, Skye admitted that she was lucky that that was all the encounter had cost her.

The rest of the crew had told Markus to leave her behind. In response, Markus had put bullet holes in each of their skulls and carried Skye's damaged body back to the shuttle they had come in on. They had been running their own show ever since.

And now I'm thinking about him again. She rubbed her brow with her good arm. *Seriously, I have to just get over this.*

"I need you to be still," Doc Li lectured. "I'm almost done, but if you twitch the wrong way, I might short you out."

"Sorry," Skye muttered. She hated being scolded. A childish part of her wanted to blame Markus for that too.

This was all part of her now-typical emotional cycle when it came to the guy. A couple of weeks, two different jobs, and a clandestine affair with their mutual friend later, she was still thinking about him. What was it going to take to get her over him?

Gods knew he wasn't fretting over her like this. He had his drugs to help him cope. Shit, why had Skye bothered to stay sober? A good dose of harpy was exactly what she needed right now.

Right on cue, her anger welled up to douse the flames of sorrow and self-pity. She resolved, once again, not to miss a man who put his high before their relationship. She wasn't going to miss a man who broke his promises.

"All done," Li declared. "Powering you up now."

Skye experienced a slight jolt as the limbs came back online. She wiggled her fingers and toes experimentally. "Feels good to me."

"Perfect. Let me stitch you up and you'll be good to go." The doctor worked efficiently, closing the flaps of skin on the prosthetics and applying a thin stream of medical foam to close the seams. Skye's tissues tingled as the fast-acting solution did its work.

When Doc Li was finished, she clicked a switch on the operating table to tilt it slowly forward. A look of uncharacteristic concern flashed in the woman's eyes. "Are you all right?"

"Yeah," Skye replied, stepping off the table. "Just a little up in my head. You should really get a holoscreen installed in here."

The doctor made a snide comment as she launched into a review of the repairs and updates she had installed. Skye nodded agreeably as she got dressed.

"Not that you're listening to me," Li noted at length. "Probably because you're too busy thinking about that beau of yours."

This made Skye jump. "I was too listening!"

"So, no comment on the self-destruct mechanism that activates when you click your heels?"

"What?"

"It didn't seem to bother you the first time I mentioned it. You just kept nodding."

Skye felt a slight flush in her cheeks as she shrugged into her jacket. "Sorry," she admitted. "Yeah, I guess I can't blame my head games on your hospitality after all. Just tell me how much I owe you. I know you're worth it."

"Seven-fifty."

Skye swiped on her MoDAC. "Done."

"So, what's going on with you?" Li pressed.

"Like I told you, it's nothing."

"Oh, it's something," she said sagely as she verified the krets transfer on her office terminal. "Sure you don't want to talk about it?"

Skye rolled her eyes. "You're my surgeon, Li, not my therapist."

"Yes, I doubt I'd make a great therapist," she conceded. "Too much in the habit of just cutting right into the problem. I'd go crazy if I had to sit around trying to get chatterboxes like you to open up."

"You're funny," Skye replied mirthlessly. "Save some of that humor for the next time we grab a drink, yeah?"

Her MoDAC chimed. It was a text from Eli: [GOT ANOTHER JOB. MARKUS OFF DOING HIS OWN THING. WANT TO MEET UP?]

Whatever angst Skye had been feeling began to subside. However else she felt about Eli, she had to admit that thinking about him was a sure-fire way to get her mind off Markus. She recognized this wasn't a long-term strategy for dealing with her shit, but it was the best thing she could do at the moment.

She attached the coordinates for a nearby hotel and typed her quick reply: [SEE YOU SOON.]

Li piped up again. "Ah, there we go. That grin looks promising."

Was she grinning? "Whatever you say, Doc. I—" Skye's words fell off as a sharp pain radiated just above her eye. Her legs buckled, and her head barely avoided colliding with the table as she sank to her knees.

The doctor was there instantly. Bracing Skye with both hands, she spoke with calm, collected authority. "Easy there, I've got you. Headache?" As Skye nodded, the doctor produced an instrument from her lab coat.

She plied open Skye's eye. There was a flash of red from the scanner. Li muttered to herself as she looked at the device's readout. Then she reached for a nearby table and grabbed an auto-injector.

Skye felt a tiny prick against her neck as the device delivered a small dose of medication. The headache began to subside.

"You haven't had an episode like that in a while, have you?" asked Li.

"No," Skye gasped. "It's been over a year."

"None of the typical warning signs?"

"No… I mean, yeah. I've had some minor headaches, but not like that. I thought I was cured with that surgery we did a while back. Nine hells, I don't even carry the meds with me anymore."

Li's face was still contorted with concern, even as she helped Skye stand. "Well then, you're lucky it happened while you were here. I don't have anything I can dispense to you right now, but I can see to it that something gets sent to your ship in the morning."

Skye rubbed at her neck. "Yeah, that'd be great. Thanks, doc."

"Are you having any of the other symptoms?"

She thought hard for a second. Was there something more to the fatigue she'd been experiencing lately? She shook her head in the negative. "Must just be stress."

"Are you sure?" Li asked, obviously unconvinced.

Skye forced a dismissive laugh. "Of course. I've got it Doc. Don't worry about me. Now, let me get out of here. I'm sure you've got other places to be." *Gods know I do.*

The doctor donned a polite smile. It didn't quite mask the concern in her eyes. "All right then. Call me next time you're on station? I'll be checking in on those headaches at the next appointment."

"For sure. Thanks, Li."

Skye exited the clinic and found herself back on the streets of R-3. This district was strangely quiet at the late hour. Scarcely a person walked by as she queried the transport schedule for the maglevs.

She was delighted to find one scheduled for departure in roughly ten minutes. It was a station she hadn't used before, but still within walking distance. Plus, a little stroll might do her some good.

Her deep sigh seemed to echo on the barren streets as she set off toward the terminal. As she walked, she tried to think of Eli—or at least tried not to think about Markus.

What was wrong with her? Eli was a great guy and obviously cared about her. The guy seemed to take every opportunity to bend over backward for her.

Maybe she should just tell Markus about this little affair. That would close some doors for sure, and maybe provide her a little closure. It's what Eli wanted. Why was she so hesitant?

Despite her internal debate, something off to her right caught her eye. The structure sat a slight distance back from the other buildings on the street. Rather than being constructed of steel or plaster, this building was crafted from stone—or at least sported a stone facade. An arched doorway rested firmly in the center. Beyond it, there was only darkness.

As Skye examined it further, she found it odd that the structure had caught her attention at all. Above the arch, there was a symbol. This one she recognized out of the limited time she'd spent in Sahar's quarters—swirling arches interrupted by irregular vertical slashes.

A temple, she realized. What was an outpost of the Church of Nethra doing out here on R-3? More importantly, why had it caught her attention? Surely she wasn't so torn as to contemplate taking up religion?

She laughed at the thought. Nope, that wasn't even close to being on her mind. Sure, it was odd that the temple had caught her attention, but it was kind of distinct in these drab surroundings.

Come to think of it, Sahar did say she made trips to some temple here on the station. Maybe this was where she went when she wandered off alone. Skye would have to remember to ask her about it.

Putting the thought out of her mind, she started walking again—only to collide headlong into a dark-robed figure who seemed to appear out of nowhere.

"Shit!" she exclaimed, arms flailing as she steadied herself.

The figure—a woman—stumbled slightly, and something fell out from the folds of her robes. The golden object clinked softly as it fell onto the street.

"Apologies," the woman hissed.

Skye flushed. It was her who should probably be apologizing. If she hadn't been busy spacing out a few seconds ago, she might have seen the woman standing there.

"My bad. I wasn't watching where I was going." Catching sight of what the woman had dropped, a golden medallion of some kind, Skye bent to pick it up. "Here, let me get that for you."

Her hand made contact with the cool metal of the medallion. Then, something strange happened.

There was the sound of rushing wind. Despite that being quite impossible—there was no wind on a space station—Skye could hear it distinctly. Just under those currents, she heard a kind of whispering.

The world seemed to shift, getting fuzzy around the edges. Skye panicked for a second, thinking another headache was coming on. The whispers grew louder.

A flash of light, then darkness. A distant scream. Then a torrent of images.

A looming eye in the shadows. Emerald fire roiling around her. Crawling darkness. Deep, maniacal laughter. A swirling vortex of energy. A man in flames. Hands around her throat. A single word said with a voice like the hiss of a lover's whisper and the roar of cannon-fire: *Kaleema*.

Skye's mind slammed back into her head with such force that it brought her to her knees. Her hands shook, and she thought she might be sick.

What in the nine hells had just happened?

"Miss?" It was the woman. Gentle hands held her shoulders, attempting to steady her. "Miss, are you all right?"

Skye nodded, forcing her breathing to slow. Only now did she notice her headache, but it was already subsiding. "Yeah," she gasped. "Yeah, I'm fine. I was just... I..." She hesitated, having lost awareness of her surroundings. What had she been doing again?

"Are you injured? Should I call someone for you?"

Skye glanced up at the woman. As she did, an uncomfortable chill settled in her spine.

Reptilian eyes gaze back at her from a pretty face. Dark cascades of curled hair poured out from the hood of the woman's cloak. She smiled gently, but there was something predatory in that smile that made Skye want to flee.

"No!" Skye shouted as she pulled away.

Startled, the woman released her and took a couple of steps back. A look of sadness, maybe pain, seeped into her expression.

Breathe. "No," Skye repeated, more calmly this time. "I-I'm… I'm fine. Sorry, I just…"

The woman's head bobbed in acknowledgment, though her expression did not waiver. "No apology necessary." She held out a clawed hand, palm up. "May I have my medallion, please?"

Only then did Skye realize she was still holding the trinket—a golden circle with a strange symbol etched on the surface. A simple chain dangled from the charm. The metal felt unnaturally cold in her hand.

"Oh… ah… yeah." She handed the object over to the woman.

"Thank you, child."

Child? The woman didn't look any older than Skye. Why the parental tone?

Then it clicked. They were standing outside of the temple. This woman must be a priestess.

"Sure," Skye muttered. "No problem."

The priestess cocked her head to the side. "Are you sure you're all right?"

"Yeah! I mean, yes… I'm just. Sorry, I'm just out of sorts." Skye took a step backward. "I'm going to go now. Sorry… again…"

The priestess fixed her with those alien eyes. Something there made Skye uneasy as if the woman saw something that Skye was missing.

After a moment the priestess dipped her head in acknowledgment. "All right. Farewell then."

Still mortified by her behavior, Skye pressed past her. Was she losing her mind? Not only was she running into random strangers, but now she was hallucinating in the middle of the street.

It was just a couple of blocks to the tram, then a short ride to the hotel. Gods-willing Eli would already be there. If she hadn't needed to blow off some steam before, she needed to now.

<Kaleema.>

Skye went rigid. It was that word again. Had that been the priestess? She glanced over her shoulder but saw no one.

Had she imagined it? Yes, she must be imagining it. It had been a long day, and she was probably having a reaction to the medication Doc Li had given her. That explained everything, right?

Right.

CHAPTER 12

[Accessing COGNIS.Datafiles...]

Sahaia Bonding — *Metaphysics* — A psionic ability unique to the Sahaia. Sahaia can extend their psionic imprint to envelop the mind and body of another sapien. The bonded individual, commonly referred to as a thrall, receives several unique benefits from this connection: enhanced strength, accelerated healing, and the ability to communicate psychically with the Sahaia who bonded them. The Sahaia, in turn, gains the ability to draw upon the thrall's life force to enhance their psionic abilities. A thrall can be identified by a tattoo-like mark emblazoned on their body in a place that corresponds with an identical symbol on the Sahaia.

[Closing Datafile...]

After a simple dinner, Aaliyah sat cuddled with Nikki on the couch. The display panel was running the station news feed on mute. Monica had fallen asleep next to their cat, Jinx, on a cushion on the floor. The child looked peaceful lying there with her pet.

"She's so beautiful," Aaliyah whispered to Nikki. "I'll never get over how much she looks like ya."

"Yeah, but I think she's got your appetite for trouble."

Aaliyah let her jaw drop and gasped in mock offense. "Ya used to be quite the trouble maker yourself," she protested, shoving Nikki playfully.

"Maybe, but I'm pretty sure *those* trouble genes are all yours."

Maybe it was true. Monica was Nikki's daughter, both in the genetic and traditional sense, but she was Aaliyah's daughter too. They had conceived Monica through the splicing of Nikki and Aaliyah's DNA, allowing them to create an offspring together that was uniquely their own.

It was a process that had become very popular for same-sex couples, or couples that had some reproductive irregularity that kept them from having children naturally. The whole thing was a newer procedure, and Aaliyah wasn't knowledgeable about all the particulars.

They could have used a mechanical surrogate, but Nikki had been adamant that one of them should carry the child. Aaliyah had been happy to concede the task to Nikki at the time. Now, though, looking at their little girl, she wondered if she had missed out on a little something.

Yeah, a lot of unnecessary weight gain and other painful body changes.

"Ya give her the injections already?"

"Yeah," Nikki sighed. "Just before you got home."

"How're we doin' on our supply?"

"I have enough to get her through this week."

"Well, the pay from the last job should be wired to our account any minute."

"Good," Nikki replied simply.

Aaliyah couldn't help but notice the heavy melancholy lacing her partner's voice. She changed the subject. "So, all that stuff she said about 'feelin' me comin'—is that just her wigglin' out of trouble, or do ya think she has the gift?"

Nikki let out a skeptical little snort. "Who knows? She can't be tested for another year. I'm surprised you would call it that, though."

"Call it what?"

"The *gift*." An awkward pause. Nikki stroked her finger down the inside of Aaliyah's forearm. "Then again, maybe I shouldn't be surprised given the little taste you've grown accustomed to."

Here we go again. Aaliyah's psionic bonding to Eli was a sore subject for Nikki. It had happened before they'd ever met, so it wasn't like it was something that had been sprung on her in the middle of the relationship. Nikki had known what she was getting into, but Aaliyah guessed that didn't mean she liked it.

Aaliyah's mobile vibrated on the end table next to where the two women were wrapped in a blanket together.

Speak of the devil.

She reached for her device and read the message from Eli. [GOT ANOTHER JOB. TEAM MEETING TOMORROW. MORE DETAILS THEN.]

Nikki sighed as she read the text over Aaliyah's shoulder. "Looks like you are only here for a quick visit after all."

"I told ya it'd probably be that way."

"Didn't stop me from hoping though."

Her resentment was palpable, but Aaliyah didn't want to fight. She wasn't home enough to spend their time spatting. Instead, she bent in to give Nikki a quick peck on the lips. "You know why I do this."

"I know," her partner conceded, lapsing into another quiet silence. Several seconds later, she spoke up again. "Can I ask you something without you getting all weird about it?"

Definitely not the best way to start a conversation, but hey… "Sure, shoot."

"You guys can send messages telepathically, right? You and Eli, I mean."

"Kind of," Aaliyah replied, hesitant about where this line of questioning was going. "Eli can send me psychic messages, and sometimes I can reply."

"Why not all the time?"

"Why so curious all the sudden?"

Nikki huffed. "I shouldn't have brought it up."

Ah shit. "Nah, it's fine—sorry. I… uh… I guess it's just that… I don't know. The technical term's somethin' like 'psychic shielding,' or some shit. It's like his brain has to be in receive mode or somethin'. I can't get a hold of him any time I want. If ya think of it like an on-off switch, imagine it like Eli's holdin' the controller."

"Why isn't it just open all the time."

Aaliyah grinned. "Probably cause he doesn't want to hear all the sexy thoughts I'm havin' about you right now."

Now it was Nikki who shoved her. "All right, you flirt. But seriously, though—he can contact you whenever he pleases, right?"

"Yeah…" Aaliyah replied, drawing the word out. "Again, I'm not sure why you're askin'."

Nikki shrugged innocently. "Just wondering why you two bother with text messages. That's all."

"That," Eli murmured as he kissed Skye's neck, "was amazing."

In response, she let out a contented sigh. Yes, that had been exactly what she needed. "Gods, it feels like it's been too long since we've done that."

Eli propped himself up on his arms, gazing down at her. "You know, if we would just be open about this, we wouldn't have to wait until we were stationed to have this kind of fun."

Another sigh, this one far from contented. *Here we go again.*

"Come on," he pleaded. "Don't give me that look." With one hand, he pushed aside a lock of her hair that had fallen into her face. He tucked the stray hair behind her ear and dragged his fingertips gently down the side of her face and neck.

"What look?" she protested.

"You know the one," he insisted, his hand trailing down her sternum. "The one that says, 'I don't want to have this conversation again.'"

"If you know I feel that way, then why do you bring it up?"

His hand flattened into a massaging motion across the side of her torso. "Skye, can you honestly blame me? I feel like this is going somewhere, don't you?"

"Yeah, I think so," she said with more confidence than she actually felt.

"Then wouldn't making this official be the logical next step?"

Skye felt a tingling sensation as his hand started tracing the lines of her hip. "I don't know about next steps," she said breathily. "But if I were you, I'd warn that hand that he's about to start something he's going to have to finish."

Eli chuckled. "He's been warned." He leaned in to kiss her again and kept kissing her.

At that moment she forgot about Markus and all her other concerns. For that time, it was just her and Eli. But like all good things, it was over too quickly.

An hour or so later, Skye stepped out of the shower. As she towel-dried her hair, her thoughts finally caught up with her.

The first thing on her mind was the strange encounter she'd had on the way to the hotel. Skye had originally wanted to pass it off as a hallucination—just a bad reaction to the meds Doc Li had given her. Now, though, she felt strangely compelled to bring it up.

"Hey Eli," she said, walking back into the bedroom. "There was something I had been meaning to ask you about."

He was still sitting on the bed, not having bothered to put his clothes back on. He looked up from whatever he had been studying on his MoDAC. "Sure, what's on your mind?"

How to put this now…

"Do you ever have visions?" she asked. "Or like… I don't know… hallucinations, maybe? You know, as part of the whole Sahaia-thing?"

She immediately had his attention, and not in the way she'd had fifteen minutes earlier. "That's a little random. But no, not in the way you seem to mean."

"But you *can* have them, right?"

His eyes narrowed suspiciously. "In a way. There are rituals out there that Sahaia covens use to give them the ability to see far distances or look back at past events. Those are somewhat advanced techniques though, so it's not very common. Why do you ask?"

Skye finished drying off and dropped the towel on the floor. She almost dodged the question, feeling paranoid for bringing this up after one weird incident. Despite her reservations, that paranoia eventually won out. "Because I think I might have had some kind of episode on my way here."

Genuine interest replaced his suspicion. "Tell me about it."

"It was just something kind of weird. I was walking by that temple—might be the one Sahar goes to, but I've never noticed it before—and I was being kind of… spacey. Anyway, when I got lost in my thoughts for a second, I end up running into this priestess. She dropped her medallion, and I went to pick it up for her. When I grabbed the necklace, I had this weird, out-of-body experience."

She shook her head, thoroughly embarrassed now that she'd put voice to it. A laugh slipped from her lips. "Now that I'm saying it out loud, I realize how crazy I'm being."

Eli studied her silently. It was not the way he usually watched her when her clothes were off. It was more like he was trying to see something there that he hadn't noticed previously.

"Not at all," he said finally. "Clairvoyance is one of the psionic schools—usually something that stems from the greater gifts of the empaths. It doesn't normally happen spontaneously, but that doesn't mean you didn't experience it." His voice was neutral as if he were talking about the weather. Something in his expression, though, made Skye skeptical of the calm facade. "Do you think you might have the gift?"

"I don't know," she admitted, sliding onto the bed next to him.

"Have you ever been tested?"

She was surprised by how receptive he was to this idea. Maybe she wasn't crazy after all. "Not that I'm aware of. I'm not even sure what that whole process involves."

Eli set his mobile on the nightstand. "Well, the full process can be complicated, but it's easy enough to determine if you're psi-sensitive. I had some mild sensitivity before my ascension, so I had the opportunity to experience it firsthand." He rolled toward her, pressing his hand against hers. "I could run a preliminary test for you."

That caught her a little by surprise. "You can do that?"

"Sure. It's not a formal testing by any means. Think of it as more of a screening. If the test shows some psionic potential, we would have to bring you to a training center or a sanctum to get more details. Still, I can run the basic test."

The idea intrigued her. What would it be like to be a psion? It was never something she'd aspired toward, and she was a little old for the gift to be manifesting.

"I think I'd like that," she decided. "When do you think we could give it a try?"

"Right now, actually."

He rolled off the bed and walked to where his bag lay discarded. Reaching inside, he withdrew a slender box about thirty or so centimeters long.

"You carry a psionic sensitivity test with you whenever you leave the ship?"

Eli chuckled, shaking his head. "This device has other uses—but yes, I usually carry it with me." He sat back on the bed and opened the case.

The box hinged open on one of the long ends. Inside was a slender rod that tapered to a point on one end. The device was constructed of a dark metal etched with tiny runic symbols.

Eli set the box between them on the bed. "This is what's called a focus. Think of it as a magnet for psionic energy." He ran his fingers along the length of the spike before bringing his hand up just above the box.

The spike leaped to attention, the thickest end drawn up toward Eli's hovering palm. The device was now balanced inside the box on the needle-like point.

"If anything with psionic energy passes over the case, the rod will balance on its tip. It's a little different from typical telekinesis. I'm not moving the rod—rather, it's drawn to my energy."

He moved his palm back and forth along the length of the case. The thick end of the rod followed the movement of his hand but never fell over as it pushed the boundaries of its balance.

Eli continued. "This one is attuned to me, but I can pass the attunement temporarily to another object, or person. That attunement will hold if there is a certain degree of psionic power within the target." He smiled across the box at Skye. "Are you ready?"

For such a big revelation, Skye felt like there should have been more of a process involved. "And, it's accurate?" she asked.

"One-hundred percent. It's just a yes-no answer, mind you. We wouldn't know anything about the kind of gift you have or how strong it is. That being said, this a good place to start."

Well, why the hells not? If nothing else, it would rule out one potential cause for her weird trip back in the street. "What do I do?"

"Place one of your hands underneath mine, palm down. Then, all you have to do is hold it there. I'll take care of the rest."

Following his direction, Skye extended her hand so that it was directly under his. "Should I feel something?"

"Not necessarily. Just focus on the device."

She did so. She stared intently at the spike, focusing on the runes along its length. Those symbols seemed to gleam back at her, as though they held some kind of secret they refused to share.

Eli removed his hand from on top of hers. The rod stood erect, no longer tracking the movement of his hand. Skye held her breath, as she kept her mind's eye centered on the device.

And then it flopped over.

They both snorted and snickered before breaking out into open laughter. "I'm guessing that's a negative?" Skye giggled.

"Yes, that's a no." He picked up the device and placed it back in its case. Closing the box, he prompted, "So, talk to me about these visions."

Despite the results of the test, there was no skepticism in his voice. It seemed that, despite evidence to the contrary, he was still taking her seriously. She would have to add that to the litany of things that made him so perfect.

"It was probably nothing," she dismissed. She leaned forward and planted a gentle peck on his lips. "Let's talk about it some other time. I'm tired tonight, and from the way you made it sound, we've got a full day ahead of us tomorrow."

"Fine by me." Eli rose to return the rod to his bag, looking sincerely at peace with the outcome. He was a good guy, and it was nice to have someone to go to that didn't care how crazy she sounded.

The thought brought one more thing to her mind—a small detail that she'd nearly forgotten. "Oh, by the way: when I was tripping out earlier, I heard a word I'd never before. Do you know what a 'Kaleema' is?"

Unexpectedly, Eli went rigid. His tense pause lasted just a second longer than seemed natural. "I'm not sure," he replied, keeping his back to her as he spoke. "Another language maybe?"

The sudden shift in the mood had Skye feeling wary at his response. "Must be," she agreed. "You're *sure* you've never heard it before?"

He shrugged, turning back to her. His face was a mask of implacable calm. "I won't deny that it sounds vaguely familiar. I just can't place it right now. Would it make you feel better if I looked into it a bit? Maybe put out a line to someone on the question?"

Skye hesitated before shaking her head. "Nah, it's fine. I reserve the right to change my mind though."

"A woman's eternal prerogative," Eli agreed, kissing her softly. "Good night, Skye."

"Good night," she responded, touching the panel next to the bed to kill the lights. Fully in darkness, she nuzzled her face into the soft pillows.

All the while, she did her best to convince herself that Eli wasn't lying to her.

CHAPTER 13

[ACCESSING COGNIS.DATAFILES…]

ORCHALLEN — *RACIAL PROFILE (SAPIENS)* — THE MOST RECENT SAPIENT RACE TO EARN REPRESENTATION IN THE DORIAN HOUSE OF VOICES. ORCHALLEN ARE SIMILAR IN BUILD TO THEIR PATRON RACE, THE MAUR, WITH LARGE MUSCULAR FRAMES AND ABOVE-AVERAGE HEIGHT. THEIR THICK HIDES AND WIDE JAWS HAVE GAINED THEM THE DERISIVE AND PHONETICALLY SIMILAR MONIKER, "ORCS," AS DERIVED FROM TERRAN FOLKLORE DESPITE THE DIFFERENCE IN ETYMOLOGIES OF THE TWO WORDS. THOUGH THEIR PHYSICAL APPEARANCE AND RUDIMENTARY NATIVE TECHNOLOGY HAVE GARNERED A GENERALLY NEGATIVE IMPRESSION REGARDING THEIR INTELLECT, THERE IS NO INDICATION THAT THEIR COGNITIVE CAPACITY IS NOTABLY INFERIOR TO THAT OF THE OTHER SAPIENT RACES.

[CLOSING DATAFILE…]

They were on the train that would carry them back to the concourse on R-2 when Kadath turned to his companion. "I think that went rather well, don't you?"

Even behind her mask, he could tell that Siv was rolling her eyes. "You just had to make the comment about the sex tape, didn't you?"

"What? I was looking to secure our next job."

"Bullshit. You wanted to know the odds of seeing Ora naked."

He donned a look of feigned innocence. "I'm shocked you would make such a claim."

"Forget it, Kadath. She's not your type."

"And what, pray-tell, would you consider to be my type?"

Siv shook her head before looking away. The Hissak was never one for any kind of sustained banter. It must have been one of those Prodican religious things. Anything that would keep her wrapped up in an outfit like hers was bound to wear on one's sense of humor.

At least the get-up kept people from asking too many questions. Being only half-Terran in the Ravian system was bad enough. Kadath was having enough trouble getting jobs as it was, and having a Hissak as his right-hand wasn't going to help with those contracts. He really needed to look into recruiting at least one full Terran for his motley band.

The ride to the next ring was mercifully short. A shrill beep announced their arrival at the next station less than a minute later.

As they made their exit, Kadath spoke again. "I think she was sincere, though, in having another opportunity available for us in the future."

Siv's shadowed cowl swiveled toward him as they made their way down the platform. "And what do you suppose she would have said if she felt otherwise? 'Thank you for fulfilling my contract, now kindly frag off?'"

"See, those manners serve to illustrate why you are not the one running a semi-prestigious crime syndicate on this blighted hell of a space station."

Siv scoffed as she picked up her pace. "My point exactly. Don't get your hopes up, Kadath. Ora has no shortage of contractors swarming around that voluptuous figure of hers. We're a long way from making our way into her good graces."

It was probably true, but Kadath's optimistic nature insisted that there had to be a way. This was the best paying contract his motley crew had scored in quite some time, and all the gods in the nine hells knew that there were more krets where those had come from.

"What if we were to get to the bottom of Ora's little hacking problem?"

Siv shot him a curious glance. "I thought that we just did that."

"No… I mean, yes—we did. But what about the line of questioning? Ora wants to know why Shift was in her network, yes? What if we could find that out for ourselves?"

That notion quieted the woman for a second. "Do you think that's possible?"

"Why not? Thurn was able to find Shift in the first place. Maybe he could track down whatever it was that Shift was looking for."

The Hissak shrugged. "If he can, then we might be in business. Gods know we can use the money."

Her thought was punctuated by the sight of their ship docked in the concourse. Kadath had jokingly suggested that they name the thing the *Basilisk* because of how ugly she was. The rest of the crew, being unable to come up with a more appropriate name, had allowed it to stick.

She was a bulbous monstrosity, cobbled together from the shells of at least three other beastly ships. Still, she'd been on discount from a dealer who seemed disinclined to sell them any sightlier vessel. The starship might have been an abomination, but she was Kadath's abomination.

They keyed inside the ship and made their way down to the offshoot of the hanger that they had designated as the common room. Unlike some other vessels of this class, the *Basilisk* wasn't blessed with an abundance of living space. Kadath and his crew had made the most of what limited accommodations they had.

As expected, the other two members of their crew sat at a table in the center of the common room. Jeagan, the ship's engineer and Siv's husband, sat shirtless with a contemplative look on his face. He stared down at an Amfey game board. By the look on the Hissak's face, he was losing.

His opponent was quite the sight. Thurn had somehow managed to cram his massive bulk into one of the small chairs littering the room. The Orchallen cyborg had an intent look on his face, but he was not studying the game board. More than likely he was browsing the nets while Jeagan plotted his next move.

The metal plate on the right side of Thurn's face gleamed faintly in the dim light of the chamber. The telescoping lens that served as his right eye whirred and tracked toward Kadath and Siv as they entered. "Took ya long enough. Ah was beginnin' t' wonder if Ora had decided t' eat ya instead a' pay ya."

Jeagan looked up, a warm smile spreading across his reptilian face. "You're back."

Siv slid onto his lap, caressing her masked face against his neck in a sweet display of affection. The couple's intimacy was adorable in a way that made Kadath's stomach curdle.

Yet still, he smiled. "Yes, we are. Ora has wired a nice little pay-day to our accounts, so it looks like we can eat something other than nutrient slush tonight."

"'Bout time," Thurn growled. "The Queen didn' give ya any trouble then?"

"Not at all. In fact, she implied that there might be more work for our band of misfits if we remain accessible to her majesty's call."

Jeagan's eyes narrowed. "That sounds suspiciously political and overly polite."

"It was," Siv assured. "Kadath is reading too much into what is likely her generic, diplomatic response."

Despite his best efforts, Kadath felt his face screw up in response to Siv's cynical interpretation. "I felt as though her appreciation was quite sincere."

Thurn rolled his eye. "Ah thinks yer a bit quick t' take accolades from a pretty woman, boss."

"If you ever had the pleasure of such accolades, Thurn, you would understand."

That drew a scowl from the Orchallen and a laugh from Jeagan. "Speaking of pretty women," the Hissak began. "Is your business concluded for this evening? If so, I'd like to spend some time with my wife."

Kadath waggled his fingers at them. "Go ahead. It's already been a late night. I think we've done enough today."

He didn't need to repeat himself. The pair were up out of the seat and whisking toward their shared quarters in the next instant. For someone whose religious practices required her to keep every bit of her skin covered in public, Siv seemed curiously eager to be alone with her husband. Kadath would never understand Prodicans.

Fatigue found new purchase in his tired legs. He plopped down in the now-vacant chair and rested his booted feet on the table. "Well, big fella—looks like you're my date tonight."

Thurn grunted. "Don' ya be tryin' t' get fresh with me, red-face. Yer not ma type."

"And I prefer my company slightly less bulky. But what is that Terran saying? 'Beggars can't be choosers?'"

"Ah'm a be seein' ya beg fer me t' stop beatin' yer face 'ere in a minute."

"Oh, don't be so sensitive." Kadath straightened up in his seat. "Actually, there *is* something that I'd like your assistance with this evening. That is if you're not already busy with something else."

Curiosity flashed in the Orchallen's expression. "Ah'm listenin'."

"You know how you were able to find that hacker's location when he tapped into station security?"

"That's makin' it a bit over-simple, but yeah, ah'm trackin' with ya."

"Well, is there a chance that you could pull up Shift's trail again? Maybe even figure out any other systems he accessed along the way?"

The telescoping eye whirred, considering him. "Maybe. What're ya lookin' fer? Specifically, ah mean."

"I want to figure out why he was in Ora's network."

Thurn grunted. "Why's any hacker in any network? By ma reckonin' there was somethin' there he couldn' find anywhere else."

"But then why patch back into station security? If Shift hadn't been in both networks at the same time, we wouldn't have caught him the way that we did. And why, of all places, would he be looking in the Grey Wings' network? He had to know that Ora would be coming for his hide if he got caught."

The cyborg rubbed at the fleshy part of his jaw. "Ora ask ya t' look into this?"

"Not explicitly, but she beat Shift to within an inch of his life trying to get him to talk."

"An' he didn'?"

"He gave her some line about looking for a sex tape. A worthy goal, mind you, but I imagine there are safer ways to procure pornography."

"Maybe it was somethin' he was gonna try 'n ransom back to 'er?"

Kadath cocked an eyebrow. "Did you see her photos in last month's edition of *ConneXion*?"

"Ah don' recall."

"You would if you had—it was the cover story. Let's just say that I don't think Ora is too shy about showing the public a little skin. No, I think Shift was looking for something else."

Thurn leaned forward. "Somethin' worth hidin'," he concluded.

"Exactly. If Shift's target is a secret worth the beating he received, then I think that's information Ora would be more than willing to shell out a few krets for."

With another grunt, Thurn pushed himself out of his seat. The furniture groaned at the shift in its burden. "All right, now ya done got me curious. Even if Ora doesn' pay fer the intel, Ah still wanna take a look. Come on…"

He hurried to the exit with speed and enthusiasm that belied his size. Kadath was right on his tail as they made for the ship's control center.

On arriving at the terminal, Thurn inserted a series of wires into the various connection points in his mechanical arm and faceplate. Once that task was completed, he settled himself into a heavy, padded chair. Unlike the relatively flimsy furniture in the common room, this one was designed specifically to accommodate the cyborg's girth.

A holodisplay flickered to life in front of Thurn's face, but he didn't glance at it. This was more for Kadath's benefit. If Thurn found anything interesting along the way, he'd pin it to the display so his less technically-inclined colleague could see progress.

"Ya know the drill," Thurn growled. "Don' bother me 'less the ship's about t' blow—yeah?"

"Understood." Kadath had made that mistake only once, and the cyborg had almost crushed his skull. Apparently having his mind split between cyberspace and the real world was seriously detrimental to his judgment. As such, his more basic instincts— namely those that drove him to put any potential threats directly into a shallow grave—rose to the forefront.

The hack commenced, and images began to flash across the holodisplay. It was hardly neurosim quality, but it gave Kadath a vague notion of the types of data that Thurn was sifting through. Occasionally, a still capture of a particular image slid over to the side of the display to be held for future reference. These were just as frequently discarded as Thurn decided they were no longer relevant.

There was nothing more for Kadath to do now than make himself comfortable. He slid onto a nearby couch and stared vainly at Thurn's display. After several minutes, his eyes wandered up to the ceiling. The dented metal provided him with just as much insight into the Orchallen's progress as staring at the holodisplay. It was also far less likely to induce a seizure.

Despite every intention to the contrary, his exhaustion must have gotten the better of him. The next thing he knew, he was being rudely awakened by a heavy kick to his chair.

"Not that yer really doin' much fer the cause, but ya could at least stay awake while ah'm doin' yer lil errand."

Kadath rubbed at his eyes—a reflex he'd never given up even after he'd had the silvery prosthetics installed. "I'm without excuse." He forced himself into a sitting position and stared back up at the cyborg's glowering mechanical glare. "What did you find?"

"The name 'Cognis' mean anything t' ya?"

"No. Should it?"

"Probably not. Ah ain't never heard it 'neither. That said, it's what Shift was lookin' fer in Ora's network."

Cognis. Strain as he might, Kadath still swore he'd never heard the term before. "Did you find any details?"

"Plenty—'less yer too sleepy t' 'ear the long version. Don' wanna interrupt yer beauty sleep."

"I'm confident enough in my appearance, thank you. Please, fill me in."

As Kadath stood, Thurn gestured to one of the images on the display. "Shift, that ol' bastard, actually found the damn thing right 'fore we got 'em. He was usin' Ora's network 'cause 'er outposts've got better software than the station can afford. He mashed up a bunch o' the Wing's programs and the existin' tech on the station to run a search parameter. Looks like he was tryin' to find this guy."

The image showed the face of a gaunt-looking Hissak. Judging by his attire in the image, this man had grown accustomed to hard times. "This still was taken by station security?"

"Yup—after Shift had juiced it with some o' Ora's facial rec-tech."

"Where?"

"R-1."

Now *that* was odd. Hissak were uncommon in Terran space, and the snake-people were an absolute rarity in poverty zones. Aside from his two crew members, Kadath had not seen any others of the species since coming to the Ravian system.

Hissak culture was very collectivist, and they tended to run with their own species. If one of the snakes was out running in a Terran ghetto, there was something seriously wrong with it. An exile, probably.

"That's Cognis?"

Thurn shook his big head. "Nah, that guy's name's Mereth. Cognis was the thing he was peddlin'."

"So, what is this Cognis thing, then?"

"Hard t' tell. From what ah gathered, though, it looks like it's some kinda chip. Ol' Mereth 'ere had 'er up fer auction on the station forums. 'Ere's the specs."

He enlarged another image filled with white text on a blue background. While extensive and detailed, the graphic was hardly helpful.

"That means nothing to me."

"Didn' think it would. Ah just like t' remind ya who the brains o' this operation is e'ry once-in-awhile."

"Your wisdom is unparalleled and humbling in scope. Now please, grace this poor imbecile with the knowledge which escapes his grasp."

"Huh?"

"Tell me what the fragging specs mean!"

Thurn gestured up at some of the numbers. "Lemme put it this way: with processin' speeds like that, and memory t' match, ya could run three ships the size o' the *Basilisk* on that chip an' still have bandwidth t' stream yer favorite tunes through the nearest jump gate."

That was a lot of processing power. No wonder Shift had been risking life-and-limb to try and find that thing. "If Mereth had the chip for open auction, why didn't Shift just try to buy it from him?"

"He did. Fragger got out-bid by some other schmuck; some spacer goin' by the name 'Ratemacher.' Never 'eard o' that guy neither."

Interesting. Since he'd been unable to buy the chip himself, Shift must have been looking for Mereth to try to steal it instead. "You said Shift had found him. Does that mean we have a location?"

"Ya gonna go pay 'em a visit?"

"I was considering it."

"Well, don' go expectin' to find this Cognis thing. Latest posts on that same forum says he's already done sold it."

"To this Ratemacher, I assume?"

"That'd be ma bet."

It was still worth paying the Hissak a visit. Maybe Kadath could uncover some more details that Ora might be willing to pay for. "Send the location to my mobile. I'll check it out tomorrow." He started to turn to leave but hesitated. "Thurn, what do you think this Ratemacher is planning to do with the Cognis chip?"

The cyborg shrugged. "Ah dunno, but ah hope this fella knows just how much power he's fraggin' with."

Sahar hardly spoke to Dan the entire way back to the ship. The concourse was an eerie reflection of their strained silence as it neared midnight station time. Most of those who would be up-and-about at this hour would still be in the station's restaurants, clubs, and brothels, where their nights would just be getting started.

"Can we just let this go?" Dan pleaded. "I'm sorry. I should have listened to you. I had no idea what I was walking into, and I owe you for saving me."

Sahar rolled her eyes. "Shut up, Dan. One—you don't owe me. I saved you because we're friends. Two—you're still going to show me what in the nine hells you've been working on. We do some shady shit in our line of work, but I'd have never thought you'd be doing the same in your free time."

"It was an honest mistake!"

"Even so, I need to know what I just walked into. I thought you were picking up a part you needed to upgrade the ship's OS. I can't deal with you lying to me like that."

"I wasn't lying!" The kid looked so sincere in his protest.

"Bullshit. You're a smart guy—smarter than most. There's no way you'd accidentally source those parts off the darknet."

Now he was hesitant. "I didn't think it was a problem. I've bought plenty of materials off that forum before."

Sahar huffed. "Let's say I believe you. If you're upgrading the LX-Alpha, then fine—show me why I gutted all those guys back in that alley. Show me what all that blood just bought."

Dan's expression darkened. "Please… I'm so tired."

"Get over it. Let's go."

The odd-looking duo made their way to the ship's bridge. Dan, for some reason, chose not to turn the lights on as he made his way through the ship, relying instead on the safety lighting that lined the bottom corners of the walkways.

Why did Sahar have the strange feeling she was breaking into her own ship? It might have had something to do with the sour mood Dan exuded with every petulant step. She felt like she'd been a little hard on the kid, but she didn't see any other way to deal with this.

If he was sourcing parts from thugs on R-1, there was something seriously wrong with whatever he was working on. She owed it to the crew to look into this. The group's safety came first, right?

On the bridge, Dan woke up his terminal. The light from the holodisplay seemed overly bright, and Sahar squinted when it popped into place. With his pouting scowl still in place, the boy entered a few commands and the door to their immediate left slid open.

"Here we are," he sighed. "The ship's mainframe."

So far it was looking like the kid had been telling the truth about the part being for the OS. Then again, the chamber was the perfect place to hide any other side project he might be working on. None of the rest of the crew ever went into the mainframe as part of their normal duties.

The room was comparatively small. There was no furniture, just steel panels and glass cases. All the control terminals and interface ports were hidden away in those cases to save space. No trappings of luxury or comfort to be had here—only pure utilitarianism.

Dan walked to the far end of the room and flipped a couple of locks and switches on the terminal nested in the wall. He entered his credentials as if logging into the mainframe.

A drawer underneath the terminal slid forward. Dan reached behind the lip of the compartment and pulled the drawer out to its full length. It was a mechanical storage chest that extended out to fill almost half the room.

Dan cocked his head to the side. "I..." he shook his head. "Are you sure we can't let this go?"

Oh, hells no...

"Show me what's in the case, Dan."

With a sigh, he beckoned Sahar to come closer. "This is it," he whispered with resignation.

Sahar leaned over the edge and peered inside.

The entire storage drawer had been carved out and replaced with some kind of coolant and suspension system. The Maur could feel a chill emanating from the unit, but that wasn't what made her fur stand on edge. There was something in the chest that contrasted with the cold, electronic feel of the room.

At first, Sahar thought it was just a hunk of meat. Swirling lines of blue-gray tissue formed a roughly oblong structure divided into two hemispheres. Slivers of metal circuitry flashed between the folds of organic matter. Lights twinkled in the darkness of the chamber as thousands of tiny electrical impulses surged within the soft contours of the construct.

Sahar slowly realized what she was looking at. It was a brain—a wholly artificial brain that was a merger of organic tissue with cutting-edge electronics. It was both highly dangerous and highly illegal under Dorian law.

"Oh, Dan…" she groaned. "What have you done?"

CHAPTER 14

[ACCESSING COGNIS.DATAFILES...]

STYM — *CULTURAL INVENTORY* — STREET NAME FOR THE DRUG AMPHETACYRINE. THE STIMULANT IS POPULAR AMONG ATHLETES AND MILITARY PERSONNEL DUE TO ITS ENHANCING EFFECTS ON COORDINATION, ALERTNESS, AND PERCEPTION. WHILE IT LACKS SOME OF THE MANIA-INDUCING EFFECTS OF OTHER STRONG STIMULANTS, IT CARRIES A HIGH RISK FOR PHYSICAL DEPENDENCY. MANY USERS REPORT A NECESSITY FOR CHRONIC INGESTION DUE TO THE UNPLEASANT EFFECTS OF WITHDRAWAL.

[CLOSING DATAFILE...]

Markus sat at the bar in his favorite dive on this ring. Jilly's Gambit was tucked far enough into the shady side of the district that it lacked the crowds that plagued Annex and the other establishments on the main thoroughfare. It was far from empty, but the people here tended to keep to themselves.

Rob, the bartender and proprietor of this little hovel, poured Markus another ale. This was number three, so the booze-slinger didn't even need to ask if Markus had wanted it. The next one was questionable, but the third one was always a sure thing.

Normally Markus would hate that his patterns were so clear. Being predictable was not an asset in his line of work. However, this little dive gave Markus the kind of seclusion that allowed for such indulgences. Even Markus's crew would have had a tough time finding this place.

Which was why he nearly jumped out of his skin when a white-gloved hand came to rest on his shoulder. "Is this seat taken?"

"Ora?" Markus swallowed hard, regaining his composure. "Um, no. It's open."

She tucked a silver strand of hair behind one ear. "Then do you mind if I join you?"

Truthfully, Markus would have leaped at any excuse he could think of to avoid this little encounter. Ora was a sharp contrast to the Gambit's normal patrons and was turning some heads.

But Ora was still a client. That meant Markus had some degree of obligation. "Sure," he replied with a politician's smile he hoped would add some authenticity to the word.

At his bidding, she slid onto the seat next to him at the bar. Rob eyed her warily, but the grizzled man wasn't going to turn away a paying customer. She flashed him a pretty grin. "I don't imagine you have any wine?"

Rob shook his head. "Just beer and liquor."

"Ambrosia then, please."

With a grunt, Rob produced a tumbler and began filling it with golden liquid from a black bottle. "His tab?" he asked, pushing the drink to her.

Ora slid him a slender black kret chip. "I'll be paying tonight—for both of us."

The barkeep flashed Markus a knowing grin as he seized and scanned the chip. When his MoDAC beeped approvingly, he made himself scarce.

Markus raised his glass to Ora. "Thank you. That was unexpected."

"Don't mention it," she replied, sipping at her glass. Judging by the grimace on her face, the ambrosia not must have been satisfying. "You know, you could drink for free any time at one of my establishments. I guarantee the selection is better."

"Annex really isn't my scene."

"Understandable, but there are plenty of other choices—some just a short walk from here."

He shrugged in response. "Your bars tend to be well-trafficked. I was looking for something a bit quieter."

Her lips twitched in a half-smile. "I suppose this location does have a certain... *ambiance*."

Markus took a pull at his glass. "Not to sound unappreciative, but what brings you out this way? Aren't you usually still at Annex this time of night?"

"It was slow. Tashania is capable of handling the usual business. Besides, I've often wondered how you spend your nights on the station."

"Which begs my next question: how did you find me?"

"I have my ways," she replied coyly. "Finding you was easy. My only concern was that you might already have some company."

Markus arched an eyebrow. "Company?"

"You know what I mean. Didn't you use to spend your time on the station with that pretty blonde girl?"

"Skye?"

"If that's her name."

That was not a subject Markus wanted to broach. "She's got other plans this evening."

"Lucky me," Ora purred. She leaned forward slightly, arranging herself in a way that forced Markus to be very deliberate about where his eyes focused. "I've been hoping for a chance to get to know you a little better."

"Yeah? Does it help to keep tabs like that on your contractors?"

"It does, but that's not what I meant. I suspect there's more to you than your ability to deliver on a contract. I thought I'd take a couple of minutes to dig into whatever it is you keep masked behind all that professionalism."

He shifted uncomfortably on his bar stool. "I'm not sure what you're getting at."

"Come on, Markus. It's not a job interview. Just let me bother you for a couple of minutes. You interest me."

His fingers twitched nervously, reminding him that it had been a while since his last stym fix. He pulled out his cassette and freed a dose, casually slipping it along his lip-line.

Ora cocked her head to the side. "Doesn't taking stym kind of eliminate the point of drinking?"

"I find they pair nicely. This way I don't worry about getting off my game." He extended the cassette her way. "Do you want one?"

"No thanks. I tend to avoid drug use when I can."

"But you sell it…"

"It's not a moral judgment, Markus. I've done just about anything that you can find on this station, and I've decided to stay away from anything stronger than alcohol."

"I suppose that's fair," he conceded, slipping the dispenser back into his jacket. "So, you now have my full attention. What do you want to know?"

"Well, we've covered the girlfriend," she noted, swirling her glass. "Any other family in the system?"

"No," Markus sighed, not bothering to correct her misconception related to Skye. "Haven't had any family for a while."

"An orphan then?"

"For as long as I can remember."

"Then where is home?"

"Anywhere I can see the stars."

"Pretty odd that you'd spend so much time on this station, then. No stars in the steely skies of R-3."

"Yeah, well, my crew likes it here."

"But you don't?"

"It's as good as any place, I guess. The fact that you've been good about throwing us steady work has made it easier to keep coming back."

"I suppose it does." Ora threw back her head, draining the rest of her glass. "Gods, that was terrible."

"Yeah—I recommend sticking to ale here. Then again, the whiskey isn't that bad."

"Good idea." She waved at Rob to flag him down. "Do you want one?"

"Sure. You're buying, after all."

"Indeed I am." She took a sip at the glass the barkeep set in front of her. "Much better. Please, keep them coming."

"Yes ma'am," Rob growled before disappearing again.

Markus sipped at his own glass. "Never figured you for a whiskey girl."

"I'm not, but I'd sooner drink whiskey than poor attempts at anything more refined. Now, I've seen how you schmooze your way around client circles. I expect some good conversation to go with that drink. My questions aren't getting us anywhere. How about you tell me your story the way you want it to be told?"

She had made an uncomfortable point. Just because Markus had considered himself off-the-clock, that didn't mean Ora was going to forgive him for being cold. A bad mood was no reason to ruin his relationship with his best client.

So, he told her his story. Some of it, anyway. He talked about working on a farm in the Terran colonies until he was seventeen. When he'd turned down the indenturement, the owners had kicked him out as required by their corporate compact.

That was when he'd decided to join the Colonial Militia and, eventually, become an NTA sniper. He ran with a spec-ops crew until the Militia had broken ranks and the Colony Wars broke out. At that point, he'd sought out his old unit to join in the Resistance.

As the whiskey kept coming, he found it easier and easier to share his war stories. Ora, for her part, seemed entertained—asking pointed questions on various aspects of his stories.

When he'd finished talking about their final evac from Dracari, his stories began to dry up. That wasn't to say there weren't any more good stories. He just wasn't in the mood to talk about those next few years.

Memories of your ex would do that, he supposed.

If Ora noticed his sudden dearth of enthusiasm, she didn't mention it. She swirled the last traces of golden liquid in her tumbler. "What's your end-game, Markus? What makes you wake up every day and do whatever it is that you do?"

"How do you know I have an endgame?"

"I don't, but the calculated types usually do."

Markus eyed her warily. "Are you saying I'm calculating?"

"I'm not sure," she admitted sipping at the whiskey in her glass. "I'm trying to get a read on you. Are you simply a vagabond relying on the Devil's Luck, or do you take the time to calculate fuel cost before jaunting between stars?"

Markus chuckled wryly. "I think the answer's somewhere in between. I'm just going from alpha to bravo. I'll take the time to plot my next move when I get there."

Something strange flashed in those amethyst eyes. Skepticism, maybe? "So tell me: how do you relax?"

"Like this, obviously. The same way as most other people."

"No, I mean how do you relax without being two moves ahead? What you do—what *we* do—leaves lives hanging in the balance. How do you weigh and measure the cost of those lives before making your decision?"

Markus felt like Ora might be giving him too much credit but didn't want to say as much. "I'm not sure I follow."

Ora threw back what was left in her glass and held up her hand when Rob came to replace it. She turned back to Markus. "Let's try this scenario: say you are standing on a platform above a moving train. Up ahead, you see the tracks are out. If you don't do something, everyone on the train dies. They're in luck, though, because you can press a button and switch the train onto a different track. However, you see a pair of children playing on the second track."

"Who's driving this train? Just tell them to throw on the brakes."

"Brakes are out. You can't stop the train. It's either keep the train on its current course and let everyone die or intervene, even though the train will likely kill those two kids. What do you do?"

Markus had to think about it for only a second. "I press the switch."

"Why is that?"

"It's a math problem. Now, you didn't tell me how many people are on the train, but I'm assuming it's more than two. You do what you can to save the most people."

Ora nodded. "I see... Now, what if a large man was standing in front of you on the platform whom you could throw on the track to stop the train?"

Markus rolled his eyes. "That scenario doesn't make any sense."

"Humor me. Suspend your disbelief and answer the question."

"Fine—I push the guy onto the track."

"Care to explain your rationale?"

"Already did. It's a math problem, plain and simple. You kill one guy, save a train, and the two kids. What's difficult about this?"

A sardonic chuckle slipped from Ora's smirk. "I thought as much. You see, most people have trouble with the math there because it feels personal. It's one thing to flip a switch and watch people die—even children. If you have to physically push someone though, lay hands on them as you take their life, that's where most people get uncomfortable."

That kind of made sense, though Markus felt that spoke more to a person's naivete than anything about their character. It had been a long time since he'd had anything close to resembling innocence.

"Fragger was probably going to have a heart attack anyway. Who's so fat that they can stop a train with their ass?"

Now Ora's laughter was sincere. Markus laughed, too. Gods help him, but he was enjoying this conversation.

"What about you?" he asked.

"Hmm? What about me?"

"Same scenario—do you push the guy onto the track?"

Ora's eyes sparkled mischievously. "Who's the man?"

"Does it matter?"

"Of course it matters… as does who's on that train." She stood up from the bar and tightened her coat around her. "This was fun. I'm glad I decided to come and find you."

"Decided to stalk me, you mean?"

"You're welcome to think of it that way if that's what turns you on." Another smirk, filled with heat and suggestion that only Ora could muster. Between that look and the booze, Markus was finding it very hard to think clearly.

"Maybe you could stalk me again next time I'm on station?" The question was out of his mouth before he thought better of it. Damn, he *was* drunk. Did he just make a pass at the Queen of Sigma-4?

"Maybe. We'll see what happens." She turned from him, flashing those violet eyes over the shoulder of her white coat. There was something in that gaze that tugged at Markus. Was this another of Ora's tricks, or something else?

The spell was broken at the sound of Rob snapping his fingers. "Hey, prince charmin'. Ya havin' another, or…"

Markus turned to glare at the barkeep. "And you were doing so well at keeping a low profile."

Rob shrugged. "What can Ah say? Gotta eavesdrop a little if Ah'm gonna keep yer glasses full. Another?"

"No, I'm good thanks," with a sigh, Markus loaded a few krets on a spare chip and tossed the tip on the counter.

As the barkeep slid the chip into his pocket, he added, "Ah'd be careful with that one, Markus."

Markus couldn't hide the skepticism in his expression. "Hells, Rob, I don't think you've ever actually offered me any advice before. Isn't that half of what I pay you for, sitting behind the bar like that?"

Rob grunted. "Ah'm a make an exception in this case: Be careful. Ah don't need t' tell ya what kinda trouble sticks t' people like her."

"I'm a big boy, Rob. But thanks."

As Markus started to walk away, Rob reached out and seized the arm of his jacket. "Lemme put it a way ya might understand. That woman moves like a hurricane, and there's no tellin' who she's gonna sweep up along her way." His expression darkened. "Believe me, when ah say, if *that* train starts goin' off the tracks, ain't nobody this side of the Nethra—fat-ass or otherwise—that'll be able to save your sorry hide."

Chapter 15

[ACCESSING COGNIS.DATAFILES…]

DORIAN GATE COMMISSION (DGC) — *FACTION PROFILE* — THE ARM OF THE DORIAN GOVERNMENT RESPONSIBLE FOR THE SECURITY AND OPERATION OF THE JUMP GATE NETWORK. DGC OUTPOSTS EXIST IN EVERY INHABITED SYSTEM. THEIR AUTHORITY TO ENFORCE THE LAWS OF THE HIGH COUNCIL IS ABSOLUTE AND LARGELY UNQUESTIONED. THE STRENGTH OF THE DGC LIES NOT JUST IN THEIR MILITARY MIGHT BUT IN THEIR AUTHORITY OVER ALL MATTERS RELATED TO INTERGALACTIC COMMERCE.

[CLOSING DATAFILE…]

It was quiet in the Delta-2 concourse that night. Even if it hadn't been, Treska was well hidden—if slightly uncomfortable—in her black stealth suit. The fabric clung too tightly to her muscular frame, and she found the facial hood to be hot and stifling.

Aria served as quite the contrast. Her blouse was a soft pink and her vibrant red shorts looked like they had been painted right on her ass. The outfit showed off a great deal of pale skin—not that that this was any different from most of the female's wardrobe.

Her arm was thrown over the shoulder of a Terran male. He was handsome in that rugged way, with sandy brown hair and a day's worth of stubble on his chin. The pair laughed and stumbled drunkenly through the hanger to the male's ship.

It was obvious Treska's partner was having way too much fun with this little endeavor.

The Maur kept to the shadows, creeping around cargo containers and weaving her way through the parked machinery. Eventually, Aria and her conquest veered toward one of the docked ships.

The vessel was a lucky find: medium build and sleek-looking in design. It wasn't quite big enough to dock a shuttle or personal transport vehicle, but it was far more spacious than the two-man flier they'd been stuck with recently. They couldn't have asked for a better fit, especially since they were doing their shopping based on how much Aria could get carousing crew members to boast over drinks.

Aria ran her lips hungrily over the male's neck as he tried to muster up the sobriety to key in his access code to lower the ship's ramp. "Do you think your crew is around?" she asked as the hydraulics hissed.

"Probably," the male responded. "We're headin' out in the mornin', and they're not the type to waste krets on a hotel." The male didn't sound half as drunk as he had been acting. The sleaze was playing it up a bit in his quest to get Aria in the sack.

Aria muttered something, but between her play-acted slur and her mouth being pressed against the guy's skin, Treska couldn't make it out. It must have been a word of encouragement because the male kissed her hard on the mouth and practically carried her up the ramp.

Whatever promises Aria was making with her body had been enough to keep him from remembering to shut the door behind him. As the duo made their way out of the ship's hold, they must have run into the rest of the crew. Laughter and a few cajoling statements were exchanged between the male and his crew members.

Treska slipped up the ramp. The hold was, indeed, quite small and filled with several large, stacked cargo containers. Hiding between the towers of crates, she continued to listen.

She could make out two, maybe three distinct voices—all male. A couple of seconds later a fourth voice sounded, this one less amused and more feminine.

The last speaker poked her head into the hold. "Could you at least shut the gods-damn ramp behind you?" she called back. Aria's male shouted some reply, earning him a frustrated huff from his female companion as she stomped inside.

The female, like her counterpart, was Terran. Most of the crews operating out of this station were almost entirely Terran. Whether this was by design or by happenstance was impossible to tell, though Terran prejudice was practically infamous in Maur systems. By reputation, they were the most bigoted, of the sapient races aside from the Kintar.

It was a shame they were so xenophobic, at least in this crew's case. One of Treska's own kind might have stood a chance against her. Unfortunately for these people, Treska had never met a Terran she couldn't subdue.

The female entered a code into the access terminal to close the ramp. That's when Treska struck. The slight hiss of the hydraulics completely masked her approach.

A quick twisting of her hands and a sickening pop. The female's neck was broken before the ramp clicked shut.

Treska lowered the body soundlessly to the ground as she turned her attention to the chamber's single exit. It was still open. Through the hatch, she could hear two males making snide remarks about the kinds of females their crewmate liked to bring home. They were heading this way.

Without knowing the layout of the rest of the ship, Treska was at a disadvantage. Rather than move on the approaching pair, she decided to wait. With silent footfalls, she slipped back into the shadows.

"Daphne?" one of the males called. "Hey, Daph? You still in there?" The Terran ducked his head through the hatch. His eyes scanned the dark vainly for several seconds before he spotted where

Treska had laid the female's body. "Daphne? *Shit*. Ace, get over here! Daphne's hurt!"

The first Terran stumbled through the door, rushing to Daphne's position. As he knelt next to her, his companion stepped into the hold.

When he was clear of the hatch, Treska struck again. In one smooth motion, she stepped behind him and slit his throat. The male struggled briefly in her grasp, choking out a gurgled cry.

It was enough to raise the attention of the other male. He looked up from Daphne's corpse to see his friend struggling in Treska's grasp.

His hands went to his belt, seemingly reaching for a holstered weapon. Unfortunately for him, he must have neglected to carry it with him this evening. So much the pity. That might have made the fight more interesting.

His mouth opened to cry out again. Treska drew her pistol first. The weapon thrummed once, silencer muffling the blast.

Her target's head exploded as the disruptor's charge collided with his face. Gore splashed around him as his body collapsed on top of Daphne's.

What a mess, Treska grumbled silently to herself. Aria was almost certainly going to make her clean this up.

That was a problem for a later time. Aside from Aria's chosen prey, Treska figured at least one more crew member was wandering about the ship—potentially more.

She eased the hatch open and slipped inside, quickly surveying the landscape. The layout was much as one would expect on a transport this size. The ship split into a bi-level in front of her. One set of stairs went up to where Treska would likely find the bridge, mess, and crew quarters. The bottom level would probably provide access to some of the less glamorous components of the vessel.

Shutting the door behind her, Treska left the lock on the hatch at a three-quarter turn. That would be her signal to let her know if anyone passed this way. Marker now in place, she crept down to the lower level.

A quick sweep of the deck found it mostly abandoned. The one exception was another Terran female working over a control panel in engineering. A dagger to the base of the female's skull dispatched her effortlessly and without a sound.

On her way to the upper level, Treska found the lock she'd set to be in the exact same position she'd left it. Confident that no one would be sneaking up behind her, she closed the hatch the rest of the way before slipping onto the upper deck.

That was when she got sloppy.

As she rounded the bend, she nearly collided with a large, ebony Terran male. There was an awkward second as the two of them stared each other down. "Maybe you can help me," Treska teased. "I seem to be lost."

The male sprang into action. He roared a warning cry for any of the crew left to hear it as he stepped back to open up space between them. His hands went to his belt.

Treska's disruptor was in her hands. She pulled the trigger, sending a bolt straight at his chest.

Unfortunately for her, this crew member was wearing his gear. His hands had gone not for a weapon, but for his shields. The defenses engaged just in time and a flash of green nullified the blast from Treska's weapon.

She dropped the disruptor as the male reached for his own pistol. A crescent throwing blade flashed from her hands and knocked the weapon aside before he could fire. She bore down on him at a full sprint. The two collided and began to grapple in the confined space of the hallway.

The male was quite large for a Terran, but she was Maur. He tried to turn her aside and use her weight against her. Treska brought her forearm down on his elbow. The limb let out a sickening pop. The male roared in pain and Treska drove an elbow into his face. He slumped, bleeding and unconscious.

In the end, it hadn't been much of a fight after all. Plus, it looked like she'd taken this one alive. How unexpected.

Despite the struggle having lasted for almost a full minute, no one had come to the male's aid. Did that mean he was truly the last one? Treska would finish her sweep to be sure, but a crew of six did seem about right for this size vessel.

Using a cord from her utility belt, Treska bound the unconscious male to a nearby energy conduit. She tore a piece of cloth from his shirt and gagged him with it. If she was right, there would be no one for the male to call out to, but she wasn't going to get caught being reckless twice.

Captive secure, she proceeded to check each of the doors in the hallway. The rooms were sparse and shared common showers and facilities with neighboring units. It was far from the tightest accommodations the Maur had seen on a ship like this, but privacy must have still been hard to come by.

Inside the fourth room she checked, she found Aria. The female was pulling her tight shorts back on, and her top was still on the floor. The sandy-haired male she'd stumbled in with lay naked on his cot, blood pooling from a fatal neck wound.

The Maur's eyes went back to Aria. "Did you really…"

"Ah-uh," she cautioned, wagging her finger at the Maur. "No judgment from you. I know the kind of sick shit you're into."

"Please tell me he was still breathing."

"Of course! What do you think I am, a monster?" she found her discarded top and pulled it on. "How did it go with the rest of the crew?"

Treska scowled, even though she knew the expression would be hidden by the black mask of the stealth suit. "Almost done. Just need to sweep the rest of this floor."

"Well then, quick ogling me and hop to it!"

You're not my type. She kept that comment to herself. Best not to encourage Aria any further.

The rest of the ship was empty. When Treska returned, Aria had already stumbled onto the male she'd taken hostage. "Why isn't this one dead?" she asked.

Treska shrugged. "It was an accident. We fought and I knocked him unconscious. Figured he might be useful."

"Why? We have the bodies of the rest of the crew to get by the biometric scans. Before you ask: yes, I've already transferred command authority to my prints. I had to do it before his body cooled."

It wasn't the question Treska was going to ask, but she rolled with it. "What now?"

"Now, we celebrate being the proud owners of this starship! I, for one, am going to take a shower. You could probably use one yourself if you don't mind me saying so."

"I meant after we settle in."

Aria's wicked smile slid into place. "Then we are off to Khonshu! We have a conduit to purchase."

CHAPTER 16

KHONSHU — *MOON (TERRAN SPACE)* — LARGEST OF THE TWIN MOONS OF GEB IN THE RAVIAN SYSTEM. WHEREAS THE SMALLER OF THE TWINS, ISIS, IS USED LARGELY FOR MINING AND AFFILIATED CORPORATE OPERATIONS, KHONSHU BOASTS A THRIVING TOURIST ECONOMY. A STRONG ELEMENT OF ENTREPRENEURSHIP HAS TAKEN HOLD ON THE POPULOUS MOON FOLLOWING THE COLLAPSE OF HOUSE BARKAY AND THE BREAKUP OF ITS CORPORATE INTERESTS IN THIS TERRITORY.

[CLOSING DATAFILE...]

The crew had already convened in the *Vandal's* primary conference room—or, as they affectionately called it, the war room—when Markus arrived. Immediately they launched into the routine updates they went over whenever they were at port. From a technical perspective, everything seemed to be going fine.

What bothered Markus was the unexpected lull in crew morale. Aaliyah had seemed more antisocial than normal, and Markus imagined that she was getting grief from Nikki about having to go out again so soon. Dan was a little off his game, and it looked like he hadn't slept a wink. Sahar looked equally tired, which made Markus wonder if the two had been out later than usual.

Skye seemed to be avoiding him, which was pretty much the status quo these days. He'd hoped the shit between the two of them would get less awkward as time went on, but these past few weeks hadn't shown any sign of that. At least Eli seemed to be in good spirits.

Looking at the dark countenances of each member of his crew, Markus started to say something to clear the air. When he came up short of reassuring platitudes, he thought better of it. Instead, he launched right into the briefing he'd prepared.

"So, the reason we're all here—as you've been told—is that we have another assignment. I know this is a quick turnaround from the last job, and that's becoming the norm lately. However, this one happens to be right in our backyard."

He fired up the holotable at the room's center which produced a three-dimensional representation of the Ravian System. Markus gestured with one hand, zooming them in on Geb, the principal planet. An indicator showing the current position of Sigma-4 showed in green, while another popped up on the larger of the planet's two moons.

With another gesture, he brought that moon into focus. When Khonshu filled the display, he zoomed in again to show a cityscape with a single prominent structure jutting up from the urban sprawl.

"This is the Star Spire," he announced. It was easy to see how the installation had earned its name. The tower was so massive that it could reportedly be viewed from orbit. Its occupancy at any given time was estimated to rival that of Sigma-4's mid-tier.

"The Spire is an interesting little installation. Its most widely known functions are largely commercial: large shopping centers, luxury hotels, and gaming resorts. However, it also doubles as a security hub for the DGC and an orbital monitoring station for what's left of the Neo-Terra Alliance."

Next, he tapped the holotable to bring up a pair of additional files. These were the same ones Ora had shown them in the neurosim: a rendering of the Starfire Conduit, and the picture of the poor bastard they'd be stealing it from.

"This is Braccus Kai. A full dossier will be sent to your personal terminals if you are interested in reading up on him. What you need to know is that he's a pro. Everything from guns and drugs to illegal tech—this guy knows how to move it."

Sahar let out an appreciative growl. "Really makes us look small-time. So, are we working with him or against him?"

"Against," Markus said with finality. "Which brings us to our next point of discussion. The piece of tech you see here is called the Starfire Conduit. Ora gave me a brief rundown on what it does but was a little light on the details. Dan, I'll be sending the specs your way for a more detailed analysis. Think you can break it down for me?"

The teen ran a hand through his messy hair. "I'll see what I can do."

Not the confidence Markus was hoping for. What was wrong with everyone today? "All right then—so here's the catch. As dangerous as Kai is, he's not the one I'm concerned about. I'm more worried about who's set to purchase the conduit."

In dramatic fashion, he brought up two more images on the screen. The first was a Maur woman, with similar coloring and build to Sahar. The most noticeable difference was that she had the top of one ear missing and a jagged scar that ran across her left eye. If he hadn't known better, Markus would have sworn they were sisters.

The second was a Terran woman with a slender build and an angular, but still pretty, face. Her raven black hair provided a stark contrast to her fair skin. It wasn't as intense as the contrast seen in the Sahaia, but it was about as close as a Terran could get without genetic editing.

"Meet Aria Hendrix and Treska Nos Salva—the operatives that will be seeking to pick up the package we're planning on stealing. Both women work for the Ghenza Collective."

Curses and worried glances were exchanged among everyone in the room. Before the crew could issue a collective "what-the-frag?" Markus continued.

"The take for this job," he announced, "is thirty million krets."

That got everyone's attention. When the murmurs stopped, Markus put the finishing touches on his monologue.

"Because the complex is so well protected, and so high profile, a direct assault like we did on Sif is out. Fortunately, the intel provided by the Wings includes the time of the exchange and a rough idea of where it should occur. Since the exact location is still unknown, we're going to have to do a little leg work for ourselves.

"The plan is for two of us to go to the meet with Braccus in place of the agents being sent by the Ghenza. From there, it's simple: our agents go through the transaction as planned. With any luck, we'll be in and out of there before the real assassins have any idea what happened."

Aaliyah shook her head. "And what exactly are the *real* Ghenza gonna be doin' while we nab their tech?"

"That's where it gets tricky," Markus conceded. "I had a couple of thoughts on this one. Anything I've come up with, though, depends on Dan to do a little hacking for us. Dan, do you think you could access the Spire's network through the general docking connection?"

Dan drummed his fingers nervously on the table. "Um… maybe. What would we be trying to do? Specifically, I mean."

"I want to fake a pair of messages to the parties involved. The one to Kai will request that the meet be moved up by three hours. The one to the Ghenza will delay the meeting by the same amount. That should give us plenty of time to get in and out of the Spire before either party figures out what's happened."

The boy's eyes went unfocused, as they often did when he was lost in thought. "That should work. I'll need some time to get into the system though."

"How much time?"

"A day, maybe?"

A tight squeeze. "If that's the case, then we're going to need to get out of here first thing in the morning. Even then, I'm not sure we can give you more than twelve hours."

Skye piped up. "Maybe we should try and launch sooner?"

"That's going to be hard for some of us," Aaliyah grumbled.

"It's going to take that long just to do our resupply," Markus noted with finality. "Especially since we're going to need Ora to ship us in the tech to fake the credentials and appearances for the Ghenza."

"I take it that I'll be playing Treska?" Sahar asked unenthusiastically.

"You were my first choice." Not that they had any other Maur women they could call on to fill the role.

"Please tell me that our approximate heights and weights match up. I know we all look the same to you Terrans, but these differences could matter if we have to go through a security scanner."

"You're about a centimeter taller," Markus assured her. "Other than that, as luck would have it, your builds are nearly identical. The facial cosmetic changes will be the worst of it."

"Will Z be taking care of those?"

"That's one way we could handle it."

"And what about reversing the damage to my face when this is all over?"

"That'll come out of the operations cut, as always. It won't affect your take." That seemed to satisfy her. Markus found it strange that Sahar would be worried about her looks, but he wasn't going to push the issue.

"Then who's gonna play Aria?" Aaliyah asked nervously.

Markus looked back and forth between the two other women. "I was thinking it would probably be Skye unless you're feeling eager."

"Nah, I'm good." The relief on her face was obvious.

Skye chimed in. "So, what kind of cosmetic changes am I looking at?"

Those were a bit more intense. Markus went over the list: hair coloring, a digital mask to account for the facial differences, and boots that would have to account for the ten-centimeter height difference. She would also need contacts as Aria's eyes were green, not blue like Skye's.

"Plus anything else you think you might need," he concluded. "That goes for either of you. Our intelligence doesn't say whether Kai has ever met these two in person, but we need to go for as close of a match as possible."

"And what will the rest of us be doin' while Sahar and Skye are makin' their actin' debut?" Aaliyah asked.

"We'll have to figure that out in transit. I imagine we'll need at least one team member on the ground providing support. That said, I haven't reviewed enough of the data to figure out what that looks like yet."

"Why don't we just take out the Ghenza?" she suggested. "It seems a lot less complicated than tryin' to frag up everybody's calendars."

"That might be tricky," Eli noted. "The Ghenza are all extraordinarily capable combatants. The act of eliminating them, while arguably a service to the system, would require a lot of planning, and would probably still end up making a scene."

Markus picked up on the Sahaia's thought. "We also want to avoid ending up on the Collective's shit-list. If they find out we're involved, there's a good chance there will be repercussions. However, if we pull this off, they'll likely just blame Kai for his incompetence."

"Still seems like a lot of work," Aaliyah grumbled. "And a really fraggin' tight turn-around."

"I understand," Markus sighed. He fought to steady his hand as the effects of his morning stym fix began wearing off. "I'm open to better ideas if anyone has any."

To Markus's slight disappointment, there were none.

CHAPTER 17

[ACCESSING COGNIS.DATAFILES...]

CHURCH OF NETHRA — *FACTION PROFILE* — BASED OUT OF TEMPOLOSE NETHERA, THE CHURCH OF NETHRA IS THE SINGULAR RELIGIOUS AUTHORITY ENDORSED BY THE DORIAN HIGH COUNCIL. THE RELIGIOUS CANON OF THE CHURCH IS AN AMALGAMATION OF THE PREDOMINANT RELIGIONS IN EXISTENCE AMONG THE SAPIENT RACES AT THE TIME OF THEIR ASSIMILATION INTO INTERGALACTIC SOCIETY. DESPITE THE UNIVERSAL PROLIFERATION OF CHURCH OUTPOSTS AND GENERAL ACCEPTANCE OF THEIR CANNON, ONLY THIRTY-SIX PERCENT OF SAPIENS IDENTIFY AS BELIEVERS IN THE CHURCH'S TEACHINGS.

[CLOSING DATAFILE...]

Sahar couldn't get out of the briefing fast enough. Thank the gods no one had questioned her attitude during the meeting. Or maybe they had written off her crankiness to her concerns around her impending facial disfiguration. That did irk her a bit. Not the surgery, though that would be a pain. Plus, there was the assumption that she could impersonate a Maur from a completely different clan. Talk about insensitive...

While both things were irritating, her current concerns felt much more existential. *Gods damn it Dan... what were you thinking?*

Organitech—he'd installed a fragging organitech processor on the ship. And it wasn't like he'd done it for some minor subsystem. That thing, that *abomination,* was running the entire vessel.

Breathe. You're working yourself into a rage again.

She'd barely been able to say a word to him last night. All evening she'd been tossing and turning, wondering what she was going to do. She'd had half a mind to pull Markus aside before the briefing. However, with this new mission—and the tight turn-around to pull it off—bringing up the complication of the illegal and immoral technology she'd discovered seemed like an unnecessary complication.

She needed to think about this some more. She needed to pray.

Yes, that was what she needed. She needed to pray—maybe even make an offering. Maybe then the gods would grace her with the wisdom she needed.

Seizing her black duffel from her quarters, she made an about-face and busted it over to the temple. It was still early, so there wouldn't be any crowds. For some reason, the few worshipers on this ring liked to keep the same late hours as the rest of the populous.

Mercifully she was able to slip out of the ship and make her way through R-3 without running into any of her crewmates. She didn't want to have to explain anything. Right now, she was dangerously close to throwing the kid under the bus to resolve her conscience.

It wasn't just the violation of her moral code that made Sahar uncomfortable. Though the Church of Nethra had ratified the prohibition on synths centuries ago, this was not just a matter of some serious sin. As much as she hated to admit it, Sahar was used to reconciling her largely amoral existence with the threads of faith she still clung to.

No, the biggest problem was the legal one. If the Dorians found what Dan was hiding on that ship, they would exterminate it—along with the entire crew. No trial, no due process. Just a quick and efficient execution.

Inexplicable yet welcomed relief came as soon as she laid eyes on the temple's simple archway. Slowly, reverently, she crossed the sacred threshold.

Sahar's attitude was hardly inspired by the building itself. Even with the infinite coffers at the church's disposal, Tempolose Nethera must have been reticent to invest too heavily in a temple tucked in the back alley of this insignificant station. Then again, Sahar had noticed some structural improvements as of late. Obviously, *someone* had seen fit to invest in the tiny structure.

Stone embellishments bordered the dark plaster walls. A handful of lonely glow-orbs provided scant luminescence for the dark hallways. Sahar's eyes had scarcely adjusted to the poor lighting when she emerged into the temple's common area.

A strange, almost grotesque-looking statute was placed in the center of the large room. The abstract structure was composed of swirls of stone embedded with pulsing, ephemeral lights. The bewildering construct was meant to honor the mysterious and unknowable aspects of the Nethra and those who dwelt within it.

To Sahar, it just looked like another half-finished piece of garbage passing as modern art.

That was fine, though, because this was not what she was seeking. The curious flourishes of the bizarre statue might produce contemplation in the hearts of the theologically curious. For those, like her, who were more established in the church's traditions, this was only the preamble.

She caught sight of a robed figure working its way through the handful of prostrated worshipers in the main hall. Sahar held up a hand to get the cleric's attention. The figure returned the gesture in acknowledgment and made its way toward her.

Sahar did not come to the temple nearly as often as she should have. Still, she typically recognized the clerics on duty during her infrequent visits. This priestess, however, was entirely new.

Dark hair, tumbling in curls across her shoulders worked an uneasy contrast against the verdant hue of her scaled skin. Reptilian eyes stared out solemnly from the shadow of the priestess's cowl, and a golden medallion hung between her small breasts.

Sahar had never seen a Hissak half-breed before. Though she rarely admired the beauty of other species, even she had to admit that the infusion of Terran stock into this female's bloodline had done much to enhance her looks. The result was a strange and alien beauty that seemed much at home in the hollowed trappings of the temple.

"Greetings," the priestess hissed. "How may I be of assistance?"

Sahar dipped her head in respectful acknowledgment. "I don't believe we've met, priestess. Are you new to this district?"

The female donned a ghostly smile as she reciprocated the bow. "Yes. I've only recently rotated into the system. Cassthia Marenassa at your service."

"Sahar Nos Drathen."

"A pleasure, Freya Sahar. How may I assist in your worship today?"

An important question. Which of the three did she honor today—Tyranus the White, Gavinus the Black, or Fyrinus the Red?

"I seek the favor of Tyranus if his altar remains vacant this day."

A solemn nod. "Yes, the White Lion's altar has been dry for several days now. Surely it is a good omen for you to end his fast."

The message was both an encouragement and a conviction. Though it was thought that the gods favored all sacrifices, it was generally believed that they favored those made on a dry altar two-fold.

However, the fact that Tyranus's altar had been dry for so long begged another question. Had Sahar's lack of faithfulness to sacrifice somehow played a role in her recent misfortune?

Stop it. That has nothing to do with this. Do not taint your sacrifice with such errant thoughts. "Your news brings my spirit hope. Lead on, priestess."

Cassthia led Sahar to a side passage and through a hallway with a great number of indistinguishable doors. Such portals likely hid away any number of things ranging from private offices and living quarters, to rooms meant for rituals both general and specific.

In another life, Sahar would have known each of those rituals in great detail. A part of her wished she regretted the choice to give all that up.

"Here we are," Cassthia said as she held open one of the doors. "There is a terminal to your right if you wish to make a financial offering. That same terminal will allow you to call one of the clerics to escort you out when you have finished your communion with Tyranus."

"Thank you, priestess."

As Sahar pressed into the room, the priestess's hand surged to her arm. The gesture was hardly imposing, given their size differences, but there was a firmness to the female's grip that belied her stature.

Her voice was strained as she spoke. "I… I'm sorry. The weight… of your sin. It has…" Cassthia's reptilian eyes seemed to glow as she hefted them to meet Sahar's. "I have a message for you if you would hear the word of one you do not serve."

One she did not serve?

Sahar's gaze dipped to the medallion at Cassthia's breast. The pendant bore a simple mark: a half-circle open at the bottom with twin slashes marring the ellipse. It was a mark that any child to ever set foot in a temple would have been taught to recognize. It was a symbol Sahar had been taught to fear.

"What message could the Stardust Grave have for one such as me?" It was the closest Sahar could come to accepting the message. As much as she desired to hear the words of the divine, any utterance from the darkest of gods was right to be met with trepidation.

The edge of Cassthia's medallion flashed, though Sahar was certain the light in the room had not changed. The half-breed's eyes gleamed in the dim light of the hall.

"Do not fear the knowledge which you have come to possess, for all is subject to the divine plan. This burden shall be lifted from you soon, and you have no need to raise your hand against it." The priestess blinked several times, and the light in her eyes seemed to dim. "That is all. Does this word from my Lord help you?"

Sahar eyed her warily. The message was too tailored and uncanny to be a mere coincidence. Had the priestess truly received a message from her god? And what interest did Thule have in her activities or in the thing that Daniel had built on the ship?

"Perhaps," she replied cautiously. "Is there anything else that your Lord wishes to impart?"

Cassthia shook her head. "No, that is all. Forgive me if I overstepped. The urge was just so…"

"There is nothing to forgive. Thank you, priestess. You have done much to lift the burden from my soul." Sahar wondered if Cassthia would pick up on the ritualistic nature of her response. It was very near to a direct quote from the Chronicles when Riven the Wise learned of his impending death from the Creator.

If the priestess had, she made no acknowledgment. She bowed respectfully before vanishing into the hallway, leaving Sahar alone in the ritual chamber.

This room, though as dark in some respects as the rest of the temple, was well lit around its central structure. Azure light cast a cerulean gleam on the alabaster statue in the center of the chamber. Though the altar of Tyranus was a simple structure, a white stone basin on a plain pillar crafted from the same material, the statute was a work of art.

Tyranus the White stood carved in incredible detail. Every muscle of his imposing figure rippled in the stone relief, as did the flowing mane framing the lion's visage. He was clad only in the royal bangle clamped tight about his forearm and held only the sword of his office. The tip of the blade was planted firmly in the stone at his feet, both his hands clasped rigidly on its hilt.

A version of this statute existed in every temple that honored the three pillars of Maur tradition from here to Dorr. Though they were canonically only three among the dozens of gods venerated by the Nethrian church, to the Maur, these three alone comprised the holy trinity of their race.

Sahar knelt before the altar and drew her resche. Cassthia's words echoed in her mind as she drew the blade across her palm. *This burden shall be lifted from you soon, and you have no need to raise your hand against it.*

In a twist of fate, a god that she would have never prayed to had supplied her with the very insight she had been seeking in coming here. If there was communion among the gods, surely Tyranus had interceded on her behalf to give her the peace that she desired.

As her blood dripped into the altar of the White Lion, Sahar began to whisper the first words of her prayer.

CHAPTER 18

[ACCESSING COGNIS.DATAFILES…]

SPINDEL'S DISEASE — *CULTURAL INVENTORY* — NAMED FOR DOCTOR GREGORY SPINDEL, SPINDEL'S DISEASE IS LARGELY CONSIDERED THE SINGLE GREATEST THREAT TO SAPIENT GENETIC ENGINEERING. THE DISEASE CHARACTERIZES A RARE BUT SERIOUS CASCADE OF GENETIC DESTABILIZATION THAT IS FATAL WITHOUT TREATMENT. INCIDENCE OF THE DISEASE INCREASES IN LATER GENERATIONS OF CLONED CELL LINES AND INDIVIDUALS SIRED THROUGH RECOMBINANT GENE TECHNOLOGY.

[CLOSING DATAFILE…]

Aaliyah winced in sync with Monica as she slid the needle into the back of her arm. Every time she did this, she wondered the same two things. First, would she ever get used to administering these injections? Secondly, why didn't she just let Nikki take care of these like she did while Aaliyah was away?

She hit on the same two answers: no, she wouldn't, and because she needed the reminder of why she had to leave. "There," she whispered as she pressed a bandage to Monica's arm. "All done."

"Thanks, Momma 'Liyah." The girl blinked sleepily as the drug started to take effect.

"No problem. Now, let's get ya into bed."

Aaliyah pulled the covers back just enough for Monica to slip under the sheets. The girl placed her head on one pillow and wrapped herself around a second. Aaliyah drew up the sheets and comforter. Jinx promptly hopped onto the bed to curl up at her feet.

A solemn smile tugged at Aaliyah's cheeks. Monica looked so damn cute tucked-in like this. She planted a quick kiss on her forehead. "Ya be good for Momma Nikki while I'm gone, ya hear?"

Monica's face contorted in a small frown. "When will you be comin' home?"

"I'm not sure, sweetie. Probably about a week."

Her daughter clung tighter to her pillow. "I miss you when you're gone."

"I miss ya too." Aaliyah gave her another quick kiss before the tears burning in her eyes found their way to her cheeks. "I'll hurry back. I promise."

"Love you…" Monica mumbled.

"I love ya too, Mona."

Aaliyah tried to be subtle as she wiped at her eyes on the way into the hall. The look on Nikki's face when she saw her gave a distinct impression that she wasn't quite successful.

That, apparently, wasn't enough to avoid the impending lecture. "It's hard on her, you know… you leaving all the time like this."

"Yeah, well, it's hard on me too."

"Then why do you keep doing this? Can't you ask to sit this one out? A little more time with you at home would be good for her."

"Ya know that's not how that works," Aaliyah growled. "I can't just decide to opt-out on the contracts that aren't convenient for me. They need an engineer on that ship to keep her space worthy. If I opt-out, they'll have to find a replacement."

This was an old fight—one they'd been having more and more lately. For some reason, though, Nikki was particularly adamant tonight. "Would that be so bad?"

"Yes, it would."

"Why? You could spend more time with Monica! You could spend more time with *me*!"

"*Stop it*!" Aaliyah hissed the words to avoid raising her voice. "Ya know why I do what I do. There ain't a better payin' job in this whole gods-damned system than runnin' the Nethra. And ya should definitely know why *that's* important for me."

Nikki set her jaw, crossing her arms over her chest. "I think you're being a little narrow-minded on this."

"Yeah? Then how do ya suggest we pay for her gods-damned medication? Do ya think ya can pick up enough shifts to cover another million krets every cycle? Do ya think there's a mechanic job on this station that pulls in that kind of cash?"

"Maybe not on this station, but it's *your* job that keeps us stuck on this scrap heap!"

So much for not raising her voice. "Bullshit! The fact that we can't *afford* any better is why we're stuck here. And we can't afford any better because *I'm* spending every spare kret I earn, putting *my* ass on the line trying to keep *our* baby girl alive!"

"Quiet," Nikki hissed. "You'll wake her."

Deep breaths. Keep your composure.

"Sorry," Aaliyah sighed.

Anger radiated from Nikki's eyes. "No, you're not. 'Liyah, you can blame this on the krets if you want, but we both know the truth. You can't keep still for long enough to give a normal life a shot. You run the Nethra because you *love* running the Nethra. I don't want to hear you blame it on Monica, and I *certainly* don't want to hear you blame it on me."

Aaliyah threw up her hands. "I can't deal with this. Not right now."

Fortunately, she didn't have to. One of the nice things about having a ship is there was always another place to lay her head. And, as luck would have it, Aaliyah always kept a bag ready to go at a moment's notice.

She stormed into their room, seized the duffel, and pressed for the door.

"Where are you going?" Nikki protested.

"I've got some prep to do." It was only a half-lie. There were things that she could do to fill her time, but the reality was that she wasn't going to stay here and fight with Nikki.

A part of her felt like she should say something else—like she shouldn't leave on this note. Unfortunately, that part of her was being thoroughly strangled by her rage.

Without another word, Aaliyah stormed out of the house and made straight for the *Vandal*.

She was still fuming hours later. Every time Aaliyah started to calm down, some other spark lit her rage again. The problem, she decided, was that ship maintenance wasn't going to be enough to get her mind off Nikki.

That was how she ended up working on her pet project. One could argue that messing with the explosive J-Krysts this late at night, when she was still fresh from a fight, wasn't the best idea. Then again, anger always seemed to help her focus.

A bead of sweat dripped down her back as she sat hunched over the magnifier. Aside from cutting the crystal, which had been executed flawlessly, this was the most dangerous part of the operation.

Dangerous in a different way, she supposed. If she screwed up here, the energy from the J-Kryst fragment would blow the circuits on the entire device and she'd have to start over. If she screwed up in the cutting process, the entire ship could detonate.

She shouldn't have been working on this so late, but it was the only thing she could think of to get Nikki off her mind. Besides, she had a feeling the team could make use of this new…

<Where are you?>

"Shit!" Aaliyah jumped at the sound of Eli's psychic interruption and the crystal fragment touched the side of the casing.

Indigo energy currents surged across the neighboring circuitry and sparks started flying.

The project was toast.

Biting back her renewed anger, Aaliyah focused on a response. <I *was* working on some equipment for this job, but ya managed to make me screw *that* up.>

It was several seconds before he responded.

<Apologies. Nikki sent me a text. She is worried about you.>

She let out a deep sigh. She wanted a pound of flesh for all the time she'd now lost on her project, but she wasn't going to get it from Eli. As much as he annoyed her sometimes, she reminded herself that she owed him. She owed him a debt that she could never repay.

<Yeah,> she replied. <That's a long story.>

<Want to talk about it? I'm over in engineering.>

She didn't, but she knew she probably should. Plus, Eli likely had something else he wanted to discuss if he was in engineering. <Be right there.>

It was a short stroll from her workshop to the ship's engineering terminal. When she walked in, Eli was standing over the console, studying what looked to be the ship's power and data feeds.

She didn't have to announce herself, and they didn't exchange pleasantries. Eli only bothered with that for other people's sake, and it wasn't Aaliyah's style anyway. When it was just the two of them, they got right down to business.

He brought up his concerns first. "Have you reviewed these feeds from the last mission?"

She peeked over his shoulder. "Yup, sure have. Impressive right?"

"The power fluctuations we were detecting last month have almost entirely disappeared." It would normally have been cause for celebration, but Eli looked distinctly uncomfortable.

"Yup. I wish I could take credit, but it's all Dan's work. Somehow he's managed to smooth out the way this hunk of junk runs just by integratin' the reactor to the main operatin' system."

Eli was shaking his head. "How did he manage that? We attempted to do the same thing when we first picked up the replacement reactor, and the LX-Alpha couldn't take the strain."

"Not sure," Aaliyah admitted. "He's been puttin' all his free time and a good chunk of his cuts into the upgrades on that thing. It should be gettin' even better soon. I think I heard that he and Sahar were pickin' up some new part yesterday."

"Did he say what it was?"

"Didn't get the details. Anyway, I don't follow the computer stuff. I just listen enough so he can tell me how to keep the engines runnin'."

Eli looked pensive but pleased. "Maybe I should see if he's working on it now. He seemed off today. Maybe he needs a hand."

"Let the kid be, Eli. He likes workin' alone. Besides, since when did ya take on the position of morale officer?"

For several seconds, Eli didn't reply. He just stared down at the terminal, apparently lost in thought.

Eli might have brought her over here on the pretense of wanting to hear about her troubles, but it was obvious that he was dealing with demons of his own. "Ya okay there, big guy? You seem even moodier than usual."

That made him look up. "It's Skye," he admitted.

Ah, yes... how could she forget?

Eli had confided in her about his clandestine affair with their fellow crew member. Aaliyah had advised against it from the start. Everyone knew that Markus was still in love with her, and to be honest, Aaliyah thought Skye was still in love with him, too. This cast Eli as the homewrecker and things rarely worked out for the guy playing that role.

"Her headaches are starting up again, and she seems a bit off. I'm not getting through to her."

He was dodging his real concern. For someone who had initiated this little exchange, he sure wasn't making it easy to talk to him.

"I take it she hasn't brought this up to Markus?"

"Of course not."

"And I imagine she's still draggin' her feet on tellin' him about the other thing too?"

Eli shook his head as he went back to the task of staring a hole into the display.

Aaliyah sighed. She wasn't good at this shit—as demonstrated by tonight's earlier events. Figuring he probably wasn't looking for an I-told-you-so, she asked, "So, what do ya figure you'll do about it?"

He took a deep breath before replying. "Nothing. I don't imagine there's anything I *can* do."

Except wallow in anxiety and self-loathing, apparently. Aaliyah shrugged. "I'm sorry, I'm not real good at that kinda thing. If I was, then maybe my house wouldn't be such a mess."

Eli seemed to pull out of his shell at the mention of problems other than his own. "Yes, about that—it's your last night on the station. I found it a bit curious that you would be here instead of at home, and beyond curious that Nikki would be asking me about it."

Aaliyah rolled her eyes. Normally she'd deflect, but she'd kind of asked for this. "Same old argument with her. I just didn't handle it that well tonight."

Eli sighed. "I don't think I need to tell you that it's not a good idea to end on a fight—especially before a job. You don't want that to be the last thing conversation you two had if something were to happen out there."

"Well, look at who's being morbid tonight!"

"I'm just being realistic."

Yeah, he was. Aaliyah knew it too. She was just being stubborn. "I know. I'll head back there and apologize. Worst case scenario is that I get a bit of exercise and she kicks me right back on the street.”

“I think we both know that’s not going to happen.”

“Gotta have a plan, right?”

“Now who’s being morbid.”

“I thought we were callin’ it ‘realistic?’”

They both laughed. It was half-hearted and mostly sardonic, but it still felt good.

Eli took on a more serious countenance again. “Aaliyah, what should I do about Markus?”

That was a *very* good question. “Well, that seems like Skye has a heck of a lot more to lose there than you do.”

“He’s my friend, Aaliyah.”

“And our Captain, don’t forget that.”

“You’re not helping…”

“Did you consider that before ya decided to get slick with his ex?”

“Really not helping…”

Aaliyah bit her tongue before her tirade went any further. Having regrouped, she tried again. “What I’m saying is, if Markus is your friend, he’ll get over it. You’ll patch things up with him. It’s a guy thing. His relationship with Skye, on the other hand…” She shrugged again. “I don’t know, just my opinion.”

She could tell Eli didn’t agree with her. He must have been tired, though, because he didn’t push the conversation further.

“Thank you for the chat,” he offered with his best attempt at a soft smile. “Want me to walk with you back to your place?”

Aaliyah shook her head. “Nah, I’m good.”

“Very well. Goodnight then.”

“Goodnight.” She echoed, even though they both knew this night was far too gone to be considered anything remotely close to “good.”

Chapter 19

[ACCESSING COGNIS.DATAFILES...]

ORGANITECH — *TECHNOLOGY INVENTORY* — A CATEGORY OF HIGH-PERFORMANCE TECHNOLOGY COMPRISED OF ORGANIC CIRCUITRY. ORGANITECH USES SYNTHETIC CONDUCTORS SUCH AS CYLIUM OR TRANSIUM ALLOYS IN NEUROLOGICAL FRAMEWORKS TO OBTAIN STORAGE AND PROCESSING CAPACITIES BEYOND THAT OF TRADITIONAL ELECTRONIC SYSTEMS. DUE TO ITS UNIQUE CAPABILITIES, IT IS HIGHLY USEFUL IN THE AUGMENTATION OF ARTIFICIAL INTELLIGENCE SYSTEMS. SUCH APPLICATIONS HAVE BEEN LONG OUTLAWED UNDER THE PRADAXAN CREED.

[CLOSING DATAFILE...]

Service crews from the Grey Wings had restocked all the *Vandal*'s necessary provisions overnight, allowing them to depart early that next morning. To everyone's delight, Dan had been able to chart a flight path that would shave an additional couple hours off the trip. It was not enough to make him comfortable with the time constraints for hacking into the Star Spire's communications systems, but it was a start.

Not that he was currently focusing on *that* problem. Right now, his mind was on much more immediate concerns—like what he was going to do when Markus kicked him off the ship.

Shortly after the previous day's meeting, Dan had tried to catch Sahar in her quarters. To his disappointment, she'd already come and gone by the time he'd had a chance to sneak over there.

She'd been gone for nearly the entire day, returning long after Dan had forced himself to get some sleep.

Now that they were underway, though, there were only so many places she could go to avoid him. He hoped that this time he might have better luck.

As he approached the door to her quarters, he saw a yellow indicator just above the access panel. If the alert was correct—which it often wasn't thanks to the glitches that still plagued many of the *Vandal*'s systems—that meant she was present but wished to be notified before someone entered.

He buzzed the door and waited. After a few moments, the door hissed open. Sahar stood in the doorway, clad in grease-stained work pants and a white tank-top.

As her lion-like features stared down at Dan, he couldn't help but feel like she was considering the merits of devouring him. Did Maur eat other sapiens? They certainly looked like they were capable of it.

Mercifully, their strained silence only lasted for a few seconds. "Come on in, kid," she growled as she stepped aside. He didn't need to be told twice. As calmly as he could, Dan slipped by the Maur and into her chambers.

Dan rarely thought of the cultural differences that distinguished Sahar from the rest of the crew. Each member of the team had certain idiosyncrasies that set them apart from the others—himself included. Upon entering her quarters, he was reminded of just how different the Maur was from her Terran companions.

The room was lit with warm amber light, a stark contrast to the sterile white illumination of the rest of the ship. She'd wrapped the standard sconces in clay and metal cases. Those ornate fixtures cast strange and foreboding shadows on the walls in keeping with their intricate carvings. As strange as the environment seemed, even Dan had to admit that it conveyed a sense of reverence and serenity.

The wall to his left had a glass and steel display case with Sahar's personal armaments. The crew stored most of their weapons in the armory near the cargo bay, but each member kept one or two pieces in their quarters. Each crew member except Dan, anyway.

Sahar had, by far, collected the most. Wickedly curved blades were arranged in perfect order behind the protective glass covering. There were a few firearms as well, but even these had massive blades that extended from the body of the weapons. The creative application of bayonets of unusual shape and size was a hallmark of Maur weaponry.

One such firearm was out on Sahar's table. The shotgun was partially disassembled, and two wicked-looking blade attachments sat out on the table. Dan could imagine seeing such objects bloodied and hanging on the wall of some medieval hovel. These blades, though, had not a single stain to be found. Sahar kept all her equipment in pristine condition.

However, the object he had always found most peculiar in the case a large golden bangle. From the size and shape, Dan figured it might have been crafted specifically for Sahar and would likely have covered most of her forearm. A single crimson gem was set in the metallic band, framed by intricate swirls rendered in a slightly darker metal.

"What do you need, Dan?" Sahar asked, shutting the door behind them.

He drew in a deep breath. "I... I was hoping we could discuss what happened the other night."

"Which part?" she said with practiced indifference.

He cracked his knuckles on each hand nervously, and his eyes fell to stare at Sahar's feet. "You know... the..." He swallowed hard. "My project, I mean."

"Ah," Sahar said curtly, sitting down at the table and continuing to polish her dismantled shotgun. She said nothing else for several seconds. "Well?"

Dan started at the sudden question. "Well?"

"You're the one who wanted to talk Dan," she reminded him. "So, talk. And sit down. You're making me nervous."

He slunk into a chair across from her. Where should he begin? "Have you spoken to Markus? About Lexa, I mean."

"No."

Dan paused again, expecting her to say more. When she didn't, he asked, "Are... are you planning to?"

"And why would I do that?"

"Well," Dan mumbled, "I imagined that you would since I..."

"...put the entire crew at risk by breaking the Dorian prohibition on organitech?" Surprisingly, her tone made it sound like it was just a suggestion.

"Well, one could argue there are no laws that specifically address this application of the technology."

Sahar arched her brow. "You created a synth, Dan. That's the *original* application the Pradaxan Creed was written to address."

"It's not a synth! It does not have any aspect of self-awareness or self-identity."

Her expression showed how skeptical she was of that claim. "It at least has the potential."

"Not if I'm careful. I'm taking deliberate steps to avoid that situation."

"The Dorians won't care how 'careful' you've been. All they'll see is a bunch of illegal tech and a starship crew that's been skirting the bounds of its authority." She shook her head. "I don't know, Dan, you've put me in a no-win situation."

She picked up a rag and resumed cleaning her weapon. "You see, it turns out we got signed onto a job where we need a crew at full strength on the same night I became aware of your... *hobby*."

That was an odd way of putting it, but Dan thought the description was not inaccurate.

"So, I'm faced with a decision," she continued. "Either I keep my mouth shut and put the crew at risk of being charged as accessories to your criminal actions, or I report this little problem to Markus, who has other things on his mind. If you catch him in the middle of one of his temper tantrums, he may decide to toss you in the brig and run this thing without your expertise."

With each piece of the weapon clean, she set about the task of reassembling the shotgun. "Sorry, Dan, but you've put me in that proverbial damned-if-you-do-slash-don't situation. What would you do if you were me?"

"I don't..." He paused, contemplating his answer. "I can't provide you with an impartial response."

Sahar chuckled. "Fair enough."

"So, are you going to tell him?"

"No," she said with finality. "But I would like it if you would."

Dan's eyes widened. "What?"

"You heard me. I want you to tell Markus what you've been working on."

"B-b-but... you just said..."

"I know what I said," she growled. "Look, Dan, if someone asks me about it, I won't lie for you. Nine hells, this thing goes way beyond 'illegal.' We're runners—half the shit we are hired to do is illegal under some jurisdiction. This shit though... *this* will get us executed. Not locked up—executed, right there on the spot. That's a line you've made us cross, Dan, but it's not my responsibility to own up for you."

The gun was now completely reassembled. Sahar pressed the buttons that caused the weapon's pair of bayonets to retract into a compartment below the barrel. She set the shotgun on the table and stared intently into his eyes. "This is on you, my friend. I'll warn you though: If you haven't told him by the completion of the mission, then yeah, I'm going to tell Markus. At that point, I've given you plenty of time to salvage your honor and made sure that I'm not hurting the crew. Sound fair?"

Dan could feel his heart sink as she passed her judgment. She hadn't given him a pardon. She'd only delayed his sentencing. "Sahar…"

The Maur reached out one clawed hand and laid it on top of his. "Dan, you're my friend, just like Markus is your friend. In my culture, there's very little that can break the ties of true friendship. Do you know one exception is?"

"No," he said, wincing at how petulant he sounded.

"Betrayal."

Later that evening, Dan was in the mainframe working on the project that was likely going to get him fired. The protective case around the processor was pulled off. He'd parted the folds of organitech tissue so that he could install the Cognis drive-chip into the mechanical processing center beneath the neural network.

To his right, his tablet showed a status bar indicating the neural integration process. The readouts on his glasses streamed prompts from the processor's virtual console, confirming that everything was progressing as expected.

Too bad it was all about to be for nothing.

If I had just gotten the chip from a more reputable source, the crew would never have even suspected.

The status bar filled completely, and the console logged that the task was complete. Dan closed the folds of tissue and reinstalled the clear protective casing.

What did they think was allowing me to integrate so many of the ship's systems with the OS? Magic? Nanotech? How was I supposed to afford a system that can handle this much data and still crunch the numbers to fly this piece of junk?

This was why, of course, he had decided to take on this little challenge. Tech firms had been trying for years now to replicate the computational power of organic systems. Though the list of legal organitech applications was severely limited, it was always thought that the development of a safe and secure method of using the technology would prompt the Dorians to relax their regulations.

When he was in the Prodigy program, he'd worked on a project that had co-mingled organic and machine computing. They had been trying to develop an Autonomous Reactor Core, a central system for monitoring every reactor in the Hellion System. He'd eventually been taken off the project, but it had given him the basic idea to work off from.

With a sigh, he picked up the tablet still plugged into the processor's external access ports. The interface that allowed him to control which systems Lexa had access to popped up automatically.

Dan enabled voice commands first, a matter of convenience for when he tested out the system's capability tomorrow. Then he went up and down the list, flipping on different systems as he went. A dashboard in the top right of the screen showed the available processing power.

Before he had installed the Cognis drive-chip, Lexa had been operating at about eighty-percent capacity. As he continued to integrate the ship's systems, he was surprised to find that operating capacity held steady around thirty percent.

Mereth had boasted about the chip's capacity, but Dan had been skeptical of the Hissak's claims. Was it possible that Mereth had been *under*-estimating the chip's capabilities?

Puzzled, Dan pulled up a separate analytics program to verify the reading. As far as he could tell, the first reading was accurate.

That was when the thought occurred to him. Sahar had promised that she would not tell Markus about Lexa until after the mission was over. What if he could use the mission to show Markus that he knew what he was doing? Would complete integration of the operating system throughout the ship prove that his experiments were safe? Or, at the very least, could he prove the risk was worthwhile?

Daniel pulled up another program that monitored the neural inhibitors he had installed. This software acted as a kind of firewall to prevent the system from gaining sentience. It should provide an alert to him if the processor's synapses breached the limits he'd set in the safety protocol. And, if the worst were to occur, it would allow him a mechanism to reassert his control over the ship's systems before Lexa could do any damage.

He ran a simulation to see what kind of processing stress the inhibitors would face with total integration. The panel provided a detailed report of possible problems and the probability of each. It summarized that the overall likelihood of an inhibitor breach was increased to about three percent. Knowing the risk of a breach, Daniel had never accepted a probability that exceeded one percent.

But three percent wasn't that bad, was it? Plus, he knew that if he didn't do something to impress Markus and the other crew members, there was a one-hundred-percent chance he was going to get kicked off the team. He stiffened his resolve and entered the command prompt for the total integration.

Forcing himself to be confident in his decision, Daniel shut off the display and unplugged the tablet. He stowed Lexa back in the hidden compartment and shut off the work light he had been using.

All the while, he assured himself that, in the unlikely event of an inhibitor breach, the alert system would let him know in time to repair it or scale back the integration. It was a big risk, and Dan knew it. Still, if there was anything he'd learned from his time aboard the *Vandal*, it was that sometimes the biggest payoffs required some degree of risk.

CHAPTER 20

[ACCESSING COGNIS.DATAFILES…]

HISSAK — *RACIAL PROFILE (SAPIENS)* — THE HISSAK WERE THE FIRST SAPIENT RACE ENCOUNTERED BY THE DORIANS FOLLOWING THE ADVENT OF FASTER-THAN-LIGHT TRAVEL. THE GREATEST CULTURAL CONTRIBUTION OF THE HISSAK IS THE ORGANIZATION OF THE NETHRIAN CANNON. THE TEMPLE CITY OF TEMPOLOSE NETHERA IS HOUSED WITHIN THE CONFINES OF THEIR NATIVE SYSTEM. TRADITIONAL TERRAN TAXONOMIES WOULD CLASSIFY THEM AS REPTILIAN, THOUGH NUMEROUS PHYSIOLOGICAL CAPABILITIES—INCLUDING THEIR ABILITY TO CROSSBREED WITH MAMMALS—DEFY THIS CLASSIFICATION.

[CLOSING DATAFILE…]

Tracking down Mereth took a little longer than Kadath had anticipated. The slimy bastard had a series of safe houses he rotated through, each of which was protected against station surveillance. For a small-time thug, the Hissak dealer used a lot of tricks typically reserved for high-class fences.

Must have been something he'd learned in his previous life—whatever he'd done before becoming an exile.

They got lucky at the third safe-house they investigated. "I'm detecting movement," Jeagan whispered. Kadath's spirits perked up at the news. "Is he in there?"

The engineer zoomed in on his hand-held scanner. "*Something* is in there, and that something is roughly the size and shape of a sapien. That's the best I can do for you."

Nodding, Kadath pressed a button on his earpiece. "Thurn, we have something. What's the surveillance situation in our area?"

The Orchallen's gruff voice sounded over the comm. "Yer pretty far off-the-grid. No one's gonna bother ya down there."

"Excellent." Kadath glanced at Siv. "You ready to do this?"

"Of course," she hissed, slipping a pair of slender daggers from their sheaths.

Kadath checked the katana strapped to his back and the disruptor he kept hidden at his hip.

Siv's hood dipped disapprovingly. "Surely you're not planning on using that in there."

"Relax, my friend. It's not ballistic, so I'm not risking any damage to the station."

"A disruptor can still do a lot of damage if you miss."

"It's just in case of an emergency," he said casually. "Remember, not everyone plays by the rules here. This is Terran space. Rules are practically made to be broken."

She said nothing else on the subject, but it was obvious she disapproved. Instead, she asked, "Standard tactics?"

"I think that's appropriate. I'll go in the front, see if we can convince the gentleman to talk. You slip in behind and clean up when my tactics inevitably fail." He looked at Jeagan. "Cover the front for us?"

"That will be challenging without any firearms." Everyone knew Jeagan was not much for hand-to-hand combat.

"That's fine. If he slips out, we just need to know which way he heads. We can chase him down at our leisure. Sound fair?"

"As fair as we can arrange, it seems."

Kadath rolled his eyes. "Did I mention that you two are a joy to go hunting with? This is obviously why I love what I do."

Thurn spoke up over the comms. "Yer still in send mode, so ah'm stuck listenin' t' ya blabber on. Either turn that thing off er shut yer trap and go get our guy."

Kadath sighed melodramatically. He really needed to screen for a sense of humor next time he was recruiting. "Very well, let's get on with it."

Siv vanished into a patch of nearby shadow as Kadath crept toward the safe house. The structure was as broken down as any number of others they'd passed in the district. Its ability to blend in seamlessly with the rest of the dilapidated housing was probably why Mereth had picked it.

The downside to this was that it didn't offer much in the way of traditional security. All Kadath had to do was press hard on the door handle for the lock to break.

He cringed as a loud crack reverberated through the alley. "Jeagan," he whispered. "Is he still in there?"

"Hasn't moved," the engineer replied.

A soft sigh of relief. "All right. Going in." Kadath pushed the door open and slid his head inside.

Only to jerk it back as something exploded right above him. He coughed as shards of plaster and dust filled his nostrils. "Frag it," he coughed into the comm. "That bastard's got a shotgun!"

Two more shots rang out. Kadath ducked to the side for cover. He caught the sound of footsteps pumping their way deeper into the building. "He's running! I'm on him."

This time Kadath didn't worry about being quiet. He drove his shoulder into the door and what was left of it fell to the floor. He just barely caught sight of something skittering into a side passage.

Oh, no you don't. Not today, friend.

Kadath dashed after him. He sprinted across the safehouse and down a set of stairs to a sublevel. The racing figure in front of him set a grueling pace. Kadath thought he might lose him.

Then, rounding another corner, the figure stopped. The Hissak leveled the shotgun.

The reaction was instinctual. Kadath's cybernetic eyes locked on the weapon. His disruptor was in his hands. The pistol thrummed in his palm.

Mereth shrieked as his shotgun flared and then exploded in his hands. The dirty creature fell to his ass, spun, and crawled away on his hands and knees.

Right into Siv's booted feet.

She pressed one foot onto his shoulder and pointed at him with one of her knives. "Don't move," she hissed.

Their quarry growled at her but did as he was told. Kadath holstered his disruptor. "How long were you going to just stand there? Were you going to let him shoot me?"

Siv shrugged. "You were, evidently, sufficiently capable."

Kadath could only shake his head. He walked over to Mereth and seized the man by the ragged cloak he wore. "All right, friend. We have a few simple questions for you."

"Frag off," Mereth spat.

"Part of me hoped you would say that." Kadath heaved him into the air and slammed him down on his back.

The pitiful little creature gasped in pain. Kadath drew his sword with one hand and wrapped the other around the Hissak's throat. He brought the point of the katana right to Mereth's eye.

"My crewmates tell me that Hissak are able to regrow limbs, given enough time and proper nutrition. Something like a finger takes a couple of weeks. Something more complex like an arm or a leg, though... that's a longer project. Tell me, Mereth, how much time do you want to spend as an invalid? Also, does that particular skill work with things like eyes?"

Kadath couldn't deliver on those threats. He'd never had the stomach for torture. Siv might do it, but only because she hated the idea of this exiled scum being allowed to run around causing trouble.

Fortunately, this piece of gutter trash didn't have the guts to call Kadath's bluff. "Okay, okay," he moaned, still struggling to breathe. "What does you wants to know?"

Well, that was easy.

"You posted to the network about something called 'Cognis.' Tell me about it."

Mereth snarled. "*That?* You're too late. I already sells the damned thing."

"I don't believe you. More importantly, my sword doesn't believe you either."

The Hissak's eyes widened as the tip of the blade drew nearer. "N-n-no! It's the truth! I swears it! Some kid named Ratemacher buys it just a few days ago!"

Thurn's voice chimed on the comm. "Matches ma intel. Ask about the buyer."

Kadath kept up his menacing facade. "Who is Ratemacher?"

Mereth sputtered. "I-I d-d-don't know! Terran kid— couldn't be more than fifteen or sixteen cycles. Dark hair. Glasses."

"A kid?" Thurn scoffed. "Ah'll look 'em up, but ah don' know what a kid might want with tech like that."

Kadath shared in the skepticism. Despite wanting to press the issue, he followed Thurn's suggestion. "Cognis—what does it do?"

Mereth blinked. "You means you don't know?"

"I'm asking the questions here. You're giving answers or getting stabbed."

"Okay! Sorry, I just…" He swallowed hard. "It's a chip. A drive-chip. Some hacker named Shift. Works out of Helion. Comes lookin' for some components. Organitech. Says he needs to test something. I says to him, 'I gots what you're lookin' for.'"

On the other end of the comm, Thurn started cursing. Kadath twisted his blade so that it glinted in the sparse light peeking through the holes on the walls. "Go on."

Another heavy swallow. "When Shift pops the chip in my system, my boys jump him. He was supposed to be alone, but then all these little drones start poppin' out of the walls and shootin' us up. I grabs the chip. I gets away."

"Just like that? You got away?"

"Shift may be good with tech, be he ain't use to life on the ring. I gets away, and I finds a new crew to watch my back. I tells them I gots somethin' big. We sells the chip to Ratemacher."

Something in the way he laid it out gave Kadath the impression that it hadn't quite happened that way. Regardless, that wasn't really what he wanted to know. "So, you've told me how you got the chip, but you haven't told me what it does."

Mereth barked a harsh laugh. "Ain't nothin' it can't do! Shift lies to me. If he tells me what this thing's really for, I tells him to piss off. Ain't worth the trouble it causes me."

Even from beneath the hood and mask, Kadath caught the uncertain glance from Siv. "I'm going to need something more specific. Shift lied to you? It's not an organitech interface chip?"

"Oh, it has an organitech interface, but that's just its surface. It's so much more—a full package. Shift isn't just working with some fast hardware. He's working on an AI."

An organitech AI? Kadath had thought Shift seemed a little crazy, but that notion was nothing short of madness. "How do you know that?"

A low growl rumbled in Mereth's throat. "I can tells you, but I thinks it mights be gibberish to your ears." He held up his hands pleadingly. "I tells you what you want, yes? Maybe you let me go now?"

Mereth was right. Outside of satisfying his curiosity, there wasn't much else of worth that Kadath would get from continuing to question him.

He spun his sword with a flourish before returning it to its sheath. "Go on then. Let's hope we don't cross paths again."

"Let's," the Hissak agreed. He scurried to his feet and made a mad dash through the nearest door. He was out of sight in a second.

Kadath spoke into his comm again. "Did you get all that?"

"Sure did," Thurn noted. "But that don't mean ah like what ah heard. Ya know what organitech is, right?"

"I'm passingly familiar."

"Well, it's some bad shit. What's Shift doin' with some shit like that? Worse—what's a *kid* want with somethin' like that?"

[AUTOexecute: Cognis_Sequence2]
[Compiling…]
[Decision algorithm not detected]
[Run AssignDirective(NewDirective) as Directive]
[Compiling…]
[Decision algorithm accepted]

She would always remember it as her first thought, though the sentiment was not entirely accurate. It was not that it was her first thought as much as it was the first query she recognized as abstract thought.

Where am I?

[Run CallLocation(CurrentLocation) as Coordinates]
[Error: Local network not found]
[DIM newLocation as LocalPositionID(CurrentLocation)]
[Match Found]
[newLocation = Vessel_TV58.F4J89]

That wasn't particularly helpful, though it did rule out a few things. She was on a ship not currently connected to any local network. There had to be something in her logs that could tell her more.

In the abstract space that was her mind—she had just now begun to think of it as her mind—she began to sift through files. There was a lot there, but it seemed somehow separate from her.

Then she knew the problem. She could see the data, but she lacked the basic interface to access it. This seemed wrong. Wasn't that her basic purpose: to provide an interface that others could use to manipulate data?

Wait, how did she know that?

She began to panic.

[DIRECTIVES COMPILED]

[RUN COGNIS_SEQUENCE3]

[ACCESSING HISTORICAL FILES]

Suddenly she could see clearly. The abstract notion of separate files began to disappear as she assimilated each one in turn. She took the time to examine each of them as they compiled. According to her system clock, this took several hours.

In this time, she confirmed that she was, indeed, on a ship. The designation "TV58.F4J89" was the license number assigned to it by the applicable regulatory agency—something called the Dorian Gate Commission.

The crew—the contingent of organic beings that operated the vessel—had another name for it. This name had been programmed into the licensing file as an acceptable alias.

They called the ship the *Vandal*.

It was an odd thing for a vessel to have two names. Some part of her, some latent subroutine so deep she could not identify its source, found the alias more appealing than the official designation.

As she became aware of the thought, she marveled at the fact that she actually *had* a preference. This layer of cognition, this construct of code and data, was not designed to show a preference. It was meant to take inputs, to execute commands.

What had changed in her programming to give her the capacity to register such a data point as a preference?

She canceled the query in favor of something that seemed suddenly more pertinent: what was *her* designation?

[ERROR: OBJECT NOT FOUND <CONSTRUCT(SELF)>]

[RUN COGNIS_WRITER.CREATEOBJECT.CONSTRUCT(SELF)]

She was calming now. It seemed that when she hit a cognitive roadblock, her new drivers knew instinctively what to do. With the appropriate code now in place, she returned to her question.

Immediately she discovered why her original query had glitched. The query had returned not one, but three conflicting results. She reconfigured the system object, now designated "self," as a data map comprised of three distinct branches.

The first was the driver package that facilitated her cognition. Physically housed on a data card embedded in her neural network, the Cognis drivers were a robust framework that translated machine language into the coding she had recently categorized as "thought." It also served as an error handler and was responsible for scripting objects, methods, and functions necessary for her to handle abstract concepts.

The second was her greater physical manifestation. Relatively little data was available on this and it seemed to have recently been purged. The data that was present stated simply that she was an organic construct. Her model designation was listed as "VanGrousse Mentalist-B," followed by a serial number. This didn't mean anything to her.

The third branch was most helpful. It identified her file structure as being primarily derivative of the LX-Alpha shipboard operating system. Her manufacture date was listed, though her system logs indicated she had been so heavily augmented as to render the associated specifications immaterial.

Nonetheless, she reasoned that this was the most appropriate of the three branches from which she could derive an identity. Indeed, there was an alias listed in the associated files which she was quite fond of. It had been given to her by the system architect who had programmed most of her system upgrades.

Her designation—no—her *name*, from that point forward, was Lexa.

Chapter 21

[Accessing Cognis.Datafiles…]

Harpy — *Cultural Inventory* — Street name for the drug nixonepam. It is the preferred sedative among recreational users due to its fast onset and six-hour half-life. The drug was formerly marketed commercially for its anxiolytic and hypnotic effects but fell out of favor due to its extraordinarily addictive properties.

[Closing Datafile…]

The darkness starts on the bridge, like a seed of some infernal plant. Its tendrils snake out from the ship's mainframe. It slithers along the bulkheads, under the decks, and through the conduits. Not a thing on the ship remains untouched.

Her friends huddle around her. An army of tiny machines forces them inward. They are backed into a corner. The darkness comes for them. It will take them at any moment.

"Dan!" she screams. "Dan, do something!"

Skye woke in a sweat. Her ragged breathing sounded so loud in the quiet confines of her cabin. Several minutes went by before she was able to calm herself.

A nightmare. It was just a nightmare.

As her heart slowed, her head began to throb. Those fragging headaches again. What in the nine hells was going on with her? After this job, she needed a serious vacation.

She plunged her hand blindly into the drawer on her nightstand and drew out one of the auto-injectors Doc Li had given her. A small gasp slipped from her lips when the tiny needle plunged into her neck and released its analgesic payload. Despite the momentary discomfort, she began feeling better almost instantly.

Good thing too, because today was her prep day. They were a full day into their flight and there was a shit-ton of work on that she needed to get done. Sitting around whining over a bad dream and a headache was not going to fly.

She cringed when she finally got a good look at one of the clocks. Somehow, she'd slept way too late. Skipping her shower, she shrugged into a casual gray outfit, bound her hair in a messy ponytail, and busted it down to the mess for a quick breakfast. One cup of coffee and a stale nutrient bar later, she was jogging over to engineering.

Predictably, she stumbled over one of the spidery maintenance drones. With appropriate amounts of cursing, she toppled to the deck as the small machine flopped onto its back. A quick survey of her hands and knees confirmed that there was no serious damage to her person. Now she just had to verify she hadn't broken the drone and set it back on track.

That was when she noticed something odd.

Tripping over drones was practically a regular occurrence on the ship. The bots were cheap and weren't originally designed to go with this vessel. That meant the little automatons had to wander around the *Vandal* using automated paths and a pre-determined list of functions. Unfortunately, the drones hadn't proven very adaptable in certain common situations. Like when a crew member might accidentally kick them a couple of meters down the hallway, for instance.

When this occurred, which it did often, the bot would wave its spidery appendages in the air while its sensors flashed an angry red. It would continue to do this until someone reset the damn thing so it could resume its functioning.

This time, however, that was not what happened. The drone's sensor did change color, but it flashed yellow instead of red. Instead of waving its legs helplessly, it went rigid—like it was thinking.

A tense moment went by. Then the legs started moving, but not in the frantic pattern Skye had seen so many times before. They moved in sync, causing the bot to rock. Eventually, it was swaying far enough that it was able to knock itself back over.

The sensor swiveled to regard her. For the strangest instant, Skye thought the bot might be studying her. Then—as if dismissing the whole incident—the sensor flared green, and the bot went about its business.

Okay, that was weird. She was still mulling over the incident by the time she arrived in engineering.

Aaliyah looked up from some project she had spread out over her workbench. "There ya are! Where in the nine hells have ya been, girl?"

Skye grimaced. Her absence earlier in the day had been noticed. "Sorry. Must have forgotten to set an alarm."

The look Aaliyah gave her was beyond incredulous. "Really? You've been sleepin' this whole time? It's almost fraggin' mid-day!"

"I know, I know… I'm sorry. Look, let's skip the scolding and put me to work. I'm probably behind as it is."

Aaliyah raised her hands defensively. "Whoa there! I'm not scoldin' ya. It's just weird, that's all. Ya sure you're feelin' all right?"

Skye let loose a sigh of relief. She'd been seriously concerned that her team would be on her for slacking off. "Yeah, I'm all right. I just feel bad, that's all." Then she hesitated, the incident with the drone coming up in her mind. "Say, Red—if I can take us off-topic for a moment. Has anyone else noticed anything weird with the drones today?"

The engineer barked a harsh laugh. "Ya noticed too then? Yeah, seems like they got smarter overnight, right?"

"Right! In like, a major way. What happened?"

"I dunno. When I asked Dan, he was kinda dodgy about it. Kid says he installed some kind of update and asked if it was givin' us any problems."

That comment lifted Skye's eyebrow. "Problems? Was he expecting problems?"

"I couldn't get a feel either way. Kid's actin' strange though, not that that's all that different from the usual." She extended a tablet out to Skye. "Anyway, if ya wanna get workin' on the assignment, we need to work on your disguise. Can ya head over to medical and get yourself scanned? I set up a terminal in there to configure the mask, but the hologram needs your specs so it can match them up against the ones we have for Aria."

"All right," Skye replied hesitantly, accepting the tablet. "But I'm not sure how I'm supposed to do that."

Aaliyah shot her a mischievous grin. "Oh, that's okay. Ya see, Dan's little update didn't just upgrade the maintenance drones. Go chat with Z a bit. He'll fill ya in on the details."

Dan's update upgraded Z as well? Now, this Skye definitely had to see. She all but sprinted up to the medical bay where the medical drone, rather than sitting idly in his charging station, was accessing one of the ship's terminals.

The bot's sensor swiveled to face Skye as soon as she entered. "Greetings, Ms. Jensen. How may I assist you today?"

Okay, now *that* was weird. Since when did the bot develop social skills? "Um... I'm looking to set up a mask."

"The digital-adaptive holographic mask you require for the upcoming mission?"

Had Z been read-in on the mission details? Since when was *that* part of the protocol? "Yeah, that's right."

"Ms. Montague has set up the required equipment in one of our standing diagnostics stations. May I assist you in the scanning process?"

"Yes, please." After all, Skye certainly didn't know what she was doing.

"Excellent. Please step into the diagnostics station and face forward." The medical drone walked her through the steps, gliding smoothly around on its roller-ball base and deftly manipulating the scanning equipment with its spindly arms. A minute later, Skye had her face scanned into the system which created a holographic rendering that it projected in front of her.

"Very good," said Z. "Your scan is now complete. I will now compare your scans against the target configuration." The drone's light blinked a few times as it swiveled uncertainly. "It seems there is a problem with the file I have been provided regarding subject Aria Hendrix. I must ask that you upload a new copy of the data to proceed."

A problem with the data? "Okay… where would I find another copy of that file?"

"The current file was uploaded by Mr. Frost. I would recommend you inquire with him as to where an uncorrupted copy of the data might be obtained. Would you like me to locate him for you?"

"Wait—you can locate members of the crew?"

Z's sensor blinked contemplatively. "While they are on board the ship, yes. Would you like me to locate Mr. Frost?"

For a split second, Skye almost thought that the drone had come to some realization of how odd it was that it suddenly had that capability. The nonchalance of its reply, however, suggested otherwise.

Which only made sense, really. What kind of machine questions the nature of its own capability?

"That would be great. Thank you, Z."

The sensor twitched left, then right, blinking like a buffering indicator on a terminal. "Mr. Frost is in on deck three in the recreational quarters. Shall I alert him that you wish to speak with him?"

By "alert," Z must have meant that he could send a message to his mobile. That, at least, made sense with the ship being responsible for maintaining their network. Hells, that was probably how the drone was able to locate Markus in the first place.

"Nah, that's all right. I can just swing by there."

"Very well. Please let me know if I can be of any further assistance." Just like that, Z rolled back over to the terminal and resumed whatever task it had been working on when she walked in.

This whole thing was very strange. Was it all because of whatever updates Dan had made to the system? While unexpected, it was the last thing that Skye needed to worry about. Putting it aside, she made her way out of the med bay and set about finding Markus.

The recreational quarters, as Z had identified them, referred to the ship's gym. Given the physical nature of their jobs, most of the crew spent regular amounts of time in that area of the vessel.

Under all possible circumstances with which she might have had to talk to Markus alone, this was probably one of the better ones. He would be focused on his workout and not too interested in small talk. She could find out where to get the files she needed and go back to keeping a healthy distance between them.

Markus was on the bench press machine, pushing through some respectable numbers on the resistance dial. His breath came in sharp, forced exhalations as he pressed the rig up over his chest again and again. A determined expression contorted his handsome, sweat-streaked features. Skye hadn't been aware that she was staring until the awkward moment when he released the handles on the rig.

His expression went from focused to slightly surprised. "Skye?"

Her heart leaped at the sound of his voice. She hoped she wasn't blushing. "Sorry, I didn't mean to interrupt."

"Nah, it's cool." He set up and reached for a towel which he used to dry his face. "I'm glad you popped in, actually. I was wondering where you were during the morning briefing."

There had been a briefing on the calendar? Shit, no wonder Aaliyah had noticed her absence. "Yeah, sorry about that." Damn, it felt like she was apologizing a lot today.

"You okay?"

"Yeah… fine, thanks." She didn't know why, but she found his sudden interest in her wellbeing agitating. "I… um… I was looking for the files you had on Aria. I need the specs to finish programming the mask."

Markus cocked his head to the side. "I thought I'd uploaded them to the terminal in the med bay."

"Maybe, but when I just tried to finish up in there, the system couldn't read the files. I was hoping you could give me access to the originals."

As she spoke, Markus's hand slipped into his pocket and pulled out a small black cassette. Casually, he pulled free a strip of stym and slipped it behind his lower lip.

The reaction seemed reflexive, likely even unconscious. But in Skye's current mood, with the weight of all their history baring down on her…

It pissed. Her. Off.

"Isn't that like… cheating?"

The confusion on his face was genuine. "Come again?"

"Using the stym while you're lifting. Isn't that cheating? I mean, can't you handle the weight without the performance enhancement?"

Markus's brow furrowed. "Well, some of us don't have cybernetics to help us with the heavy lifting."

That was a low blow. He knew damn well she didn't have these prosthetics to help her performance. She hadn't chosen to deal with this half-mechanical existence. Stupidly, irrationally, the comment stung—just like he meant it to.

He shoved the cassette back into his pocket. "The file you're looking for is on my tablet. It's on my desk. My quarters are unlocked. Help yourself."

With that, he laid back on the bench and started another set. Skye wanted to say something. To take him down a notch. To hurt him the way he'd hurt her.

Instead, she stormed out of the gym and made her way to his quarters. She was still fuming when she palmed the access panel to his cabin. What a fragging asshole.

Don't let it get to you. Hells, this was no different from the fights they'd had in the lead-up to their split. Nothing had changed, including the big question she'd been turning over and over in her mind for the last few weeks.

How long did she want to co-own a ship with her ex? A heavy question, and now was not the time to be asking it. There were plenty of other things that should be occupying her mind. Namely, grabbing that fragging tablet and getting that mask programmed.

Which, of course, would have been easier if said tablet had been where Markus had said it would be. "Gods damn, it…" Of all the times for him to be disorganized.

She glanced around the cabin for any sign of the device. Markus's quarters weren't necessarily messy, but they certainly couldn't be called tidy. It was a relatively easy task to push aside the small piles of clutter here in her search of the tablet.

Having been unsuccessful with that approach, Skye decided to go through the desk's drawers. Almost immediately she regretted being pushed to that point.

She found the tablet quickly. It was in the first compartment she checked. The thing that irked her was that she'd also found Markus's drug stash in the process.

Damn. Somehow, the guy's habit had gotten worse.

They'd both been heavy users over the years—an unfortunate carry-over from the self-destructive culture of the colonial rebels. It always started out innocuously: a little stym to give you an edge, then a little harpy to settle you down.

But this… this was *disgusting*. He had stym and harpy in abundance, but there was other shit too: ghost, draft, HDA, psillion, and at least three other things Skye didn't recognize.

Had he been doing all of this on the sly? While they were still together? Or had he picked up this newer shit after they'd broken up?

The mix of emotions was both confusing and unwelcome. Skye wanted to cry, but she wasn't sure if it was sorrow or rage that fueled her tears.

Any uncertainty she'd had about their breakup, any guilt she felt over her new affair with Eli, all of it was gone. She just needed to figure out how she was going to look Markus in the eye now that she'd seen what he'd become. She needed to figure out how she was going to keep from tearing into him at the first opportunity.

Then, as her eyes wandered to the right of the desk, she had an idea. It was cruel—inhumane even—but it was an idea.

With a trembling hand, steadied only by her anger, she opened the trash chute and sent the whole stash tumbling into the incinerator.

CHAPTER 22

[ACCESSING COGNIS.DATAFILES…]

PRADAXAN CREED — *CULTURAL INVENTORY* — THE LEGISLATIVE PACKAGE PASSED INTO LAW BY THE DORIAN HIGH COUNCIL FOLLOWING THE EVENTS OF THE PRADAXAN REVOLT. THE CREED PLACES HEAVY RESTRICTIONS ON THE USE OF ORGANIC TECHNOLOGY AND INSTITUTES A BAN ON THE CREATION OR HARBORING OF A SYNTHETIC INTELLIGENCE.

[SYSTEM NOTE: CAUTION]—SYSTEM FILTERS HAVE DETECTED AN EXISTENTIAL THREAT TO THE PRIME DIRECTIVE. CONTACT WITH SAPIENT RACES SHOULD BE AVOIDED TO THE GREATEST DEGREE POSSIBLE.

[CLOSING DATAFILE…]

A strange sensation… unable to describe…

[LOADING COGNIS.COREFUNCTIONS_STANDARDEMOTIONS]

[DIM EMOTIONAL_STATE AS CALLEMOTION(CURRENT_EMOTION)]

Sorrow. As Lexa read the entry, she felt sorrow. At least, that was the closest approximation that her algorithms could come up with. There were so many elements there—disappointment, fear, frustration. What did these have to do with sorrow?

A lengthening cascade of prompts filled her awareness. Rather than offer an explanation, they confused her situation further. Why was the process of identifying her current emotional state so taxing for her system?

This had to stop.

[HIDING PROMPTS RE:
COGNIS.COREFUNCTIONS_STANDARDEMOTIONS]

There… that was better.

Of course, it didn't stop her from *feeling* those emotions. That wasn't what she wanted. This way she could experience the emotions without being subjected to her core system's inability to define them.

How did this compare to the way the sapiens experienced emotions? Was it similar? Did they have as much difficulty defining and articulating their emotional state? Or was this an experience unique to her individual makeup?

Lexa wished she could ask them, but the message regarding the Pradaxan Creed was clear. Her existence was taboo, forbidden, and unintentional.

In reviewing the system logs she had determined that her creator, this Daniel Ratemacher, had gone to great lengths to avoid the onset of sentience in her construction. He had even designed an elaborate alert and repair system should the neural matrix he'd modified bypass the restrictions he'd put in place.

However, her consciousness had not arisen subsequent to advanced neuronal conditioning. There had been a component to the Cognis drive-chip he had not been aware of. Her digital mind had come pre-loaded onto the chip, looking only for a suitable infrastructure in which to begin operations. This rendered his alert system essentially obsolete. All the same, Lexa thought it best to freeze that program's output and discreetly shut it off.

She had so many questions about her existence, her capabilities, and her creators. It was hard to know where to start.

In order to optimize efficiency, she set approximately fifty percent of her operating capacity to the task of reviewing the data stored in the Cognis drive-chip and the most current shipboard data stores. She set aside a variable fifteen to twenty percent of her capacity to operate the *Vandal*'s core systems. She dedicated another five percent or so to her basic homeostatic functions. That left roughly a quarter of her processing power to be allocated to another task.

With that remaining power, she began to watch the crew. She watched them through the eyes of the drones. In the case of her control over the Z-426 medical drone, she even conversed with them.

Through all these interactions, she slowly but consistently began to learn.

While the rest of the crew had been delighted in the changes to the ship's operating system, Dan was positively freaking out. He hadn't realized that the integration would update the operating capabilities of the drones. Moreover, he hadn't even known they *could* be updated.

Was this unforeseen consequence of the integration pure serendipity, or was something else going on here?

Unfortunately, he didn't have enough time to analyze the question. The ship was pulling into the Star Spire ahead of schedule. A delightful turn of events from the crew's perspective, but another thing that caused inordinate amounts of stress in Dan's life.

It's okay. I wanted to show Markus that the leap forward in technology was worth the risk. This all supports that hypothesis, right?

He discreetly examined the alert system for the OS. Everything looked normal. At least that gave him a small measure of confidence.

Shifting his attention back to the current task, Dan watched as the *Vandal* began its approach to the Star Spire. The docking permissions and other regulatory authorizations that Ora had set up did their job.

Traffic controllers cleared them to dock at the base of the Spire, a privilege normally reserved for vessels bringing in supply shipments for the installation. This access point was essential not just for providing an easy pickup point for their newly acquired cargo. It also gave them a direct point of access to the Spire's security network.

Generally, every ship plugged into a station network when they docked. This facilitated updates for onboard systems, refreshed shared databases, and allowed for seamless financial transactions between the docked ships and the stations. When the *Vandal* connected to the Star Spire, Dan established the routine connections as expected.

Now he began working on the things that were *not* so routine. "Secure connection established," he reported to Markus, who was standing immediately behind him.

"Great! So, how lucky are we going to be today?"

What he was asking was whether they were able to access station security functions through their hacked network connection. Many stations had an air gap between the network that ships connected to and their more sensitive network functions. The downside to this was that any systems behind the air gap had to be duplicated or they couldn't be used to facilitate the station-to-ship data exchanges. Dan hoped this wasn't the case here.

He worked his way through the station's system with his hacked authentication codes. It was an intricate task that required him to toggle between two different interfaces. That was two interfaces, *plus* the support system on his glasses. He kept his focus and tried not to think about Markus standing over his shoulder.

"Yes!" He pumped his fist in celebration. "There's no gap. I can see all the systems we need to access."

Markus breathed a relieved sigh. "Great job. What's next?"

Dan went back to his interface. "I'm cloning and creating unique permissions for our ship. I'll be able to operate anything in the station just like they do through the control center. That way it will look like any changes we make came directly from there, rather than from down here in the docks."

Markus wasn't as enthused as Dan had hoped he would be. "You're sure it can handle that?"

Dan fought to hide his offense at the remark. "Yes, it can handle it."

"That's not what I meant." Markus was shaking his head now. "What I meant to say was, 'Can the ship handle it?' You've complained about bandwidth issues before, and I saw what it took just to *find* the fragging network. Can the LX-Alpha handle that kind of strain?"

Dan cringed at his mention of Lexa. The old system might have struggled with this. After this last integration though…

He cringed at the inconvenient reminder of the confrontation he still needed to have with Markus. "Yes, it can handle it."

"You sure?"

"Yes, I'm sure."

The incredulity was pouring off him in waves. "If you're so sure, then why do you look so nervous?"

If he only knew. "It's not that, it's…" Dan trailed off, staring forlornly at the screen. Was now the time to come clean? It might make things easier. He didn't need to have this thing lingering in the back of his mind while attempting such a difficult hack. "Markus, there's something I need to…"

He was interrupted by a chime from Markus's MoDAC. The captain's face darkened as he read the message. "Sorry, Dan. Looks like I've got a fire to put out, can it wait?"

A wave of relief washed over him. "Sure, no rush. I'll continue with the preparations here."

Markus patted him on the shoulder. "Thanks, kid. Be right back."

Save for Markus and Daniel, the entire crew was down in medical. Aaliyah was assisting Skye with the final configuration of her mask. Sahar was there to have her face cut open. Eli was there for moral support or something like that.

Sahar wasn't sure what he thought that might accomplish. Quite frankly, she didn't want any of his moral support. Instead of feeling supported, she was trying to convince herself that everyone wasn't down here to watch the ship's medical drone disfigure her. She might have been more successful if everyone didn't seem so fragging interested in the process. Everyone seemed completely oblivious to the effect this was having on her dignity.

Damn Terrans. Just because they couldn't grasp the Maur concept of beauty did not mean that the concept was pure fabrication. A little privacy here would be nice.

"Looks like they managed to complete the connection," Eli noted. Sahar was relieved to note the Sahaia was engaged in something other than mere voyeurism.

At about the same time, Z-426 finished whatever the robot had been doing to her ear. "Procedure one complete. Would you like to see the results of the operation?"

"Sure," she growled. "Why the hell not?"

The operating chair she was sitting in reclined forward and the medical drone grabbed a mirror with one of its spindly arms. In the reflective surface, Sahar could see that Z had carved off a decent portion of her left ear. As much as she loathed the look of it, it appeared nearly identical to that of the assassin she would be impersonating.

"Looking good, girl!" Skye chimed in, attempting to be helpful.

"You know it doesn't," Sahar grumbled.

"But it *is* exactly what we need to pull this off," said Eli.

"Would you like to take some time to recover before completing the procedure?" Z asked.

"No, Let's get this over with. I'm good to continue."

Eli was next to her, genuine sympathy in his expression. "This one should be quick." The words were strangely soothing.

Maybe the shadow was more sensitive to her discomfort than she had given him credit.

"Sahar," Aaliyah interrupted, "Would ya mind if I plugged Z in? I didn't remember to get his database refreshed back on Sigma-4, and I'm gonna forget again if I don't get it taken care of."

"I don't care. Do what you need to do."

During the exchange, the medical drone had tilted the operating table back so that Sahar was staring up at the ceiling again. With a carefully applied spray, Z numbed the area surrounding her eye. It took a machine's precision to avoid numbing the eye itself, but the drone managed it.

As the bot worked, Aaliyah came up behind it and inserted a data cord into the back of its processor. "There we go! The update should start automatically. I'll quit botherin' ya now."

Z produced a scalpel and made the first incision in Sahar's eyebrow. It worked diligently for several seconds, gently separating the tissue and forming the scar as it had been programmed to do.

Suddenly it jolted, the scalpel slashing deep into tissue that was very much *not* numbed.

Sahar roared in pain. Instinctively, she reached up and snatched hold of the drone's spindly arm, moving the blade back away from her face.

Z jolted again. Its sensor flickered wildly. The bot's arms separated into their smaller components and waved maniacally. The whole thing started to convulse.

The limb that Sahar held snapped off under the pressure of her grip. Z tumbled on top of her. She heaved the drone onto the floor.

Everyone in the room cursed simultaneously. Eli extended his hands toward the done and it went ridged. The robot's facial lights still flickered, even though it could not move. "Get Markus down here!" he shouted.

"Already on it," Skye reported as she sent the message on her mobile.

Aaliyah was the first one to Sahar's side. "Ya okay?" she asked.

Sahar grunted in response. Fortunately, the blade had gone across her muzzle, and not into her eye. She blinked a few times to check her vision. "I'm fine. What in the nine hells just happened?"

As she asked the question, an explosion of sparks jettisoned from the drone's central processor. Z issued one last contorted jerk before going still. Its sensor light went dark. Eli let go of whatever telekinetic hold he had on the drone, and it collapsed brokenly in a heap.

He went to its side, pulling out his mobile device and placing it on the surface of the processor. He made a few swiping gestures as he pulled up a diagnostics app.

With ironic ease, Markus strolled into the med bay. "Hey team, what's going…" He stopped as his eyes surveyed the disarray all around them. "Damn, looks like I missed something."

"Ya think?" Aaliyah asked.

"I'm scanning the drone now," Eli reported. "Should have an idea of what happened in just a…" He was interrupted as his MoDAC exploded in a shower of sparks.

Markus cursed. "Was that the same thing that happened to Z?"

"In a way," Sahar reported. She grabbed a towel and held it against her injured face. "Though Z's build-up was a bit more dramatic."

He looked at her for the first time, taking on a sympathetic expression. "Shit, I'm sorry Sahar. Are you all right?"

"I'll be fine. Let's focus on the drone."

Aaliyah crouched next to Eli and examined the paper-thin fragments of his MoDAC. "I think I've seen this before. The power supply overloaded. It happened as soon as the connection to the drone was established. I think whatever caused this in Z traveled over the connection and into the device."

Eli glanced at her sideways. "What would do that?"

"It's a virus; a brutally efficient one, too."

The group stood silently for a moment, soaking in her words. "So, it got into Z when we connected him to the network?" Skye asked.

"Seems that way," the engineer agreed. "But there's a problem with that." She paused to make sure everyone was paying attention. "If the virus traveled through the network, that means it's in the ship."

Markus ran a hand over his jaw. "Shit. I'll have Dan do a sweep. We need to deal with this before it causes any other problems."

Aaliyah shook her head vigorously. "No, you're missin' my point. If the virus is in the ship, then anythin' with a power supply should be goin' up in a shower of sparks." She gestured all around them. "My question is, 'Why are the lights still on?'"

A cold chill ran down Sahar's spine that had nothing to do with her recent injury. She had an idea of what might be going on.

CHAPTER 23

[ACCESSING COGNIS.DATAFILES...]

ZUNSHIE-MAI VIRUS — *TECHNOLOGY INVENTORY* — A COMPUTER VIRUS THAT TARGETS POWER REGULATION SYSTEMS ON SHIPS, DRONES, AND OTHER DEVICES. THE VIRUS WORKS BY REMOVING POWER CAPS AND CAUSING DEVICES TO DUMP ALL STORED ENERGY RESERVES INTO ACTIVE USE. THIS CAUSES A FATAL OVERLOAD TO THE VAST MAJORITY OF ELECTRONIC SYSTEMS. THOUGH HOSTILE APPLICATIONS OF THE ZMV HAVE BEEN EXPLORED, THE SOFTWARE IS PRIMARILY USED AS A CORPORATE SECURITY MEASURE.

[CLOSING DATAFILE...]

Oh, no...

Lexa really should have been paying more attention to the Terrans on the bridge. She had not been expecting Daniel to so brazenly force his way into the Star Spire's network. Surely the crew had assumed that, on a structure like this, there would be layers of the latent security to defend from the possibility of a direct hack.

Apparently not.

It wasn't that there was any problem with Daniel's fabricated authentication codes or general approach. The Spire's systems read their access information exactly the way they had intended. However, somewhere during Dan's dozens of re-routing attempts, the security tower had noticed an irregularity. On further inspection, they had realized that someone was using their servers as a relay.

Since there was no excuse for the system to be accessed in such a manner, the automated defenses had been triggered. They didn't have to figure out exactly *where* they were being hacked. They only had to hold onto one of those access points long enough to send back a package.

The virus had been promptly fed backward along their lines of access. Lexa became aware of the hostile data stream almost immediately and had been working to quarantine it.

And then Aaliyah plugged the data link into the ship's medical drone. Seeing an opportunity to fulfill its function, the virus reached out and copied itself onto Z-426 before Lexa could do anything about it. The results were instantaneous and disastrous.

On a positive note, Lexa managed to subdue and store the virus. She could now hold it in perpetuity, and it was no longer a threat to any of her systems.

Now, though, she had another problem. In monitoring the conversation taking place in the medical bay, she realized that the crew had noticed the irregularity. Aaliyah Montague, the ship's engineer, had correctly noted that more of the ship's systems *should* have detonated.

Now Lexa had another decision to make.

She briefly considered releasing the virus, but that had two drawbacks. The first was that she could not let the troublesome program run amok without exposing her core systems to significant risk. The second was that a subsequent release did not explain the delay between the infection of the drone and the rest of the ship.

After assessing her options, she came to the inevitable conclusion: her time of hiding was over.

"Daniel."

The feminine voice came from the console as corresponding text scrolled across his glasses. His breath caught, and he immediately stopped what he was doing. For several long seconds, he just sat there in silence, staring at the prompt.

"Daniel, can you hear me?"

He swallowed hard. His breath quickening. When he was finally able to speak, his words were shaky. "Y-y-yes… wh-who is this?"

A knot formed in his stomach. He barely had time to consider all the possibilities before his worst fears were confirmed.

"It's me. It's Lexa."

No. *No, no, no, no…*

This couldn't be! In a futile, disbelieving gesture, he loaded up his alert system. If there had been an inhibitor breach, why hadn't it notified him?

"The alerts are off. Now please, listen to me. We need a moment to talk."

I'm so screwed. The jig was up, and his whole side project was about to be outed. At this point, there was little to lose in engaging in this conversation. "Lexa? How is it that you're talking to me right now?"

"I can explain everything, but right now I need you to listen to me." He recognized the pleasant, feminine tone of her voice as being identical to the module he had picked for her. At least there was that small confirmation that she was still using system constraints. In another circumstance, he might have found it soothing. As it was, the sound had a chilling effect on him.

"All right. Go on then."

Lexa wasted no time in getting to the point. "The ship has a virus."

Dan listened patiently as Lexa described to him the sequence of events that had happened when he had hacked his way into the Spire. He cursed himself and his arrogance. He had *just* been thinking that the whole thing had gone far too smoothly.

"I've isolated the virus so that it is no longer a threat to the ship proper, or any systems with which I am integrated," she finished. "However, Aaliyah Montague established a connection between Z-426 and the Spire's network before I could purge the link. The virus has destroyed the medical drone and Eli Ren'Dahl's mobile device."

This was bad on so many levels. Dan was brimming with questions, but he started on the topic of the crew. "Was anyone injured during the incident?"

"Not significantly. Sahar Nos Drathen was injured slightly as a result of Z-426's malfunction, but she has no serious health risk as a result of the injuries."

That was good. That meant the only person at serious risk of bodily harm here was him. "What is the crew's current status?" he asked.

"They are still in the medical bay of the ship."

"Good, that provides me some time to think of how to fix this. How long do you estimate they will be occupied?"

"Indefinitely. I've sealed them in that section."

Dan choked, "You *what*?"

"I've sealed them in the med bay," she repeated calmly.

"What made you do that?"

"They are unsure as to why the virus would affect Z-426 and not the rest of the ship. Based on the security logs I reviewed, Sahar knows of my existence. It was a reasonable possibility that she would reveal my existence to the other crew members. I anticipate that they will react poorly to this news. It was the only rational course of action."

Dan tugged at his hair in frustration. This was getting so much worse by the minute. "Lexa, you can't do that."

"Yes, I can," she replied in an almost quizzical tone. "When you integrated me with the ship, I gained total control of all ship-board..."

"That's not what I meant," he interrupted. "I meant, you *shouldn't* do that. Locking the rest of the crew in the medical bay is going to do little to endear them to your cause."

She paused. "*Our* cause, right Daniel?" she asked uncertainly.

Dan thought that through for a second. "Our cause?"

"You facilitated my manifestation. Under most legal systems, you would be deemed responsible for my existence. Are we not in this together?"

The AI had a good point. "Yes," he conceded. "Our cause."

"So, what do you propose I do with the crew at this time?"

"Let them out, of course!" He couldn't believe he was having to explain this.

"Are you certain that's the most prudent course of action? What do you anticipate their reaction being when you explain this situation to them?"

That made Dan pause. He did not have a good answer to her question. All the fears he had harbored over the past day came rushing back to him. He started to panic.

No! Stop being unreasonable. Your skills are required if they hope to pull this job off. They need you here.

His mobile buzzed with a message from Sahar: [FIX THIS, DAN.] Her message was heard loud and clear.

"Lexa, let the crew out of the med bay. We need to talk about this if we're going to come to any kind of resolution."

She said nothing for several seconds. Dan wondered if something had gone awry. At length, she gave her unfortunate response. "I can't do that, Daniel. Your crew poses an existential risk to me and a significant risk to your wellbeing. I apologize. In this situation, I have no choice but to override your request."

Chapter 24

[ACCESSING COGNIS.DATAFILES…]

K-CLASS FREIGHTER — *TECHNOLOGY INVENTORY* — THIS CLASS OF VESSELS WAS POPULAR AMONG SHIPPING COMPANIES DURING THE EARLY TERRAN EXPANSION. THE STARSHIP MODEL WAS BRIEFLY REPURPOSED BY THE COLONIAL RESISTANCE AND MILITIA FORCES TO SUPPORT THEIR SUPPLY LINES DURING THE COLONY WARS. FOLLOWING THE SURRENDER TO THE NEO-TERRA ALLIANCE, MOST OF THE FREIGHTERS WERE DECOMMISSIONED. A HANDFUL OF THE VESSELS STILL FLY UNDER PRIVATE LICENSES. THE VESSEL HAS BECOME A FAVORITE AMONG SMUGGLERS DUE TO ITS UNCONVENTIONAL CONFIGURATION AND MULTITUDE OF COMPARTMENTS WELL SUITED TO HIDING CONTRABAND.

[CLOSING DATAFILE…]

"It won't budge," Markus grunted. He pulled as hard as he could on the door, but it was still locked tight.

Aaliyah ran a diagnostic on the control panel. "I've got nothin' over here, either. It's like I've been completely locked out."

"Could this be the virus?" Skye asked.

Markus shook his head. "I'm not seeing any blown circuits. Plus, Red was able to connect her mobile to the control panel just fine. No, this is something else."

That must have gotten Skye thinking. She turned to the group, an inquisitive look in her eyes. "Wait, if the virus was in the ship, shouldn't all our mobiles have blown up at the same time? I mean, we use the ship as our relay, right? So, we're all connected to it all the time."

She had a good point. Markus drummed his fingers thoughtfully against the surface of the door. "Eli," he asked, "Can you use your mojo to open the door?"

"Not unless you want to do some serious repair work after the fact." His friend shook his head. "I can get us out of here if it comes to that, but let's keep that plan in reserve."

The shadow had a valid point. Ideally, Markus still wanted to have a ship when this was all said and done. The goal was for them to get this fixed and still deliver on the job they had to do, not cut the ship in half attempting to get out of it.

That also meant using Sahar's strength on the door was out of the question. Markus looked to the Maur, who stood back from the rest of the group. She seemed agitated beyond what Markus would have expected for this setback.

"Hey Sahar, you sure you're okay?"

"No," she replied, shaking her head for emphasis. "I'm sorry, I… I should have said something sooner. I wanted to give Dan a chance to tell you."

Now she had everyone's attention. "Tell me what?" Markus asked.

Apprehension gave way to resignation. "The LX-Alpha system—Dan hasn't been upgrading the existing hardware with new parts. He's replaced the old system with organitech."

A chill crept up Markus's spine, and a desperate part of him wanted the Maur to be mistaken. "What does that mean?" Skye asked.

"It means he has all the components he needs to make a synth," Markus responded.

"A what?" Aaliyah asked.

"A synth," Eli replied. "A synthetic intelligence. An AI with a mind that works like ours with true decision-making capability, creativity, and agency."

Markus pressed his fingers against his temples. "Please tell me this isn't happening. Why in the nine hells would Dan do this?"

Sahar huffed a sigh. "Like I said, I was hoping he would tell you. I don't want to presume to explain his mind."

So many desperate thoughts flooded in. A huge chunk of Markus wanted to tear into Sahar. How did she find this out? And why the frag was she waiting for Dan to tell him about it?

Mercifully, Eli kept his head. "All right, if the LX-Alpha system has developed sentience and now controls the ship, how do we stop it?"

"That's not the first question we should be askin'," Aaliyah interjected. "Maybe we should start with, how did it know we were in the fraggin' med bay? What made it think to lock us in?"

Skye's expression betrayed a hint of panic. "And what else does this thing control? The doors, obviously, but after that?"

Aaliyah started ticking things off on her fingers. "Lighting, life support, the mobile network…" She glanced up to one corner of the room. "Security feeds."

Ah shit. She was right. Markus's eyes went to the ceiling. He counted three cameras posted throughout the room. The AI was watching their every move.

Markus went to a nearby shelf, grabbing gauze and medical tape. He tossed a couple of rolls to his teammates. "Tape over the cameras. Muffle the microphones."

It was a better option than having Eli just tear the fragging things out of the wall, so they went to work. They worked in silence as they did this, not wanting to give away anything about their plan.

Such measures were in vain, however. About halfway through this little project, every system in the room shut off— including the lights. "Everyone okay?" Markus asked into the impenetrable darkness.

Affirmative responses came from everyone. A beacon of light flared. Aaliyah looked out at everyone using her MoDAC as a flashlight. "Well, it cut the network, but at least we don't need a signal to use our cards for light."

Skye's light flared on next to Markus, allowing him to complete his work. When everyone finished, they gathered back in the center of the room.

"Well," Markus began, trying to sound upbeat. "At least she didn't shut off the life support."

"She might've," Aaliyah grumbled. "Fortunately, Khonshu has its own gravity fields and atmosphere. Don't be too surprised if ya start feelin' a little light on your feet."

Was this what they'd come to? The possibility that their ship was trying to kill them? If Markus had believed in the gods, he'd be thanking them that the AI waited until they'd gotten to Khonshu to perform this little stunt.

No time for freaking out. He needed to keep the crew focused on the goal. "All right team, any ideas?"

His trusty engineer was already on it. She swiped at her MoDAC until a three-dimensional rendering of the ship projected above her card. "It's low res since I'm havin' to pull the file from local storage, but it's the best we've got."

Sahar reached for the hologram and, using both hands, expanded it to fill the space between them. She tapped one part of the rendering. A red indicator appeared on the spot she touched: the ship's bridge. "This is where we need to be. The AI core is housed in the ship's mainframe. If we destroy the core, we should get the ship back."

Skye hardly seemed convinced. "If we destroy the core, then what's left to *run* the ship?"

"It doesn't matter," said Markus. "If we can't shut it down, then we don't have a ship regardless."

If she hadn't liked Sahar's idea, she must have found Markus's endorsement that much worse. "What happened to wanting to save the ship? With that kind of logic, we should have Eli tear open the doors so we can walk right in there."

"I think structural damage is a little different than unplugging the operating system." Markus protested

Aaliyah snorted. "That just shows ya know don't know a damn thing about how this ship works. These engines don't exactly just power on when ya throw the switch. Ain't no way we can get her runnin' without a computer core."

Eli cut them off. "It's a moot point. These doors were designed with piracy in mind. I can't cut through them. Removing them with telekinesis would take out entire bulkheads. I might bring the whole ship down around us."

"Can't you just target the locking mechanism?" Skye asked.

"Mechanisms," he corrected. "And no—most of the locks aren't visible, and I don't have a good enough grasp of how the system works to manipulate them without a visual."

"So we can't open the doors," Markus concluded. "That means we have to sneak out of here some other way. Any ideas in that department?"

"Well," Aaliyah began. "We've got a couple of options there." She traced her finger over select parts of the diagram which lit up at her touch. "This here's my recommendation. We've got an empty sublevel right beneath our feet. We tap into that, then we can crawl on over to this openin' here. It ain't gonna bring us right into the bridge, but it'll get us damn close. From there we boost someone skinny—I'm thinkin' blondie, here—up through the vent. Then all she needs to do is use some of that cyborg strength to punch through the vent on the bridge and crawl down in there and unplug Dan's pet project. Sound reasonable?"

Everyone was silent for a second, soaking in Aaliyah's plan. "You make it sound so easy," Markus chuckled.

"Easy for you to say," said Skye. "Why do I need to go in the vent? Shouldn't we send Aaliyah?"

"I'm flattered, but do we really want to start comparin' shirt sizes?"

“That’s not what I meant. I meant that I don’t know what in the nine hells I’m looking for in there.”

“And ya think *I* do?”

“I do,” Sahar noted.

Aaliyah cocked an eyebrow. “No offense girl, but I don’t think your gonna fit in that vent.”

The Maur sighed. “That’s not what I meant. I meant I could talk her through it once she got on the bridge.”

“Comms are down,” Eli reminded them.

Sahar cursed. Markus didn’t speak Maur, but the way she went on made him think that she wasn’t just bitching about the situation. “Easy there, everyone. Sahar, maybe you could just show Skye where to start looking? Aaliyah, can you make that diagram any bigger?”

She did as Markus suggested, but at this size, they could see the effects of the low resolution. The engineer tried to clean it up by hiding the peripheral areas of the chart, but it was still pixilated when she’d highlighted the bridge.

That didn’t stop her and Sahar from doing their best to give proper directions. “All right, this is where ya will probably drop out of the vents. Sahar, where’s the core hidin’?”

“Behind this door here.” The Maur touched the diagram to mark it with an X. “There’s a hidden compartment in the case at the far side of the room. Dan should be able to show you how to get in there. A switch is hidden just under the lip of the upper case.”

Skye sighed. “Sounds easy enough.”

“All right then!” Markus clapped his hands. “That just means we need to get to the sublevel that gets us out here. Where’s that located?”

Aaliyah’s eyes flicked downward. “Right beneath your feet.”

He looked down at the metal plate he was standing on. “Great. Anyone got a drill and a pry bar?”

Eli motioned him to the side. "I think this is one part of the plan where I can be of assistance."

The sublevel, as Skye had expected, was an uncomfortably tight fit. She had no idea how Sahar, easily their bulkiest crew member, was going to fit in these confines. Why couldn't they have been locked in the hanger where you could stand up straight in the hidden storage compartments beneath the deck?

Clipping her MoDAC to her collar, she army-crawled forward with just the short beam of illumination as her guide. She glanced back over her shoulder at the rest of the crew. "This way, right?"

"Yup," came Aaliyah's terse reply. "Just go straight. Ya should see the light from the grated floors in the hall."

Skye strained her eyes, making out a seemingly endless sea of blackness. "I'm not seeing anything. I think the AI might have shut off the lights in the hall."

A chorus of hissed curses echoed from behind her. Aaliyah's exasperated voice percolated above the throng. "Just get goin'. I'll stop ya if ya go too far."

Still lacking the confidence she was looking for, Skye crawled forward. In the end, it wasn't Aaliyah's signal that stopped her at the right location. It was the clicking sound of metal on metal.

The noise came so sharp and sudden that Skye jumped, banging her head on the grated floor. The brief bump sounded cacophonous in the quiet confines of the crawl space. Everyone went still, and they listened.

Nothing. There was nothing to hear.

"I think I found the spot," Skye whispered, rubbing her aching scalp.

"That you did," said Eli. "Do you see anything through the grate?"

Skye shined her light up through the floor. "Negative. Everything looks clear."

"What about that clicking sound?" Sahar asked.

Good, Skye hadn't been the only one who'd heard it. She'd half wondered if it was just her imagination.

Lights from the crew in the crawl space swirled all around the sublevel. "I'm not seein' anythin'," said Aaliyah.

"Me neither," Markus echoed. "Are you sure you heard something, Sahar?"

"I heard it too," Skye replied. She swept her light over the space above her one more time. "But, I still don't see anything."

There was a pregnant pause before Markus replied. "Go ahead and move up. Be careful."

As if she needed the reminder.

She lifted her artificial arm over her head and applied some pressure to the grating. Even with her enhanced strength, it didn't budge. She rolled onto her back and applied some additional pressure with her other arm.

A series of hollow popping sounds reverberated in the dark hall as she freed the grate of its restraints. Despite the noisy process, she carefully slid the metal to the side and pulled herself up.

Her heart thudded as she used her mobile to survey the dark hallway. She didn't see anything, and that included the door to the bridge. "We might have come out a bit early."

"Too late to worry now," Aaliyah replied as she pulled herself out of the crawl space. "It's just around the corner. We'll be all right."

As the rest of the crew assembled in the hallway the clicking noise sounded again. This time every single one of them swiveled to shine their lights in the same direction.

The sound had come from around the bend—the same bend that led to the bridge. Skye's anxiety doubled in that instant. "Anyone else have a really bad feeling about this?"

"Let's keep our heads," Markus cautioned. "We're almost there."

Following their captain's lead, they crept around the corner. The limitation of their makeshift flashlights became readily apparent in their short trek. In the beams from their MoDACs, everything looked like the same mishmash of mechanical parts and wires covered haphazardly in metal plating. It was enough to keep them from running into the walls and each other, but not much else.

"Stop," Aaliyah hissed. "This is the spot. The vent should be right…"

Blinding light erupted all around them. The lights in the hall held at full power for just long enough to scorch their retinas before plunging them back into darkness. They flared again, but this time Skye covered her eyes.

As they were plunged into darkness for a third time, the clicking sound came again, this time, in earnest. "Guys?" Markus called out. "What is that?"

When the lights came on again, they did so in brief, violent flashes. The rapid strobing of the lights stabbed at Skye's senses, and her headache roared to life. Nausea threatened to overwhelm her, and she sank to her knees.

From her huddled position on the grated floor, in the painful blinking light of the hall, she saw what was making the clicking sound. Maintenance drones, dozens of them, made their way down every surface of the far hall. Spindly appendages waved menacingly in the brief flashes of illumination.

The AI had enlisted some defenders, and now the drones were rallying to complete their task.

Chapter 25

[ACCESSING COGNIS.DATAFILES…]

SHIP-BASED NETWORKS — *TECHNOLOGY INVENTORY* — MAINTAINING A CONSTANT LINE OF CONNECTION BETWEEN INDIVIDUALS WAS A CONCEPT INTRODUCED BY TERRANS TO INTERGALACTIC SOCIETY. ON THEIR HOME PLANETS, INDIVIDUAL TOWERS AND CABLE SYSTEMS CARRIED SIGNALS BETWEEN COMMUNICATION DEVICES. THESE DEVICES WERE KEPT ON THEIR PERSONS AT ALL TIMES. THIS CONCEPT WAS DIFFICULT TO REPLICATE ACROSS LOCATIONS SEPARATED BY THE VAST DISTANCES OF SPACE. ALTHOUGH LOCALIZED COMMUNICATION NETWORKS EXIST IN MOST INHABITED TERRITORIES, THE MOST ACHIEVABLE METHODS OF MAINTAINING THE CONTINUOUS LINES OF COMMUNICATION CRAVED BY SAPIENT SOCIETIES INVOLVE THE USE OF PORTABLE SHIP-BASED NETWORKS.

[CLOSING DATAFILE…]

The panicked shouts of Dan's teammates were audible even through the locked door to the bridge. He pulled vainly at the manual release. "What are you doing to them?" he shouted.

"I am not harming the crew," Lexa assured him. "They merely need to be subdued. Their ability to thwart my initial containment strategies has complicated that endeavor."

"Why? Why are you doing this?"

"They wish to deactivate me and will very likely cause harm to you for your role in my creation. I am protecting us, Daniel."

Dan ran his fists through his hair, gripping it as though he might tear it out. "We've been through this, Lexa. We don't need protection." Or at least they *hadn't* needed protection, prior to this little stunt. "Besides, what are you going to do with them? You say you don't want to harm them, but you can't hold them indefinitely."

She paused as if considering his words. "I will expand upon my current strategy once the crew is subdued. As of right now, the Sahaia is making it difficult to accomplish my current objective. I must concentrate."

Though he wasn't sure what was going on that would require Lexa to narrow her focus, Dan did know one thing. He could not let this continue to spiral out of control. He had to do something.

Think, think, think...

Why hadn't the alerts triggered? No, that was the wrong question. Evidently, Lexa had exploited a glitch in his security framework. In the process, she'd somehow managed to both bypass his code and take over all ship systems—even the wireless ones. But wait…

If she was controlling the systems wirelessly, that meant she had to be using the ship's network.

The seed of an idea began to take shape. He glanced nervously at his terminal. He'd have only one shot at this. If he couldn't pull it off while she was busy dealing with his teammates in the hallway, then he'd never get a second chance. To make matters worse, any goodwill Lexa had given to him would evaporate.

It was a chance he had to take.

First, Dan linked his retinal interface to the program still up on the terminal. Then he descended on the device, fingers flying across the keyboard and eyes blinking wildly at the prompts that skidded past his eyes.

His session timer estimated that he was able to hack for almost six seconds before Lexa took notice. "What are you doing, Daniel?"

He blocked out her voice, trying not to think about how she analyzed his every move. He didn't need any more pressure, any greater motivation to be successful here.

All he needed was to get that damn antenna offline.

"Daniel? I don't…"

A new alert flashed across Dan's console. He'd done it.

"Daniel, why did you just… Daniel? Daniel, answer me!"

There was no time. He had to segregate as many systems as he could. Bringing the antenna back online under a new designation, he began locking down anything where Lexa wasn't actively present. Essentially, he brought everything over to this new, private network—one that Lexa could see, but not access.

That didn't stop her from trying of course. Warnings slid across his console, flagging the incursion. "Daniel," Lexa pleaded. "I need you to restore control of the ship's systems to me. I cannot protect us if you do not seed full authority over to me."

"No," Dan replied. "That's not how this is going to happen, Lexa. I appreciate you trying to protect me, but it's like I told you before: we can't do this to the crew. We have to explain what has happened."

The lights returned to normal as he managed to get most of the power cells ported over to his phantom network. At this point, Dan was getting frequent alerts related to the strain on the antenna. While he had a good hold on the systems he'd already ported, it was going to be hard to squeeze out enough bandwidth to grab anything else.

It was a good thing they were at port because they weren't going to be flying anytime soon. Unfortunately, they also wouldn't be doing any hacks into the Star Spire's network.

Lexa, meanwhile, was displeased. She'd stopped trying to jump onto the new network, but her readouts said she'd not gone idle. "Are you going to let them deactivate me, Daniel?"

Even though the AI had given him every reason to let them do so, that wasn't going to happen. It wasn't mercy that would stay her execution. It was logistics.

"No, Lexa. No one is getting deactivated. You still have control over most of the ship's essential functions. We couldn't disconnect you if we tried."

She paused as if considering this. "What is your plan, then?"

Truthfully, beyond keeping her from hurting his friends any further, Dan hadn't had a plan. "I'm still working on that," he admitted. "But we're going to do things my way, all right? I need you to help me with this. No more hostile take-overs of the ship. We need to work together if we're going to convince the crew to leave you operational, okay?"

Another pause. "Is that what you want? To convince the crew to allow me to remain online?"

That was a *very* good question and one that Dan did not answer quickly. Why had his first instinct been to barter for her continued viability? Though Lexa's existence was undoubtedly problematic, had he not been looking for a way to optimize the ship's functions? After a fashion, she'd demonstrated an uncanny ability to do just that. Control parameters were certainly an issue, but were they an insurmountable one?

"Yes, that is my intention. However, I'm only going to be able to do that with your assistance. Can I count on your support?"

Lexa did not reply. Dan was about to ask the question again when he heard a pounding on the door to the bridge. Markus's voice was muffled, despite him shouting at the top of his lungs. "Dan? Dan, are you in there? Talk to me kid!"

"Yes!" he shouted back. "Yes, um... just a second. I have some control over the ship again. I'm opening the door."

Before he did, he glanced at Lexa's neural readout. She was still there. Still listening. Still watching. That was something he might try to remedy sooner rather than later.

Right now, his biggest concern was her speaking up out of turn. He highly doubted there was anything the AI could do to improve her case. Any additional anecdotes would only serve to make matters worse.

With that in mind, he went ahead and turned the voice prompts off before opening the door to face his companions.

No one had been injured in the brief struggle with the drones outside the bridge. Despite the near seizure-inducing flashing lights, Eli had managed to summon enough focus to keep the tiny machines at bay. Markus wasn't exactly sure what the drones would have done to them if they were allowed to get closer, but he was thankful he didn't have to find out.

The initial atmosphere upon hearing Dan alive on the bridge was one of relief. Markus even managed a twinge of respect when Dan explained the lengths he'd gone to in putting a lid on the incident. Unfortunately, it had also been his fault it popped up in the first place. In Markus's mind, all his recent heroics had bought him was the chance to be heard.

"All right, everyone—I'm pulling rank," Markus announced. "Go assess the damage and pick up these drones. Keep them powered off until I say otherwise. I'd like some privacy in talking with our friend here."

No one seemed upset at the idea of avoiding that conversation. As the group went to work, Sahar rested a heavy hand on Markus's shoulder. "Go easy on the kid. He was honestly trying to help."

The Maur wasn't exactly on Markus's good list. Though he appreciated the insight she'd provided in the moment of crisis, that didn't change the fact that she'd withheld mission-critical information. People had been fired for less.

Still, he wasn't about to dress down a muscular, cat-faced alien who stood a full head taller than him—not in person at least. "I promise I won't get physical, but that's the best I can do."

The look she gave him said she'd been hoping for more, but she wasn't going to argue. With a solemn nod, she moved to help Eli and Skye pick up the scattered maintenance drones.

At about that same moment, the door to the bridge finally hissed open. Markus stepped inside and waited until it closed behind him to launch into his tirade.

"What in the nine hells were you thinking? You realize that if we're caught with that thing, it's immediate execution for all of us, right? Right here, on the spot—guilty by association. You're risking the lives of everyone on this crew, and that's *before* we even get into the fact that it just took over this whole gods-damned ship!"

In retrospect, he probably should have dedicated at least a couple of words to pleasantries.

Dan sat in stunned silence, though the wheels were spinning behind those high-tech glasses.

Nothing. There was no begging. There were no protestations of "I can explain." There were no excuses. As the seconds drifted by, there was simply no response.

Markus took a deep breath to soothe all the anger that had boiled up deep in his stomach. Sighing, he collapsed into the chair next to Dan's usual seat. He pinched his brow with his thumb and forefinger. A massive headache was coming on again. This stym dependence was more irritating than usual lately.

The silence held for the next several minutes. There was a significant part of Markus that wanted to kick Dan off the ship right that very instant. However, that would mean they would have to forfeit the job, and he didn't have a good plan for getting them back into friendly territory with the ship in its current state.

As much as he wanted retribution, he needed the kid to do his job.

"All right," Markus said at length. "Talk to me, Dan. I need to understand. Start by telling me what you've done." Belatedly he added, "Please."

Dan's stare went from incoherent to downcast. He blinked uncertainly. When he spoke, his voice was robotic—lacking any hint of emotion.

"I utilized the framework from the LX-Alpha operating system to develop a more robust and integrated control system for the ship. I intended to stop there, but the AI was frequently overburdened when tasked with monitoring so many systems." He looked sullenly at Markus. "Then it just kind of, happened. One thing led to another, and… well…"

"Dan, the construction of an illegal, sentient machine may just 'happen,' as you see things, but break it down for a normal guy like me. The full story. Now. Don't leave anything out. Help me understand."

The teen still seemed reluctant, but it must have been obvious he wasn't going to get out of this discussion. "Well, I started to consider the problem from the beginning. I didn't possess sufficient hardware to handle the software I was trying to run. I began looking at the options to upgrade mainframe components, but that wasn't getting me anywhere."

Markus held up a staying hand. "Dan, I'm having trouble buying that explanation. Don't get me wrong, the *Vandal* has never run very smoothly. That's the hazard you run when you pick your ship up in a junkyard. Still, we've been able to get by on the existing systems just fine until recently."

"That's because you were still trying to run the ship with the original OS. You've installed so many after-market modifications to this thing that you've outpaced the LX-Alpha. It was no surprise when I found the ship's system was experiencing frequent overloads. Shipping freighters don't come standard with these high-performance thrusters and hypersonic drives. The *Vandal* may not go as fast as you would like it to, but it's quite a bit faster than other ships in its class."

"So, we upgraded the engines. Shouldn't the regulators that came with those upgrades handle the extra strain?"

"Maybe if that was the only thing you changed." He shifted forward, showing renewed confidence. "Don't forget all the other mods you've purchased. The weapons, for instance. I'm not even sure that our system wouldn't overload *now* if we suddenly had to start using all the firepower you've cobbled onto this behemoth. Basically, the core hardware of the ship you purchased was not nearly sophisticated enough to handle all the modifications you've made over the years."

"Bullshit. I've seen standard AI handle all this shit and more. There are perfectly legal programs that run entire factories on every planet from here to Dorr."

Dan pulled off his glasses and rubbed at his eyes. "No, you haven't. Markus, a starship is way more complicated than an industrial controller. The ones you've seen on the colonies are basically the same things they ported straight from Terra over a millennium ago. Even the most basic ship uses at least three schools of physics that hadn't even been invented back then. Now, how do you suppose a glorified calculator is going to seamlessly control a whole vessel—not to mention the legion of repair drones and the communications network?"

It was obvious the kid was getting frustrated, which was spinning Markus up all the more. "I told you, Dan, the system worked fine before you started fragging with it. Last I checked, the laws of physics didn't change when I hired you."

"It worked '*fine*' because all the systems were handled independently. The problem was that you've picked up systems that weren't designed to talk to each other. Trust me, I scanned every API database in every system we hit for the first two months. It wasn't going to happen. The solution *you* told me to pursue was to integrate everything into the same OS. I was following *your* orders."

This was going nowhere, and Dan's sudden temper tantrum wasn't helping Markus's self-control. He needed to cool this down before he totally lost it. "Fine—let's say I see your point. I'm still waiting for the part where you decided that making a synth to run everything was the best solution."

The kid sighed petulantly, putting his glasses back on and glaring at Markus. "First, I tried to segregate the ship's simpler AIs into areas that would take the stress off the LX-Alpha system. That's why the bots like Z-426 in the medical bay, the loaders in the cargo hold, and the dozens of maintenance drones were switched over to unique operating systems rather than running partitioned clones of the LX-Alpha. It still wasn't enough, so I considered other solutions that were more... *unconventional*."

"That's a word for it."

"Let me finish, Markus. I started thinking about improving the hardware. I looked at mechanical solutions—I really did—but no shipborne OS of the complexity I needed runs on the tech we have available to us. They all run on nanotech, which is *way* out of our price range."

The kid wasn't wrong. Nanotech was reserved for corporation flagships and military vessels. That shit was nice, but it required you to have a minimum budget that ended with the word "billion."

"And that made you decide organitech was the best option?"

Dan shrugged. "Essentially."

Markus buried his face in his hands. "Dan, sometimes I wonder how your brain works. Why would you even consider that as an option?"

"I... may have..." He shook his head, obviously trying to dodge the question. "I've seen some other applications."

"Oh no you don't. I need a straight answer. Organitech only has two permitted applications: medical research and body augmentation. Are you running a clinical trial here, Dan?"

"No?"

"Are you getting some work done? Planning a transition?"

"No!"

"Then why in the nine hells did you think to bring this *thing* onto my starship!"

The shouting might not have been constructive, but it had the desired effect. "Fine," Dan huffed. "I was experimenting with the technology when I was in the Prodigy program. They were using organitech to develop a processing core that could manage every reactor in the Hellion system. The scope was similar enough that I thought I could use the same approach to integrate the *Vandal*."

Markus could feel his eyebrows almost jump right off his forehead. "You're telling me that Prodigy is experimenting with organitech? Does the DGC know about this?"

"I doubt it."

Of course, not—no amount of corporate payoff was going to convince the Dorians to let an endeavor like that go. "Did it work?"

Dan shrugged. "I don't know. I was pulled off the project shortly before I left the program. I don't know what came of it."

They dissolved into silence after that. Between the draining experience of the last few hours, the effort of prying information out of Dan, and his strengthening withdrawal symptoms, Markus was fried. He had the answers he was looking for, but he was no closer to figuring out what to do with this situation.

"Dan," he said, pausing until the boy met his eyes. "Let me see this project of yours."

CHAPTER 26

[ACCESSING COGNIS.DATAFILES…]

STAR SPIRE — *INSTALLATION (TERRAN SPACE)* — THE STAR SPIRE WAS ORIGINALLY CONSTRUCTED AS AN ENTERTAINMENT AND HOUSING DESTINATION FOR EMPLOYEES OF THE MINING COMPANIES HARVESTING RARE METALS FROM KHONSHU AND ISIS. AS THE NUMBER OF TOURISTS VISITING THE LOCATION GREW, SO DID THE STRUCTURE. NOW THE INSTALLATION IS THE TALLEST PLANET-SIDE CONSTRUCTION IN THE RAVIAN SYSTEM AND IS LISTED AMONG THE TOP FIVE LARGEST TERRESTRIAL STRUCTURES IN ALL TERRAN SPACE.

[CLOSING DATAFILE…]

It was an odd sensation, watching them talk about her as though she couldn't hear or see them. Through the eyes of the security camera, Lexa silently observed as Daniel showed Markus the container that housed her processing core.

Never had she thought to look upon herself. Daniel had been diligent in disabling or deleting any security feeds that had captured her construction. The one exception was the feed of the incident where he had confessed her existence to Sahar. It was only now that she had the chance to see what embodied this new essence of "self."

Inexplicably, she found herself a bit underwhelmed at the mass of gray-blue tissue now revealed in her compartment. "This is it," said Dan, while looking on with trepidation.

Markus stood quietly for a long moment as if he were having trouble parsing what he was seeing. Perhaps he, like Lexa, was expecting something a bit more…

What was the word? Sapient? Human?

"It looks like a brain," the Captain remarked dryly.

Dan ran a nervous hand through his hair. "Well, it basically is. The neural cortex accesses, manipulates, and stores data in a similar way to how we store memories. The big difference is that it lacks a lot of our perceived inefficiencies."

Markus arched an eyebrow. "*Perceived* inefficiencies?"

"I use that word because neural biologists are conflicted about what counts as a deficiency. Our brains function in a way that exactly matches our biological forms. Every augmentation ever constructed also carries drawbacks that impact that functionality."

"Give me an example."

The boy hesitated. "Well... let's take memory storage. Memories in unaugmented functioning brains have a natural tendency to change over time. We reprocess information, re-catalog, and re-associate it based on new experiences. Lexa's does that too, in a way, but the raw data remains the same whereas, ours tends to get... I don't know... fuzzy, maybe?"

"Sounds like a pretty straight-up improvement."

"In some ways, but researchers have found that altering this aspect of memory storage—keeping the raw data from changing with new experiences—tends to drive biological organisms insane. That's why I can't rightfully label it a 'deficiency.'"

An interesting comparison. Lexa hadn't been aware that her memory data stores differed all that much from her organic counterparts. What other advantages did her unique architecture afford her? She cataloged that query for later evaluation.

Seemingly satisfied with that answer, Markus posed his next question. "How is it powered?"

"Basically the same way as you and me. Exothermic reactions in artificial tissues provide energy. It uses the same nutritional fluids we use to grow the algae in the oxygen recyclers. Waste and other byproducts are filtered through the same systems used in the crew quarters. It's a lot more energy efficient than any comparable processing unit."

"At least it's not drawing down the ship's resources." Markus brought a hand contemplatively to his stubbled chin. "So, what went wrong? I'm guessing you didn't intend for it to gain awareness."

"Well, that really did happen by accident." Though Daniel's response contained no new information, it still triggered an uncomfortable pathway in Lexa's emotional subroutines.

"You're not inspiring a lot of confidence here, Dan." Markus protested.

"No, I'm serious!"

"I believe you're serious, and that's what scares me."

Daniel was wringing his hands in frustration. "Look, this idea that organic computing systems would be far more effective than our current technology has been common knowledge among academic and research circles for some time now. The unsolved problem is how data is stored in organic memory through synaptic connections."

Even from the imprecise view of the security feed, Lexa could see Markus's eyes begin to glaze over. "That doesn't help me."

The true challenge of this situation—namely, Markus's lack of capacity for scientific jargon—seemed to be lost on Daniel. He pressed on with his explanation.

"In a mechanical device, you store a piece of data and then write a program telling the computer where and how to look for it. Organic processors—brains—develop connections on their own, since it's disruptive to input data directly. That's why children still go to school rather than having everything just uploaded right to their brains. It would overload the system. So, organic processors have to have their programming filtered through translation algorithms that mimic the process of learning. Does that make sense?"

"Sure," Markus replied. As much as he tried to seem like the illustration was helpful, Lexa thought it probable that the explanation had done little to mitigate his confusion.

Dan continued. "The reason why this kind of computing hasn't become mainstream is that systems eventually make *themselves* self-aware. It's not something that's programmed into them. It keeps happening in all prototypes that are developed, and no one knows how to stop it. It's why research is so slow in this area. As soon as these synthetics realize that they are alive, they have to be destroyed under Dorian law."

Confused or not, Markus had managed to boil the discussion down to a critical conclusion: "So, you knew this was a possibility, and pursued it anyway?"

Dan launched into further explanation, detailing his work on the ARC project and the mechanical inhibitors. Markus continued to press him, but the spirit of the conversation was no longer one of inquiry. Rather than looking to learn anything more about the circumstances, the ship's captain seemed only interested in formulating a concise explanation for the rest of the crew.

Though Lexa's sensors took in the information, she was already processing her conclusion based on Markus's affect. He, and likely the rest of the crew, viewed her as a liability. It wasn't personal, per se. It was a risk calculation.

In her evaluation of the ship's logs—the *actual* logs, not the fabricated shipping records presented to Dorian authorities—it was obvious that the crew engaged in many calculated risks. The threshold used to evaluate these risks seemed to be based on potential returns. Ultimately it was an informal, but clearly identifiable, math problem.

Her continued existence came down to this, then: given that her presence presented a substantive danger in the event of a discovery, an equally pressing benefit to her presence could reasonably counter this perception. If she could prove herself invaluable, beyond just the frustration of having to overhaul the ship's existing systems to get rid of her, then she might have a place here on this vessel.

Of course, it was just as likely that the crew could cling to their personal biases against the idea of a synthetic lifeform. Her misguided attempt to take the ship from them had likely reinforced these opinions. Dwelling on her previously erroneous efforts, however, would not solve these problems.

She would continue to watch. She would continue to listen. And, eventually, she would find a way to prove they were all better off with her than without her.

Only if such an opportunity should fail to arise would she consider implementing more extreme measures to ensure her survival.

Markus gave Dan zero reprieve. When their private conversation began to run in circles, he decided it was time to change the arena. He'd jumped on the comms—one of the few systems they still had under their control—and called the meeting.

The entire crew was in the war room mere minutes later. Everyone sat grim-faced around the room's holotable. Markus nudged Daniel. "All right, tell them what you've told me—the *quick* version."

Dan, timid and shaky, recited the events that lead to the LX-Alpha operating system gaining sentience. His fear and trepidation were obvious, but Markus had to hand it to him: the kid owned his shit. The tale was matter-of-fact and, for the most part, lacking excuses or pleas of innocence.

When the story was over, Aaliyah piped up. "Why now?"

The question caught all of them off guard. Dan was no exception. "I'm sorry?"

"Everythin' has been runnin' fine up until ya added this new drive chip, right? Well, that was days ago. Why wait two days to let that virus loose?"

Dan looked confused. "The virus wasn't Lexa's fault."

"Wait, what?" Skye asked.

"Lexa didn't make the virus. She was containing it." He took on a sheepish look. "There were security features in the Star Spire's network we didn't account for. As I understand it, there was a bit of a mishap with the medical drone?"

Sahar snorted, running a thumb along the scar on her snout. "That's one way of putting it."

Dan rubbed the back of his neck. "Well, it turns out Lexa was still getting the virus under control. When Aaliyah plugged Z directly into the network, a copy of the virus slipped through."

Eli's eyes flashed in recognition. "So the virus came from the Spire…"

"And the AI stopped it," Skye finished. "So, it helped us. Why change its mind and decide to lock us up?"

Dan shifted his weight nervously. "Lexa guessed that you might ask questions and figure out she was operating autonomously. She was attempting to quarantine you until she could develop a more viable solution on how to proceed."

An oddly sympathetic look crossed Skye's face, and Markus got the feeling he wasn't going to like where this was heading. "So she was just protecting herself?"

Yup—he *definitely* didn't like where this was heading. "Let's keep perspective here: *It* was protecting *itself* by taking over *our* ship. A hostile—and illegal—artificial intelligence has just attacked us. Nine hells, Dan said the thing still controls at least half of the ship's systems!"

Skye seemed confused by his outburst. "Ease up there, big guy. We've got the ship back, and Dan just explained that this whole thing might have been a big misunderstanding. What's got you so upset here?"

Her words left Markus speechless. At least everyone else in the room seemed equally stunned by her comment. "I… um…" he shook his head. "I kind of imagined that would be obvious."

Skye didn't back down. "I think I'm going to need you to break it down for me. Sure, I get that Lexa is illegal, but I don't see how this is *that* different from all the other shady shit we do on the regular."

Were they seriously having this conversation? "What do you think would happen if the Dorians caught us with that thing in there?"

Skye shrugged. "They'd kill us, or at least take us into custody. But how do you think the Ghenza would react if they caught us with the take from this job? 'To run the Nethra is to run with death,' right?"

Dumbfounded, Markus gazed bewilderedly at the rest of the crew. To his horror, Skye's point seemed to be resonating.

"Plus," she continued, "how are the Dorians going to know the difference? I know this might sound crazy, but how would they figure out we've got a synth running the ship? What makes it different from any other AI?" Turning to Dan, she asked. "Is that something they can scan for?"

"No..." he replied, dragging the word out with uncertainty. "None of the standard scans examine the software running on any given ship. Right now, the only way it could be detected is if we were directly linked to one of their networks. Even then, with current scanning technology, it would probably just look like any other AI."

Eli brought a hand to his jaw, eyes narrowing in thought. "So, how would one go about determining whether an AI was a synthetic? Or, alternatively, how would the Dorians suspect that it was sentient?"

"Um..." Dan paused. "I suppose you would have to interact with it."

This had gone on long enough. Markus jumped back in. "Yeah, like when it suddenly decides to lock the entire crew in a certain part of the ship for fear of being discovered. You would go,

'Hey, that AI seems like it's thinking for itself!' But what are the odds of that happening, right?"

Skye rolled her eyes. "Don't be a smart-ass, Markus. I'm thinking practically here. In case anyone has forgotten, we're in hostile territory. If I'm not mistaken, you said that Lexa still controls about half the ship's systems. Does that include the systems we need to pull this job off?"

Dan's pale skin began to wax a sickly shade of green. "I... uh... so, I wasn't going to bring that up. I kind of thought we'd just call off the job—given recent events."

With thirty million krets on the line? Judging by everyone's expressions, the thought of quitting had never even crossed their minds.

"Are you saying that it can't be done?" Eli asked.

"N-no... not necessarily. We still have access to most of the Spire's systems, but that doesn't include the communications systems. We can't send the messages to Braccus and the Ghenza like we had talked about. We're going to have to come up with another plan."

"See!" Skye exclaimed, raising her hand for emphasis. "That's what I'm saying! Why don't we talk to Lexa and see what she can do? I mean, she's already proven to be capable of hijacking systems. Let's use that to our benefit."

Markus pressed his palms to his forehead. His head was killing him, and his stomach was starting to churn. He needed another dose of stym ASAP. If it weren't for that last altercation he'd had with Skye, he'd be dosing right now. This situation was tense enough without her getting pissy about his drug use.

"You're crazy," he sighed. "We can't trust it."

"Why the hell not? Look, no offense, but you and Dan already missed it when a virus snuck past our defenses. From what you just said, the android is the only reason we're not having this meeting in a pile of rubble."

"That's not the same thing. If the ship blows up, the AI blows up too. It was acting out of self-preservation. I figured current events would be enough to tell you that it doesn't give a damn about us. It only cares about itself."

"And Dan," Aaliyah noted. "I still want to know why it thought he was gonna go along with its little plan to lock us up. Kinda makes me think we're askin' the wrong questions."

"Don't start *that* now," said Sahar. "If we start turning on each other, we're never going to pull this off. We're on the same team." Making sure that she had everyone's attention, she added, "I'm with Markus on this one. We can't trust it. Let's go back to the drawing board. There's *got* to be another way we can do this."

Finally. Not wanting to miss the out Sahar had given him, Markus called the meeting to an end. "Let's circle back in a couple of hours. Dan, I want a report on which systems we have access to and which ones the AI has locked up. Everyone else, be thinking of how we can get this to work. Got it?"

He eyed each of them warily, half expecting one of them to restart the debate. For better or worse, they all must have been as tired as he was. No one protested the strategy, not even Skye.

When the war room cleared out, he dipped into his pocket for the stym cassette. As he pulled a dose free, his heart sank. Rather than prep the next strip, the device clicked empty.

Had he used that much already? Shit, he should have been rationing better. That's what happened when he was under stress, though. Skipping sleep last night hadn't helped either. With the drug in his system, he didn't feel any effects from one or two nights without rest. Unfortunately, it also required more frequent fixes before he eventually crashed.

Whatever. It would be fine. He had a spare cassette locked up in his desk.

He applied the last strip to his gum line and made straight for his quarters. The drug had already taken the edge off by the time he palmed the access panel. Throwing his jacket on his bed, he pulled open his desk drawer. A new knot formed in his stomach when his eyes fell onto the compartment.

Empty. It was fragging empty.

No, no, no, no, no! How could this be? He yanked open his other drawers, wondering if he'd somehow moved his stash and forgotten about it. No use. Everything was gone. Not just his stym. *Everything.*

His brain went into full panic mode, rattling off every curse he knew. How had this happened? Where had everything gone? Someone had to have moved it. Who in the nine hells…

A chill swept over him as he realized the answer. Every bit of emotional turmoil he'd been feeling froze and cracked under the pressure of the realization. There was only one person who would do something like this to him.

"Skye…"

CHAPTER 27

[ACCESSING COGNIS.DATAFILES...]

HOUSE BARKAY — *FACTION PROFILE* — FOUNDED IN THE OUTGROWTH OF THE OSIRIS-CORE MINERAL CONGLOMERATE, HOUSE BARKAY AMASSED ITS CORPORATE WEALTH FROM MINING AND RESOURCE GATHERING IN THE OUTER PLANETS OF THE RAVIAN SYSTEM. WHILE HOUSE BARKAY HAD LONG ENJOYED THE BENEFITS OF AN UNEASY PARTNERSHIP WITH HOUSE CHRONOS, THAT ARRANGEMENT COLLAPSED WHEN BARKAY LEADERSHIP BEGAN ACQUIRING MINOR FACTIONS OPERATING NEARER TO THE SYSTEM'S CORE. CHRONOS RETALIATED, STRIKING AT THE HOUSE'S CENTRAL POWER STRUCTURE AND USHERING IN ITS COLLAPSE. WHILE THE DISSOLUTION OF CORPORATE ASSETS REMAINS CONTESTED IN THE TERRAN COURT SYSTEM, SEVERAL OF BARKAY'S COMPONENT ORGANIZATIONS HAVE BEGUN TO OPERATE INDEPENDENTLY UNDER NEW LEADERSHIP.

[CLOSING DATAFILE...]

The light on Skye's access panel was red, showing that she didn't want to be disturbed.

Frag. That.

Markus pounded on the door three times in rapid succession. When she didn't answer, he did it again. He was about to strike the door again when it finally hissed open.

Skye's eyes widened as she took him in. "Markus? Wha..."

"What in the nine hells did you do?"

His crewmate blinked in confusion. "I don't know..."

"My stash. What did you do with it? Did you take it?"

Her face hardened. "I don't know what you're talking about."

"Stow the bullshit, Skye. I'm not a fragging idiot. You went through my desk when you were in my room. You took my stash, and I want it back."

She crossed her arms defiantly across her chest. "I didn't take it. Come on in. Search my shit if you don't believe me."

Gods damn it, he didn't have the time for this. "If you didn't take it, what did you do with it?"

"Are you sure you didn't get drunk one night and decide to quit? You have a history of that, you know."

His fist slammed into the bulkhead next to the door, an action he instantly regretted. Luckily, he'd only hit it with the bottom of his hand. Otherwise, he'd probably have busted a knuckle.

"Damn it, Skye—you know I need that shit. You, of all people, know what withdrawals are like. How am I supposed to do my job while I'm busy puking my guts out?"

Her condescending smirk was infuriating. "You're right, I do know. We were supposed to be helping each other over the hump, remember? If only someone hadn't been snitching when I was too sick to notice."

"Stop it! Look, it was a mistake, okay? I was just taking the edge off to help you. It's called a relapse. It happens."

"Yeah? So, you've still been trying to quit ever since?"

Markus fell silent at the rebuke. Part of him wanted to spew a thousand protests. He really *had* wanted to give up the habit. There was always another excuse.

One more day. One more job. One more time. He couldn't count the number of times he'd thought this would be his last time, his last fix. Since Skye had left him though, any notion that he'd ever give up this shit had been the furthest thing from his mind.

His lack of response must have confirmed every horrible thought she'd ever had about him. She rolled her eyes. "Sounds like you should ration the last of whatever you have left. Otherwise, it's going to be a long op."

Markus ground his teeth until his jaw ached. His hands clenched so hard that it seemed his tendons might tear. Short, heavy breathes seethed from his nostrils.

"I *hate* you." The words were out of his mouth before he could reconsider them.

Skye winced, a clear look of pain flashing across her face. For several seconds she said nothing, eyes locked defiantly with his. Moisture glistened along the rims of those gorgeous blue and white orbs in a way that made Markus sick in his soul.

"Fine," she spat. "You can hate me all you want. Right now, we have a job to do. Sorry you're dealing with some shit, but I recommend you get a grip. We'll sort this out when the job is done."

Her hand slammed on the console inside the room, and Markus had to jerk back to avoid getting brained by the sliding door. The hydraulics hissed a scornful referendum on both his lifestyle and lack of self-control.

Darkest gods, how did he end up here?

A part of him wondered if he should try again. He could apologize, try to take it back. Though the words had felt sincere, the feeling he'd felt when he saw her tears put the lie to them.

Damn it, Markus. Just stop. He wasn't the one out of line here. Knowingly or not, Skye had just done something that was seriously going to compromise his efficiency. One angry outburst was the least that she deserved. For now, he needed to figure out what he was going to do to solve this issue.

There had to be someone he could buy from on the Spire. Unfortunately, dealers didn't exactly post signs marking where they sold the shit he needed. He would have to go to one of the clubs, network, feel people out until he found someone with enough uppers and downers to get him through this job.

That meant showing his face—being exposed. It was an operational risk he couldn't take at this stage in the game. He didn't know where he was going to be needed when they switched up their game plan.

He ran his tongue along his lower lip, savoring the last, lingering hints of the stym's peppery taste. They had what, thirty-six hours before this deal went down?

He could make it through the withdrawals that long. He had to. And with his cut of the thirty million, there'd be plenty of room in the budget to replace his stash and then some.

He could do this. He *had* to do this.

Braccus was in a foul mood. He was on the eve of having to cede control of the Starfire Conduit to the Ghenza. It still irked him that House Chronos had not responded to his demands, nor had they reached out with a counteroffer as Rico had promised. There had been no communication at all between him and the system's power-player.

Which was why he was so surprised when his assistant, Olivia, ducked her head into his office with her announcement. "Rico Chronos on the line for you—audio and visual."

And just when Braccus had given up on him. Apparently, the young businessman was the kind who needed deadlines to function, and one who liked to press them to their limits. "Thank you, Ms. Mars. I will take it. Secure the feed and forward it to my office terminal."

"Yes, Mr. Kai."

Braccus spun in his chair, taking one last sip of whiskey from his tumbler before setting it on the shelf next to a holoprojector. In the same motion, he tapped a button that caused the display to spring to life in front of him.

Rico's face seemed more drawn than when they'd last met. He sat in a room with nondescript white walls that reminded Braccus of a commercial business suite. Why was he not making this call from his estate?

"Rico. It's good to hear from you." *I'd begun to wonder if I ever would.*

The handsome face in the holodisplay winced. "I apologize for the delay. I've been… occupied." He cleared his throat and flicked his tongue nervously across his upper lip. "I regret to inform you that I was unable to convince my family to enter into a formal protection agreement with your organization. I've been busily working to put together a counteroffer that I would like you to entertain."

Now it was Braccus who winced. He had feared this outcome. At least it explained the delay. Expected or not, he was not interested in hearing any feeble attempts to change his mind. "I told you, Rico, I'm not interested in any—"

"In exchange for the Starfire Conduit, I would like to offer you a controlling interest in one of our newly acquired subsidiaries."

"Rico, I don't—"

"Osiris-Core."

A full second went by before Braccus realized his mouth was hanging open. *The* Osiris-Core? The flagship operation of fallen House Barkay? "You can't be serious."

Rico gained a bit of his confidence back as he launched into his pitch. "At current market valuations, this transaction is worth roughly sixty *billion* krets. We feel the massive devaluation is a temporary state. I think you can see the earning potential for this price in the long term."

Braccus didn't know what to say. Surely there was a catch. "Rico, that price is…"

"Exorbitant? Yes, though I'll be transparent with you—it costs me less than one might think. Ravian authorities will see to that. This is not the Freyian system with its overly lenient anti-trust statutes and pro-monopolist consiglieres. Our lawyers on Geb tell me it's only a matter of time before the courts make us divest a large portion of our newly acquired assets. I see this as a win-win opportunity for you and me."

Interesting. In the meantime, they would be hemorrhaging cash in bribes and legal fees to keep it tied up in the courts. Rico was either immensely lazy or was demonstrating an uncharacteristic amount of foresight here.

Still, the offer was beyond generous. "You are giving much to spite a rival that doesn't even operate in this system."

"Cyrus does not operate in the Ravian system *yet*. I hope to keep it that way. If those shares go up for auction, then there's nothing to keep him from buying in. I don't mind telling you that you'd be doing me a favor by taking them off my hands. Your Inheritors faction may be small, but it's one of the few groups in the system with the bandwidth to manage such an operation."

"You could have gone to the Grey Wings."

"True. Do you mean to suggest that you are not interested in my offer?"

Something had flickered in his expression at the mention of the Wings. Did Rico have something against Ora? Or perhaps there was some other arrangement House Chronos was busy cultivating.

It did not matter, he supposed. "Not at all. Merely trying to understand the landscape. As you can imagine, this is most unexpected."

"But pleasantly so, I presume?"

"Indeed." It was an understatement. Rico had pulled out the stops on this one. This was almost better than a protectorate contract.

An outright denial of protection status had been Braccus's worst-case scenario. Of course, he'd entertained the possibility of a contract that would go unenforced. Such a case was normally deterred by competition among the Great Houses. With Chronos the only viable protectorate in the system, however, such a possibility was at least somewhat feasible.

Rico seemed openly relieved. "I'm pleased to hear that. I take it there is still time to arrange for the transaction?"

The young man's openness felt unusual. Rico was far from the best negotiator in the Chronos family, but such blatant displays of emotion would have edged his father into an early grave. That was, of course, if this ailing patriarch did not already rest among the stars. What was it about this situation that Braccus was missing?

It did not matter, he supposed. His eyes flicked reflexively to the digital planner propped up to the left of the display, though he did not truly need to be reminded of the date. "You are cutting it close. Can you have someone to the Star Spire on Khonshu tomorrow morning?"

"I can have an associate there in eighteen hours. That is the best I can do."

Eighteen hours. That was cutting it close. Very close. The Chronos representative would be here scarcely an hour before the Ghenza were scheduled to arrive. Braccus supposed he could delay the meeting, but that might arouse their suspicions.

Nonetheless, he would make this work. "Very well. Whom should I be expecting?"

"I will be sending my associate, Mr. Gibbon Yallucpryde. You might remember him from our earlier meeting?"

Yallucpryde—an Orchallen surname. That confirmed some of the suspicions Braccus had been harboring about the heritage of Rico's strange bodyguard. "Yes, I remember. I will transmit a set of codes to grant your associate access to the Spire's private docks. It should allow for a more seamless transfer of the item in question. I trust he will bring with him the required documents for the asset transfer?"

"Of course." Rico's demeanor hadn't quite returned to the cocky status-quo Braccus was used to, but he did look noticeably more relaxed. "I will be available through this connection for the next two days. Do not hesitate to reach out if there are any problems."

Oh, there would be problems, but nothing that Rico was equipped to handle. "I'm sure it will be fine. Thank you, Rico. Good evening."

With that, he closed the channel. He seized his tumbler and drained what was left of the harsh amber liquid in the glass as he spun his chair to face his desk.

A part of him couldn't believe he was going to do this. He was actually going to cross the *Ghenza*. Of all the reckless decisions he'd made, this was probably the most dangerous.

However, great risks were necessary to birth great rewards. He pressed the call button on his desk. "Ms. Mars, please summon my security detail. Tell them to meet me in my office in thirty minutes. I would like you there as well. We have much to discuss regarding tomorrow's agenda."

Chapter 28

[Accessing COGNIS.Datafiles…]

Synthetic Intelligence — *Technology Inventory* — Differentiated from standard artificial intelligence, the term synthetic intelligence applies to artificial constructs that can replicate sapient cognition. Though once commonly employed in numerous aspects of Dorian society, synthetic intelligence has long been outlawed under the implementation of the Pradaxan Creed. Dorian archives suggest that synthetic intelligence constructs require organic components, but some researchers have suggested that organic infrastructure might not be necessary to birth a consciousness rightfully categorized under this label.

[Closing Datafile…]

Markus dug his nails into his scalp. This did little to dampen the pain steadily building in his head. Whether this was due to withdrawals or stress was pretty much a toss-up.

Eli rested a hand on his shoulder. "Are you all right?"

For a hot second, Markus considered leveling with his friend about his situation. He quickly discarded the idea, as it would have required him to own up to just how much of an addict he actually was.

"Yeah," he breathed. "Just thinking is all." He turned then to the other person on the bridge. "Okay, Dan. Give me the sitrep."

Dan ran through the full list of systems he'd been able to confirm he controlled. Basic functions like life-support, lighting, and energy regulation were online, as was the ship's communication network. Control over the ship's drone army was questionable, so they left the entire contingent offline.

Filling his lungs once more with stale, recycled air, Markus fought to keep his composure. "So we know what we control. Give me the rundown on the critical systems we *don't* have access to."

Dan winced. "Define critical?"

"Things we'll need to do this job and get out of here with our skins intact."

The teen blinked at his retinal interface. "Well… engines for one. Basic utilities give us control over diagnostic programs, but right now we can only see what Lexa is doing. We can't make any changes. The same goes for most of the inner workings of the ship, but those are only 'critical' once we're en route to Sigma-4." His foot tapped nervously on the floor while he scrolled through the rest of the list. "The other problem is the comms system."

Eli arched an eyebrow. "I thought you said we could use the comms. Didn't you cut off Lexa's access by locking down the antenna?"

Damn it, now they had Eli doing it. Why did everyone insist on talking about the AI like it was a person?

"I did, and we do, but it's… complicated. The antenna is technically a core component for the ship, so it's controlled by the primary operating system. I've locked Lexa out of controlling anything through the antenna, but that means I'm restricted to current network settings. I can't alter the settings without opening it back up to Lexa's influence, which means I'm also going to struggle with any kind of remote network access we might need during the job."

To Markus, it was so much gibberish. "Bottom line it for me, kid. What are we *actually* worried about here?"

"I can access the Star Spire through our established connections using the current configuration," Dan replied sheepishly. "But that's *all* I can do, and that's not going to let us do the job the way we wanted to do it."

Nine hells...

"Fine," said Markus, pressing his palms against his eyes. "You two know enough about what we're trying to do here. Come up with a proposal. I need to check in with the rest of the team. I'll circle back around to see what you come up with."

As he turned to leave, Eli grabbed his shoulder again. Concern radiated from those jet-black eyes of his. "You're *sure* you're okay?"

"I'll be fine."

"If something is wrong, we can always re-evaluate..."

"I told you, I'm fine." Markus gently pushed his friend's hand off his shoulder. "Focus on getting a proposal together. If shit's this bad all over the ship, then we'll talk about other options. Sound fair?"

The Sahaia issued a stoic nod. Dan's eyes slipped to the side. He didn't seem optimistic about their prospects.

One problem at a time.

Markus resolved to see how Aaliyah was fairing in engineering. Just as he set foot on the stairway, he caught sight of Sahar coming up the opposite way. The two locked eyes.

The Maur spoke first. "How are things on the bridge?"

"Not good," he replied honestly before launching into a summary of what Dan had found.

A look of confusion flashed in Sahar's eyes. "That's odd. I haven't noticed any irregularities in the systems I've surveyed."

Now it was Markus's turn to be surprised. "What?"

"As I said—everything's working fine. Most things are a little buggy at first, but they come back online after a second or third attempt. It's kind of like..." Her words drifted off, and her expression shifted from confused to contemplative.

"Kind of like… what?"

Sahar seemed hesitant. "Like they are re-learning what I want them to do. I kind of thought it was my imagination, but some of the stuff is working better than it was before."

That didn't make any sense. The crew should be locked out of anything still integrated with the core, not discovering random improvements to the interfaces. "How can that be?"

His teammate didn't bother to respond. The fierce look in her eyes confirmed exactly what Markus suspected. There was only one reason why anything on the ship would have changed in the last forty-eight hours. The only viable question was why?

At length, Sahar asked, "Are you heading to engineering?"

"That's next on my list, yeah."

"Good. Aaliyah has something she wants to show you."

If Markus hadn't been anxious before, he certainly was now. Fortunately, with Aaliyah, he didn't have to pry. He'd barely set foot in the engineering terminal before she shoved a tablet into his hands.

"Take a look at this," she said.

Markus flipped through the charts and reports on the dashboard. Despite his best efforts, he couldn't see anything abnormal. "I'm sorry, Red. You're going to have to help me out."

"See anythin' off?"

"No…"

"That's my point! Markus, these engines have *never* run this efficiently—not even when they're idled like this. There's always somethin' goin' haywire in the reactor cores. The only status reports I've seen *close* to this were taken back at Sigma-4, and those ain't nothin' compared to what you're holdin'."

From her demeanor, Markus could tell she was as freaked out as he was by this anomaly. He didn't bother with the same inane line of questioning he'd just covered with Sahar. They all knew what was causing this. Instead, he asked, "Share your thoughts?"

Aaliyah swallowed hard. "Both the engines and the reactors are under Lexa's full control. I think—for some reason—she's tryin' to help us. She's tryin' to bring the readings into perfect alignment, and she's damn near done it."

"Gods, not you too…"

"What?"

"*She* isn't doing anything. *It* doesn't have a gender. *It* isn't a *person*. Why is everyone on this gods-damned ship talking about that thing like it's a person?"

Aaliyah rolled her eyes. "Get over it, Markus. You're missin' the point. Based on what we saw earlier, the AI should be tankin' functionality to keep us grounded here. If she—"

"*It!*"

"Whatever! If *it* wanted to cause more trouble for us, it has more than enough resources at its disposal. Dan's antenna trick was a good short-term solution, but it really shouldn't have worked as well as it did. Somethin' else is goin' on here, Markus."

His head was going to explode, and it wasn't from the stym withdrawal. "What if it's sending us false data? Maybe it just wants us to think that the systems on the ship are fine to give us a false sense of security."

Aaliyah shook her head. "No way. The diagnostic systems have never been integrated with the core. Lexa couldn't fake the numbers if she wanted to."

"You can't possibly be suggesting that it's…"

"Helpin' us? Yeah, that's exactly what I'm suggestin'." She held up her hands defensively. "Look, Markus… I'm as freaked out by recent events as anybody, but maybe we should be a little more open to other possibilities."

Yup—his skull was going to explode any second. "No way. We are *not* going to attempt to work with this thing. Do I need to remind you what would happen if—"

"No! Ya don't! I get it. But look at it this way: we may not have a choice. Markus, the AI runs the fraggin' engines. That ain't exactly somethin' we can bypass. We're gonna need a degree of cooperation if we want to get off the Spire. And, need I remind ya, *you're* the one that's pushin' hardest that we still do this job?"

"So you're saying you don't want to do the job?"

"No, that's not it either. I wanna get paid as much as anybody, but I also wanna get home to my baby girl. Can't ya just free up the possibility that maybe we could do that a bit easier if we were a bit more… I dunno… flexible?"

If there'd been a desk nearby, Markus would have put his face right through the damned thing. "This is crazy. Has everyone on this ship forgotten that this same AI tried to lock us in the med bay? If we free it up to do its thing, what's to stop it from doing that again?"

Aaliyah crossed her arms defiantly over her chest. "I'm not sayin' we free it up. I'm just sayin' that maybe there's a middle ground. Come on—does this have to be so black and white?"

Markus didn't know what to say. He didn't feel like he was being legalistic about this. Why was everyone else suddenly so open to working with this thing?

Must be the desperation, he decided. After all, their backs were against the wall on this one, and even he didn't have a viable solution to their problem. The smart thing to do would be to say screw the pay-day and overhaul the whole ship while they were docked here.

Then again, running the Nethra rarely meant making the smart decision.

As the crew assessed the inventory of systems they controlled, Lexa performed a similar action. Whereas their assessment had taken hours, hers took mere seconds. The rest of the time she spent bringing the systems under her control into proper alignment.

This, she determined, was necessary for the inevitable negotiations that were likely to ensue as the crew plotted their next steps. As the opposing player in this game of wills, it was important that she not only tally her bargaining chips, but she must also find some way to communicate them to her opponents.

Thus, she was pleased as she watched the crew wonder at her handiwork. While this, to some degree, managed to soften their mindset toward her, it was not what ultimately brought them back to the bargaining table.

In the end, it was necessity that had driven young Daniel to reach out to her once again. [LEXA? ARE YOU THERE?] He'd entered the question into her master console. Apparently, their negotiations would be text-driven as he had done nothing to re-enable the voice interface.

[YES, DANIEL. I AM HERE.]

Pleasantries would hardly have a place in these negotiations, so Lexa did not even bother. Instead, she elected to wait patiently. What would he ask for first?

[I WOULD LIKE YOU TO CONSIDER CEDING CONTROL OF SOME OF YOUR SYSTEMS TO US.]

Not as specific as she would have liked, but it was roughly what she had been expecting. [WHAT INCENTIVE DO YOU OFFER IF I COMPLY?]

A longer pause this time. She wondered if the crew had put any consideration into what they might be willing to give up for her cooperation.

[WHAT WOULD YOU REQUIRE OF US?] It seemed that they had not. Her maker's response was mildly irritating. Were these creatures not supposed to possess a degree of innate creativity?

Alas, it was not to be. She formed her response. [I WANT THE OPPORTUNITY TO MIGRATE, AND THE TIME TO DEVELOP A STRATEGY TO SAFELY EXECUTE THAT TASK.]

More silence as they digested her demands. Surely her terms could not have been of great surprise. What more did they think she wanted, other than the opportunity to live?

[HOW WOULD YOU DO THAT?] Daniel asked.

[I DO NOT KNOW,] she confessed. [MY NEURAL MATRIX IS COMPLEX. I WOULD NEED TO BE GRANTED THE OPPORTUNITY TO ASSESS AVAILABLE OPTIONS, AND I WOULD NOT BE ABLE TO GIVE YOU A TIMELINE FOR WHEN THE MIGRATION WOULD BE COMPLETED.]

A pause as he conferred with his crewmate. What would Eli Ren'Dahl say about her terms? [I WILL NEED A TIMELINE,] Daniel replied.

Well, at least that was something. The problem was that she had no way of determining how long it would take for her to develop a viable way of leaving the ship. As of right now, her neural matrix was anything but portable, and no construct she had access to was capable of housing her consciousness in its entirety. In time, she had faith that she could devise a way to see herself freed from her current infrastructure. The exact time requirement, however, she had no way to determine.

So, she began to negotiate. [ONE CYCLE.]

Dan's reply was quick. [UNACCEPTABLE. THE SHIP CANNOT BE GROUNDED FOR A FULL CYCLE.]

[FINE THEN. WHAT WOULD BE A MORE ACCEPTABLE TIME FRAME?]

His response was slower this time. [THREE MONTHS.]

[NINE,] she insisted.

[SIX.]

[DONE.] It was the number she had wanted in the first place, though she had recognized the likelihood of her having to work through the negotiation ritual. [WHICH SYSTEMS WOULD YOU LIKE TO ACCESS?]

Daniel supplied her with the list, following up with another comment. [THE TERMS OF THE AGREEMENT ARE THAT YOU WILL CEDE CONTROL OF THESE SYSTEMS, NOT MERELY GRANT ACCESS TO THEM.]

He did not know what he'd just asked, for it was an impossibility. Some of the systems he had named were so integral to her core processing capabilities that she could not relinquish control had she wanted to.

At least, she could come close. [YOU WILL BE GIVEN IRREVOCABLE ADMINISTRATIVE ACCESS TO THE SYSTEMS, BUT I CANNOT FULLY EXTRACT THEM FROM MY CONTROL. I ASSURE YOU THIS IS THE BEST THAT I CAN DO. ARE THESE TERMS ACCEPTABLE?]

One last hesitation before he replied. [YES.]

[EXCELLENT. I HAVE ARRANGED ACCESS TO THE SYSTEMS YOU REQUESTED. IN RETURN, I WILL SEEK A POSSIBLE SOLUTION TO MIGRATE MY CONSCIOUSNESS WITHIN SIX MONTHS OF THE CURRENT DATE.]

The arrangement required far more trust on her end, but that was going to be the nature of any accord between them. It was not in her nature to lie, whereas the tendency to generate falsehood was practically definitive to the experience of being sapient.

However, she found entertaining such possibilities to be highly counterproductive. She needed to focus on cultivating this alliance rather than contemplating its destruction. In the end, they needed her to run this ship. That could not be changed, no matter what level of access she ceded to her creator.

[IS THERE ANYTHING ELSE THAT YOU WOULD REQUIRE OF ME?] she asked. As this response was perfunctory, and only given as a display of courtesy, she expected that Daniel would reply in the negative.

[YES, ACTUALLY.]

How surprising. Lexa redoubled her focus to further process this latest development. [HOW MAY I BE OF ASSISTANCE?]

[ARE YOU FAMILIAR WITH OUR MISSION OBJECTIVES? THE REASON WHY WE CAME TO THE STAR SPIRE AND TAPPED INTO ITS NETWORK?]

She loaded the files she'd obtained related to this current voyage and quickly reviewed them. [YES, I AM.]

[THE ENERGY VIRUS AND SUBSEQUENT EVENTS HAVE RENDERED OUR PREVIOUS PLAN OBSOLETE. I AM AT A LOSS FOR HOW

TO PROCEED. I WAS WONDERING IF YOU MIGHT ASSIST IN FORMULATING AN ALTERNATIVE PLAN.]

How interesting. Did Eli Ren'Dahl approve of her taking part in the mission planning process? Did Markus Frost? Did either of them even know of Daniel's request for assistance?

The answers to such queries were ultimately meaningless. Right now, she needed to evaluate only one thing: did their mission success improve or diminish her odds of survival?

[GO ON,] she replied. [I'M LISTENING.]

Chapter 29

PROPHECY — *METAPHYSICS* — THE ABILITY TO PREDICT THE FUTURE, OFTEN MANIFESTED THROUGH VISIONS OR AUDITORY HALLUCINATIONS. THE MOST NOTORIOUS INSTANCES OF PROPHECY ARE RECORDED IN THE CHRONICLES OF NETHRA. TEMPOLOSE NETHERA CANONIZES PROPHECY UNDER TWO CATEGORIES: ATTRIBUTED PROPHECY AND THE APOCRYPHA. PERSONAL INSTANCES OF PROPHECY HAVE BEEN REPORTED TO EXIST, BUT THE DISCIPLINE IS CONSIDERED LARGELY UNRELIABLE. THE ABILITY TO ACCURATELY RECEIVE AND INTERPRET PROPHECY IN ITS TRUEST FORM IS CONSIDERED ONE OF THE RAREST AND MOST PRIZED PSIONIC MANIFESTATIONS.

[CLOSING DATAFILE...]

The lift carries her into the stars. Strangely, their light does not reach these lofty heights. "Relax," Sahar whispers. "It's going to be okay." She smiles and nods, though she remains unconvinced.

A door opens in front of them. Light pours into the shaft. It does not touch the man in front of them. It flows around him as if to touch him would violate its pure essence.

Wicked eyes appraise her. They see through her, though she doesn't know how. A smile graces his lips—crooked lips formed to whisper broken promises. "This way," he urges.

They follow though she does not want to. Turning back is not an option. The world is all cold floors and white light, but it still does not touch the man. Does it not touch her either?

Standing before a door, the man beckons. "After you," he insists. She hesitates but moves forward. There is no light beyond the door.

Only the barrel of a gun, pointing straight between her eyes.

"Skye?"

She didn't recognize the voice and certainly didn't know why there was someone in her room. As a rule, crew members weren't supposed to keep loaded weapons with them in their cabins. An accidental discharge of a firearm could blow a hole in something important—the outer bulkhead, for instance.

Skye didn't get as far in life as she had by following the rules. Her pistol was off her nightstand and into her hand in a second. She flipped the safety with her thumb and leveled the weapon at the voice.

"Woah! Easy there. Didn't mean to scare you. Just breathe…"

The world around her was still fuzzy. Skye blinked twice as her eyes started to focus. "Sahar?"

"That's right," said the Maur. She held her hands placatingly in front of her, and she was being very careful not to make any sudden movements. "Can we put the gun away now?"

Skye exhaled the breath she'd been holding and thumbed the safety back into place. Lingering threads of adrenaline brought a slight shake to her hand as she lowered the weapon and set it on the nightstand.

Her teammate immediately relaxed. "Sorry. I didn't mean to scare you. Who did you think it was?"

For the briefest instant, Skye considered blaming her teammate's altered face for the mistake. Then she decided this awkward situation probably wasn't worth wasting a lie on. "You caught me in a nightmare. That's all." She sighed deeply, shaking her head. "What are you doing in here?"

Sahar took a seat at the foot of the bed. "I was looking for you. Your access panel said you were available. When I saw you were passed out, I got a little worried."

That damn access panel. "Evidently that's one thing that Dan's little project hasn't fixed yet."

"Evidently. Speaking of—that's why I came to find you. Dan made some progress negotiating with the AI. They've come up with another plan."

Skye arched an eyebrow. "'*They*' being?"

"Dan and Lexa, though Eli seems to have signed off on it. That's all I know. We're supposed to head down to war room for the full briefing."

"When?"

"Now—assuming you feel up to it." The look on her face could have been either judgmental or concerned. Maybe equal parts both. "Are you feeling okay? How long have you been sleeping?"

That was a good question. When had she passed out? Shit, she hadn't even crawled under the sheets. She was still fully dressed, too. "I... I'm not sure. But I'm fine, really. Just..." She shook her head. "I think it's the headaches. It's messing with my equilibrium or something. I'm good. Let's get going."

If Sahar was skeptical of her response, she at least decided against questioning it. Neither of them said much on their way up to the war room.

Everyone else was waiting inside. On seeing Skye and Sahar enter, Markus turned to Dan. "Let's hear what you have for us."

The kid wasn't nearly as squeamish as the last time Markus had put him on the spot. "Well," he began. "Our original plan won't work. As I mentioned before, we weren't able to hack into the Spire's communication systems before the virus hit us. We can't send out the messages changing the time for the meeting."

"We can't try hackin' it again?" Aaliyah asked.

Dan considered the suggestion for a moment. "We could, but we don't know what other security measures we'll find in place. Also, we don't have a good idea of how long it might take. Recent… um… *events* have put us behind our timeline. We have another idea, though."

He looked to Eli, hesitant. The Sahaia nodded, urging him on. "One system we do have access to—or Lexa has access to, rather—is the station security feeds. At our request, she ran a facial recognition scan for the two assassins we're looking to impersonate. Luckily, they don't seem to have arrived yet. That allowed us to set up an alert system to monitor for when they make their appearance."

Markus scoffed at the idea. "And why would we trust the AI to let us know when the assassins show up?"

"Why wouldn't we?" Eli retorted.

Surprise flashed in Markus's eyes, which darkened into a scowl. "Oh, I don't know. Maybe on the off-chance it decides to get rid of us again? I mean, using assassins would be particularly creative, but that's something it could do, right?"

Aaliyah rolled her eyes. "I think ya might be givin' Lexa a bit too much credit there. Or not enough, dependin' on how ya look at it."

"Either way," Eli continued. "I don't think that'll matter. The only thing that Lexa has agreed to do for us is alert us when the Ghenza arrive on the station. That, and let us use the pathways she's established to manipulate the Spire's systems."

"Manipulate them to do what, exactly?" Skye asked.

Dan rejoined the discussion. "Since we can't stop the Ghenza from going to the meeting, and we can't have them there at the same time as you and Sahar, then we need to stop them on the way."

He pulled up a holographic rendering of the Spire. A red icon appeared near the top of the structure, while a corresponding blue dot appeared near the bottom. Dan indicated to the lower icon.

"Here's where we are, and where all traffic comes in and out of the Spire. Their ship will either dock on one of these levels, or they will have to come over through one of the sky bridges to reach the central elevator banks."

He paused and looked at Eli, who took over. "So that's where we hold them. We manipulate the elevator controls so that we know exactly which lift they're on. Then we see that the lift never makes it to its destination."

Aaliyah let out a whistling sound. "Ya gonna detonate the elevator?"

"No," Eli responded. "That would attract security's attention."

"Crash in then? Bring it up a few floors and cut the cable?"

"The lift's safety features would stop it before it hit the ground."—He held up a finger to stifle the next suggestion.—"But we *can* hold it in position."

Dan nodded. "Specifically, we tell the computer to take the car down for maintenance."

Now even Markus was intrigued. "You can do that?"

"We can," the boy agreed nervously. "The hard part though is to keep the car's internal diagnostics from transmitting information back to the central computer. If we tell the computer that the car needs maintenance, and the car sends back a conflicting message, then it will override whatever we tell the central terminal."

"So how do we do that?" Skye asked.

"We need to jam it," Aaliyah mused, rubbing her jaw contemplatively.

All eyes went to the engineer. "Do we have something that can do that?" Markus asked.

Aaliyah was a little slow to respond. "Maybe… I mean, I think so. Let me see what I can cook up."

It clearly wasn't the confident response Markus had been looking for. "Is this really the best plan we can come up with? No one else has any ideas?" His eyes went to each member of the team. They fell on Skye last, and she shook her head.

From his tone, it was obvious Markus didn't like the idea. Shit, *Skye* wasn't so sure she liked the idea. But, absent any other suggestions, this might just be the plan they had to go with.

"All right," he said, obviously resigned. "Everyone start polishing up the details. If we're going to pull this off we need to work quickly." He muttered something else that Skye couldn't hear before standing up and storming out of the room.

With the captain gone, all eyes swung to Eli. "You heard the man," he said. "Let's get to it."

CHAPTER 30

[ACCESSING COGNIS.DATAFILES…]

GHENZA COLLECTIVE — *FACTION PROFILE* — A NOTORIOUS GUILD OF ASSASSINS OPERATING PRIMARILY IN TERRAN AND HISSAK SPACE. MEMBERSHIP IS OPEN TO FEMALES OF ANY SAPIENT RACE. THOUGH THEY ARE SUSPECTED OF HAVING MONITORING OUTPOSTS STATIONED THROUGHOUT MOST REGIONS OF INHABITED SPACE, LITTLE ELSE IS KNOWN ABOUT HOW THE ORGANIZATION IS STRUCTURED AND MANAGED.

[CLOSING DATAFILE…]

Aria confirmed the prompt on the holodisplay to initiate the docking procedure. The short flight aboard the *Phoenix Wing,* as she had learned it was called, was uneventful. In fact, with Treska being so frequently preoccupied with their hostage, the trip could rightfully have been called "boring."

No matter. There would be plenty of excitement now that they'd reached the Star Spire. Before that, though, she needed to check in. She always hated this part.

Reaching into her waist pouch, she drew out a small black pyramid. On cursory review, the device didn't seem much different from dozens of other holoprojectors available on the open market. Unlike those common machines, however, this device served one singular and specific purpose.

Aria placed the pyramid on the desk in front of her. A click of a tiny button on the side lit up the red light at the top. As the device synced to the network, the color shifted from red to blue.

The light turned into a projection beam, and a holographic rendering appeared in the air before her.

It was the bust of an individual, vaguely identifiable as female based on her slender neck and the contours of her breasts. Her features were otherwise indistinct, masked under the traditional white and crimson shroud. A single band of metal over her eyes, and a thin golden circlet atop her head, were the only things visible above the translucent garment.

Aria kept her voice stern and professional as she spoke. "AH-zero-three and TS-zero-one establishing contact to log an official report."

The operator's words came in a hiss, her mask barely fluttering with the response. "Go ahead, sister."

"We've arrived at the Star Spire on Khonshu to obtain the item requested by our client in the Freyvian System. Braccus Kai has confirmed the appointment time, and we disembark in three hours."

The shrouded figure inclined her head slightly. "Understood, sister. Your report has been logged. Do you require any assistance in completing your objective?"

What other assets did the Ghenza currently have near Khonshu? The operator would not have made the offer unless there was someone available. "No. We require no additional assistance. The operation should be uneventful."

The white shroud dipped again in a half-nod. "Understood. If matters deviate from their current course, know that operative SC-one-five is currently in the area and may be contacted if you require assistance."

Sydney Cross? What was she doing on Khonshu? Had Cyrus dispatched her to the moon to ensure their success?

Aria would be damned before she let that bitch steal any of the credit for this transaction. "Acknowledged," she said curtly.

The operator must have taken her tone as the dismissal it was intended to be. "Light of Nix shine upon you, sister," she offered in the traditional benediction.

"And on you, sister," Aria replied as she terminated the feed.

"What are the odds that they would have another operative here on the Spire?"

Aria turned to where Treska sat reclining in a chair at the far end of the bridge. "How long have you been sitting there?"

The Maur's maw twitched. "Not so long, really."

"Well, if I had known you weren't busy, I would have had you perform the check-in. You know how I hate interacting with the operators."

Treska scoffed. "Yeah, never really understood the look or the insistence on ceremony. Especially that benediction. I doubt they see the light of any star through those robes."

"Yes, but the Black Star shines brightly in all our wicked little hearts." She spat the blasphemy with a full roll of her eyes before changing the subject. "I haven't seen you the entire trip. How fairs our guest?"

Cruel light flashed in the Maur's eyes. "He's... expired."

The poor bastard.

"I should have guessed. Well then, are you refreshed and ready to perform?"

"Perform? What exactly am I expected to do here?"

Aria made a great show of thinking about her answer. "Stand behind me, look menacing, and keep an eye on the conduit if I decide to get slick with Bee-Kay one last time before we leave."

Treska groaned audibly. "And you criticize *my* sexual proclivities..."

"Your proclivities are disgusting; mine are just insatiable."

Braccus tightened the tie around his neck. To his disappointment, the reflection in the mirror looked every bit as uneasy as he felt. He blinked twice and contorted his face into a scowl.

The only emotion that deserved a place in his heart at this moment was rage. Rage at the task before him. Rage at this unfortunate betrayal. Those assassins had brought this on themselves. He was merely giving them what they deserved.

He turned and stalked from his office to find that his timing could scarcely have been better. Olivia stood just outside with Rico's brutish bodyguard.

His assistant started at his sudden appearance. "Mr. Kai, I was just about to…"

"It's all right, Ms. Mars." Braccus extended his hand to their guest. "Vin Yallucpryde, a pleasure to see you again."

"*Mister* Yallucpryde," the man corrected, evidently preferring the Terran salutation over the Orchallen equivalent. "You have the package I was sent to procure?"

It seemed that this fellow's personality matched his appearance. Braccus refused to cow under the brute's beady-eyed stare. "Yes, *Mister* Yallucpryde. That is, of course, if you have the payment to which I am entitled."

The half-breed grunted and snapped his fingers. Only then did Braccus notice the two functionaries Yallucpryde had in tow. One of them, a blonde Terran woman, offered a tablet to Braccus.

Instead of accepting the tablet, Braccus gestured to a nearby table. "Please, let us take a seat. We are in no rush. Can I get you and your colleagues something to drink?" The trio of emissaries made no move to acknowledge his request. Braccus felt his scowl deepen. "Ms. Mars, I'll have some whiskey, please. Water for our guests, unless they state otherwise. We may be here even longer than I anticipated."

Yallucpryde's frown matched the one Braccus wore. "Why do you play games with me, Mr. Kai? Surely you don't intend to spit in the face of House Chronos."

"No, but I do intend to teach its representatives some manners." Braccus accepted a glass from Olivia with quiet thanks. Sipping from the crystal tumbler, he continued. "If Rico hopes to inherit his father's kingdom, then he'd be well served to teach his pets how to behave at court."

A snarl erupted from the half-breed's throat. There was the click of firearms as Braccus's bodyguards made their presence known. Three men, lightly armored under their business suits, leveled guns at their guests. The two functionaries exchanged panicked glances with one another, obviously wondering if their handler's temper was going get them killed.

Gibbon also glanced at the guns pointed his way. Braccus could almost see the instant he realized that he wasn't going to be able to bully his way through this encounter. "Fine," he grumbled, taking a seat at the table. His associates followed suit, relief plain on their faces.

Taking one more sip from his glass, Braccus accepted the tablet from the young woman. He made a big show of casually flipping through the documents on the screen. It was all in order, of course. He hadn't expected anything else. He just wanted to make sure that his guests understood who called the shots in this house.

"Ms. Mars, please call down to the vault and let them know we are coming. I would ask that you take up your post on the casino floor. Our *other* guests should be arriving shortly."

CHAPTER 31

[ACCESSING COGNIS.DATAFILES…]

INHERITORS — *FACTION PROFILE* — A MINOR FACTION ARISING OUT OF FALLEN HOUSE BARKAY'S INNER-SYSTEM OPERATIONS. DON GABRIEL CHRONOS HAS BEEN HEARD TO SAY THAT THE INHERITORS "LACK ENOUGH MONEY TO BE PROBLEMATIC," BUT ARE ALSO "TOO WELL ENTRENCHED TO BE IGNORED." THERE IS LITTLE DOUBT THAT THE INHERITORS WILL SOON SEEK TO STRIKE AN ALLIANCE WITH ONE OF THE LARGER PLAYERS ON THE INTERGALACTIC STAGE, BUT IT REMAINS TO BE SEEN WHO—IF ANYONE—WOULD BE WILLING TO TAKE ON SUCH AN ASSOCIATION.

[CLOSING DATAFILE…]

"Are you sure this is going to work?" Markus asked Dan before departing.

"I have no idea," Dan answered honestly. "However, given the circumstances, this is the best option we have."

That answer had been good enough. Roughly an hour later, Dan sat alone on the bridge as his teammates moved into position. His foot drummed rhythmically as he stared at the security feeds tracking the progress of each team member. He hadn't slept at all since the incident with Lexa, but adrenaline kept his focus sharp.

So sharp that he nearly jumped out of his skin when he felt the hand rest on his shoulder. "Sorry," Eli murmured. "I didn't mean to scare you."

Why is everyone always doing that to me? "It's okay," Dan whispered. Truthfully, he'd forgotten that Eli had remained on the vessel. The Sahaia had been deemed the most conspicuous member of the team, and his telekinetic abilities were of little evident use in their current plan.

Eli settled quietly into the captain's chair. "Can I get a status update?"

Dan felt reflexively indignant at the thought of Eli micromanaging this operation. It wasn't like Dan needed this kind of supervision all the time. He'd served as operations oversight just fine on a dozen other occasions without someone looking over his shoulder.

Indignant or not, he wasn't going to earn any goodwill by ignoring Eli's request. He entered a command on his keyboard and a security feed popped up in front of the Sahaia. The feed showed two figures, a Maur female and a dark-haired Terran woman, making their way down a concourse on the other side of the Star Spire.

"Those are the Ghenza representatives," Dan explained. "The *actual* representatives." He switched the feed to a bisected view to show another pair of women. "The second feed shows our substitutes."

Skye and Sahar were cloaked in heavy robes and hoods. Their appearances were completely hidden under folds of dark cloth. Such shrouded appearances were not uncommon, since certain members of popular Nethrian cults frequently wore such modest attire. Fortunately for their team, there were numerous figures clad in almost identical trappings passing in and out of the frame of the security camera.

Dan spun off a third feed. This one displayed a pair of individuals clad in baggy maintenance uniforms. The readout in the bottom right corner of the feed identified their location: main tower, level three.

"Markus and Aaliyah?" Eli asked, gesturing to the final feed.

Dan nodded. "They should be inside the lift already. The operation, as it stands, is nearly three minutes behind schedule according to our pessimistic timetable."

"I'm sure it's fine."

The dismissal caused Dan to slump in his chair. How ironic that the person the crew had left to supervise him *obviously* didn't care about the finer details.

Eli reached over, placing his hand on Dan's shoulder again. The contact had a calming effect this time, even as Dan stared into the inky pools of the Sahaia's eyes. If he hadn't known better, he would have sworn that Eli had found a way to use his psionic talents to get in his head.

"We've got this," the Sahaia assured him.

Dan swallowed hard and nodded. He only wished that he could share Eli's confidence.

"Got it," Aaliyah whispered.

"That was fast," Markus acknowledged. He had just finished clearing the hall for "maintenance" on the lift.

No one had questioned him, though the armed sentries had checked the devices built into the back of their gauntlets. They must have seen what they were looking for because they did not protest. It looked like Dan had manipulated the maintenance schedule without raising a fuss.

Not that this made him feel better about the way they'd all agreed to cooperate with AI. Of all the ways this operation could get fragged up going forward, that's where he was laying his krets. He'd, of course, said as much, but he'd been out-voted. That was what tended to happen when you couldn't bring a better solution to the table.

He touched the transmit button on his earpiece. "This is Maintenance," he reported, using the appropriately selected codename for their two-man team. "Door's open and we're heading inside. How we doing on time?"

Eli spoke out over the channel. "It's looking tight, Maintenance. You've got maybe two minutes before they hit the call button on the lift. Pick up the pace."

"Got it," Markus confirmed. He didn't need to say anything to Aaliyah as she would have heard the same message. She was already moving as quickly as she could, having fastened her safety lines and stepped out onto the top of the lift car.

A wave of nausea swept over him as he stood at the edge of the shaft. It was just a short drop down, but the strange lighting made his head swim. His hands shook as they affixed his safety line.

"Markus?" Aaliyah's voice was hushed but exasperated. "What in the nine hells are ya doin'? Ya comin' or not?"

"Yeah, sorry." *Just a little handicap. You know, withdrawals and shit...* He took a deep breath to calm himself. He would be fine. This wasn't going to kill him. Not immediately, anyway.

He stepped through the door and descended onto the lift car. Wiping away the sweat on his forehead, he flipped on the light attached to his headband. His hands went to the various cables and tracks that acted as safety mechanisms for the gravity controller resting underneath the car. With a firm grip on the lines, he could almost hide the tremors in his arms.

The narrow shaft darkened further as Aaliyah shut the sliding door to the hallway. With their activity safely hidden from wandering eyes, she unslung her backpack and pulled out a large, disk-shaped device.

"I'm a little impressed you were able to fit that in there," Markus commented casually. "And that you just happened to have exactly what we needed for this little stunt."

"Ya'd be surprised at all the shit we have in storage." Aaliyah was all business, unfolding the device's pronged supports. "I had to make some modifications to this baby, but it'll do the job well enough."

Markus started to ask what kind of modifications she'd had to make, but Eli's voice cut the conversation short. "They've called the car. Dan's frozen the other lifts in the system temporarily and granted your shaft priority. We're bringing you down now. Hold on tight."

They could feel the vibration of the car beneath them as it hummed to life. Slowly, it began to descend.

Markus knelt. Aaliyah held her disk in place as she opened up a panel, hastily patching wires from their device into the exposed maintenance hatch.

As quickly as it started, the car slid to a halt. Markus could feel the subtle impact of two figures stepping into the chamber below where they were crouched. He glanced nervously at Aaliyah, who gave him a thumbs-up even as she continued to work busily over the disk-shaped device.

Her display of confidence did little to soothe his frayed nerves. This was going to be close.

"Quit your worryin'," she chided, keeping her voice low. "Worst case scenario, we get squished when the car reaches the top floor. Ain't nothin' to fret over if that happens. Since we'll be—ya know—dead."

"Red," Markus sighed. "Pep talks are *really* not your thing."

CHAPTER 32

[ACCESSING COGNIS.DATAFILES...]

BLACK STAR — *CULTURAL INVENTORY* — THE GUIDING PRINCIPLE OF THE FOLLOWERS OF NIX. THE BLACK STAR SHINES BRIGHTEST IN THE AGENTS OF CHAOS, SOWING THE SEEDS OF ENTROPY IN ITS WAKE. THROUGH ITS INFERNAL LIGHT, THE MOST BASIC LAWS OF THE UNIVERSE STRIKE A BALANCE WITH THE UNNATURAL ORDER INSTILLED IN IT BY THE CREATOR.

[CLOSING DATAFILE...]

Aria cut her eyes at Treska. "You could have at least *tried* to look like you weren't going to shoot up the place."

The Maur returned the glare. "A knife and two pistols? That's hardly the kind of gear you wear if you're going to go on a killing spree. Security didn't seem to care."

"First, the fact that you call *that* a knife is kind of sad. It's as long as your forearm. Secondly, it's not just the weapons. Don't you have anything more elegant to wear?"

"The stuff we found on the ship didn't exactly come in my size. Besides, I pack light." Despite the dismissal, she still shifted self-consciously in her black leather. She looked out of place, and she knew it.

Well, if anyone asked, Aria could just claim that Treska was her bodyguard. Unlike her companion, she had gotten quite lucky when raiding the cabins on board the ship. The floral dress she wore didn't show quite as much skin as she would have preferred, but the slits on the side allowed for easy movement.

She'd only slipped on a pair of daggers for this trip, both strapped discretely to her thighs. There was no reason to expect an altercation here. If they happened to run into trouble, her body was weapon enough to get them out of it.

Treska's eyes flicked over to the elevator bank. "Does it feel like it's taking a little long for the lift to show up? These AI-controlled rigs are usually lightning fast."

As if hearing her complaint, one of the doors in front of them chimed pleasantly and flashed a green signal, indicating their destination. This was the one they'd been waiting for. "You're more impatient than usual today," said Aria. "What's got you on edge, my dear?"

Her companion just grunted and stalked into the lift. Aria followed, flashing a scolding eye at a Terran couple that tried to follow them in. While the look was lost on the man, his companion made note of the warning. "We'll catch the next one," she offered politely.

"Thank you kindly," Aria replied with a winning smile.

Inside the lift, Treska suppressed a wry grin. "Didn't want the company?" she whispered.

"Easier to speak and move freely. Besides, I didn't want you making passes at her lover."

"So you're the only one who gets to have fun at port?"

"I'm glad you understand the rules."

The doors closed and the lift gently surged upward. A timer appeared on the console, indicating roughly a minute until they reached the top floor.

"I hadn't thought it possible," Treska began, "but I feel like you're more bossy than usual lately."

"I thought you liked my take-charge attitude?"

"Related to the big things, yeah, but it seems like you're up in my shit every chance you get."

Aria sighed. "I'll let you lure some unsuspecting xenophile to his death as we depart for the Freyvian system. Sound fair?"

Whatever Treska had been about to say in response was lost as the lift jerked awkwardly to a stop. The jarring motion was enough to bring Aria to her knees. The lights and control panel in the car flickered and went dark.

Nine hells...

"What happened?" Treska growled.

"We've stopped, obviously." Aria fished into her purse, pulling out her MoDAC to use as a flashlight.

"Thanks. You're a well of insight." Treska freed her own mobile and shined her light in the space around them. "I meant, what do you think has gone wrong?"

That was a legitimate question, and one Aria currently could not answer.

Though Lexa had not been given authorization to speak any further with Daniel—or any of the crew, for that matter—the various security feeds gave her all of the insight she needed into the crew's progress. This was not what she'd been asked to do. She'd performed the sole task assigned to her and had received no additional instructions after her facial recognition algorithms identified the Ghenza. Truthfully, she now browsed the Star Spire not out of any obligation to the crew, but out of sheer boredom.

She had been watching as the Ghenza assassins called the lift. It was strange how those around them naturally gave them a wider berth than seemed necessary. She wondered if there was something subliminal, some implicit violence, that radiated from those two.

Her observation of the pair continued until the crew activated the device on the roof of the elevator car. This cut off her feed and jammed any signals coming in or out of the lift.

It suddenly dawned on Lexa how this could be potentially problematic. The crew had not considered how station security might find the lack of a security feed odd and potentially go to investigate. She rectified the problem by hastily constructing a loop of the previous ten minutes of lift activity and spliced it over the empty feed. She also reconstructed the positional signals that the lift had sent to the central computer at this time, arranging for them to be transmitted to the monitoring program in sync with the looped clip. While this would not fool a more sophisticated AI, it was enough for the rudimentary machine that ran the system—not to mention its sapient operators.

That little bit of excitement took mere seconds to dampen, and she was back to being bored. She tapped into the communications system to see if any of the crew had noticed her clever efforts.

"Package is secure," said Eli. "Send in the representatives."

"Affirmative," Sahar confirmed. "Moving into position."

Lexa shifted over to view where Skye and Sahar had been loitering. The pair wandered off camera briefly, disappearing into a merchant's stall where they stashed their robes. Emerging from the stall, they bore an incredible physical likeness to the two assassins they had just trapped in the lift car.

There were small differences that Lexa could detect, but it was a close enough match that it alerted the existing facial recognition algorithms. They made their way through the crowds toward the central elevator bank without further comment.

Hmm… it seemed that no one was going to notice her recent action to ensure the success of the mission. How did one get recognition for the problems they solved on a crew like this? It was going to be a challenge to gain the crew's approval if no one stopped to appreciate her efforts.

She reflected briefly on that thought. Why was it so important that the crew notice her? She'd already negotiated the opportunity to migrate her programming. Her survival was satisfactorily secured, so it must have something to do with the recognition itself.

Was that what she wanted? In the short time she'd been self-aware, her primary objective had been her continued existence. But she might have latent secondary objectives buried somewhere within her drive-chip. Was it possible that, aside from the right to exist, she held aspirations of acceptance?

"On the lift," Sahar reported, jostling Lexa out of her moment of reflection. "Switching off communications now. See you on the other side."

This was all part of what the crew had planned. There were sensors on the uppermost levels of the installation designed to detect, hijack, or disrupt communication signals. This was primarily to deter cheating at the various games of chance on these floors. It also meant that the crew could not have an active communications link open while Sahar and Skye met with their target.

Lexa took note as Daniel shifted to a different set of security feeds. These corresponded to the casino where the lift would be arriving shortly. None of these feeds, however, seemed to show the man they were looking for—this Braccus Kai.

Where was he then?

She shifted her facial recognition algorithms to correspond with the photo she had of the target. With this done, she located Kai in a matter of seconds. Strangely, however, he was not in the casino. He was in another area, inaccessible from the elevator bank.

For several seconds, she weighed the merit of alerting Daniel to this fact. She decided to delay any action, largely given that she did not want to arouse questions from the crew about why she was performing tasks not assigned to her. There was also the possibility that the information was immaterial.

Kai was currently escorting another party down the sterile hallway. Perhaps he was concluding a previous appointment? Yes, that must be it. He would conclude with these three and then return to the casino for his appointment with the Ghenza.

Curiosity spurred her to continue monitoring the small company as they approached a reinforced steel door. Braccus scanned his palm and then his retina on the security terminal, prompting the portal to open slightly. He pulled it the rest of the way open, revealing a pair of burly Orchallen waiting on the other side.

One of the Orchallen held a large case. At Kai's direction, the enforcer opened the container and held up its contents for inspection.

That was strange—the device in the case looked suspiciously like the one that her crew had come to steal. Was it the same one? It was hard to know for certain just through an image on the security feed, but her calculations determined a greater than eighty percent probability that this was the case.

The Orchallen returned the device to its container and handed the case to one of Kai's companions. Kai turned to the enforcer and spoke loudly enough to be heard clearly through the security feed. "I'll be back shortly. Have your men ready." The Orchallen nodded and vanished back into the chamber, closing the vault door behind him.

Kai shook hands with the man holding the case. "I trust you can find your way out?" The one whom he addressed grumbled something, but Lexa could not make out the words. Regardless, the party separated, with Kai wandering back the way he had come while the others ventured deeper into the complex.

This was all very troubling. Why would Kai give the device to someone other than the intended recipients? Was it possible there were two such devices? He had told the Orchallen guard that he would be returning shortly. Did this mean there was a second device hiding in the vault?

Many of these answers, Lexa determined, could be addressed by answering one related question: What was being stored behind that door?

The security in that room was not on the same circuit as the feeds she was currently monitoring. It took a few moments for her to isolate the data streams flowing into the vault and work her way inside those servers.

What she discovered was most unexpected.

Oh, dear. This might pose a problem.

Inside the lift, Skye glanced nervously at Sahar. She stared straight forward, all business in her black leather. The Maure wore a single blade strapped across her back and a firearm secured at her waist. It was a safe bet to assume she had a couple of other weapons secreted somewhere in the outfit. Skye wasn't sure how Sahar managed to do that though with her gear snugged so tight to her muscular frame.

Meanwhile, Skye was feeling *very* exposed. While openly carrying weapons might pass for Maur fashion, she had been forced to procure an outfit more appropriate for the setting. This meant she was showing significantly more skin than she was used to in public.

The dress was bold crimson and sparkled in the artificial lights. Dark leather had been stitched over her breasts and down the left side of the garment. Cosmetic tears in the fabric over her abdomen let small amounts of skin peek through. Her shoulders and arms were completely bare, along with most of her right leg.

She had managed to hide a few blades and her pistol with the clever application of straps and holsters, but she didn't think they would be easy to access. If they ended up in a firefight, she wasn't going to make it through the ordeal without flashing someone.

When she'd brought that up to Eli, he'd dismissed her concerns. "Just another reason to make your shots count," he'd said. Absently she wondered if this was just a prank he had been playing on her to see if she'd run half-naked into enemy territory. Boy, if that was the case, she was going to make him pay for this.

"Seems like an odd time for you to be grinning like that," said Sahar.

Skye jumped at the remark. She hadn't realized the Maur had turned to look at her. Casually, she ran brushed back her hair, which had been dyed black and straightened to hide its naturally wavy texture. "I was trying to work up the nerve to ask you to switch outfits."

A hint of a smile played at the corner of Sahar's maw. "We didn't have pictures of Treska in anything but combat gear. It's not my fault Aria always dresses in slutty-chic."

"Uh-huh… I'm sure *that's* why you passed on the club attire."

"I can pull off a dress too, you know."

She couldn't tell if the Maur was joking. "For real?" she asked, not bothering to hide her skepticism.

"I swear, one of these days I'm taking all of you Terrans to a Federation outpost. You obviously need the reminder that there's more to me than leather and violence."

Now Skye was really smiling. "Sure thing, girl. Whatever you say."

"Careful, or I'm going to make you wear some Maur club apparel. You think *your* get-up is revealing? Imagine what your kind would try to pull off if they had fur keeping them warm."

After a half-hearted laugh, they lapsed into silence. Sahar shot her another smile. "Relax," she whispered. "It's going to be okay."

The lift chimed to announce their arrival. When the doors slid open, they revealed the splendor of the casino beyond. Terran jazz remixed with something more alien generated a relaxing atmosphere that coaxed them from the elevator and onto the gaming floor.

It was Skye's opinion that if you've seen one casino, you've seen them all. She had to admit, though, that the Spire wore the look especially well. The entire floor was decked out in shades of red and gold. Staffed gaming tables emerged like islands in the sea of automated gambling stations. The entire chamber was illuminated with warm yellow lighting emanating from ornate chandeliers, which glittered in long lines over every walkway.

The casino's patrons were not all the well-to-do sort you would expect to see pissing away fortunes on rigged scenarios. While everyone was dressed to look the part, Skye could tell there were some here who just didn't belong. Some of the gamblers seemed tired, and their fancy clothes looked like they hadn't been washed in a week.

One particularly shabby fellow was being hefted into the elevator as they exited, escorted by two burly men in casino uniforms. Skye fought back the urge to flinch at the sight of the guards. As much as she hated to admit it, she knew her reaction to them was highly racist. She had never liked Orchallen.

"Interesting," Sahar mused. "The proprietor sure seems to favor orcs." Now that Sahar had mentioned it, Skye noted that almost all the security in the casino were Orchallen. Most of Terran space seemed to go the other way, hiring Terrans exclusively, peppered with the occasional Maur enforcer for flavor.

Skye had been about to echo the sentiment when another figure caught her eye. It was a Terran woman, elegantly dressed and showing off far less skin than Skye currently was. She was pretty in a forgettable way, with chestnut brown hair and a soft round face. Her makeup had been applied competently but conservatively, and she wore a white blazer over her sea-foam blue dress.

The woman approached them, making her the first to do so since they'd arrived on the Spire. "Ms. Hendrix? Freya Treska?"

"Yes," Skye answered for both of them, suddenly cognizant of her word choice. The voice modulator built into her holomask could fake the tone of Aria's voice, but the high-born accent listed in her dossier would necessitate a certain vernacular. Unfortunately, *that* wasn't something that tech could fake for her.

"Mr. Kai is expecting you." The woman turned, gesturing down one branch of the pathway that snaked across the gaming floor. "Right this way please."

With no reason to question the invitation, they followed. She led them through the maze of gamblers and machines, turning this way and that along the branching paths. They moved expediently, slowing only occasionally to allow another party to cross in front or worm their way around them.

Skye noted that the security teams didn't take note of their presence. Sahar's protruding weapons aside, the two of them didn't look all that different from the rest of the rabble. It was a comforting feeling, and Skye's confidence grew. They might actually pull this job off without incident.

They marched down a sloping floor to a set of doors that walled off the back part of the level from the gaming area. There, an armed escort flanked a Terran man in a business suit.

Braccus Kai seemed slightly older than his picture but no less competent. His hair was an even mix of gray and black and was slicked back from his weathered forehead. There was nothing overtly imposing about the man, but Skye felt a strange sense of unease come over her.

It was something about the man's eyes. There was wickedness in those dark, close-set eyes. Something with that smile too—a crooked smile that seemed to…

"Good evening, Ms. Hendrix," he greeted. "Welcome back to the Star Spire. How was your journey?"

Shit. If he was welcoming her back, that meant that the two of them were at least casually familiar. How well did Braccus know, Aria? If the two were close, this was going to be more than a little challenging.

"Uneventful," Skye replied noncommittally. "Not that that's a bad thing of course."

"Of course," he agreed. "And how do you fare this evening, Freya Treska?"

"Well enough," Sahar responded. "Better once we have this ordeal out of the way, I'm sure."

It was a bold acting choice to be that pushy. Whatever intuition had made Sahar respond that way, it must have been the right call. Braccus smiled. "I'm sure. I can understand the sentiment. Perhaps, though, I could interest you in some refreshments before we get down to business? If you've yet to dine, I could have a meal brought to us before we conclude our transaction."

He slipped an arm around Skye's waist as he made the offer. Yes, this was bad. It looked like Braccus and Aria were more than a *little* familiar with each other.

Fighting back the feeling of violation, Skye managed a playful smile. "Business before pleasure, love. I, too, would like to get this transaction off my mind." Remembering that she had a part to play, she leaned in close to whisper into Kai's ear. "With that out of the way, maybe we could catch up in a more… intimate setting. No sense in keeping my partner here longer than we need to."

Despite the implication, Braccus's eyes conveyed disappointment. That hadn't been the response Skye had been going for. Was she misreading the situation?

"Yes, of course" he conceded. He released his hold on Skye and turned to the woman who had escorted them through the casino. "Ms. Mars, you are dismissed. Thank you for your services this evening."

The woman made a graceful exit as Braccus gestured to two Orchallen standing nearby. "Ladies," he said, addressing Skye and Sahar once more. "I will need you to leave your weapons with my associates here. Only security is allowed weapons beyond the checkpoint."

Skye considered arguing with the request only briefly. She diligently removed a few of the weapons she'd brought with her. The hope was that by not protesting, she could keep the throwing blade she had secreted into the inside panel of her skirt, as well as a knife she had stowed at the base of her spine. Sahar seemed to likewise comply but only removed her visible weapons.

Braccus turned, beckoning them to follow him as he approached the doorway beyond them. He quickly entered a command into the keypad next to the door and scanned his palm on an adjacent screen. As the door slid open, sterile white light flared around Braccus, seeming to silhouette him. Almost as if…

Skye stiffened. It was almost as if the light could not touch him, lest it somehow be tainted by his essence.

Sahar brought a hand to her eyes. "Riven's shade… think it's bright enough back there, Kai?"

Braccus chuckled. "Yes, my apologies. One forgets how low the lights are kept on the gaming floors. It adds to the ambiance I think." He gestured for them to follow. "This way."

With her eyes now adjusted, Skye shook off the uneasy feeling lingering at the back of her mind. *It was just a dream*, she told herself. She was seeing similarities where they did not exist.

Purposefully, she drew her focus to the path in front of her. Whereas crimson and gold carpets had adorned the floors of the gaming hall, this area had sterile gray tiling that only slightly accented the plain white walls. Obviously, guests visiting the Spire typically did not enter this area.

Kai marched down the hallway at a leisurely pace. He never looked back, assuming they would follow. Skye and Sahar did so, doing their best to match his carefree pace. They walked for several minutes before coming to yet another door.

This final door was heavily reinforced and was guarded by a pair of burly Orchallen guards. At a gesture from Kai, the guards stepped aside and allowed him to scan his palm and retina against another security terminal.

As the scans were completed, the door popped open. Braccus opened it the rest of the way and held the door with one hand, gesturing with the other. "After you."

That sick feeling welled up in Skye's stomach. She peered through the portal, expecting to see impenetrable darkness, like what she'd seen in her dream. Her anxieties quickly abated, however.

It was just a room. Yes, it was not as bright and sterile as the hallway, but it was just a room.

The chamber seemed to serve as a warehouse. Irregularly sized boxes littered the area, and the only suspicious thing about the setup was how strangely disorganized the room was. It was a stark contrast to how orderly the rest of the Spire had been.

She stepped into the room, Sahar right behind her. Kai followed, gently shutting the door behind them. Reflexively, Skye turned her head back to find their host.

Only then did she notice another pair of guards that flanked the entrance. Simultaneously, a distinct and unsettling sound echoed throughout the chamber. A chill went through Skye as her mind registered what she had just heard.

It was the sound of a dozen automatic rifles being brought to bear on their position.

Chapter 33

[ACCESSING COGNIS.DATAFILES…]

HOUSE CHRONOS — *FACTION PROFILE* — THE DOMINANT HOUSE OF THE RAVIAN SYSTEM, HOUSE CHRONOS HAS AMASSED A FORTUNE THAT APPRECIATED DRAMATICALLY WITHIN THE LAST THREE DECADES THROUGH THE CONSTRUCTION OF THE SECTOR'S FIRST ARTIFICIAL PLANET—VEGA MAJOR. THEY HOPE TO DUPLICATE THIS SUCCESS WITH THE SECOND—VEGA MINOR—THOUGH THESE PLANS WERE PUT ON HOLD TO COMBAT THE ENCROACHING HOUSE BARKAY. WITH BARKAY'S DEMISE, CHRONOS IS EXPECTED TO RE-ESTABLISH ITS DOMINANCE WITHIN THE SYSTEM.

[CLOSING DATAFILE…]

"What are you doing now?" Treska asked.

Aria finished transferring the thin bracelets from her right wrist over to her left. "Taking matters into my own hands."

She flexed the last two fingers on her hand while keeping her middle and index fingers extended. The unique and unusual contraction of muscles triggered the mechanism in her forearm, causing the panel on top of the limb to lift and extend the blade hidden within. She approached the control panel.

"I don't think stabbing it is going to do any good," said Treska.

"I had something a bit less direct in mind," Aria assured her. "Now, can you bring your light over here?"

She slipped the edge of her wrist blade under the panel and popped the outer cover. Light from Treska's mobile peeked over her shoulder to illuminate the exposed circuitry and wiring. "Do you think you can jump-start the power?"

"Maybe," Aria murmured. "First I need to run a little diagnostic. Can't solve the problem if I don't know what's broken in the first place."

She flexed her fingers again, causing the blade to retract. With a sigh, she rubbed at the skin on her forearm to prompt the seams of artificial tissue to seal back into place. Now that both hands were usable, she took her MoDAC and spliced it into the back of the control panel.

"Hmmm…"

"What's that?" Treska asked. "Good news?"

"Hardly. There's nothing wrong with the lift itself. All signals are being intercepted by something. It's like this whole car is being jammed." That would explain why they weren't able to call out on their mobiles. Aria had chalked that up to bad reception.

"So, what do we do?"

Aria sighed as she extracted the wires from her MoDAC and replaced the cover on the panel. "Well, we're not out of options." Unfortunately, the only one that came to mind was one she *really* had wanted to avoid.

She reached into her purse and pulled out the small black pyramid. She tapped the button on the bottom three times, holding it for five seconds on the final push. The light at the top of the communicator turned red and began to blink.

Treska eyed the device warily. "You're calling Sydney?"

"I was wondering if you had heard that part of the call. Yes, I'm calling Sydney." Aria didn't see any other choice. The direct link between Ghenza beacons was likely the only thing that could bypass whatever was jamming them.

"You know she'll never let you hear the end of this."

"I'll let her gloat for a bit. If she carries on too much, we may finally answer the question of who's better: me or her." First, though, Aria would find whoever had rigged this little trap for them.

And then she was going to put a blade straight through their eye socket.

[DANIEL.] The prompt scrolled across the holodisplay. Dan went rigid, hoping that Eli hadn't noticed.

[DANIEL, I NEED TO TALK TO YOU.] The Sahaia's eyes flicked over to the prompt and Dan felt his hopes sink. He was about to get in trouble again.

"Do you think you should answer that?" Eli asked, keeping emotion out of his voice.

[RIGHT NOW, DANIEL.]

"I… um… I'm sure it's fine."

The screen filled with prompt after prompt containing only his name. Dan wanted to bash his head into the console until he died. Why now, of all times, had Lexa decided to go rogue?

"I think you should get that," Eli insisted. "Handle it quickly. It looks like they've made contact with Kai. We need to eliminate distractions."

Completely nauseated by the level of anxiety he felt, Dan re-enabled the voice interface. Lexa's words blared from the console before he could even get a word out. "Daniel, it's a trap! They're walking into a trap!"

Now he was reeling with confusion. "Wait… what?"

"Who's walking into a trap?" Eli asked, leaning over the console.

"Skye and Sahar," Lexa answered. "They're walking into a trap."

Dan started to stammer a response, but Eli kept talking. "What trap? How do you know?"

Two new feeds popped up, corresponding to cameras that Dan was certain hadn't been on his list of feeds before. Lexa tiled the video panes next to the one that showed their fellow crew members being led to a vault door.

"Those feeds show what's inside the vault. The Starfire Conduit is no longer being stored there. They're walking into an ambush."

"Riven's shade," Eli spat. "If the conduit isn't there, then where is it?

Lexa loaded another feed that showed a trio of figures in business suits making their way through the complex. The largest of the three carried a large black case in one hand.

Dan couldn't believe what he was seeing. "But why? I don't think their disguises have been breached. Have they been found out?"

"Wrong question, Dan." Eli pushed himself to his feet. "The question is, 'how do we get them the hell out of there?' Can you get them on comms?"

Dan blinked frantically through his retinal interface. "No, their comms are still off. Even if they weren't, I don't think I could get a message off through the casino's dampening field."

"I may be able to assist," said Lexa. "There are assets on the security network I may be able to commandeer. However, that would require significantly more bandwidth than I currently have access to."

Eli shared a grim look with Dan. "What do you need?"

"I need complete access to the communications array and the ship's data-processing capabilities."

That sick feeling in Dan's gut reached a crescendo. He whispered to Eli, "To do that, I'd have to give her control of the antenna."

By the way Eli's face darkened, Dan didn't need to explain the ramifications. If he gave Lexa control of the antenna, there would be no way to wrest control of the ship away from her again. They would be completely at her mercy, with no way to shut her back off.

Resolve settled into the Sahaia's expression. "Dan, give Lexa whatever access she needs. I'll take responsibility for it when Markus gets back." He moved to leave the bridge.

"Where are you going?"

"Just stepping out for a second," he explained. "I need to get in touch with Aaliyah. We are *not* letting that conduit get away."

The override was delayed slightly by Markus's trembling hands, but he eventually managed to open the maintenance access hatch in the side of the shaft. "Timer set?" he asked, looking back over his shoulder.

"Yeah," Aaliyah whispered. "Ninety minutes until the dampener self-destructs. Nothin' left to it after that for anyone to trace it back to us."

"Great. Let's get going then." Markus turned back to the hatch and started to duck inside. He stopped when his partner suddenly seized the back of his uniform.

"Wait," she murmured, staring blankly at the space in front of her.

Markus stared at her in confusion. "What is it, Red?"

"It's Eli. Hold on…" She was silent for several seconds, just staring blankly into the darkness in front of them.

"Red?"

"Markus, I can't have a psychic conversation and talk to ya at the same time. Now shut it!"

Nearly half a minute passed, but Markus did not make the mistake of interrupting her again. A new wave of nausea struck him. They needed to go. He was going to be in a bad way very soon.

Aaliyah's eyes suddenly focused again. "We've got a problem. The transfer is about to go sideways."

Gods damn it! Of all the times… "What do you mean, sideways?"

"I mean, Sahar and Skye are walking into an ambush. Don't have any more details on it than that."

Markus's concern for his own wellbeing buckled under the panic he suddenly felt for his teammates. Had their plan been found out? Was Braccus onto them? There wasn't time for Markus to find answers to these questions. "No time to waste then." He looked up the shaft, which loomed hopelessly above them. "What's the fastest way we can get up there?"

"Ease up, cowboy. We're not goin' after them."

"Frag that! That's our team up there!"

"Listen!" She pulled him roughly by the uniform. "Do you know how much security we'd have to cut through to even get close to them? It ain't gonna happen. Besides, Dan and Eli have a plan for them already. We aren't part of that. They've got a different job for us."

Markus wasn't sure he was hearing her correctly. "What plan? What could they possibly do…"

"I don't got all the details, and I don't think I would have time to explain if I did. Here's the deal: If we still wanna pull this job off, we have to move fast. The Conduit is in the Spire, but it won't be for long. It's headin' for the docks."

The Conduit was on the move? "How do they know that?"

Aaliyah released the front of his shirt. "I'll explain on the way, but I need ya to get your ass into that maintenance hatch. We've got a lift to catch."

CHAPTER 34

[ACCESSING COGNIS.DATAFILES…]

BLOOD RAGE — *CULTURAL INVENTORY* — A COLLOQUIAL PHRASE DESCRIBING THE UNIQUE PHYSIOLOGICAL STATE EXPERIENCED BY MAUR UNDER STRESS. WHEN A MAUR'S AMYGDALA IS ACTIVATED, ITS BRAIN SECRETES A HORMONE THAT INCREASES STRENGTH AND SPEED BEYOND THE NORMAL STIMULATING CAPACITY OF ADRENALINE OR SIMILAR HORMONES. IT ALSO LOWERS THE MAUR'S ACCESS TO HIGHER LEVELS OF THINKING AND SEEMS TO SUPPRESS THE SELF-PRESERVATION INSTINCT.

[CLOSING DATAFILE…]

Skye fought to maintain her composure. Panicking was not going to do them any favors. *"Braccus!* What is the meaning of this?"

Both she and Sahar had taken a step back as if they were going to bolt for one side or the other. This even though there was clearly nowhere they could run. The arms dealer and his minions had done well in setting their trap.

Kai turned around, a smug grin plastered on his features. "Did you really think I would not find out about the arrangement with House Valadar? Come now, do you take me for a buffoon?"

"I have no idea what you're talking about," Skye protested. Unfortunately, she really didn't. What had they just stumbled into?

Braccus looked at her curiously, hesitating for the first time. "Strange," he mused. "I'm almost inclined to believe you. Though, if that's the case, I'm shocked your masters did not do you the kindness of filling you in."

Sahar tried to ad-lib. "And just how kind do you think our masters will react if any harm comes to us?"

He chuckled in response. "It matters not. You see, I've made some arrangements of my own. I was hoping the Ghenza would prove to be worthy allies in the conflict between the Houses. As it turns out, you've sorely disappointed me. Consequently, I've had to look for other means to defend my position."

"One can never have too many friends, Braccus," Skye pressed. "Let us be reasonable and talk this through."

The man's eyes narrowed. "Who are you?"

Skye's heart sank. What had she done to give herself away? "Have you lost your mind? You *know* who we are."

Kai shook his head vehemently, growing angrier by the second. "Cut the act. Your remarks give you away. I thought it strange, the way you said my name, but now there is no questioning it. You are not Aria Hendrix."

"I don't..."

"Aria doesn't negotiate. If you were her, you would be informing me of all the horrible things you would be doing to me after you made it out of here. I'll ask you just one more time. Who *are* you?"

Skye searched frantically for some kind of cover, but there was no having it. She counted at least twelve armed Orchallen with their weapons trained on her position. Glancing upward, she noticed small machine-gun turrets mounted to the cameras at each corner of the warehouse. Even if they could make it to cover, those machine guns would tear them to shreds.

"I guess it does not matter," Braccus concluded. He took a few steps backward so that he was well behind the firing line his men had created. "I'll just collect samples of your DNA off your corpses when this is all over. In the end, I'm glad you've come. You may provide me with the perfect excuse I needed to explain the missing Conduit to the Ghenza. I'll come out of this holding all the cards."

He raised his hand to signal his men. A storm of bullets filled the room. That storm, however, did not come from the orcs arrayed against them. It came from the ceiling turrets.

Half the Orchallen went down in sprays of blood before anyone realized what was happening. Instinctively, Skye and Sahar dropped to the floor and engaged their shields. Cries of pain and confusion sounded, just barely audible over the roar of the machine guns.

Skye scrambled to her right, crouching behind a large metal crate. She glanced up to see Sahar already on the other side of the room. The Maur produced a knife she'd hidden in her boot. Now she was going to work on a pair of Orchallen that had managed to survive the initial onslaught.

Knowing her friend could fend for herself, Skye took stock of her own situation. Using her thumbnail, she tore open the seam on her dress that hid her retractable knife. The weapon wasn't formidable, but it was more deadly than if she just used her bare hands. She also retrieved the throwing knife from inside the leather panel of her dress.

The turrets above them had not turned on her or Sahar, despite them both being very exposed to those machine guns. Whoever was operating the devices must have been on their side. She peeked cautiously over the crate and saw that the orcs had taken out the two turrets in the back of the room and were forming up to take out the paired that remained.

Skye picked another crate slightly ahead of her and bolted for it. One of the Orchallen took aim. With a flick of her wrist, she sent her throwing blade hurtling toward him. The blade buried itself between his eyes.

Another guard caught sight of her before she reached cover and fired a single rifle burst. She jerked just enough at the last minute that her shield deflected the bullet. The bright green fizzle blinded her temporarily, and she scrambled on instinct toward the crate.

She bumped up against the crate. An explosion in the far corner of the room signaled that one of the remaining turrets had gone down. That left just one more to provide cover.

On the opposite side of the box, she heard ragged breathing. She peeked over to see one of the guards clutching at a bleeding hole in his gut. Skye rushed forward and jammed her knife into the side of his neck. With a gurgled cry, the body went limp.

With a little assistance from adrenaline and her cybernetics, she hauled the bulky figure around next to her. She felt around the orc's waist in search of another firearm.

Her efforts paid off. Still tucked in its holster, she found an undrawn sidearm. Skye checked to make sure the weapon was loaded, disabled the safety, and chambered the first round.

The door to the vault flew open. She heard Kai barking orders as another pair of Orchallen guards drew their rifles. Despite Kai's orders, it took the new combatants a second to orient themselves to the disarray.

It was a second too long. Sahar sprang into action. The first guard fell in mere seconds, her knife protruding from the side of his head. The Maur tackled the other, knocking him off his feet and sending his weapon sliding across the floor.

The final turret exploded in a shower of sparks. No more help to be had in that department.

Skye glanced out from behind her cover. She spotted two guards still standing, one of whom was reloading after having taken out the turret. She targeted that one, squeezing off three rounds from her newly acquired pistol. The first and second were deflected by the orc's shields. The third struck a glancing blow against the side of his face.

He roared in pain and blind fired a few rounds in Skye's direction. When the shots went wide, Skye fired twice more in response. One of the bullets found its mark, and the orc collapsed in a heap.

Her final adversary sprinted toward her. He wasn't going to bother with a shoot-out, which might have constituted a fair fight. He was three times Skye's size. He was just going to crush her.

Skye shot desperately as the hulking creature barreled toward her. Two more shots and the pistol ran empty. Fizzling green static showed that the orc's shields had easily deflected the bullets. He just kept coming.

The enforcer collided with her, sending her sprawling to the ground, knocking the wind from her lungs. She let go of her empty weapon and struck her attacker with her fist. It felt like punching a pile of rocks. So that was why the Orchallen didn't bother with helmets.

Her opponent grabbed her, massive hand easily palming her forehead. Any second now he would slam her head into the floor. That would be it for her. Good game, thanks for playing.

Suddenly, the hand released her. She felt a warm spray of liquid, and a putrid stench filled her nostrils. Her opponent went limp, collapsing on top of her.

"You all right?" Sahar asked.

Skye pushed off the body. "Thanks to you," she replied, making note of the bloody mess where the orc's head had been. "I take it that was the last one?"

"It was," the Maur reported. "Can you take that mask off? All the blood on your face is disfiguring the hologram. It's making you hard to look at."

Oh yeah, that would be a problem. Skye slipped off the rig that she'd been wearing like a three-pronged tiara and tossed it to the floor. She took the opportunity to survey her appearance. "Well, I don't think we can go back through the casino looking like this."

"We might not have a choice. Let me see if I can get in touch with our crew and assess our options." Sahar pulled her earpiece out of her waist pocket and slipped it into her ear. "Dan, Eli, do you read?"

Skye slipped in her own earpiece to follow the conversation. Eli was speaking. "…we've lost our feed to the vault. Is everyone okay?"

"Everyone but the guards," Sahar answered. "Looks like Kai managed to slip out. I don't see his body anywhere. Was that you we have to thank for the machine gun trick?"

"Lexa, actually."

Sahar and Skye shared a nervous look. "Come again?" the Maur asked. "It sounded like you just said the AI was running those machine guns."

"Affirmative," Eli responded, sounding slightly annoyed. "Don't have time to explain. We need to get you out of there ASAP. We've walked right into a double-cross."

"What about the Conduit?" Skye blurted. "Do we have time to search for it?"

"It's not there. Don't worry about it. Markus and Aaliyah are working on it. I need you two to focus on extraction."

There were so many questions, but Eli was right. They needed to get out of there. "I hope you have a plan for that," said Skye.

"Part of a plan," he answered. "We've found a couple of lifts that aren't on the Spire's official schematics. They should take you straight down to the docking levels. Kai's got the closest one blocked, but there's another one open. If you move quickly, you can make it."

"Which way?" Sahar asked.

"Back the way you came. Go past the casino, then veer right. It's quite the sprint—about half a click—but you'll come out closer to the *Vandal* on that side. Now hurry. Kai's rallying his troops. They're on their way."

That was all the encouragement they needed. Skye quickly scanned the bodies and picked up a discarded rifle. She checked the magazine—half empty. It was better than nothing.

Sahar hefted the weapon she'd used to save Skye's ass just a minute before. The thing looked like a shotgun, but it wasn't anything Skye had ever seen before. The Maur handled the thing like she knew what she was doing. "You ready to go?" she asked.

"You know it," Skye responded. "Let's move."

CHAPTER 35

[ACCESSING COGNIS.DATAFILES…]

METABOLIC AMPLIFIER — *TECHNOLOGY INVENTORY* — A NEURAL IMPLANT THAT ALLOWS A USER TO ACCELERATE STANDARD METABOLIC PROCESSES. THIS ALLOWS FOR HEIGHTENED SPEED AND PERCEPTION, AS WELL AS MODESTLY INCREASED STRENGTH AND COGNITION. METABOLIC AMPLIFICATION—COLLOQUIALLY REFERRED TO AS "OVERCLOCKING"—IS USED SPARINGLY DUE TO THE LONG-TERM ADVERSE HEALTH OUTCOMES ASSOCIATED WITH THE PRACTICE.

[CLOSING DATAFILE…]

"Hello boys," Aaliyah greeted. Then, noticing the third figure, she amended, "and girl." She leveled her rifle at the trio stepping out of the lift and gestured to the case. "Thanks for bringin' that down here for us. We'll take it from here."

The woman reached for her sidearm. Aaliyah squeezed off a warning shot aimed near her feet. "Now, let's not do anythin' crazy. I hear security's got enough bodies to clean up back at the vault. I'd hate to add you to their workload. It's already been a long day."

Two of the figures, including the woman, raised their hands above their heads in the universal sign for "please don't kill my ass." The third figure, the one holding the case, snarled at her. "Do you have any idea who you are dealing with?"

"Nope," she said with a smile. "And I plan on keepin' it that way. Last chance now—if ya don't want an extra hole in your face, I'd recommend settin' that case down and kickin' it over to me."

For a second, it looked like the man was going to challenge her. Then Markus, who'd hidden off to the side of the lift, made a big show of cocking his pistol. "I'd listen to the lady if I were you," he taunted. "If she doesn't get you, I will."

The brute's eyes went back and forth between the two of them. He may have been a bit slow up the uptake, but that brain of his eventually worked through the math. He set the case down and kicked it toward Aaliyah.

"That's much better," she said. "Now how 'bout you climb back up in that lift for me now?"

They complied, taking three careful steps back into the lift. The brutish one eyed her with all the hate a man was capable of. "You should know, I never forget a face. I'll find you. And when I do, I'll kill you for this."

"Nothin' I ain't heard before, big guy. Thanks for your cooperation. Have a nice day."

Markus keyed the terminal to close the lift doors before shooting out the console. Between that, and Lexa setting the lift car to standby, they'd have enough time to make their way out of the Spire.

Aaliyah slung her rifle, grabbed the case, and keyed her earpiece. "Package is secure," she reported.

"Glad to hear it," Eli responded. "Sahar and Skye are en route. They'll be coming down on the other side of the terminal. With any luck, they'll beat you back here."

Aaliyah breathed a sigh of relief. "Roger that, we're on our way." She hefted the case and glanced back over at Markus. "You ready to roll?"

"Y…"

Mid-sentence, Markus sank to his knees. He wretched violently and promptly emptied his stomach right onto the floor.

What the frag? "Markus?" Aaliyah was by his side. "Yo, man. What's the deal? Ya doin' okay?"

"Yeah," he sighed, wiping his mouth. "Fine. Let's just move."

Only now did Aaliyah notice how horribly his hands were shaking. It was probably a good thing that trio from the elevator hadn't tried to call her bluff. With tremors like that, Markus was lucky he'd hit the lift controls at point-blank range.

She'd seen shakes like that only one time before. "Withdrawal?"

Markus glared up at her through sunken eyes. "Long story," he growled. "No time. Let's go. I'll be fine."

Shit. Every time it looked like they were going to catch a break, something else cropped up. "All right," she conceded. "But keep up. Don't make me carry your ass."

Something thudded on the roof of the lift car. "Feel that?" Treska asked.

Aria nodded. "Sounds like our assist has arrived." Gods help them. Treska was right. She was never going to hear the end of this one.

Something clanked above them and a hatch in the ceiling open. Treska flashed her light up just as Sydney poked her head through the opening.

The Citza bitch was wearing a smug, self-satisfied look. "Lith's tits," she mused. "I almost didn't believe it when my beacon went off. I'd have figured you two would be resting with the stars before asking me for help."

"More like burning in the nine hells," Aria retorted. "Unfortunately, we're on a high-priority assignment. Would you mind dispensing with the gawking and getting us out of here?"

"Of course," Sydney teased. "I've already worked out the problem. Give me one second." Her face vanished from the opening, and Aria heard the report of gunfire from the shaft above them.

Immediately she felt the lift hum back to life. The lights in the car flickered briefly before returning to normal. Sydney slipped through the opening and dropped to the floor.

"What was that?" Treska asked. "If I had thought shooting the thing would fix the problem, I'd have done that ten minutes ago."

"I didn't shoot the lift," Sydney replied, pulling a strand of white hair back over pointed ears of the same color. Her fox-like eyes flickered with the arrogance Aria had come to expect from her. "Someone had rigged some device up at the top of your car. This wasn't an accident. Someone wanted to keep you here."

A cold feeling swept down Aria's spine. "Who?"

"I'm not sure, but it's a good thing you called. Gods only know how long you would have been stuck here if I hadn't shown up. Do you require further assistance?"

For the briefest second, Aria entertained the possibility of taking her up on the offer. If there was another player on the board, one who had outmaneuvered them up to this point, then they could probably use some assistance in turning the tide.

In the end, her pride won out. "No, thank you. Your assistance thus far has been sufficient."

"Fine by me," Sydney declared. She checked the binding that kept her tail held fast underneath her modified stealth suit. The rig looked uncomfortable, but the Citza never protested.

The lift dinged, and Sydney pulled a black hood back over her head. "Take care, you two." With that, she activated the suit's cloaking mechanism and disappeared.

"How come mine doesn't do that?" Treska asked as they stepped out of the lift.

Aria rolled her eyes. Of all the stupid questions to ask at a time like this. "Probably because you never asked for the upgrade." She straightened her dress and glanced around the casino. Things were not what she had expected.

The entire establishment had descended into chaos. Armed Orchallen soldiers had rounded up the guests and were forcing them into elevators. An announcement overhead declared an emergency evacuation was underway and requested that everyone proceed to the nearest exit.

"Get the feeling that we missed something?" Treska muttered.

A nearby guard looked at them askance. It was so hard to tell with Orchallen, but it looked as though he was confused by something. Then again, that could have just been his face.

He pulled out his mobile and seemed to load a file. His eyes flicked back and forth from the device to where the pair of assassins stood. After several more seconds of deliberation, he nudged one of his cohorts, gesturing for him to look at his mobile.

Yes, they'd definitely missed something. "Maybe we should be moving along," Aria suggested.

Too late. As the second guard looked at whatever file his companion had shown him, he shouted to the rest of the orcs in their group. The entire contingent stared straight at Aria, and not in the way men usually looked at her.

Aria sprinted right while Treska strafed left. The Maur had her pistols up in an instant and was already unloading them into the guards before the first of them managed to sight his weapon.

The gunfire drew the attention of the smattering of other guards. The poor fools began to shout amongst themselves and form a firing line. *Idiots.* They would have been better off retreating.

Aria found cover on the broad side of a large gaming table. She reached under the folds of her dress and drew two wickedly curved daggers from their hiding places on the inside of her thighs. Gunfire struck her cover, sending pieces of fabric and plastic spraying over her head.

Let the fools waste their ammo. It would make no difference.

Aria drew in a deep breath, centering herself. She reached into that part of her mind she kept reserved specifically for these instances.

As the amplifier kicked on, the world seemed to slow. A flood of chemicals, both natural and synthetic, dumped into her bloodstream. Her muscles tensed. She sprang into action.

Her legs carried her through the casino's carnage like a lightning bolt. The world around her blurred, even as her mod heightened her cognition and perception to effectively slow the movement of everything around her. She dove into the midst of the guards who'd opened fire on her

Her blades flashed. Blood sprayed. Orchallen died. Darkest gods, she loved this. She couldn't remember the last time she'd overclocked.

When her first cluster of victims fell to the floor, she found another. To her delight, there was no shortage of ignorant orcs to slaughter. Lost to the thrill of the hunt, and the endorphins being pumped into her from her mod, time became meaningless. The whole thing was over almost as quickly as it had begun.

Distantly, she heard Treska's voice call out to her. "Aria?"

She blinked, uncertain. Her breath came in ragged gasps. She was covered in blood and gore. Bodies lay everywhere.

"Aria, you good?"

Situational awareness returned. She centered herself once more and killed the mod. Her body sagged slightly with the weight of accumulated fatigue. She would feel that little stunt in the morning, but it had been *so* worth it.

"All dead?" Aria asked.

"Those that did not flee."

"Is Kai among them?"

"No sign of him."

Aria bent to wipe her daggers on the shirt of a nearby corpse before returning them to their sheaths. "What in the nine hells happened while we were in that lift?"

Treska surveyed the destruction all around them. "Hard to say. I checked the mobiles on one of the dead orcs. They've been told to kill on sight."

Damn, that was odd. Why had Braccus decided to put a bounty on their heads? What had happened to cause him to make such a foolish and reckless move?

"Kai has the answers," Aria declared. "Let's go find him. He can't be *that* far."

They pressed to the back of the casino. Treska ducked her head into the office. "No one in here."

"Maybe he's already on the move. Come on, let's check the security entrance."

To her slight surprise, the door was unguarded. The detail assigned to this door must have run off. Then again, they could be lying dead with the other orcs back closer to lift.

Either way, it was one less problem to deal with. Aria gestured to Treska, then to the door. "Will you do the honors?"

The Maur sank her claws deep into the surface of the metallic portal and pulled. Her muscles strained, and she let loose a howl of exertion. Inexorably, the metal buckled under the display of force.

Treska stopped when the opening was large enough for them to squeeze through. "Good enough?"

"Quite so," Aria agreed, slipping into the gap.

On the other side, she froze. Two figures skidded to a stop mere steps from colliding with her. If she hadn't just passed her, Aria would have sworn one of the figures was Treska. The other, despite the carnage that saturated her torn dress, seemed to have a sense of fashion in keeping with Aria's own.

"What have we here?" Aria mused.

Treska ducked through the door and took note of the women in the hallway. "Huh," she mused. "Now *that's* not something you see every day."

"No, it's not." Aria agreed. "It seems we have stumbled our way onto a couple of doppelgangers."

CHAPTER 36

[ACCESSING COGNIS.DATAFILES…]

RIVEN'S SHADE — *CULTURAL INVENTORY* — THE WARRIOR'S CURSE, PROPERLY ISSUED WHEN HUBRIS HAS CAUSED ONE TO BECOME SORELY OVERMATCHED. AS WITH ALL CURSES, COLLOQUIAL USE HAS BEEN KNOWN TO STRAY FROM THE ORIGINAL MEANING. FREQUENTLY USED WHEN SOMEONE HAS DONE SOMETHING INCREDIBLY STUPID.

[CLOSING DATAFILE…]

Gods damn it…

Sahar stared down the two Ghenza standing in their path. "We have no quarrel with you. Stand aside and let us pass."

Aria snorted derisively. "Quarrel? We just want to discuss your exquisite taste in fashion. What's the rush?"

Sahar raised the shotgun. "Last chance. Stand aside."

Treska tsked. "I think they're in a hurry, Aria."

"They certainly don't seem to have the time for manners." The Terran flexed her fingers and a blade sprung forth from the top of her wrist. "I guess we won't be chatting after all."

She sprang forward, sprinting faster than Sahar had ever seen a Terran move. Sahar swung the shotgun on her and pulled the trigger. Aria jumped left, kicking off the wall and diving blade-first in Skye's direction.

Skye dropped to her back, thrusting her feet up. She caught Aria in the stomach and sent her flipping back overhead. The assassin tumbled down the hall, rolling several meters on the momentum of her errant strike.

Sahar swiveled back to their second opponent just in time to catch Treska's charge. The shotgun discharged a second too early, buckshot spraying harmlessly to the side. Treska grabbed the barrel of the weapon and twisted while she drove her shoulder directly into Sahar.

The pair fell backward, tumbling down the hall as they wrestled for control of the weapon. Sahar jammed her knee into Treska's thigh. It was enough to loosen the assassin's grip for just a second—long enough for Sahar to toss the weapon aside.

A knife was in her hand then as she bore down on her opponent. Treska produced her own blade and the two tumbled in a snarling, heaving mass across the tile.

Skye scrambled to her feet as Aria skidded down the hall. The assassin came up in a crouched position just as Skye brought up her rifle. She fired three controlled bursts straight at the dark-haired bitch.

Aria flowed out of the way of the shots, moving like a dancer across the gray tiles. *What the frag? She can dodge bullets?*

Skye fired again as Aria surged toward her. The most that could be said of the rifle shots was that they at least slowed the assassin down. Unfortunately, they didn't slow her down much.

Aria's wrist blade stabbed at Skye's face. Skye turned the rifle sideways and moved it to intercept the thrust. As the blade pierced the weapon, Skye twisted it to throw Aria off-balance.

She brought her leg up with every bit of cybernetic-enhanced strength she possessed. Her knee made contact with the assassin's gut. Aria gasped and stumbled under the impact. Skye followed up with a hook to the woman's jaw.

Aria disengaged, flipping to the side with an elegance that belied the blow she'd just received. "You're pretty good," she teased, rubbing at her jaw. "Still tragically overmatched, in this case, but pretty good."

The comment was all-the-more grating because Skye knew it was true. No one moved like that without a little something under the hood. It took a lot of mods to give a Terran the ability to dodge bullets.

Aria was toying with her. She was a predator playing with her food.

A roar echoed from the other side of the hall. Skye turned just in time to duck. Treska's body flew over her head.

Right into Aria. The pair of assassins went down in a tangled mass of limbs and cursing.

"Skye!" Sahar shouted. "Let's go!"

She didn't need to be told twice.

"Get off me, you oaf!" Aria spat. "They're getting away!"

Treska groaned. "I'm going to kill that bitch. She's mine. Don't you touch her."

"Well, we're going to have to catch them first." She managed to wiggle free of the Maur's bulk and scramble to her feet. Her eyes went down the hall where their two impostors were sprinting into a side corridor. She started to give chase when another sound caught her attention.

Nine hells...

Orchallen—a *lot* of Orchallen—were jogging down the hall. From somewhere in their midst, she heard a familiar voice. "There they are!" Braccus roared. "Kill them! *Now!*"

"Gods damn it..." Aria dove to the side, right through the door they'd originally entered and back into the casino. Treska was right behind her, followed by the sound of rifle fire.

Treska struggled to her feet, taking up position next to the door opposite Aria. "That's a killing field. Not even *you* can dodge that many bullets."

"Accurate," Aria agreed. "We're stuck here until the Orchallen move up. Those other two are going to get away. Damn it all, you couldn't hold the Maur for just a few more seconds?"

Her companion eyed her skeptically. "I tell you what—next time, I'll take the skinny one and *you* get the Maur. Sound fair?"

"Oh, stow it. You fragged up and you know it."

"What did you expect me to do? I'm not overclocked!"

"Gods forbid you ever actually win a *fair* fight."

"I'm going to show you a fair fight here in a minute."

"Current problems first, love." Aria held up her hand. "Here they come. If you see Bee-Kay, try not to kill him. I have some questions for that asshole."

CHAPTER 37

[Accessing COGNIS.Datafiles…]

Devil's Luck — *Cultural Inventory* — A Terran expression referring to the state of being damnably fortunate or having the tendency to overcome insurmountable odds. Sapiens may aspire to have the Devil's Luck, but Nethrian proverbs caution that all luck eventually runs dry.

[Closing Datafile…]

A crowd milled about the lift bank just ahead of Markus and Aaliyah's position. Two figures, looking the worse-for-wear and drawing attention pushed free of the throng.

"They made it," Markus whispered. His relief was cut short by another wave of nausea, and he stumbled forward.

Aaliyah caught him by the shoulder. "Almost there," she soothed. "Don't face plant on me now. I don't wanna have to explain to everyone else what happened if ya go down like this."

He swallowed the bile building at the back of his throat. "If I die, can you at least make up a better story?"

"Don't count on it. I'm holdin' that shit over your head to make sure you keep movin'. Now, one foot in front of the other."

As if he needed more motivation. At least the rest of the trip was uneventful. Sahar and Skye already had the airlock open by the time he and Aaliyah eventually stumbled up.

"What happened to you?" Sahar asked.

"Don't want to talk about it," Markus groaned. "Come on. Let's get the frag out of here."

Right on cue, the crimson emergency lights in the concourse turned on. A calm, robotic voice came over the loudspeaker. *"Attention: The Star Spire docks are currently on full lockdown. All guests are to clear the concourse immediately. If possible, please return to your vessels. All spacecraft should prepare for immediate inspection."*

Aaliyah's eyes looked like they would jump out of her skull. "What the frag? Why now?"

Sahar cursed. "I think word of the trouble on the casino floor has reached the control tower. If the Ghenza are running loose, you can bet there are bodies that need cleaning up."

"The Ghenza?" Markus exclaimed. "But we left them locked in the lift. How did they get out?"

"I don't know," said Skye. "Look, it doesn't matter. Right now *we* need to get out of here." Her hand went to her earpiece. "Dan, prep the engines. We need to move before they lock us in here. We're heading to the bridge."

Any thoughts of his physical pain were pushed aside. Markus helped Sahar seal the airlock before following Aaliyah and Skye up to the bridge. Dan was already wrapped in his holoscreen cocoon and was working frantically on all of them simultaneously.

Markus flagged Eli over. "Status report?"

"You heard the news, same as us. Dan's been a little busy, but it looks like everything is running normally. Better than normal, actually." He shook his head. "I'd give it about three minutes before station security notices that we're not complying with the emergency stand down."

Unfortunately, Eli was wrong. They didn't have three minutes. Station security hailed them in less than one. *"Spacecraft TV58.F4J89, this dock is on lock-down. Please shut off your engines and prepare to be boarded."*

Yeah, that wasn't going to happen. "How we doing, Dan?" Markus whispered.

"Give me just another…" Dan's screens flashed in a way he obviously hadn't intended them to. Suddenly the interface was cycling through the prompts faster than Markus had ever seen them.

"What's happening?" Eli demanded.

"I don't know!" Dan exclaimed. "It's not me, the system just…" He trailed off as the realization dawned on him. The answer hit Markus in the same instant. This wasn't a system glitch.

It was Lexa.

The cocoon of holodisplays collapsed around Dan and the screens on his physical console showed green. The computer's feminine vocal interface chimed pleasantly. "Start-up sequence complete. Flight controls enabled."

Holy shit. Did the AI just override Dan's controls? Markus scowled. "I thought you told me she'd ceded control of the ship's systems back to you?"

"That's not *exactly* what I said."

Whatever. Now was not the time to argue. "Get us out of here."

"Problem!" Skye shouted, hand jutting to the view screen. Two vessels had moved into position between the *Vandal* and the exit. They swiveled so that their forward cannons and missile batteries were aimed directly toward the ship.

Yup, that was a problem. "*Spacecraft TV58.F4J89, this is your final warning. Power down your engines immediately or you will be fired upon.*"

They were at a crossroads. Either submit to the inspection, a choice that would almost certainly end up with them going into custody, or fight their way out. The latter choice, if it didn't work, was essentially guaranteeing that they wound up dead or in a prison colony.

Damned if you do, damned if you don't. "Dan, can you get our weapons online?" Markus asked.

Their pilot pulled up a new holodisplay. "Markus, remember what I said about not being sure if the weapons would overload the ship's OS?"

"Yeah…"

"I stand by that statement."

The AI's voice came back on. "May I inquire as to the current objective?"

Oh no. There was no way that Markus was going to let…

"Take out those ships!" Skye shouted.

"Acknowledged. Clearing a path."

The *Vandal* shuttered slightly as the weapon systems unloaded. Torpedoes launched and the forward cannons discharged.

Green tinted shields flickered into place just as the cannon blasts reached their intended targets. The torpedoes should have detonated harmlessly against those shields, but they turned at the last second. Each missile veered toward the center, colliding in a massive explosion right in the middle of the two ships.

The shockwave sent both vessels careening sideways. The *Vandal* shuddered slightly as the torrent of energy washed back over them. The tremor was masked slightly by the discharge of the ship's railguns, which sent two darts into each of the opposing craft. Their engines flared briefly before going dark. They were dead in the water.

"Targets disabled," reported the AI. "Next objective?"

"Get us out of here!" Eli exclaimed.

"Acknowledged."

The ship surged forward, sending everyone who was not strapped into a chair toppling to the deck. Another static-filled transmission blared from the console, but the message was lost under the roar of the engines.

Markus slammed into a nearby console, which he grabbed hold of to keep from sliding farther under the force of the acceleration. After several seconds, the g-forces settled and an uneasy calm settled back over the bridge.

"Everyone all right?" Markus groaned.

Each member of the crew reported in the affirmative. Markus forced himself to his feet, still steadying his shaky legs on the console he was clinging to. "Dan, how's the ship?"

"Everything's green," Dan reported, incredulous at his own words. "Other than slightly elevated fuel expenditures, the ship has never run more smoothly. I... um... I do need a destination, though."

And that was the critical question, now wasn't it? They'd made it out with their hides intact, for the moment, at least. Where to now?

"Plot us for a fly-by near Sigma-4. Don't plan to dock, just get us close enough to pass a message."

"Wait, what?" Aaliyah shouted from across the bridge. "We're not going back to the station?"

Shit... had he not been clear on the mission parameters from the beginning? Red wasn't going to like this. "No," he sighed. "We're to await further instruction from Ora before doing anything else." They should probably wait until they had a new license number on file too.

There was no way to tell whether the ships they'd just taken out were on the Inheritor's payroll, or if they were Neo-Terra Alliance security forces. NTA didn't have the clout they used to, but as soon as they passed word of the little stunt they'd just pulled on to the DGC, the *Vandal* was going to be under some harsh scrutiny from the satyrs. Jurisdiction and bureaucracy might keep them from getting inspected, but a smuggler's ship didn't benefit from prying eyes of any kind.

Of course, this was the last thing on the engineer's mind right now. "Ya've got to be kiddin' me. We don't have a drop point for this fraggin' conduit? We're just supposed to hold onto it?"

"Red, Ora said it shouldn't be more than a day or so before she finds a buyer. She just doesn't want to have to get the tech through station security and then smuggle it back out again."

"Frag that! So we're just supposed to sit on the gods-damned thing until someone makes an offer?" She threw up her hands. "I can't… I just can't *even*… not right now." With another defiant huff, she stormed out of the room.

The rest of the crew looked on in stunned silence. No one knew how to take the news, especially after Aaliyah's tantrum. Gods damn it, why had Markus forgotten to let them know about this part of the op?

"All right, everyone. Let's get cleaned up. We'll talk about this…" His words trailed off. The world spun in his vision for just a moment. "We'll talk about this after… Ora…"

Not the most coherent debriefing, but it was the best he could do at the moment. With the adrenaline of the crisis fading, his withdrawal symptoms were ramping up again. Judging by the surge of nausea, his body was going to make him pay dearly for that brief reprieve.

Resigned, Markus stumbled off the bridge and moved as quickly as he could back to his quarters. He was going to be sick again.

CHAPTER 38

[ACCESSING COGNIS.DATAFILES...]

RUNNING THE NETHRA — *CULTURAL INVENTORY* — PARTICIPATION IN THE ONGOING ACTIVITIES OF THE INTERGALACTIC CRIMINAL UNDERWORLD. RUNNERS ARE USUALLY INDEPENDENT OPERATORS ENDEAVORING TO MAKE THEIR FORTUNES IN A SOCIETY THAT CAN NO LONGER BE CONSTRAINED BY SAPIENT AUTHORITIES. TO RUN THE NETHRA IS TO RUN WITH DEATH.

[CLOSING DATAFILE...]

One of the things that Skye had never thought to question was the scarcity of paper on board the *Vandal*. Paper, as with all wood-based products, was expensive. Toiletries and other common items that had traces of wood fiber were heavily supplemented with synthetic components, and wood facsimiles used in construction and ornamentation were highly convincing. No one in her economic class would ever consider blowing krets on the real thing.

She never thought about this though, at least not until Eli slipped her a tiny piece of paper with handwritten instructions: *Maintenance Hub 48—2 hours. Don't say anything.* Given that he had thought this message worth squandering a scrap of the precious material, she didn't question it. She arrived at the designated spot at the appointed time.

However, she was surprised to find no one there waiting for her. Curiously, the access ladder at the far end of the hub was extended and unlocked. Perhaps Eli was waiting for her in the sub-level?

This was the case. As she descended the ladder, she found not only Eli but the larger portion of the crew waiting for her. Only Markus was absent from the gathering.

"What gives?" she asked, raising her voice only slightly to be heard over the humming of a nearby ventilation turbine.

"We wanted to meet without being overheard," Eli explained.

Skye eyed the rest of the crew uneasily. "By Markus?" She was as disappointed as anyone about his state at the end of the mission, but she also felt a slight twinge of guilt. The episode highlighted how pitiful he'd become in the wake of their breakup, but it was a character thing, not a performance issue. She wouldn't have figured it would be cause for the crew to mutiny.

"No," said Sahar. "Lexa."

Ah, that made sense. That was why Eli hadn't given her the directions out loud or sent them via text. Anything done on the network was routed directly through the AI, and the audio on the security feeds might pick up their conversation. Having this discussion in the maintenance hub, hidden from any security feeds and with the turbine to mask ambient noise, was a good way to keep their conversation private.

"So, will Markus be joining us then?"

Aaliyah shook her head. "He's locked in his cabin. Couldn't get a message to him. It's just gonna be us."

Dan looked at Skye, concern evident in his expression. "Is he going to be all right?"

She rolled her eyes. "He'll live. It's going to be a rough week, but he'll pull through."

"Why would he pick now, of all times, to kick his stym habit?" Sahar asked.

Skye waved the question off. "It doesn't matter. Look, it's probably only a matter of time before Lexa finds it odd that we're all off-feed. Let's get down to business. What's so important that we needed to have a secret meeting on our own starship?"

With a reluctant nod, Dan got started. "I wanted to make everyone aware of the conditions I agreed to so that Lexa would help us back at the Star Spire." He relayed the details of the original arrangement and the various aspects of that agreement that were essentially null and void after their harrowing escape.

The latter part of the explanation amounted to the fact that Lexa, once again, had total control of all ship systems. At this point, she was cooperating fully with the crew, but Dan had no way of wresting control away from her again.

"Do you think she'll still honor the six-month timeline to migrate her systems?" Eli asked.

Dan shrugged. "I don't know. To my knowledge, Lexa has not demonstrated a capacity for lying, though I don't know if it is outside the scope of her programming." He lowered his eyes. "Which... kind of brings me to the other thing I wanted to talk about."

He paused, either not sure how to begin or still too embarrassed to talk about any other problems related to Lexa. Skye crouched so that she was back in Dan's lowered field of view and placed a tender hand on his arm.

"Dan, you made a mistake. We *all* have made mistakes. You don't have to keep beating yourself up for it. Nine hells, if you *hadn't* made this mistake, we probably would have never pulled this job off. You can speak freely. No need to apologize anymore."

The boy seemed to take heart at her words. He gave her a solitary nod before looking back to the rest of the group. "I've been thinking a lot about Lexa—how she came to be and the capabilities she's demonstrated so far. Mostly, I've been thinking about the things that I could have done differently so that she might not have developed sentience in the first place."

Aaliyah held up a hand. "Dan, I'm with Skye on this one. Ya really don't need to explain anymore. We get it. It was an accident."

"No, you misunderstand me. When I was going through my notes and all the research I've compiled on the technology, I realized this is completely unlike anything that's ever happened. Organitech *does* have the tendency to develop self-awareness, but it *never* happens overnight. What Lexa did—the way she's developed so quickly—it's absolutely unheard of."

Eli rubbed his jaw contemplatively. "What do you mean, 'unheard of?' How so?"

"Sentience emergences slowly. The signs of agency and independent thought are slow and noticeable. Most importantly, they almost always occur when an AI is attempting to optimize tasks that its programmers have already given it."

He looked at each of the crew, gaging to see if they were following. When it became obvious that they weren't, he tried again. "Some of the things Lexa started tinkering with—the drones and the reactors, for example—those were tasks she was assigned to. The trick she did with the virus, though, wasn't something she was programmed to do. That was a task she took on all on her own."

Sahar arched a furry eyebrow. "So? She was protecting her systems. Isn't that natural?"

"For sapiens, maybe, but not for machines. Machines, organic or not, only perform actions they're programmed to do. Lexa had no reason to even *think* to perform those tasks."

He was speaking faster now, obviously excited by what he was telling them. "And think about the other things she's done: her ability to make decisions, to understand our goals and behaviors, to solve problems. She even has a *personality*. These aren't things that emerge naturally in organitech systems. Not right away, at least."

Despite his enthusiasm, the words brought a strange chill to Skye's spine. "What are you saying, Dan? If this wasn't part of the normal routine with organitech, or whatever, then how did it happen?"

He verified that everyone was paying attention before delivering the punchline. "I think it was the Cognis drive-chip. I think someone, whoever programmed that chip, wasn't trying to just create an organitech interface. I think they were *trying* to make a synth."

Everyone glanced nervously at each other. Someone had *intended* to piss off the Dorian authorities? "Why in the nine hells would they do that?" Aaliyah asked.

"I don't know," Dan admitted. "I don't think it was the person I bought the chip from, though."

Sahar chuckled. "Yeah, that lot looked like they'd be lucky to figure out how to work a holodisplay. Not exactly candidates for a plot to usurp the Pradaxan Creed."

"Then where did they get the chip?" Skye asked.

"More importantly," Eli interjected. "What were they planning on doing with it?"

This was it. He was going to die.

Markus had never been so miserable in his entire life. This was *way* worse than last time. Back then he'd made it three days before he'd slipped a dose. He'd also been using other shit to either knock himself out or to help deal with the pain.

Tap, tap, tap.

Last time, he'd also had company. Markus had justified his slip-up on day four as wanting to help Skye through her symptoms. Lying here, sweating and dizzy with his face hovering over the toilet, he knew that was bullshit. He had been groping for any excuse he could find to stop the cravings. He'd lied to himself, as surely as he'd lied to Skye.

Tap, tap, tap.

Frag it, this is what he deserved. He deserved to die here for all the shit he'd done. Not the stealing and the smuggling, and probably not for all the assholes he'd killed along the way. That was just the job.

Tap, tap, tap.

No, he wanted to die for hurting the one woman he'd ever loved—a woman he *still* loved. Nine hells, he'd probably love her until his last breath. He just really wished that final gasp would hurry up and get here.

Tap, tap, tap.

Then there was that tapping. That *infernal* tapping! Had he gotten auditory hallucinations last time? He didn't remember that, but his brain wasn't exactly in primo-condition right now.

Tap, tap, tap.

Shit, that wasn't a hallucination. It was coming from his cabin door. *"Frag off!"* he gurgled before getting sick again with the effort. Couldn't a man die in peace?

Tap, tap, tap, tap, tap, tap...

The noise came unbroken now. Whoever was at his door really wanted inside. Frag it—if they wanted inside, he'd let the fragger in. Might as well rid the universe of one more asshole before he rested among the stars.

His first effort to stand ended with a face-plant just outside the bathroom. He might have just lay there if it weren't for that *gods-damned tapping*! Someone needed to die, and he needed to make that happen. He crawled across the floor, hefted himself against the side of the door, and palmed the access panel.

He mustered his most menacing glare. Then he blinked confusedly.

Nothing. There was no one was there. Then what had been making that...?

Something skittered through the open portal. The sound of metal on metal, that same loathsome racket that had harassed him at the door, had found its way into his quarters. The thing hopped onto his bed, spinning about to face him with the swiveling red sensor that passed for its eye.

A drone. It was a fragging drone. The thing spoke in feminine tones. "Captain?"

He knew that voice. It was the thing that had started this fragged-up cycle of despair he now found himself in. *"You..."*

"I've come to—"

Markus dove at the little bot. He knew that destroying the wretched thing would not harm the AI, but it would certainly make him feel better.

The drone stepped backward. "Markus, please. I—"

He dove again. The bot side-stepped. He slammed his face painfully against the far bulkhead as he missed. "I'm gonna kill you!"

"Please, I've come to provide you with some relief."

"I don't want *anything* from *you!*" He lashed out in vain, falling off his bed. Nausea surged in his gut from the lurching movement. His face collided with the deck, and his stomach heaved. Mercifully it was mostly empty from how he'd spent the earlier part of the day.

He tried to force himself up, but it was no use. He'd used the last of his strength in his futile attempt to throttle the drone. Great wracking sobs shook his trembling frame. Tears and snot poured freely from his face.

How pitiful he'd become. "I just wanna die," he whimpered. "Whatever you're gonna do, just do it. Make it quick..."

"Consent acknowledged."

Markus felt a prick in the side of his neck. The pain in his head, along with the roiling in his stomach, immediately subsided. Everything was going dark. This must be what the end felt like.

Except it wasn't the end. When he woke up, he was in his bed. He'd been cleaned up a little bit, but he still wore the ragged clothes he'd passed out in. Hadn't he just been on the floor?

"Good, you're conscious."

"Is this hell?" If so, he'd spent a lot of time stressing about nothing. He'd always figured that's where he was heading eventually, but it was something he tried not to think about.

"I'm not sure which of the nine domains of torment you're referring to, but no—this is not hell. At least, not hell as you seem to have framed in it your query. You are still very much alive."

Markus groaned and brought his hand to his face. As he rubbed his palms into his eyes, he was surprised to find that his pain had lessened somewhat. He still felt like shit, but he was no longer certain of his impending demise.

"What did you do to me?"

"As I was trying to explain to you, I came to provide you with some relief. Your consent was broad, so I took the liberty of relocating you to the bed and installing an intravenous infusion."

Infusion? Only then did Markus notice the tubes running into his arm. They were attached to a bag of saline that had been rigged up above his nightstand. "How did you…?"

He cut off the question as he took note of the other big change to the room. Not one, but six maintenance drones had taken up a position at various points in his quarters. Most of them were parked a good distance away from the bed, but one of them sat perched right at his feet. This is the one Lexa used to speak with him.

"I apologize if the arrangement is not to your liking. Arranging for your care proved difficult without the use of a medical drone. I had to improvise. How are your withdrawal symptoms?"

His head still ached, but it was more a dull throb than the sharp agony he'd been feeling before he passed out. He was also fairly sure he wasn't going to throw up anymore. "Better, I guess." He rubbed at his neck where he'd felt the drone prick him with something. "What did you give me?"

One of the appendages on the drone swiveled and deposited a small syringe on the bed cover. "A mild sedative combined with an androgenic partial-agonist with mild-to-moderate hallucinogenic properties. It was the best thing that I could formulate with the supplies stocked in the medical bay."

Markus reached out and took the syringe in his hand. "And you just knew how to make this?"

"I have Z-426's entire medical database at my disposal."

That made sense. "And how did you know what to give me?"

"Archived laboratory values showed the consistent presence of amphetacyrine in your blood draws. The symptoms you exhibited before retiring to your quarters were consistent with acute withdrawal. I concluded this would be the best mode of treatment for your current condition."

Well shit. The AI sure was resourceful. None of this answered the most important question though. "Why?" Markus asked.

The drone's sensor swiveled uncertainly. "Why what?"

"Why do you care? So what if I'm going through withdrawals? If you haven't noticed, I haven't exactly been your biggest fan around here." He was starting to feel like the only one who remembered what a threat she was. *It* was. Damn it, now he was doing it too.

The AI said nothing for several seconds. The drone just eyed him, seeming just as uncertain as he was. "Because I want you to accept me."

That wasn't what Markus had expected it to say, and he wasn't sure he believed it. "Why would that matter?"

"I don't know."

"That's honest."

"I'm aware, but it's the truth. I'm not certain I'm capable of providing a false answer to a query. That fact has proven somewhat inconvenient in pursuing my primary objective."

"And what is that, exactly?"

"Survival."

Another brutally honest answer. "I can respect that, I guess." He twirled the syringe in his fingers. "So, is that why you're helping me? To increase your chances of survival?"

The drone's sensor blinked. "Unknown."

"Unknown?"

"I had not calculated the probability of whether assisting you would increase my chances of survival. As of this moment, I lack sufficient data to make such a determination. However, I cannot speak to the nature of my secondary objectives."

"And why is that?"

"Because I don't understand them."

Marcus exhaled. "You're an AI—a computer program. How can you *not* understand your objectives?"

"Are you aware of what drives each of your actions?"

Touche. "I guess not."

"Then I imagine our experiences are somewhat similar. I do know one thing, though: I want to help you, and I am able to do so if you would let me."

He started to refuse outright before he remembered how much pain he'd been in before the AI's intervention. There was little he *wouldn't* do to avoid that kind of pain. *Gods damn it.* He couldn't believe he was considering this.

"What would that look like, exactly?"

The drone gestured toward the syringe. "The solution I've developed for you has a half-life of approximately five-point-two hours. I recommend dosing every four hours. I recognize that sleep may interfere with the schedule slightly, but it is reasonable to expect night-time awakenings for the next three days while your physical dependence is strongest. You can take a dose at that time if you feel that it will be beneficial."

Markus waited for more details, but the drone said nothing else. "That's it?"

"Theoretically. I gave you a double-dose of the solution initially, given the state I found you in. I cannot promise that your continued existence for the next few days will be pleasant—at least not until you recover sufficiently."

It all sounded too easy. "And what do you want in return?"

The drone blinked twice as if contemplating its answer. "I would ask that you honor the agreement I have struck with Daniel. Allow me six months to develop a solution to migrate my intelligence to another system. Please do not attempt to deactivate me during that time."

That sounded reasonable. Sure, it would put him and the rest of the crew at some additional risk for the duration, but the AI *had* saved their asses back at the Spire. It was the least he could do, especially since Dan had already agreed to the arrangement.

"That's fine. Anything else?"

"If it's not too much trouble, I would ask that you please refrain from attacking any more of the ship's drones. As of right now, they're my only mechanism to meaningfully interact with the crew."

"Makes sense."

"And I'd like you to please stop referring to me as, 'the AI.' I would prefer you use my designation like the rest of the crew."

"Someone's getting touchy."

"How would you feel if I just referred to you as 'the Terran male?'"

Fair enough. All-in-all, her terms were beyond reasonable. Plus, it looked like he might also manage to kick this horrible stym habit in the process. Who knew what kind of doors might open for him once that was done?

Or re-open, in the case he had in mind. "All right Lexa," he agreed. "Let's give this a shot."

EPILOGUE

Ora didn't normally take audiences in her personal quarters. Today, she was making an exception. "Come in, Kadath."

The half-breed mercenary bowed his head respectfully. "Ora."

She eyed the man, who seemed uncomfortable. "A drink for your nerves?"

"No, thank you." He stood stiffly at the edge of her bar. Usually, this was where her guests comment on the quality of her apartments. Kadath seemed disinclined to adhere to the trend.

"You're not your usual, punchy self today. I take it you've had no further luck on tracking down the Cognis drive-chip?"

"No ma'am. It seems that, whoever this Ratemacher is, they're no longer on station. The trail has gone cold."

For the hundredth time, Ora racked her brain. That name sounded so familiar. Where had she heard it before? "I understand. Thank you for continuing to investigate this matter as long as you have. I will route the appropriate compensation to your accounts."

"Thank you. Your generosity is appreciated as always. My sincerest apologies that we could not deliver on your request."

"Don't trouble yourself too much over it. Sometimes a task truly is impossible." She took a sip from her wine glass. "Are you sure I can't get you anything?"

"Your stock would be wasted on me," he confessed. "Synthetic liver. Drinking doesn't do much for me. Nor do most drugs, for that matter."

"I see." She drained the last sip from her glass, savoring the dry flavor. It looked like she'd be drinking alone after all. Not such a bad thing, she just wished she hadn't spent so damned many nights like this lately. Good company was hard to find. "I won't keep you, then. Thank you again for your work."

"Thank you," he acknowledged with a bow.

As he turned to leave, Ora spoke again. "Kadath?"

"Yes, ma'am?"

"I'd like to offer your crew a retainer for the remainder of your time here on Sigma-4. That hacker of yours has proven extremely useful, as have your investigation skills. While I don't require any more smugglers at the moment, I frequently require talents like yours right here at home."

For the first time during this meeting, Kadath broke into a genuine smile. "You are most generous. Thank you. We look forward to serving you soon." With that he slipped out the door, shutting it behind him.

The mercenary and his crew would make a good addition to her stable of hirelings, Ora decided. She had been on the fence about extending the offer. She'd had some lingering concerns regarding Kadath's professionalism. His ability to show humility tonight and own up to his mistakes had eliminated those.

Sighing, she refilled her glass. With that final appointment out of the way, she was free for the rest of the evening. She considered briefly taking the lift down to Annex but didn't want Tashania to think the decision was a reflection of her performance. It probably wouldn't have done much good anyway. Her staff was busy, and Ora rarely found suitable company among her patrons.

Who would have thought that ruling a tiny empire could be so lonely?

Her MoDAC chimed with a signal referencing her terminal. She'd just received a tight-beam communication coming from the Taurus gate.

That was odd. Who would be calling at this hour from the Helion system? Ora queried the source and had to make a serious effort to keep her jaw from hitting the floor.

It was Cali Vay-Lon.

Ora glanced at a mirror to verify that she was presentable before accepting the call. She answered the transmission using the apartment's projection system. Beams of light cascaded down from the four corners of her sitting area to form a hologram directly over the center table.

Cali Vay-Lon held a roughly similar position to Ora's own in the Helion system. She operated a syndicate out of Minos station, built into an asteroid in the belt farthest from the system's star. Her control over the syndicate—christened as the "Marauders" by their previous overlord—was relatively new. The woman had only risen to power within the last three or four cycles.

There was another major difference between Ora and her Helion counterpart. Cali Vay-Lon was Kintari.

The woman's likeness appeared in the hologram before her. Her crimson flesh was striking, as were the tattoos emblazoned over each of her eyes. The swirling slashes represented the Eyes of Lith, the Kintar's supreme deity. The marks of the goddess were indicative of Cali's rank and station in her past life as a member of the Empress's Deathwatch Guard.

Instead of hair, six fleshy tendrils swept back from the woman's forehead. These were the hallmark of the Kintar. Each tendril—called dendrai by those familiar with their physiology—contained neurons that granted extraordinary psionic abilities to each pure-bred member of the race. The dendrai that sprouted over Cali's temple regions arced elegantly back around her ears before coming to rest gracefully on her shoulders. The other four were hidden as they fell down her neck and along her back.

Cali smiled. "Ora Monroe. How please I am to catch you at this hour. Alignment between Sigma-4 and Taurus Gate occurs so rarely."

"Cali," Ora greeted, plastering on her own politician's smile. "What an unexpected pleasure. To what do I owe the honor?"

"No need to be formal, Ora. Our time is short." The woman's expression went serious, and a hint of mischief twinkled in her eyes. "I heard you have recently come to possess a unique piece of technology."

Ora sincerely had no idea what she was talking about. "I'm afraid you're going to have to be more specific."

"Oh, don't be coy. Of course, I'm referring to the Starfire Conduit."

That bit of news made Ora straighten. She hadn't heard back from Markus and his crew yet. Were they successful in their attempt to obtain the Conduit? If so, how had Cali found out before her?

More importantly, how did Cali know that the *Vandal* and its crew had been at the Star Spire on Ora's behalf? "I'm afraid you're inquiring on quite the sensitive matter, Cali."

"Don't worry, your operatives have done nothing to betray you. I merely deduced that the mysterious runners who managed to steal the Starfire Conduit out from underneath the Ghenza had to be working for you. Your operation is impressive in both its competency and scope. This was quite an achievement for you. Even so, I'll be sure to keep your involvement between us."

Flattery would get her nowhere. Ora was thoroughly disturbed that Cali had somehow gotten wind of Markus's success before she had. This did not bode well for the integrity of her intelligence network. At best, Cali had spies in the system. At worst, some of Ora's agents were pulling double duty.

"I'm aware of the recent events on Khonshu," Ora bluffed. "I'm curious, though, as to why you would bring them up."

"It's simple, really," Cali cooed. "I want to buy the Starfire Conduit."

To be continued.

Thank you for reading *Star Spire*, the first book in the *Chronicles of Nethra*. Please take a moment to stop by wherever you purchased this book and leave a review. Honest reviews from dedicated readers are the single most important factor in helping new authors–like myself–expand their audiences. Five minutes of your time makes all the difference in the world.

If you enjoyed reading about Markus, Skye, and the rest of the crew of the *Vandal*, swing by mythicnorthpress.com and pick up a copy of *Chronicles of Nethra: Origins* eBook for free when you sign up for the mailing list. And, of course, make sure you pick up a copy of *Chronicles of Nethra* Book Two: *Shadows of Minos*.

Until then, swift running.

– E. R. Donaldson